The Tangled Knot

A Novel of the English Civil War

by

Lizzie Jones

**Grosvenor House
Publishing Limited**

This book is published by
Grosvenor House Publishing Ltd
28-30 High Street, Guildford, Surrey, GU1 3EL.
www.grosvenorhousepublishing.co.uk

A CIP record for this book
is available from the British Library

ISBN 978-1-908596-64-2

Also by Lizzie Jones

Mr. Shakespeare's Whore - the story
of Aemilia Bassano.

*Dedicated to the memory of all those who lost
their lives during the conflict, and friends and
fellow re-enactors who are no longer with us but
who shared our passion for this period of history.*

CHAPTER 1

OCTOBER 1644

The sign creaking on its metal bracket showed a rough and weathered likeness of a man in the clothes of the last century under which was inscribed in faded lettering 'The Lord Leycester.' However it was a long time since anyone of so illustrious a title had set foot in the crooked timber and plaster building with its thatch sagging forlornly like a useless straw hat in the drenching rain. The young man ran eagerly into the inn, relieved to be within its shelter, even though its exterior did not promise much in the way of comfortable provision and there was only a dim light glimmering from the bowed window with its tiny panes cracked and dirty.

He pushed open the door and was not surprised that no warm blaze of cheer greeted him as he stepped over the threshold into a long, low-raftered room that was depressingly gloomy and chill. Once inside he took off his grey wool cloak and the water dripped onto the flagged floor which was already wet and muddy. Whilst he was doing this his wary eyes, an unusual deep brown, were raking the crowded interior. He pulled the wool cap from his head and ran his fingers through his hair, a dark chestnut shade and cut short so that it barely covered his ears though it fell thickly across his forehead, ostensibly to ruffle it dry but again using the few seconds to survey his surroundings. The room was smoky for the mean fire in the chimney corner smouldered grey and sluggish, emitting an acrid smell of damp wood as well as thick curls of black smoke which mingled with the fug of countless tobacco pipes. The inhabitants were mainly of the working sort, clad in rough fustians and leather jerkins with mud-caked shoes, though one or two looked as if they might be tradesmen or craftsmen. They surveyed the stranger suspiciously then turned back to their drinking, satisfied that a traveller on this bad night was entitled to seek a respite, for he was not the sort to draw attention. Of little more than middling height but of sturdy build, he wore a doublet of faded russet and the plain collar of his coarse linen shirt was none too clean. His breeches were of grey wool but his boots were of good leather, pulled up to the thighs for riding but which could be turned down below the knees. And his hands were not those of a manual worker. Though they were brown and strong they were smooth, the fingers surprisingly long and slender.

Walking to the board where the harassed landlord plied his trade he awaited his turn patiently and after being served with a tankard of ale looked around for a spare seat. They were noticeably few but on one of the corner settles a man was sitting with a canvas bag beside him, perhaps a bag of craftsman's tools. He strode towards the gloomy alcove. "Would you mind removing your bag so that I can sit down," he demanded curtly. The middle-aged man with grizzled curly hair and brown lined skin did not even look at him but removed the bag and continued to drink his ale. The young man squeezed his sturdy frame into the empty space. "A bad evening," he volunteered conversationally.

"Aye, but what can ye expect for the time of year," the other grunted, seeming disinclined to talk. It was difficult to make oneself heard in any case for talk all around was coarse and loud, harsh with argument and interspersed with frequent oaths. The young man made several more banal observations about the difficulty of working on the land in the unusually wet autumn weather and with all the disruptions caused by the war. Then in the same tone of voice he said, "The night after tomorrow. The supply train, silver as well as coin for wages, leaves Cirencester for Oxford". There was merely a grunt from the other. "They will make it look as if they are heading for Cheltenham but after five miles or so a small party will swing eastwards towards Whitney with the loaded cart, leaving the main convoy as decoy."

"I do not need to ask if you are certain of this," the other replied. "Good work." He drained his ale then after a few minutes silence the young man went to refill his tankard. When he returned the older man was making ready to leave. As he bent to retrieve his bag from the floor he muttered, "Thursday week, the same hour. At what place?"

"The Olive Branch, Alcester," came the prompt reply. "I am bound for Stratford."

The older man straightened and moved from the bench nodding a curt, "Goodnight to thee."

The young man waited a while, sipping his ale slowly. Then he too stood, leisurely wrapping his cloak around him and replacing his cap, and with a "Goodnight to ye," thrown to his immediate neighbours, he left the inn. Retrieving his horse from the stable yard he mounted in a swift easy leap and set his head towards the Stratford road. He was well satisfied with himself as another mission had been successfully completed. He might be temporarily incapable of fulfilling his normal role in the Roundhead army but he was still able to serve the Parliament in a useful way. He kicked his heels into the horse's flanks and set off at a gallop, both horse and man well used to cavalry charges.

Lady Mary Hesketh stood in the curve of the wide mullioned window, looking across the park to where the lake was darkening slowly in the diminishing light as gathering black clouds brought an early twilight and threw a ruffled mantle across the placid surface of the water. The chill October air seemed to invade the spacious parlour, usually a pleasant retreat with its tapestries and fine furniture, and she shivered, pulling the silk shawl closer round her shoulders. A feeling of sadness engulfed her, vague and unidentifiable, yet bringing with it such a sense of loss that her whole being seemed to empty itself into the familiar scene. The door into the hall stood open but she was not conscious of her husband's entrance, even though his boots sounded on the polished floorboards for a moment until he paused tentatively when he saw her so still, her slender figure outlined in a pose of controlled sadness where the pallid glimmer from outside the great window kept at bay the shadows encroaching from the corners of the room. His first impulse was to retire and not invade her privacy but the intensity of her emotion was communicated to him and he moved towards her, putting his arm about her shoulders. Even the familiar protection of his body did not immediately comfort her and they stood together in silence, their eyes following the slope of the park as it dipped towards the lake and plunged into the shadows of the wood.

"I feel as if the whole world is coming to an end," she said at last, leaning against him and feeling the soft lace of his collar brush her cold cheek. "As if all this is going to be taken away from us."

"That would only be the end of our world," Sir James Hesketh said gently. "God's world is far more substantial." Even as he said the words he was aware of the starkly etched trees already dissolving into a darkening sky and the earth melting into the water's edge, as if indeed the world outside was slipping away.

She realized that for the first time he had not attempted to allay her fears and she shivered again. "I hate the winter. I have a premonition that something dreadful is going to happen."

"You have no grounds for thinking so," he reassured her. "Come let us light the candles and rid ourselves of this autumn melancholy. Everything is going well. William is safe and will no doubt soon be home again. Prince Rupert and the King are on their way back to Oxford and the winter will bring a lull in hostilities, time to rethink and replan." As well they needed to after the summer's catastrophic defeat at Marston Moor, he mused, as he found the tinderbox and lit the two candles standing in their tall silver candlesticks on the table. The flickering light made little difference in the large room except to shed a warm glow over the deep crimson of the table rug, making the intricate scrolls and lozenges of the closely worked design take on the brilliance of an illuminated manuscript.

Lady Mary continued to stand in the window alcove but her thoughts had drifted from the apprehensions of the future to the security of the past. She was remembering a bright sunlit Mayday more than twenty years ago when she had first come to Hesketh Hall in her wedding finery. She could clearly recall her emotions at the sight of the house with its golden stone glowing warm in the spring sunshine for, despite the dominance of the castellated porch revealing the age of the original building, it was a welcoming family house.

Above the porch a beautiful rose window with trefoil heads softened the defensive aspect, and though on the north side the old range stood square and strong with crocketed pinnacles and small casement windows with leaded lights, on the south side the newer wing rose in an elegant gabled elevation set with large mullioned windows. The facade was mirrored in the waters of the lake, remnant of an old moat, and stood open to the rolling parkland as if it offered a smiling face to all comers after the winding driveway had skirted the edges of a little coppiced wood. A walled garden was tucked away through an archway between the bothy and the stables where the sun-baked walls trapped a little haven of scent and colour, and another arch led through to the box-hedged knot garden and the herb garden which had become her own particular province. Beyond were the kitchen gardens bounded by the meandering stream which fed the lake. How happy she had been here and how she had grown to love this house and its owner, having come to both as a stranger. But it was the house she had loved first. She had lain in the great tester bed that night, feeling the man beside her even more of a stranger after the distressing ordeal she had just experienced, but willing to endure anything so long as she could live here as the mistress of the Hall.

She was about to turn to her husband when instead her attention was caught by a phantom-like shimmer of movement across the grass and up the steps to the front door. "There goes Arabella. I wonder where she can have been," she murmured in some puzzlement.

"If it were much of a secret I doubt she would have used the front entrance," laughed Sir James indulgently.

"Well her slippers will be wet, I must go and have a word with her." Lady Mary put aside her private musings and returned to the essentials of the moment as they presented themselves in the welfare of her elder daughter.

Sir James watched her go, noting the gracefulness of her step as still that of a young girl. Standing close to her he had seen the fine lines around her eyes and the deepening furrow between nose and mouth but she was still amazingly beautiful, more so even than when he had first seen her in the garden of her father's house, dressed in a gown the colour of the sunflowers she had been gathering. Her hair was still the same rich brown with hints of copper in certain lights but maturity and years of wealth and comfort had enhanced her fine-boned face with an added serenity. Theirs had been an arranged marriage that had brought them both deep contentment with little to cloud their happiness until two years ago when the war between King and Parliament had begun to encroach upon their complacency and demand from them a fortitude and resilience for which their privileged existence had not prepared them. He did not feel as confident of the future as he had tried to appear. Affairs had been going badly for the Royalists since the summer and it was essential for them to turn the tide back in their favour. That evening they were entertaining Colonel Miles Griffin of the King's Lifeguards and Sir James had little doubt that the visit would bring a request for him to return to arms.

Arabella Hesketh's fleetness of foot had evaded her mother's solicitude and she ran upstairs to her chamber, calling quietly for her maid Abigail to bring dry stockings and slippers, though it was her younger sister Henrietta who appeared instead on the first floor landing.

"You have been to meet your lover again haven't you Arabella? I can always tell by your face," she whispered conspiratorially but Arabella ignored her, pushing past her into their chamber where she hastily began to remove her damp footwear. Henrietta followed and stood looking down at her sister perched on the edge of the wide canopied bed they shared so that she was stung into replying crossly, "You know I haven't got a lover."

"Then why did you come through the wood instead of by the road?" Henrietta said triumphantly, noticing the wet brown leaves clinging to the hem of her gown of shimmering grey silk, now noticeably dirty.

"I don't see why I should have to explain my actions to you, Henrietta," Arabella replied loftily. "I do so merely to stop this inquisition. When the sun was shining this afternoon I decided to take a walk into Felton. I am sorry I did not ask you to come with me but I wanted to be alone. Then it suddenly got dark and damp and so I ran home the shortest way through the wood knowing that mother would be cross if she knew."

Henrietta was well aware that the shortest way from the small market town of Felton was not through the wood but she realized it was useless to question her sister further. She herself had an open nature like their brother William, (though in all honesty she had to admit that William was indiscreetly frank), but Arabella guarded her privacy more jealously.

"Well I don't suppose you were secretly meeting Ambrose Hardwicke," she conceded giggling, and Arabella laughed despite herself.

"I see enough of him as it is."

"Will you ever marry him?" asked Henrietta, suddenly serious, seating herself beside her sister on the bed.

Arabella did not reply immediately and sat rubbing her cold feet. "I don't know," she said at last. "We've been friends for a long time and it is difficult to keep refusing when mother and father would like it of me."

"Only because he's a Catholic and wealthy and because theirs was an arranged marriage that happened to work out well. I shall never marry a man I do not love."

"It isn't always easy to find a suitable husband and some-one you can love," said Arabella from the superiority of her twenty one years. "The two ideals are often contradictory. You know I have been using the war as an excuse to delay committing myself but the war can't go on for ever."

"Who says it can't?" said Henrietta gloomily. "We don't seem to be getting anywhere do we? First one side seems to be winning, then the other."

It had all seemed so exciting at first when the Cavaliers were going to have a swift glorious victory over the King's opponents, but two years of indecisive results seemed an eternity for an eighteen year old. The only compensation for their curtailed social life had been the Cavalier officers brought home by their father and brother, though visitors had been scarce since the great Royalist defeat of the summer.

"You shouldn't talk as if you think there is a chance we might lose the war," Arabella admonished her sister. That was a prospect too awful to be contemplated but one which Arabella never seriously considered, even in their lowest moments.

"Of course I don't," Henrietta retorted. "I just wish we could have a decisive victory soon. Though I wouldn't accept Ambrose at the end of it all. Why he couldn't even get wounded in a proper battle, it had to be a skirmish with a dozen Roundheads." Arabella was about to protest but she went on, "I want some-one more dashing. My lover is a real Cavalier."

"Who? Philip Halsall? I don't know why you always call him your lover because he doesn't even notice you," mocked her sister.

"He will," said Henrietta complacently. "I was only a child the last time he saw me but I am nearly eighteen now. If William brings him home at Christmas I shall make sure he notices me." She smiled confidently. She was very glad she was the younger daughter and the dull Ambrose Hardwicke was not destined for her.

When Abigail Hart came into their chamber she saw them sitting side by side on the tester bed, unrecognisable as sisters with the elder fair like their father and the younger dark like their mother. Abigail thought privately that Arabella's porcelain skin was too pale for her light blonde hair, (though any suspicion of vapidity was dispelled by the spirit in her grey eyes), while Henrietta's round rosy face faintly sprinkled with freckles bore little resemblance to Lady Mary's finely-chiselled features and her hair was a true brown, lacking the copper glow of her mother's. Abigail was intensely proud of her own vibrant glowing auburn hair and she hated to hide it under her coif. At night she lay with it spread over her pillow and dreamt that her lover buried his face in the luxuriant tresses. Not that she had a lover. Abigail did not know what sort of lover she might find but it was certainly not one of the fieldworkers who ogled her when she took them something to drink, or the blacksmith's lad who had tried to put his hand up her skirt in the darkness of the smithy, or even the lawyer's clerk who licked his lips and smiled obsequiously whenever he saw her. Her lover was faceless and nameless but at night she imagined what it would be like to be with him.

"Remember there is a visitor for supper," she said as she rolled the silk stockings over Arabella's small feet. "Lady Mary says be sure you are not late."

"Colonel Miles Griffin," said Henrietta, "I wonder if he will be young and handsome."

"Why should it matter to you seeing you already have a lover," mocked her sister mischievously. "Anyway if he is a friend of father's he will probably be at least forty."

Henrietta lost interest in him at that, except to ask, "Why do you think he is coming? To ask father to go and fight again? With both father and William away there will be small chance of company in the future."

Abigail knelt back on her heels and studied the blackened hem of Arabella's dress. That would take some scrubbing! She wondered where her secretive young mistress had been but said aloud, "Are you ready for me to dress your hair?"

"Would you curl my fringe again," replied Arabella while Henrietta, who had jumped up and was surveying herself critically in the silver hand mirror on the table beside the bed, asked, "Do you think you could fasten my hair in a knot at the back to make me look older? And I'll have my yellow dress out of the closet because I believe yellow is the most fashionable colour at Court this autumn."

Very occasionally Abigail wished she could wear one of the girls' beautiful dresses instead of her own plain sombre clothes. For most of the time she was not tempted, because before she came to serve the Heskeths she had been reared in a Puritan family and vanity was not part of her nature, but sometimes when she was pressing the soft silks and taffetas she imagined what it would feel like to have such materials against her skin. Her tall slender figure could display a gown to full advantage whereas Henrietta was no more than average height with an adolescent plumpness and Arabella was decidedly petite with a waif-like fragility. Henrietta had already let her bodice and skirt fall to the floor and was standing in her petticoat and shift, screwing up her curls behind her head and pulling faces into the glass, so Abigail picked up the hairbrush from the table and set to work.

Later when they descended the stairs both girls were impressively elegant, Arabella's apple- green satin gown complementing Henrietta's buttercup yellow, and Lady Mary smiled at her daughters approvingly. Together they entered the oak-panelled dining room where a fire glowed in the hearth to offset the encroaching damp of the October evening, and the candles in silver candlesticks flickered on the polished surface of the long table and the plate set ready to dine. Sir James proudly introduced his daughters to Colonel Miles Griffin of the King's Lifeguard. The stranger was not young but he had a handsome leonine head of silvering hair and a sun-browned face framed by a lace collar. His ease of manner would have distinguished him, apart from his well-cut doublet and breeches of dark red silk trimmed with gold braid, as he bowed low over their hands and complimented them with a suave assurance Noting that his eyes twinkled appreciatively Henrietta felt bold enough to ask with her usual impetuosity, "How fares His Majesty, sir?"

"He is very well and full of hope for the future", the colonel answered, smiling at her enthusiasm and adding, with a significant look at Sir James, "but he is greatly in need of the support of all his loyal subjects."

"As we have always given it," said Sir James evenly, tapping the surface of the marble chimneypiece while his wife tightened her lips and looked apprehensive.

Throughout the meal the conversation turned mainly on the war and no-one would have had it otherwise. The Heskeths were particularly eager for news of Prince Rupert because their only son, twenty year old William, was with the Prince's cavalry whose losses had been so great at the battle of Marston Moor. William had written to tell them of his safety and how after Rupert had managed to regroup his scattered forces he had begun recruiting again in Lancashire and Chester to replace the men he had lost, but they had heard nothing further. Colonel Griffin was able to tell them that the Prince had then moved south to the safety of the garrison at Bristol where he was the governor and where he had been training his new recruits. However he was now on his way to join up with the King, who had almost reached Salisbury after a successful campaign in the South West. "The defeat of the Earl of Essex's army in Cornwall has been a notable victory for us this autumn," he said, "and has in some measure compensated for our defeat at York. Undoubtedly that was a serious set-back for us and we have lost control of a large part of the north, but we have regained the south -west. We must not underestimate our recent successes nor lose heart."

"It was a pity we allowed Essex himself to escape," said Sir James in the tone of one with previous experience of the tactical errors of the Royalists.

"But he has been discredited as commander of the Parliamentary forces and the blow to their morale is intense," the colonel insisted.

"Some of the Roundheads were glad to see him go, including Oliver Cromwell. Does not this leave the position open now for Cromwell, who is more to be feared than the Earl of Essex," countered Sir James.

"Parliament is not likely to offer Cromwell the post of Commander-in-Chief. He is too outspoken and his views are too extreme to find favour with many of his party, especially the Presbyterians."

"I am not so sure, Miles. Their victory at York was largely due to him, didn't Rupert himself call him old Ironside? He put an end to the belief that our cavalry is unbeatable."

"He is a force to be reckoned with," agreed Colonel Griffin.

"But he is an old man," protested Henrietta. "How can he do such great feats at his age when he has not even been born and bred a soldier?"

The colonel smiled ruefully for at forty-five Cromwell was some years younger than himself, but Lady Mary replied quietly, "Because he is the son of the Devil."

There was silence for a while, broken only by the ring of spoons on dishes and the spluttering of the candles.

"I am afraid you have come to take my husband away again," said Lady Mary at last, unable to defer any longer the question uppermost in her mind since the colonel's arrival. Sir James had been at home all the summer, busy seeing to the harvest, drilling the militia and organising the defences of Felton, as well as the normal administration of law and order in his capacity as Justice of the Peace. The colonel regarded his hostess with a measure of sympathy but he had seen too many estates left in the care of the womenfolk while their men were needed on more urgent service and Hesketh Hall was, relatively speaking, only a small manor.

"As I told you before, Prince Rupert's forces are trying to join with the King's army to get safely back to Oxford, but unfortunately this is not going to be easy because Parliament is either controlling or besieging some of our flanking garrisons - Banbury, Abingdon, Basing, Donnington. They are trying to circle us round and keep the King from his base. It is not without probability that another pitched battle might be necessary. But we dare not let the surrounding defences fall before the main army can get back to us and quite frankly there are not enough of us left in Oxford to supply the hard-pressed garrisons with the reinforcements they need."

Sir James Hesketh had made his decision a long time previously so he made no pretence of giving the matter some thought. "I will get my militia and house servants together and join you as soon as I can," he promised.

"I'll recruit for you, father," said Henrietta mischievously, to which indecorous suggestion Lady Hesketh was volubly shocked, an outlet for the fear which overtook her now that the inevitable conclusion had been reached.

But Colonel Griffin had not yet finished with his demands upon their loyalty to the Royalist cause. At the close of the meal, before they removed from the dining room, he leant forward with his elbows on the table and looked intently at his hosts, the candle flames flickering over all their serious faces. "I have not come only to ask Sir James to return to arms," he said. "I have come with a message from His Majesty asking you to make another sacrifice." There was a small intake of breath from Lady Mary while Sir James contemplated the dregs of wine in his goblet and Arabella and Henrietta studied their visitor with apprehensive fascination. "We are desperately short of money - in fact we are in dire straits. If we are to continue this war we need more arms and more men - and we have no money to pay for them. We stand in more danger of losing the war through lack of money than through anything else."

"We have given all our money," said Lady Mary defensively. "We sent donations to the King in forty-two, in forty-three and again earlier this year. We have no more capital." She looked at her husband. They had told no-one, not even their children, how low their own finances were.

"Give your valuables," the colonel said relentlessly. He looked at the uncleared table. "Your silver, your jewelry, pictures, tapestries - anything that can be sold or melted down to raise money." There was a momentary hush and Arabella instinctively fingered the emerald pendant which hung in the low neckline of her green gown. "We are begging you to make another sacrifice for the cause we all fervently believe in - the preservation of the monarchy and the overthrow of rebellion in England," the colonel's voice took on a note of passionate intensity. He knew he was asking a lot but there were now so many impoverished Royalists that he had ceased to feel compunction in begging from those who still had anything to give. They had come too far to turn back; they had no alternative but to go on; no matter what the cost. "I would not ask you to do what I have not already done myself," he said, as a guarantee of his sincerity, not as a boast of his loyalty. "If we cannot raise another army, if we cannot bring the Parliament forces to defeat, then England as we know it will cease to exist."

"You can take all my jewelry, everything I have," cried Henrietta impulsively, already slipping the rings from her fingers and unfastening the pearl necklace from her throat. "I will do anything I can to save the King."

Sir James and Lady Mary looked at each other across the table but Colonel Griffin had not yet quite finished. The warning was unmistakable as he said, "I should also remind you that the Roundheads will make no such request. Should your valuables be left to swell their coffers........," he left the sentence unfinished.

"You may have everything you need," said Lady Mary quietly but decisively. "When are they to be collected?"

"I shall send a waggon and a troop of horse in a few days," replied the colonel. "We are deeply grateful for your loyalty and generosity and I know that His Majesty will personally express his indebtedness to James when he comes to Oxford. Let us pray that all these sacrifices will be rewarded by God granting us victory."

They sat for a time in silence, realizing the magnitude of what they had promised, whilst the guttering candles shed their flickering light for the last time on the table silver and Lady Hesketh's jewels.

Abigail Hart opened the casement of her chamber under the eaves and leant out as she heard a groom leading the visitor's horse round to the front of the house. Colonel Griffin's leave-taking was brief and brisk and she watched him swing himself into the saddle and gallop away along the driveway. She wondered what moves were afoot with the Royalist army and how any new developments might affect the Heskeths. She had been in service with them for seven years now, since she was fourteen and Arabella had been of an age for a personal maid. Her parents had died and Aunt Keziah was proud to have found her a position in such a fine household, even a Catholic one, though Uncle Jacob had uttered strong misgivings about Papists and warned her to keep herself pure from their heathen ways. She had been afraid of entering the large intimidating house but meeting the gentle Lady Hesketh had allayed her fears and she had discovered to her surprise that these Papists were neither monsters nor heathens. Although most of the servants were Catholics also and participated in the household religion, Lady Mary never pressed her to conform or interfered with her own Puritan preferences while making it clear that she would welcome her to share their faith. She valued the girl's proper behaviour, her industry and honesty, and had no wish to lose her. And Abigail was never tempted to forsake her Puritan convictions even though sometimes she might envy the colour and gaiety of the Heskeths' lives. Upon the outbreak of hostilities between the King and his Parliament she had been merely confused. Then when Uncle Jacob had fallen at Edgehill in the first pitched battle of the war old loyalties had been resurrected. Instinctively her sympathies had veered towards the Parliament cause and she recollected the injustices of the King - unfair taxes on the common people and the ear-clipping of Puritans like William Prynne who had dared to speak out against attempts to curtail religious freedom and impose uniformity of worship. Yet the Heskeths, who had chosen to support the Royalist cause, had a claim on her allegiance after taking care of her all these years and she counted Hesketh Hall her home in all respects. She felt torn both ways and it was difficult to reconcile her hopes for a Parliament victory with her fears for the household to which she was inexorably bound, though she had learnt to deal with her divided loyalties by ignoring the problem as much as she could. As the hoof-beats faded into the distance she stood for a time watching the rain clouds veil the moon. Then closing the casement she knelt beside her bed to recite a psalm as she had always been accustomed to do before she slept. This night she chose Psalm 46 - "He maketh war to cease unto the end of the earth; He breaketh the bow and cutteth the spear in sunder; He burneth the chariot in the fire. Be still and know that I am God."

Downstairs in the parlour the Hesketh family gathered around the dying embers of the fire and knelt for their evening devotions as usual. As the well-loved words of the litany to the Blessed Virgin floated on the darkness, Henrietta, touched by their emotion, thought how romantic it would be to be poor and how she could impress Philip Halsall with her tragic simplicity. Arabella tried to think about the words she was saying but kept seeing Kit Verney's face with the upward tilted mouth that kissed so sweetly, and the mocking blue eyes that seemed to be permanently questioning the absurdity of life. On his way to Oxford that day he had contrived to steal an hour alone with her but she did not know when she would see him again. A falling coal jolted her from her reverie and she made an effort to bring her thoughts back in line with her prayers. How could she expect her prayers to be answered if she did not pray with sincerity?

To her amazement her prayers were answered in a surprising way, in spite of her inattention. A few days later when Miles Griffin's troop of horse came for the bounty of Hesketh Hall the colonel was not with them and the troop was led instead by Captain Kit Verney. Arabella and Henrietta were sitting with their mother and Abigail in Lady Mary's upstairs parlour, repairing some worn lace on one of Lady Mary's old gowns which she had decided to resurrect into service as an economy measure. Henrietta, who was seated facing the window, was the first to see the horsemen approaching the house and rose eagerly, seizing the opportunity to abandon a tedious task. The others followed and Sir James was summoned so that when the officer in charge had dismounted the whole family were standing on the steps to greet him. Arabella's heart seemed to stop when she saw that it was Kit Verney, but he was intent on introducing himself to her parents and only when these courtesies were completed did he make his salutations to her and their eyes met in secret acknowledgement.

The loading of the waggon was swift and ordered. In the past few days everything had been sorted and packed most carefully in pieces of old cloth and sacking. As the plate and candlesticks, the contents of jewelry boxes, some paintings and Flemish tapestries, had all been surrendered, so the associated memories had been bequeathed with them - memories of times and events, of people and places. The memories had been packed away with the objects and now they were merely indeterminate bundles, removed without ceremony or regret. Sir James supervised the loading and Lady Mary, dignified and composed in a brown satin gown which enhanced the rich tints of her hair, went to arrange food and drink for the soldiers.

"Please join us in some refreshment before you leave, Captain Verney," she invited him when all was finished. "Your men will find pies and ale awaiting them in the kitchen."

Leaving two men on guard, Kit dismissed the others to the kitchen precincts and joined the Hesketh family in the dining room where wine and cold meats were laid out. Arabella had been in a torment of impatience while Kit had been involved in the loading and had made answer to Henrietta's chatter from long habit without hearing a word of what she said. All her attention had been fixed on the tall figure in red velvet breeches, the gold-braided sleeves of his red doublet showing beneath the buff leather coat over which was draped a crimson silk sash of office, his black beaver hat set at a rakish angle on his long dark hair. Now it was an aching sweetness for her to sit demure and still as he talked to her parents. It gave her a deep pleasure to dwell on his lithe handsome form and to follow the curve of his cheek and the quirky line of his mouth as he turned away, but she ached for the feel of that mouth upon hers and for his smile to be hers alone.

She thought of the time she had first met him, in the spring six months earlier at a supper at the home of

Ambrose Hardwicke. The gathering had been numerous and light-hearted and the Hardwickes had entertained with their customary grandeur. The young Cavaliers present were reckless and carefree for they were fresh from a series of successful triumphs and as yet oblivious to the fact that the Roundheads were massing in the north and waiting to conjoin with the army of the Solemn League and Covenant preparing to march down from Scotland. Mistress Hardwicke, a stout woman of loud voice and indomitable will, liked to take every opportunity to display the dainty well-bred Arabella as the prospective bride of her only surviving child, though she chafed at Arabella's reluctance to commit herself to a formal betrothal. Ambrose Hardwicke was an agreeable unassuming young man, fair and stout, without any particular qualities to distinguish him apart from a devotion to his childhood companion. All the young people had gathered in the spacious hall with its square dimensions and marble tiled floor to dance some country measures and Arabella and Ambrose were dancing together when a stranger audaciously cut in and to Ambrose's chagrin whisked his partner away.

"You are much too graceful to be tied any longer to such a clodhopper," he laughed. "Kit Verney at your service, Mistress Hesketh, reputed to be the best dancer in this present company. We are well matched I think."

Arabella looked up into the quizzical face and for the first time in her life fell in love, the symptoms of which she recognised immediately from the French and Italian romances she read with such avidity. He was the most handsome man she had ever seen, tall and elegant with black hair that fell straight and thick to his shoulders, piercing blue eyes and a finely drawn moustache outlining the sardonic curve of his mouth. With a nonchalant assurance he foiled all Ambrose's attempts to reclaim his partner and when the music changed he kept hold of her hand and led her to where another set was being formed. Ambrose watched with ill-concealed displeasure and at the end of the dance reclaimed her hastily.

"It is not proper that you should dance so long with a stranger, Arabella," he remonstrated, his plain good-natured face creased in a frown.

"If I am to marry you, Ambrose, I hope you will not be a jealous husband," she replied haughtily, knowing that any mention of marriage would pacify him. She took his arm as they made their way to get something to eat from the long table laden with tempting dishes set out in the dining room, but her eyes surreptitiously sought out Kit Verney and once he caught her looking at him and smiled, making her flush with embarrassment.

When they returned to the hall the musicians had begun a coranto and saluting Ambrose with an exaggerated show of politeness the audacious Kit whisked her away again with an alacrity that defied rejection. At this final disregard of his interest, Ambrose decided it was time to make searching enquiries as to Kit Verney's intentions and it was with considerable satisfaction that when he reclaimed Arabella he was able to report smugly, "Captain Verney has a wife so I am told, somewhere in the West Country."

Arabella's face registered no reaction but it seemed to her that the myriads of candles had suddenly all been extinguished. She returned both physically and in spirit to the familiar circle of her old acquaintances, averting her eyes from where she knew Kit was and evading all his attempts to reach her. Eventually however he managed to accost her in one of the intervals between the dances and said reproachfully, "My adorable Arabella, why are you neglecting me for the attentions of Master Hardwicke, a worthy boy but no reward for your matchless beauty."

"Do not belittle either of us," retorted Arabella with spirit. "Ambrose Hardwicke and I are almost betrothed."

"So I have heard," he acknowledged, amused by the flash of anger in her grey eyes, "but nothing definite or I would not offend my hosts."

"Yet you offend me, sir, by pretending courtesy and being possessed of a wife."

"Ah, my fame travels before me I see. Of what use is it to say that my wife is a hundred miles away and you have captured my heart." He was completely unrepentant and a sardonic smile played around his mouth.

"I find your sentiments offensive, sir, please speak to me no more," said Arabella as firmly as she could, yet well aware that her voice trembled a little.

He bowed courteously and left her, keeping her command for the rest of the evening. Yet when the time came to leave, in the hustle and bustle of farewells, she had turned and seen him watching her and for a moment their eyes had met in a fatal last encounter.

Throughout the spring and summer Arabella had thought longingly of Kit Verney. Perhaps if her life had been more exciting she might have forgotten him, but company was scarce as nearly all the young men of her acquaintance were away fighting, including her fun-loving brother, and the warm pleasant days had a lazy monotony that lacked any diversion. So Kit's image fleshed out the romances she read and intruded into her dreams. When the Royalist armies marched north to dispel a conjunction of Scots and Roundheads she presumed he must have gone with them. Then in July had come news of the devastating defeat at Marston Moor near York. Foremost among their anxieties was William because Prince Rupert's cavalry had sustained terrible casualties losing half their force of some fourteen thousand men, and it was weeks before they learnt that he was safe. With this comfort secure, Arabella's visions of Kit were divided between imagining him dead on the field of battle or safe at home in the arms of his wife, either picture too painful to contemplate for long. She decided it was time to put him from her mind and whenever she met Ambrose she was patient and obliging, leading him to hope that she would soon consent to a betrothal.

Then when the harvest was being garnered in the fields she received a letter from Kit saying that he was on his way back to Oxford and pleading for a brief meeting and she had agreed, not without misgivings, to meet him secretly. They had walked by the river, concealed by the alders, and he had held her in his arms, kissing her with the confident assurance of a man experienced with women and making her tremble with a frisson of excitement. Her only experience of a man's affection had been Ambrose's hesitant salutations, and Kit's intimate hold on her body sent the blood throbbing through her veins. Yet some instinct warned her to be careful. She knew that what they were doing was wrong and dangerous and that it was not honourable of Kit to ask it of her. But she longed to have an experience of love before she had to settle into the dreariness of an arranged marriage, and the excitement helped to compensate for the tedium the war had imposed upon the women in contrast to the dangerous lottery played by the men.

"You are looking sad, Mistress Hesketh," Kit's voice broke into her reverie and she started.

"Not intentionally, sir. My thoughts were far away," she replied calmly, though his intrusion had alarmed her and she looked around anxiously at her family.

"I am going to join the King," he whispered under cover of retrieving his glove which had dropped at her feet. "Secure me an invitation for Yuletide." Then turning back to his hosts he said, "I must be on the road, Lady Hesketh. The sooner my consignment is in safe hands the better. My thanks for your hospitality and your great generosity." To Sir James he added, "I believe I shall see you in Oxford shortly, sir. Know that you have the gratitude of all who serve the King." He made a deep bow to all the family then replacing his hat he put on his gloves, picked up his sword, and sent one of the guards to gather the men from the conviviality of the kitchen where the servant girls were hanging onto their every word. Then with a swift command they were away without further ceremony or delay.

"Let us pray they reach their destination safely," said Sir James as the cavalcade wound down the driveway, for he was well aware that Roundhead patrols were on the lookout for such consignments.

"Amen," said Lady Mary fervently. "But Captain Verney seems a very capable young man. Perhaps we could invite him for Yuletide, I am sure William would like him."

"Blessed Virgin thank you," breathed Arabella.

"Didn't you dance with him once at the Hardwicke's?" Henrietta asked. "I am sure I remember his face. How strange that he made no mention of it, though I did think he seemed to look at you in a familiar manner."

"I think I did dance with him once but it was only for a brief space of time," her sister answered airily. "I don't suppose he even remembered me."

Riding at the head of his troop and keeping a sharp lookout in every direction, Kit Verney wondered again what he was doing. Unfortunately Arabella Hesketh was not a lady of the Court whose easy virtue presented no great obstacle to pleasant dalliance, like most of his conquests in Oxford. She was the exquisitely virginal daughter of a wealthy titled Catholic Royalist and he was a married man. He had begun the flirtation because her innocence combined with the spirit that flashed in her grey eyes had presented an irresistible attraction and he was interested to see how long it would take before she succumbed to his charms. It had proved easier than he had anticipated and because of his experience with women he was in no doubt that she was in love with him and his for the taking if he continued with the seduction. But an unexpected element had crept into the situation and one for which he was totally unprepared, because he feared that he was in danger of falling in love himself. The memory of the slight figure in the luminous gown of ivory satin, her grey eyes fixed on his face as he took his leave, moved him in a way he had not thought possible. He had never felt like this before. He could well have asked for her hand in marriage except that he was already a married man. Sweet Jesus, what was he to do? Then as he rode a solution of a sort came into his mind. Once she was married he would perhaps be able to take her as his mistress for then it would be an acceptable situation, especially as she was certainly not in love with the dull young country landowner. The waiting would be tedious but could be offset by some pleasant flirtation in anticipation of what was to come. His spirits rose at the thought.

In the last week of October, on a morning bristling with hoar frost, Sir James Hesketh left for the garrison at Oxford in company with the menservants from the Hall. In Felton he was to collect the local militia, though they were largely men without enthusiasm. The winter had begun early and promised to be a hard one. Men were not keen to leave their homes and families once again for a cause they did not wholeheartedly believe in, for many of the local tradesmen and yeomen supported Parliament in their hearts and many more were indifferent. But Sir James was their local landowner and master so they had to follow him. The Hesketh family stood on the steps to watch him out of sight and he rode away, leaving the Hall in the care of women, apart from an old retainer and a young boy. As they turned back into the welcome warmth of the house Lady Mary cast her eyes over the bare walls and the denuded surfaces of tables and chests. At least if the Roundheads do come they will find very little to take, she thought.

CHAPTER 2

NOVEMBER 1644

The winter had indeed come early and a bitter frost continued to clamp the land in its iron grip. In Hesketh Hall the women were glad of the timber from their own woods as they stoked the fires, though with only a handful of servants there was little time to sit by the hearth and enjoy pleasant diversions like reading and music. Arabella and Henrietta donned aprons and helped with brewing and baking, preserving and distilling, pounding away with mortar and pestle to mix potions for cooking, for medicines, for perfuming linen and for sprinkling on the bowls of dried flowers and herbs around the house. There were wax candles and balls of soap to be made and, when there was time, sweetmeats ready to pack into little bags as gifts for the approaching Yuletide. Sewing seemed never ending, repairing sheets and trimming bolsters as well as the more agreeable tasks of seeing to their gowns for the Yuletide festivities. The severe weather combined with the unsettled conditions in the countryside meant that there were few pedlars abroad so little opportunity to buy new trimmings and they spent hours taking off the lace and braid from old gowns and re-using them on others to give an appearance of newness. Every Wednesday they sent young Timothy into Felton to meet the carrier's cart but he was never able to purchase what they wanted, either through forgetfulness or unavailability, and one week it never came at all because a skirmish between a raiding party of Royalists and a passing patrol of Roundheads necessitated a diversion. If the girls went up to Felton to make purchases they would sometimes be able to buy a news sheet or pick up scraps of gossip but it was often inaccurate and always out of date so that it was difficult to know what was happening in the world at large. But they learnt that the King had returned safely to his base at Oxford on the first of November. Even though Prince Rupert had been unable to reach him with a protective escort, he had successfully resisted a large Roundhead force at Newbury which had tried to prevent his passage home. It had been a considerable triumph for the King and now that both he and Prince Rupert were back in Oxford and the garrison reinforced, the women felt more secure and their anxieties for Sir James were lessened. There was also the prospect of William's imminent return though when they heard nothing from him they were ignorant of the fact that the army had marched away again to the relief of Donnington Castle, one of their flanking garrisons still under siege by the Roundheads. It was Ambrose Hardwicke who rode over with the news that Donnington had been relieved and he was greeted with such an excessive welcome that he began to think the tide was turning in his favour as well as for the Royalists.

"It goes to show how starved of novelty we are when Ambrose can inspire such fervour in us," laughed Henrietta when he had gone. Nevertheless it had been a pleasant day as they had found time for a game of chess and Henrietta had played on the spinet while they sang together. Even Lady Mary had felt gay and hopeful for the future as Banbury had also been relieved and it seemed as if the Royalists were re-establishing their superiority. And soon it would be the blessed season of Advent. Then an incident occurred which shook their new-found complacency and jolted them into an awareness of the unpredictability of their present situation.

One afternoon Arabella and Henrietta were sitting in the little parlour on the old side of the house because it was cosier and warmer. Henrietta had been reading aloud while her sister, with infinite care and the most delicate stitches, embroidered pink roses across the bodice of her favourite ivory satin gown. As dusk was falling Henrietta stood up to light candles and Arabella went to draw the tawny linen curtains across the small diamond-paned window which looked towards the wood, when an unfamiliar noise alerted her and made her peer more closely into the deepening shadows. She thought she discerned movement amongst the trees and whispering to her sister to stay the lighting of the candles she stood motionless behind cover of the curtain, straining her eyes into the twilight. To her great alarm she made out a group of five or six men, bedraggled and in disarray but unmistakably foot soldiers, creeping stealthily out of the wood and round the side of the house to the back. With a swiftness born of necessity she ran to find the two pistols kept in readiness in the hall, sending Henrietta first to the kitchen for their old ostler Silas, then to alert the others.

"I don't know if they are on our side or not but they are acting suspiciously and seem to be intent on making a surprise entry," she said when Silas hurriedly joined her in the back passageway, followed by Timothy with the servant girls nervously behind him.

"I think they must be Roundheads," said Silas, taking the pistol she offered him. "Do you want to give the other one to Timothy?"

Arabella had already spanned the wheel-lock as her father had taught her. "No, I will go upstairs and fire from one of the first floor windows so that they will think our numbers are greater than they are," she replied with presence of mind, already starting to run up the back staircase. She had never fired a pistol but her father had given her careful instruction before he left and the feel of it in her hand gave her a sense of security.

Silas took up his position behind the door, his hand lightly holding the latch, his pistol levelled. The old man was not unduly worried for the main element of a surprise attack was surprise and this had already been denied the intruders. It was the only advantage in attempting an entry at the back for the passageway was now too constricted - behind him stood Timothy brandishing a large meat hook and the girls had grabbed whatever makeshift weapons they could from the kitchen. Lady Mary hovered apprehensively at the rear but Henrietta and Abigail had pushed their way onto the staircase, each clutching a heavy pewter candlestick. Silas motioned everyone to be still and straining his ears for the sound of movement outside he suddenly flung open the door and fired at close range into the little group of men. At almost the same time Arabella fired her pistol from upstairs, the recoil jerking her back against the window frame where she had been supporting herself. The explosions sounded loudly in the still air followed by a moment of silence, broken only by the decelerating click of the ratchet as she rewound the pistol. But there was no need, for to everyone's amazement and relief the survivors began to run away, shambling in confusion towards the shelter of the wood and leaving the body of their companion lying on the threshold.

"Mistress Henrietta, tell Mistress Arabella to stay where she is for a time in case they decide to return or there are others lurking about," said Silas. "I shall stay here with Timothy, although I think we have seen the last of them. I think they were just a few deserters or stragglers from some skirmish, they looked in a bad way."

"What about this man?" asked Lady Mary, who had now come to the front of the little group. "We must do something for him," she continued as the stricken soldier began to moan and they realized he was not dead.

Abigail went and knelt down beside him whilst the others waited, and when she rose she gave his pistol to Lady Mary saying, "He is very badly injured, the ball has gone right through his chest."

"Let us get him inside," said her mistress, handing over the firearm distastefully to Silas. His limbs were a dead weight and splayed grotesquely in his unconsciousness but together they managed to carry him into the kitchen and lay him on the floor there. The maids found cloths and water but they could see that it was useless and there was nothing they could do for him so one of them used the water to sponge away the blood which had dripped on her own skirt.

Arabella had come back downstairs and only now did she realize the full implications of what had happened. She leant against the kitchen door, shaking slightly. "I think I killed him," she said.

"No you did not, Mistress. I killed him. Your shot went wide," Silas reassured her, taking the pistol from her shaking hand.

Nevertheless she stood looking down at the man in shocked pity. It might have been she, Arabella Hesketh, who had killed him. When she had fired her father's pistol it had been towards an unknown enemy. Now she could see he was just a poor middle-aged man who was probably some-one's husband and father. He was dirty and unshaven with grizzled hair, his boots were worn into holes and the blood seeped through his stained ragged coat. His eyes opened for a brief minute though they were glazed and unseeing. "No harm,.......wanted food,...... walked.......many miles," his voice, scarcely audible, died away altogether. Then after a moment he uttered something so faintly that Abigail had to put her face close to his to catch the words.

"He wants us to pray for him," she said.

Lady Mary made the sign of the cross but Abigail requested gently, "Let me pray for him, my lady, in the words he understands." She knelt beside him and taking hold of his hands made a simple prayer commending him to God's care and mercy. Then she closed his eyes.

Henrietta had begun to cry. "He looked as if he could have been the father of any of those poor children in the village. He didn't mean us any harm, he was only hungry."

"They were intent on plunder, or perhaps worse, no matter what he said," declared Silas, completely unmoved by what he had done, for the protection of his mistress and her family was his first priority. "They must have heard that the house was unattended and might have done much mischief. Have no regrets, Lady Hesketh. Sir James would not have hesitated to kill any of them."

"That may well be," she acknowledged, "but it has been a very troubling incident. Tomorrow you and Timothy must give him decent burial. Meanwhile let us remove the body to the hall and cover it with a sheet."

They left the curtains undrawn that night and Silas and Timothy stayed on guard. Nobody slept, anxious in case the Roundheads had been part of a larger group marauding in the area and who still might return. Arabella and Henrietta crowded into their mother's bed and Abigail wheeled out the truckle bed and slept beside them as she used to do when they were sick. But no-one came and all was still. In the hall the eerie figure of the dead man covered by a cloth kept its silent vigil.

The next morning they buried him but it was not so easy to bury the memory. The incident had disturbed them and made them aware of how vulnerable they were, but for Lady Hesketh it was more than that. For the first time since she came here there had been a death in Hesketh Hall, for she did not count the two babies who had never opened their eyes to the light. And it was they, the inhabitants, who had killed a man - an ordinary, pitiable man who could have been one of their tenants. They did not know whether he would have done them harm or not, but under the conditions of war they had been forced to believe the worst. The war had invaded the precincts of their home, imposing its conditions upon them, enacting its tragedies. But eventually the memory began to fade in the busyness of the day-to-day routine, and though for a time they were more than usually vigilant they recovered their confidence and life went on in its usual pattern.

As November entered its fourth week Abigail prepared to go and see Aunt Keziah, her only surviving relative to whom she paid a twice-yearly visit at Midsummer and near Christmas. Lady Hesketh had tried to dissuade her from going this season by insisting that the weather was too cold and the roads icy. She was also afraid that she might fall into the hands of disreputable soldiers on the journey. But Abigail's own arguments were convincing. "I always go at this time, she will be expecting me and will be afraid I have come to harm if she does not hear from me. It is less than twenty miles to Stratford on familiar roads and I am young and strong."

Lady Mary could have commanded her obedience but she understood Abigail's loyalty to the aunt who had reared her and the girl asked for so little time off. So she had a generous parcel of food packed up and insisted that she took the pony, the only transport still left to them as their other horses had been commandeered for the King's army.

"No, I cannot possibly do that, you may have need of him yourself," Abigail demurred.

But her mistress was insistent. "If you make the journey quicker then you will return to us the sooner."

Abigail left the Hall with the first glimmerings of dawn and reached Stratford well after mid-day for she had not overtaxed the pony. But he had been company for her, especially in the open countryside between the hamlets, although there were other travellers on the highroad and the only soldiers she had seen had thankfully been going in the other direction though they whistled and shouted to her. Stratford had changed hands more than once during the course of the war as the town lay on the borderline between Parliamentary Warwickshire and Royalist Gloucestershire and she was not sure where its present loyalties were disposed. However as she neared the town she could see that it was still held by Parliament as on her last visit, albeit tentatively. She was relieved to have completed her journey safely as she crossed the old stone bridge across the river, some of its fourteen arches showing damage from gunshot, and turned left along Waterside until she came to Sheep street. She was very cold, her fingers numb inside her gloves and her cheeks and lips stinging even though she had pulled the hood of her cloak as closely round her face as she could. The street was busy and noisy with townspeople shopping and chatting, carts clattering and two or three buff-coated soldiers trying to look purposeful, but it was now familiar ground to Abigail as she guided the pony to the timber and plaster cottage leaning crookedly at the end of the row.

Her legs and feet were so stiff that she almost stumbled as she dismounted and thankfully lifted the door-latch of her aunt's tiny homestead, calling happily. As she stepped immediately into the front room the contrasting warmth made the blood pulse painfully in her face for a fire was burning cheerfully in the hearth though the room was empty. She put her bag down on the broad oak settle beneath the small casement window and went through into the back room which was larder and store-room with neatly stacked shelves and a large stone sink. She expected to see her aunt preparing food or scouring pots but that too was empty. Then a young man carrying a leather bucket of water entered from the yard and they stood looking at each other in surprise and some mistrust.

He was in his mid-twenties, just above average height and sturdily built with dark brown hair thick over his forehead but cropped around his ears and falling short of his collar. His features were well defined, agreeable if not strikingly handsome, with a straight nose, firm chin and a resolution in the thin line of his lips. His face was tanned as if he spent much time out of doors, but it was the deep brown eyes with a steady bold gaze that Abigail was most aware of, giving him a composure and confidence that compelled attention, even in the coarse linen shirt and leather jerkin he was wearing. For his part he saw a tall girl, her slender figure noticeable even beneath the grey cloak whose hood had fallen back to reveal a white coif from which peeped tendrils of auburn hair. Slanting green eyes, tinged with apprehension, were set in a perfect oval face and her cheeks glowed with the cold.

"My aunt, Keziah Hart, where is she?" she asked nervously.

The firm line of his mouth relaxed into a smile and having put down the bucket he came towards her saying, "Then you must be Abigail. Don't worry, Keziah is only with Meg Cooper a few doors away, helping with a birthing, she'll be back soon. Come close to the fire, you must be freezing. Let me take your cloak. Would you like something to eat, I can get you some bread and cheese and mulled ale." Abigail felt his concern pleasing after her long journey, but she was still puzzled by his presence and he felt her uncertainty. "I am sorry," he said contritely, "I know of you through your aunt but you of course do not know me. My name is John Radcliffe and Keziah is my mother's second cousin." His smile was disarming and she took the hand he held out to her.

"If you don't mind taking my pony round to the shed and bedding him down I would be very grateful," she said apologetically, and he was off immediately whilst she settled herself thankfully on the chair tucked in the chimney corner. When he returned she had thawed out and was beginning to feel pleasantly relieved and at ease. She studied the young man more closely and could not forbear asking curiously, "What do you know about me?"

"That you are twenty-one years old, that you have been employed by the Hesketh family of Felton for several years, that you come to visit your aunt twice a year, which she looks forward to with great anticipation because you are kind and generous and she is exceedingly fond of you." He laughed, but while he was talking he had been finding food and now presented her with a wooden trencher of thick bread and cheese and a mug of ale into which he had plunged the hot poker from the fire. Not realising how hungry her journey had made her, having saved her lunch to share later with her aunt, she was soon eating with relish and not able to question him further. He had seated himself opposite her on a stool at the other side of the hearth and when she had put aside the plate and mug she began to study him again. She liked his resolute mouth and his bold eyes, especially when they creased into a smile and softened the serious expression of his face.

"And do you live in Stratford, John Radcliffe?" she asked. "It is strange that we have never met before."

"I do not live in these parts," he replied. "I come from Huntingdon."

"General Cromwell's town," said Abigail. "Then it surprises me you are not fighting with the army of Parliament."

"I have done so," he acknowledged. "At present I am recovering from a wound in my shoulder."

Abigail thought there had been little sign of that when he was lifting the heavy bucket, but at that moment Aunt Keziah bustled in, uttering cries of delight alternated with apologies when she saw her niece, and soon they were in each other's arms, kissing and hugging each other.

"Well now, and I never thought you would come in such cold weather," she said. "What about something to eat? Oh I see that John has already been taking care of you and that you have become acquainted. I'm afraid that having John with me means you will have to share my bed, Abigail."

"That's no problem, Aunt, I must only stay two nights. I don't like to take advantage of Lady Hesketh's kindness and be gone too long while the men are away.

Anyway my mind is at rest now that I see you are in good health and stand to be well looked after."

"It's so good to have a man about the house again, you know, some-one to cut wood and carry water," said Keziah looking at John fondly. "Last week he mended the roof for me, a leak that had been troubling me since spring, and yesterday he caught a hare so that we can have a good nourishing stew."

Abigail's fine-arched brows lifted at this paean to the young man's accomplishments and catching her glance he shrugged deprecatingly, saying with a twinkle in his eye, "Oh I can turn my hand to most things."

But Aunt Keziah's garrulous tongue could not be stopped. "Of course I wasn't expecting him which made the surprise so much the better. I hadn't seen him since he was a child, though he hasn't changed at all, so like his mother. We tried to keep in touch over the years but these things are not easy and it was thoughtful of Rachel to send John while he was recovering from his wound. Sadly I had to give him news of my dear Jacob."

There was silence for a moment and Abigail thought of her uncle who would sit quietly in the chimney corner smoking his pipe whilst his round cheerful wife chattered about everything under the sun. When he did speak it would be a gruff burr, but she had understood that under the hard shell was a loving soul, incapable of expression.

"He died fighting for what he believed in. We are all very proud of him," she said softly, seeing her aunt wipe away a tear.

"He died fighting with a pitchfork against the King's young gallants," cried Keziah bitterly.

"The army of Parliament no longer fight with pitchforks." John Radcliffe's voice was intense. "The war is nearly over and your Jacob's death will be vindicated."

Abigail looked at him in surprise, seeing the stony expression on his face. "Do you really think the war is nearly over?" she asked.

"One more pitched battle and that will be the end. The Royalists know this and have been evading it. But come spring we will seek them out and bring them to their Armageddon." He saw the fear in Abigail's eyes and looked steadily at her. "Get away from the Heskeths. You are on a sinking ship."

"I have not been happy about you being there of late," said Aunt Keziah. "Why don't you stay here with John and me where you will be safe."

"I won't be here much longer," John interrupted, "I must be away when January comes in. But I think you should consider it, Abigail. If I were you I wouldn't stay in a Papist household."

The little room had grown dark and the fire burnt low. "I cannot leave them now," said Abigail after a pause. "I've been with them too long." Her aunt sighed heavily and she could feel John Radcliffe's eyes boring into her.

Later that night as she lay beside her aunt in the matrimonial bed she found it difficult to sleep. The straw mattress was hard and lumpy and the blankets rough against her skin, and she was conscious of her aunt snoring beside her. She was also conscious of John Radcliffe in the room next to theirs. She was sure she could hear him moving about and wondered what was keeping him awake too. Once she even thought she heard the door open and close. She heard the watchman call every hour until after midnight then she fell into a restless slumber, tormented by dreams which she could not recollect in the morning but which left her feeling disturbed.

When she awoke she was conscious of something different. The low room under the eaves seemed extraordinarily light and there was a strange hush as if all sound hung suspended. Bending her head to look out of the little casement she was surprised to find a dense blanket of snow enveloping the town, with thick flakes still falling.

"Well that's an end to any idea of you going home tomorrow," said Aunt Keziah as she served them breakfast of bread and ale, and Abigail detected a note of satisfaction in her voice.

Afterwards she and John tried to clear away the snow from around the house and their part of the walkway using a broom and a long-handled shovel. Their exertions were strenuous but useless as the flakes continued to whirl and replace their efforts with fresh falls. As they stood leaning on their tools and gasping for breath, their healthy faces glowing in the tingling cold, John said, "You have a snowflake right on the end of your nose," and as he flicked it off with his fingers they began to laugh helplessly. Abigail thought she had not had such fun since she used to shovel snow with William Hesketh and it had always ended in a snowball fight, usually with William as victor. When Aunt Keziah called them in for a hot posset she found them laughing and talking in an easy companionship that belied their short acquaintance. They sat with their feet against the fire-dogs, hands warming on the hot pewter mugs, and felt also the warmth of each other's regard.

Abigail's enforced stay lengthened into a week. It was not a comfortable week. The snow seeped into every corner of the cottage, under the doors, between the window frames, under the eaves, and feet and skirt hems were constantly wet. There was little in the way of fresh food but John made forays to the market and Aunt Keziah made bread and griddle scones and pancakes. They had to go carefully with their stock of wood and at night it was unbearably cold as they shivered in their beds, Abigail lying close to Aunt Keziah's bulky form. Often she thought longingly of the warmth and comfort of Hesketh Hall. And yet deep within her some tremulous expectancy kept her wanting this time to continue.

Forced into such close and unavoidable proximity with John Radcliffe she became even more aware of his masculine attraction. He made a sled, broke the ice in the water butt every morning, rubbed down his horse and her pony, fought a losing battle with the leaks and walked out every day to find out what news there was, but even so there was much time left together. Sometimes they played guessing games, or nine men's morris and draughts with makeshift pieces of wood or stones and a board marked out on the scrubbed pine table. The enforced inactivity would have frustrated most men but John was calm and patient, though Abigail would often feel he was deep in his own thoughts. Despite their closeness she felt she knew little about him. He would talk about his boyhood in the countryside of Huntingdon but little about his time with the army of Parliament or his plans for the future other than saying he would return home at the beginning of January, for Puritans did not keep the festivities of Yuletide. For her part she was eager to chatter about life at Hesketh Hall, about her adoptive family and their present deprivations, knowing that Aunt Keziah was interested in all her doings but sometimes vaguely conscious that John had led her on. Sometimes she would look up and find his gaze on her, a gaze so unflinching that she would have to turn away. She suspected that a great fire burnt within his virile frame and although well dampened down at this moment the anticipation of its sudden kindling excited her. During the times when Aunt Keziah struggled to her neighbours, leaving them alone together, Abigail was aware of stirrings within her that she had previously only experienced in her daydreams and as she watched his strong body performing household tasks she longed for some physical contact with him.

One day she was bending over the fire stirring a barley stew and as she straightened he took her in his arms in one swift movement, clamping his mouth onto hers with a fierceness that took her by surprise. She had imagined his strong arms holding her and his lips touching hers but her dreams had been pale in comparison. He let her go and they stood apart but with their eyes still fixed upon each other questioningly. Then slowly and deliberately Abigail put her hands behind his neck and pulled his mouth onto hers again, pressing her body tight against him. She felt his passion rising as he put his arms around her again and her eager body responded as fire surged through her loins. When they moved apart it was John Radcliffe who looked at Abigail Hart with surprise and consideration. He didn't speak but turned aside, running his fingers through his hair, and at that moment the door opened to Aunt Keziah.

He made no attempt to touch her again, not even the next day when they were alone together, and Abigail's eyes followed him questioningly as he busied himself about the house. Under his touch her vague half-formed desires had blossomed into fully developed physical longings and she ached for him to embrace her again. As he brushed past her in the confining space she seized his hand, imprisoning it in hers as she cried, "Don't you want me, John Radcliffe? Why did you kiss me like that yesterday?"

He looked at her steadily. "Yes I want you, Abigail. But it isn't the time or the place."

Abigail was as tall as John and could look straight into his eyes as she took his face between her hands.

The slanting green eyes were tempting him. He crushed her to him, his hands pressing in the small of her back to pull her into the hardness of his body, the pressure of his mouth making her gasp for breath. Then his lips moved to the hollow of her throat above the white shift peeping from the neckline of her bodice.

"There is Aunt Keziah's bed upstairs," she whispered, her breath coming in quick, short gasps.

The words sobered him and he made a great effort to stem the rising tide of his passion, pulling away resolutely as he fought to regain control of himself. "No," he almost shouted, "that would be fornication. We are Puritans and keep the commandments of the Lord." Knowing how close he had come to losing control the anger was for himself as he continued savagely, "I am not one of your Cavalier seducers."

She turned away from him then, tears of hurt and disappointment stinging her eyelids, and they stood with the breadth of the room between them, she humiliated and he ashamed.

"I am sorry," he said after a while.

"I have never known a man," she whispered. There was silence and the snow could be heard slipping from the roof.

He approached her humbly. "Forgive me, Abigail, it was wrong of me." She did not know if he meant his kisses or what he had said. "You are very beautiful and we have been too close this week. But let us not rush things, let us give seeds time to grow."

Abigail now knew the identity of the faceless lover she had often dreamed about and to whom in her dreams she had surrendered herself completely. But she turned to him and said with dignity, "I like your honesty, John Radcliffe. I would like to know you better."

In that moment as she stood before him in her simple bodice and skirt of brown wool with her linen coif covering her magnificent hair, neither coy about her feelings for him nor resentful about his rejection, he liked her more than he had ever done.

For the rest of the time they returned to their previous companionable relationship, avoiding all physical contact, but it was not the same and they could not recover their first spontaneous enjoyment. Abigail was ready for home and by the week's end the roads were clear enough for her to return.

"I'll come with you almost as far as Felton," John proffered. "I want to make sure you are safe. You can ride pillion behind me, it will be more comfortable and a little faster."

Wanting his company for a little longer Abigail did not demur.

Aunt Keziah clung to her tearfully. "Take good care of yourself, Abigail, and don't forget, if things get too difficult come back here to me, we'll manage between us somehow."

"I promise, dear Aunt, farewell and God keep you," said Abigail kissing her affectionately.

Then John swung her up onto his powerful stallion and they were away with the pony on a leading rein. They did not save much time because they were forced to keep the pony's pace though she trotted faster unladen, but Abigail found it comforting to have some-one taking care of her on the journey back and not having to worry about meeting soldiers. It was also much warmer as she rode with her head pillowed against John's broad back, shielded from the worst of the wind which blew the odd flurry of snow from the still leaden sky. When they were within a mile of Felton she appealed to him to go no further so he obeyed and lifted her down. He kissed her gently, without passion, and she held onto him, not wanting him to leave her now that the moment had come.

"May I come to see you before I leave Stratford?" he asked.

She was surprised by the request and her heart leapt with happiness that he still wanted their relationship to continue. "Oh yes. But come secretly. I think it best if the Heskeths did not know, under the circumstances."

This suited well with John's own wishes so he acquiesced without demur. "I will come two weeks today, the third Friday in December. Look for me by five o' the clock or thereabouts, just after full darkness."

"Come through the wood, it's only a spinney really, but you can leave your horse there. I will be waiting for you by the back door, there will be no-one abroad, there are but few of us."

He nodded agreement and said, "If the weather is too bad, or anything happens whereby I must fail the appointment, then I will come the next day at the same hour and so on for three days. If you hear nothing from me by the fourth day then you must presume I am dead."

She looked at him sharply but he was smiling, that steady smile that was so confident but it lacked mirth. He helped her mount the pony and watched until she was out of sight round the bend of the road that led straight into Felton. Then he turned his horse and galloped away at speed, cross country. The pace was exhilarating after the enforced canter and his horse felt it too, snorting with delight as he gave him his head. As the hooves rang on the hard frost his spirits soared involuntarily and he experienced again the excitement he always felt in a cavalry charge - Captain John Radcliffe of Oliver Cromwell's celebrated Ironsides. Soon he would be back again with the army of Parliament, ready to crush the Royalists once and for all.

As Abigail reached the familiar approach to Hesketh Hall she was vaguely aware that something was wrong without knowing why. Then she realized there were no trees. All that remained of Hesketh wood was a conglomeration of sawn-off stumps, misshapen trunks and some young saplings. Ahead, in plain view to all comers, Hesketh Hall stood naked and vulnerable. As she turned into the driveway the pony recognised his own territory and trotted happily the last few hundred yards even though the ground was rutted and slippery with frost and the remains of snow. Perplexed by what had greeted her she was dismounting by the mounting block when Arabella and Henrietta came running to meet her.

"We are so glad to see you, Abigail," cried Henrietta. "We were so worried when the snow came. Have you been safe?"

"Yes I have been quite safe and well, but whatever has happened to the trees?"

"They came and cut them all down whilst you were away," Arabella replied.

"The Roundheads?"

"No, the Royalist army," snorted Henrietta in disgust.

"They needed the timber," Arabella explained. "I fear it will be a cold winter for us."

Well if John Radcliffe does come he will find no wood to hide in, Abigail mused regretfully as they went into the house together.

CHAPTER 3

DECEMBER 1644

The horse came galloping up to the house as if possessed by the Devil and its rider had leapt from the saddle while it was still in motion. Taking the steps two at a time he ran into the hall shouting, "Have those God-damn Roundhead scum been here? Christ's blood there will be vengeance for this." He threw his plumed hat onto the settle by the livery cupboard and his eyes travelled to the bare plaster where used to hang an English tapestry of a hunting scene.

"William!" Arabella and Henrietta came running into the hall with shrieks of glee and Lady Hesketh appeared on the staircase. William Hesketh was beside himself with rage, sweeping his arm around the room as he continued, "When did this plundering take place? And the wood?"

Lady Mary looked down at her son's furious face, the face that had haunted her dreams when she had known he was in the forefront of danger and which she had so fervently prayed to see again. But her voice was icy cold as she commanded, "Control yourself, William. How dare you enter the house in this manner. And with a guest too, whose welcome should be your first concern," she added, seeing another figure standing hesitantly outside the door.

William had the grace to look abashed and Henrietta rushed in, "You are a noddle, William, it was our army that chopped down the trees, and we gave them the tapestry, and other things as well."

"You should put your brain where your mouth is," said Arabella with an elder sister's licence.

"You really ought to be less impulsive and find out the facts before you charge in like a bull," his mother reproved him severely, then she could contain herself no longer and ran to him, putting her arms around him and kissing him in a wordless welcome. "Now bring in your guest and we will explain everything to you."

William extricated himself thankfully and containing his impatience to know the facts presented his companion. "It's Philip Halsall, you have met before. Come in Philip. Excuse my exhibition of misplaced passion," he grimaced ruefully. "It seems things are not as I thought."

"We are very glad to see you again, Master Halsall, even though you find us in straitened circumstances," said Lady Mary. "Forgive my son's bad manners. No doubt you are well used to his impulses."

Feeling slightly embarrassed by the furore attendant upon their arrival, William's companion stammered his courtesies and hoped they would pardon his presumption in accepting William's invitation to share Yuletide with them as it was not possible for him to return to his own home in Lancashire. Lady Mary smiled at his earnestness. Many of the young gallants around the Court in Oxford had adopted the affectation of a stammer in deference to the King's own disability, but with Philip Halsall the occasional impediment was a natural manifestation of his diffidence. As she led him into the parlour, assuring him of the warmth of his reception, she wondered not for the first time what this serious, modest young man should have in common with her irrepressible son, though she hopefully conjectured he must have some steadying influence upon William.

Once William had heard the most important news of the last months he turned his attention to more pressing matters. "Where is Abigail?" he asked Henrietta quietly, though he had to repeat the question, the second time accompanied by a poke in her ribs, because his sister was gazing at Philip, lost to all else.

She turned her attention reluctantly from the tall, serious-faced young man to answer off-handedly, "She is in our dressing room I think."

Abigail, who was pressing two of the girls' gowns which they had recently been altering, had heard the commotion William caused and was expecting him, so that when she heard his light springing step on the stairs she was not surprised.

"Didn't you hear me, Abigail?" he asked, bursting in on her without ceremony.

"It would have been difficult not to," she murmured, concentrating on pleating the frills of Arabella's sleeve with the goffering tongs.

He strode over to her. "Aren't you glad to see me? I have dreamt about you for nearly a year, I have come back from perils you would not suspect existed, and yet you do not care enough to welcome me." There was a teasing mockery in his tone, but also reproach.

She looked at him directly, laying down the tongs. "That is your family's prerogative. I am not family, William."

The sight of her after his long absence set his pulses racing as his eyes drank in every detail of her tall slender form in the simple grey wool bodice, the skirt of a lighter hue hitched up above a dark blue linen petticoat, tendrils of bright hair escaping from her coif and framing her lovely face. He had dreamt of her so many times in the silks and velvets he would love to buy for her and her hair braided with jewels or, in his less controlled moments, naked with her gorgeous hair loose to his touch. More than one of his whores had been imagined with Abigail's face.

"You know I love you," he said. "I always have."

She bent her head and took up the tongs again for the words were said with his habitual jocularity. "You are a fool, William Hesketh. I am older than you, you are a mere boy."

"One year older than I am, that is all. You are the fool, Abigail Hart," he cried with an unexpected flash of anger. "I am no boy. Look at me! I have fought battles, real battles, not with toy soldiers. I have killed men and watched my friends die in agony. And I have known women too, women are ten a penny for Royalist officers."

"I suppose they are." Her tone of voice made him realize he had said the wrong thing. But she looked at him carefully and saw that her teasing companion of old was indeed a man, his golden hair curling nonchalantly past his shoulders, his face clean-shaven apart from the thin moustache carefully outlined above his upper lip in imitation of his hero, Prince Rupert, and his grey eyes stormy with frustration. She spoke reasonably. "You are a Catholic, I am a Puritan; you are a Royalist, my sympathies are with Parliament; you are the heir to Hesketh Hall, I am a servant. How many more differences can there be between us, William? I think my appeal lies chiefly in these obstacles. You always did attempt the impossible," she added, smiling ruefully.

He smiled too and shrugged in half-acceptance. She held out her hand to him then. "I am truly glad to see you back safely."

William resisted the impulse to kiss her on the mouth and instead took her outstretched hand, brushing it lightly with his lips. He knew there was probably some truth in what she had said, he had always been wayward.

When William had left her, Abigail felt too disturbed to return immediately to her ironing. She paced the closet pondering uneasily on the mischance that had arranged William Hesketh's homecoming on the same day John Radcliffe had planned his secret visit - the third Friday in December.

In her place at the head of the table Lady Mary felt well content. For the first time in almost a year she had all her children about her and watching their animated faces and listening to their bantering chatter it was easy to believe that everything was as it had always been. Yet whatever the conversation turned on sooner or later talk of the war intruded, for Arabella and Henrietta were eager to know all that had been happening and William and Philip were only too happy to relate their adventures.

"Life has been so tedious without you, William. Tell us what it has been like for you," Henrietta invited.

"Sometimes tedious for us too," smiled Philip, for although Henrietta's words had ostensibly been addressed to her brother she had looked at him. "We spent some time recruiting on the Welsh marches but once we had volunteers they had to be trained."

"And because Prince Rupert believes in his men being well trained that meant lots of drill and discipline, no holiday I assure you," William continued. "Then we went down to Bristol to seek more reinforcements there." He stopped as he caught Philip's eye. Some of the happenings in Bristol were not fit for the ears of women as the Cavaliers, jaded by the tedium of marching and drilling and still smarting from the defeat at Marston Moor, had gone on the rampage.

"Finally we met up with the King's army and came back to Oxford," Philip concluded. "The only real action we have seen lately, apart from odd skirmishes, has been when we relieved Donnington castle."

"Not as exciting as a battle though," said William. "It was a pity we missed the battle at Newbury and the King's army got all the glory. They have seen more action than we have of late."

"But recruiting men must be very important," Arabella ventured, "especially after so many were killed or wounded at Marston Moor."

"Or ran away," said William drily, "or were taken prisoner, or just changed sides."

"What was it really like at Marston Moor?" she asked, thinking involuntarily of Kit Verney as she watched Henrietta's absorption in Philip Halsall.

"It was a disaster," said William in disgust. "The point is we were caught out. We were sitting on the ground eating our supper, us, Prince Rupert's crack troops, when the Roundheads attacked. By the time we had got ourselves organized they were upon us."

"It was seven o' clock at night you see," explained Philip, "and we had been in position all day, just waiting."

"Waiting for God-damn reinforcements that should have come at dawn," said William. "If they had arrived on time we would have been able to attack the Roundheads who were by then only drawing up their battle lines. But the slow-arsed Newcastle only arrived on the field with his troops at mid-day so by the time they had got into place it was towards evening. Everyone then considered it was too late to join battle that day and Rupert gave permission to eat. But the Roundheads attacked, like the devious bastards they are."

"Wasn't that somewhat negligent of Prince Rupert?" Henrietta asked innocently.

"We hadn't eaten all day," began Philip, but William burst in angrily.

"'Sblood, you don't fight a battle in the evening Henrietta. It's bad enough trying to distinguish your enemy in the daylight when you all look the same, but when the shadows begin to lengthen..."

"The Roundheads apparently did," interrupted Henrietta calmly.

"Yes, well, they aren't professionals. They have no idea of professional soldiering and the rules of war."

Philip could recognise the irony of his friend's words more than William himself did, perhaps prompted by the expression on Henrietta's lively face, and he said, "The whole battle was a shambles. A thunderstorm broke and we fought in torrential rain so that with the growing dusk we were unable to see anything. Some of our men ran away, but when all is said and done, it was chiefly Cromwell's cavalry that won the battle for Parliament."

"When all is said and done it was chiefly because we were outnumbered," retorted William hotly. "Every time we have lost to Parliament we have been outnumbered three to two. It is common knowledge that Cromwell never fights unless the odds are in his favour."

Lady Mary had remained silent during the conversation because she preferred not to know what conditions were like for her husband and son when they were away, but now she proffered, "That seems to me a very sensible decision. If that is true then there is neither mystery nor supernatural power about his success."

"You are quite right, Lady Hesketh," agreed Philip. "Cromwell is no sorcerer but merely a very able and cunning man and we must beat him at his own game.

That is why our recruiting campaign has been so important this autumn."

"Well we have tried to help," said Henrietta. "I think the Heskeths must have paid the wages of quite a few soldiers."

"Henrietta!" cried her mother reprovingly, but she was gaily unrepentant and still in her irrepressible mood she continued, "Let's go and collect evergreens tomorrow. We can scour the countryside now that you have brought horses. It is wonderful to have you home, William." She smiled also at Philip, including him in her enthusiasm, and was rewarded by a returning smile which transformed his long, rather melancholy face, and gave him a vitality he seemed to lack in repose.

As darkness fell Abigail was praying that no-one would see John Radcliffe arrive, and fearing that William might either press for her company with the family or seek her at her duties she had pleaded a headache and made a request to keep to her chamber. She strained her ears for any unfamiliar sound when at the appointed time she quietly unlatched the door at the back of the house, but all was still. The family were in the large parlour on the other side of the house and the servants were taking their supper in the kitchen.

"Oh God, please let him come tonight," she prayed, "I cannot possibly go through all this again tomorrow."

"Abigail!" The barely perceptible whisper revealed John's dark figure in the shadows, though she had neither seen nor heard him arrive. She closed the door carefully behind them then without either of them speaking she led him silently by the back stairs to her chamber on the second floor. Even in his boots he managed to walk as quietly as she did and, despite the tension, he was looking about him carefully, observing every detail of the house and its layout.

Once they were safe in her chamber Abigail closed the door thankfully and leant with her back against it until her trembling stopped. Then she lit a candle and placed it on a small table near the bed where its light spread evenly about the room. John looked about him. The room was spacious and airy with a casement window overlooking the front of the house and across which she had already drawn the curtains of cream linen embroidered in blackwork. Under the window stood a panelled oak chest, there was a tall-backed chair near the empty hearth beside which stood a spinning wheel, and another chair opposite with a cane seat. The bed along one wall had a green wool counterpane embroidered with a design of fruit and flowers in crewel work and on the walls were framed samplers of intricate designs interlaced with Bible texts, obviously worked by the same hand. There was a Bible on the table near the bed together with a worn volume of Fox's Book of Martyrs. It was a pleasant room, furnished with care and considerable comfort for a girl who was a servant.

"Sit down, John," she said, taking his thick wool cloak and leather gauntlets from him and motioning him to the tall chair. She seated herself opposite on the other chair and he was able to look at her properly for the first time. She took off her coif and let her unbound hair fall to her waist, then she smiled at him hesitantly. "I am most glad to see you but you could not have come at a worst time. Today William Hesketh came home with a fellow officer and I am afraid he could come looking for me."

"Does he pester you with his attentions?" asked John sharply.

"Oh no, he's barely twenty, but he's friendly and .....observant."

"Don't worry, no-one will see me, but I must not stay longer than an hour or so."

"So short?" cried Abigail, impulsively leaving her chair and going to kneel beside him. "I excused myself from supper saying I did not feel well. Tell me everything you have been doing."

"All is the same in Stratford as when you left it. Keziah is well and life goes on exactly the same."

Nothing else was forthcoming so she asked, "Where have you left your horse? I am sorry about the wood, the Royalists cut it down while I was away."

"Did they indeed. Well it doesn't matter, my horse is well and truly hidden."

Her hair was falling onto his knees where she leant against him, burnished copper in the candle glow and fragrant with rosemary and other scents that wafted upwards into the shadows of the room. He began to stroke her hair, almost unthinkingly, and she stopped listening for sounds outside the door and put her head against his knee, feeling the coarse wool of his breeches against her cheek. After a time he said carefully, "Abigail, you say William Hesketh and another officer is here. Will Sir James be coming back also?"

"He promised so, yes. He will probably bring friends with him too for Yuletide."

"A fine little nest of Royalist officers." She looked up at him and he cupped her face in his hands. "Will you do something for me?"

"Of course."

"Will you try to find out what the Royalists plan to do in the new year?"

Her eyes widened and she drew back from him involuntarily. He stood up and pulled her with him, holding her close. "I told you, Abigail, we have to bring this war to an end. It is ruining our country and bringing hardship to both sides. Parliament is going to win in the end so the sooner we have the victory the better for everyone."

She looked into his eyes but despite the closeness of his hold there was no desire in them, only a far-seeing look. "They do not talk to me, I am only a servant. How can I discover anything?"

"They must discuss the situation in general conversation. And you say William Hesketh is particularly ..... friendly."

"Yes," she admitted hesitantly. "Sometimes William talks to me."

"Well then, anything you can pick up. It doesn't matter how trivial it might sound, any snippets of information."

She wanted to ask him why it mattered to him so much. It did not seem to be merely curiosity. She wondered what this kinsman lodger of Aunt Keziah's actually did. She looked up into his face. He was so serious. It seemed such a long time since they had laughed carelessly together and she wanted to coax him into a loving mood again, to caress his face and his hair, but he was holding her too tightly to move. Yet despite her great desire for his love and kisses she felt an uncomfortable reluctance to do what he asked of her.

"It would be disloyal to report what is said in a place of trust," she murmured tremulously.

He put her from him at arm's length and looked into her troubled eyes. "You are one of us, Abigail. We are two of a kind. We know the strength and worth of ordinary people - honest, God-fearing people who have been excluded too long from their rights. The King refuses to rule by the will of the people and overturns the laws of the land. Oh he makes promises but they are all vain promises, because if he were to regain his power he would dissolve Parliament again and subject England to his own whims and those of his dissolute advisers. I have nothing against the King personally but he must not, cannot, over-ride an elected Parliament working for the good of all men, nor hold the established laws of England in such contempt."

Abigail was moved by the passion in his voice, low though it was, but she said, "The Heskeths are kind and God-fearing."

"They are fighting for an order that is not God's order. And they are Papists who, if they had the power, would bend all to their religion as they did in the past, who have called upon foreign armies to crush the Protestant faith, and who are at this very moment organising the Papists of Ireland and France to come and destroy the Parliament cause."

Abigail could feel his intensity mesmerising her as his hands dug into her shoulders. She was both attracted to him and afraid of him. "I don't know," she murmured, "Oh I don't know," her emotions in turmoil and her voice catching in a sob.

He began kissing her then, gently and persuasively, and her mouth responded hungrily to his.

"I give you my word of honour that no harm will come to the Heskeths themselves," he said.

"Who are you that you can promise such things?" she asked wonderingly, drawing back from him again. "What sort of influence do you have to guarantee such indemnity?" Once again she felt afraid.

"The Heskeths are small fry," he said dismissively, "but they know some important people." He began to kiss her again, more insistently and demandingly. "You must help our cause, Abigail. You must help me." His hands began to move over her body with a cool mastery as he caressed her. She felt herself melting under his touch and her desire for him was overwhelming. But still she was unsure.

"I don't know if I can," she murmured.

"Yes you can, you must. Will you help me, Abigail?" His voice sounded insistently in her ear as he kissed her throat and neck.

"Yes, oh yes, if you will love me. Oh love me, John, love me." He put her away from him then and she cried impulsively, "I promise, John," fearing he was going to leave her. "If you will love me I will do anything for you." Her breath was coming in quick short gasps and she clutched his shoulders compulsively.

There was a moment's hesitation then he began to unlace her bodice. She trembled as his capable fingers drew the lace and his hands found her breasts beneath the coarse linen of her shift. Her skirt and petticoat fell to the floor as he unloosed the ties and he carried her to the bed where she lay in her shift shivering with cold and anticipation. Looking up at the rafters dimly visible in the candlelight she heard his boots and his belt fall to the floor, then he was beside her, taking her into his arms and pressing his mouth onto hers. She gasped as his hands took control of her body but she knew it was what she wanted more than anything and she was willing to pay any price. Briefly she thought of what the consequences might be, then all other considerations were forgotten as his hands moved up along her thighs and she instinctively opened herself to him.

Much later John Radcliffe was on his way back to Stratford, having collected his horse and left Hesketh Hall without being seen or heard, being well used to such clandestine activities. But instead of the exhilaration he usually experienced on the conclusion of another successful mission he felt a disturbing sensation of unease that intensified as he rode. Many times in the past two years he had had to do things that troubled him, Cromwell had once made him whip a deserter in the market place in Ely, and he had no taste for the brutalities of war. But tonight the feeling of unease was touched by shame and this was an experience he was not used to. He remembered how in the cottage in Stratford he had angrily told Abigail he was no Cavalier seducer. But the insistent drumming of the hooves on the highway spelt out to him the realization that what he had done was worse. He had not even seduced a girl for his pleasure, but for his calculated purpose. Oh it had been pleasurable, intensely so. Abigail was beautiful and passionate and he had made love to her with the hunger of long abstinence, a hunger she had fed with her innocent ardour into a fierce desire. But initially he had not thought of his own pleasure. The first time he had kissed her in Stratford had been an instinctive response to a beautiful woman with whom he had been cooped up close for too long and he had lusted after her, but he had tried to draw back when he saw into what dangerous paths it was leading him. Then he had perceived the opportunity to make use of her desire for him and once set upon that course it had been all too easy to satisfy his lust. It was unjust to reflect that Abigail had needed little encouragement and that she had tempted him with her passion as well as her beauty. She was a virgin and had declared her love for him, but for his own ends he had used her without loving her. The worst was that he had a genuine liking and regard for her. He was twenty-six years old and no virgin, but he had tried to keep himself pure and live by the tenets of his Puritan faith. Cromwell expected high moral standards from his troops, especially his officers, saying that if you chose godly honest men as captains then honest men would follow them. The weight of his sin pressed upon him as the miles passed.

Suddenly, on an impulse, he reined in his horse and sat mounted by the lonely roadside, aware of nothing but the breathing and snorting of the animal, the soughing of the wind in the trees and the heaviness in his heart. He offered up a silent prayer. He was well aware that people made sport of Puritans for enjoying sins, especially fornication, then showing exaggerated remorse after the deed was done. But he felt a genuine reproach for his behaviour and a shame that he had fleshed out the likeness drawn by his enemies. He prayed for forgiveness, and that any errors of judgement he had made in the furtherance of a cause he believed to be right and divinely sanctioned might not prove irreversible. But all the way home he could not rid his thoughts of Abigail Hart who had given him her first, unasked-for love.

Abigail lay undisturbed all night in the bed which would never feel the same again because it had borne John's imprint and something of his energy still remained there. She had no wish for sleep, lying in the wetness because she wanted to keep reliving the pain and the ecstasy. She did not want the memory to be weakened by even a short time of oblivion because she knew now that even the sweetest dreams fell short of reality. She wondered if there might be a natural consequence of their act and recollected how the laundrymaid Betty Grice had had to leave the house, though Lady Hesketh had made careful provision for her in Felton. She believed that John would not abandon her and yet even in her happiness, even despite her inexperience, she knew that though he had made love to her with a fierce urgency she had not lit the flame which burned deep within him and which she had recognized from the beginning of their acquaintance. She was well aware that the flame had only flared into life when he spoke of the Parliamentary cause.

The following day the expedition to gather evergreens went ahead as planned and Abigail was invited to go with them. "You look a little peaky this morning, is your headache no better? asked Lady Hesketh concernedly. (William gave her a quick look and she averted her eyes.) "A breath of fresh air will do you good and there isn't anything to attend to that cannot be done just as well by Dorothy."

"We can ride behind you two and Abigail can take the pony," suggested Henrietta.

"No, Abigail is riding with me," contradicted William. "Arabella can go with Philip and you can have the pony." Henrietta took him aside for a moment then he announced, "I have changed my mind. Henrietta is too heavy for the pony so she can ride with Philip, his horse can take the extra weight. You are lighter, Arabella, so you can have the pony to yourself."

While satisfied with the change of plan Henrietta glowered at her brother for his reasons, but when she was mounted behind Philip Halsall her annoyance slipped away as she put her arms around him. He turned and said to her, "You are as light as a feather, Henrietta. William is very unkind," and she smiled back at him in gratitude.

Abigail had to hold tightly to William because he set off at a galloping pace on the horse that was as high-spirited as he was but she was determined not to give him the satisfaction of alarming her. She was in no mood for his teasing and was remembering how the last time she had ridden pillion had been behind John on the way back from Stratford. Thinking of John however made her recall her promise to him and realizing this was an ideal opportunity she chattered eagerly to William about the Royalist cavalry. He was pleased to find her taking such an interest and thinking she wanted to make up for her coldness to him the day before was in great good humour. Abigail felt a spasm of guilt but also a quiver of triumph that she was hoodwinking the quick-witted William Hesketh and that for once she was calling the tune. But she still contrived to keep Arabella close beside her when they stopped amongst the trees so that William should have no opportunity to reverse the situation.

Consequently it was not too difficult for Henrietta to lure Philip further into the woods on a seemingly accidental drift away from their companions. The undergrowth became thicker and more tangled as they pressed on and suddenly Henrietta seemed to catch her foot in a twisted root and was thrown to the ground. Philip was immediately beside her but when he tried to help her rise she grimaced in pain. "I think I have sprained my ankle," she said apologetically, gingerly trying to put her weight on it but finding it too painful to walk.

"Let me find you somewhere to rest and I will go and alert the others," he said concernedly.

While she clung to his arm and hopped on one foot he led her to where the cloven trunk of a mis-shapen oak formed an ivy covered angle wide enough to sit in and she sank down thankfully with her head resting against the bark and her eyes closed. He knelt beside her and began gently to rub her foot in its white silk stocking.

A considerable time later the others found Philip sitting on the ground, careless of his well-tailored breeches of fine black wool, while Henrietta with her green velvet hood framing her rosy face, was listening with rapt attention to his account of the siege of Lathom House. Philip was describing how he and William, as troopers in Prince Rupert's cavalry, had been on the way to York in the spring of the last year when Rupert had made a diversion to relieve Lord Derby's great fortress which was being besieged in his absence by a large Roundhead force. The event had a special significance for Philip because his family were neighbours and tenants of the great Lancashire lord and the telling of the tale had given him the opportunity to describe his home set in the flat, fertile countryside dominated by the medieval stronghold with its nine towers. Henrietta was captivated by the picture of the redoubtable Countess Charlotte contemptuously defying the threats of the Roundheads and holding out against them for three months until Prince Rupert had been able to bring his cavalry to their deliverance.

"How wonderfully brave," she sighed. "I should love to do the same if the Roundheads tried to take Hesketh Hall."

Everyone was most concerned about Henrietta's accident, (though Arabella tartly remarked that it was fortunate they had gathered enough evergreens for their purpose), and Philip lifted her onto his horse, this time setting her in front of him where she leant happily against him.

Later whilst they were occupied in putting up the holly, ivy, laurel and mistletoe in the Hall, an activity accompanied by much laughter and merry-making, Henrietta lay on a day bed, which the servants had carried into the parlour from Lady Hesketh's chamber, her foot resting on a pillow.

"It doesn't look very swollen to me," Arabella commented drily. "I do think you could have used more originality. All the romances we read show a depressing similarity with the heroine either fainting or spraining her ankle to gain the hero's attention."

"Men don't read romances," replied Henrietta unperturbed.

William was making plans to perform the Saint George play "as it is certain the mummers won't be coming this year, all the men being away, and we can't disappoint the household of their Christmas entertainment. It will give Philip and me a chance to show off our sword fighting but you had better be recovered by then Henrietta or Abigail will have to take your place in the performance." He winked mischievously at Abigail for he knew she never joined in their Yuletide festivities, shunning all attempts at playacting, gaming and dancing. "Are not you secretly glad, Abigail, that you do not live in a Puritan household where you would never have the chance to celebrate Yuletide at all. Christ's mass, that dreaded word, accompanied by all sinful merriment and heathen practices."

Abigail knew he was tormenting her as was his habit and she replied more prudishly than she intended, "Puritans believe that every day is special to the Lord and therefore have no need of festivals or holy days."

"Well give me festivals any day. Any excuse for a celebration, with plenty to drink," he laughed. "How about an hour's shooting, Philip, while the weather holds good?"

"I think I will stay and keep Henrietta company," his friend answered. "Shooting has palled a little of late."

"Better keep in practice or you'll be in a pall of a different sort," laughed William irrepressibly and went off whistling to get his carbine and a couple of the dogs. Any long period of inactivity was tedious to him.

"What will you do when the war is over?" Henrietta asked Philip when they found themselves alone together. "Will you go back to Lancashire and farm your lands?"

"I am only a third son," he said. "I shall have a small property.......but not much." The stammer intruded and

Henrietta guessed there was more within the words than he had actually said. "My mother wanted me to be a priest and my father a lawyer but I don't think I have much aptitude for either preaching or wrangling." He hesitated then continued, "I want to be a merchant, a successful one, specialising in importing glass." She looked at him in surprise and awakened interest and he felt bold enough to continue. "Glass is going to be one of the most important developments and the best glass comes from Italy. You should see the beautiful glassware the King has had specially imported. I am going to go to Venice and learn all about the craft personally and also the merchandising. There has been glass production for some time where I live in Lancashire, mainly to serve the needs of Lathom House, but it is on a small scale and done by local craftsmen. I want to bring Italian methods to England so that our local artisans can learn how to produce incredibly beautiful work themselves. "

When Lady Mary entered she found two heads bent over the globe from Sir James's study, while Philip Halsall, his serious face unusually animated, was tracing a path with his finger and discoursing at length upon a subject obviously close to his heart.

By the afternoon of Christmas Eve all preparations were completed. The Hall was decorated and the kissing bough they had made added to the greenery, Abigail evading William's attempt to lure her beneath it while Henrietta surveyed it expectantly. Young Timothy had ceremoniously brought in the Yule log on a sled and it was laid in the hearth ready to be lit later with the last brand kept carefully from the previous year to ensure good fortune. The kitchen maids had finished preparing the food with the help of their mistress and the girls, and the mince pies and plum porridge stood ready, with the goose prepared for the oven. Yet despite the overall atmosphere of jollity there was a noticeable air of disappointment for there was still no sign of Sir James. Lady Mary was preoccupied with preparations for the morrow when the poor of the town would make their way to the Hall for their customary gifts of food and drink, but still kept wondering what untoward occurrence could possibly have detained her husband. Arabella meanwhile was dejectedly accepting the fact that Kit Verney would not come after all and the time and effort spent refurbishing her gowns had been for nought.

It had been a dull, dark day with heavy skies threatening rain, or snow, and dusk fell early. They were all together in the parlour and Lady Mary was half-following a game of piquet played by the young people while at the same time checking her household book that all tasks had been completed and the inventory of food and stocks adjusted, when she caught sight of Silas in the doorway behaving mysteriously. She rose to answer his strange gesticulating, exasperated as she often was by the fact that their few remaining servants no longer had their proper designated roles and everyone had to turn their hands to whatever was required. She thought nostalgically of the time when Hesketh Hall had its footmen and serving men, gardeners and stable boys, cooks and kitchen boys, dairy maids and laundresses. Now the few women had to do the men's jobs with only Silas and Timothy to help with the heavier tasks like attending to the fires and carrying wood and water.

"A visitor for you, Lady Hesketh," Silas whispered conspiratorially, leading her to the back door. She followed him, puzzled and a little uneasy at his manner and wondering why the visitor did not use the front entrance, until she recognised the dark figure in the doorway.

"Father Edmund," she cried joyfully as she grasped his hand. "Come in, come in, we are all together apart from Sir James who is expected anytime. Everyone will be so glad to see you. Have you come far?" she asked in concern as she noted his weariness now he was out of the shadows.

"Far enough, Lady Hesketh. I am on my way north but I thought you would like me to say a Mass for you. And I wanted to see you all again, to know how you were."

"That was so kind of you," she said, knowing the risks he took. "And a Christmas Vigil Mass is something I had not dared hope for. Come into the parlour and I will bring you some wine and something to eat."

"I must only stay an hour at the most. If we could have the Mass as soon as possible I could put many miles on my journey before dawn."

Lady Mary knew how important it was for priests to work only under cover of darkness and led him immediately to the parlour. As soon as she opened the door the warmth within wafted the aromatic scent of evergreen boughs and applewood logs into the chill of the hallway. They had turned from cards to music and were merrily singing carols with Henrietta playing the spinet accompanied by Arabella and William on lutes and Philip on recorder. Father Edmund stood in the doorway listening to them with pleasure and feasting his eyes on the scene of harmony, but now he was in the light Lady Mary could see how tired his eyes were and how grey and sunken his cheeks. She led him to a chair by the fire and the songsters broke off their choral to greet him with delight. His acquaintance with the Heskeths stretched back many years for he had been tutor to William, and also to other boys in the neighbourhood who used to make their way to the Hall to receive a very adequate education. They were all aware of the risks he took to pay them a visit now with no cover of being a schoolmaster, for a priest saying Mass was under penalty of death.

"Father Edmund will hear our confession and then say a Mass for us, but it must be soon," Lady Mary said, hoping that her husband would arrive in time for this unexpected benison.

Just before six o'clock they opened the concealed door in the panelling of the rear passageway and made their way down the stone steps to the tiny chapel hidden below ground at the back of the house. Behind them came most of the servants and a few Catholics from Felton who had been hastily summoned by Timothy. The sacred vessels were taken from their hiding place and set on the altar, the candles lit and the missals opened, and as the familiar words of the Vigil of the Nativity poured over them with a rush of memories, the chapel door opened quietly and Sir James came to take his place amongst them. Lady Mary, intent on her prayers, did not look round but with a rush of happiness heard his voice join with theirs. Arabella opened her eyes and knew a deep disappointment for Kit Verney had not come with him.

CHAPTER 4

JANUARY 1645

It was New Year's Eve before Kit Verney made his tardy appearance. Giving his apologies to his hosts Kit did not tell them the truth - that he had been detained in Oxford by a certain Lady Carstairs whose favours forbade his departure until the return of her husband, and even the thought of Arabella was not sufficient inducement to make him leave a pleasant and profitable affaire. His feelings for Arabella were of a different kind to any he had ever felt for a woman before, including his wife, but it was not in his nature to refuse a tempting offer in order to wait for a future promise. Kit Verney's philosophy was to have his cake and eat it, and since his brush with death at Marston Moor he was even more likely to take all life's little opportunities with a careless acceptance. However when he saw Arabella again with her fair curls and her pale luminous skin, he was inclined to regret the time he had lost. She really was quite entrancing to a man of his jaded palate. He was amused to find that she greeted him coolly with a hint of resentment in her grey eyes, and it stimulated him to realize that he would have to recapture her favour. The challenge would enliven his visit and he made a wager with himself as to how long it would take to charm her again. William, who missed very little, had seen the communication that passed between him and Arabella when they met, and though not understanding the import he was certain that there was some intimacy between them, not openly acknowledged. He looked again at the tall slender Cavalier lounging arrogantly at ease, at the thin interesting face with its cynical mouth and mocking blue eyes. A good fellow to drink and wench with, he surmised, but dangerous surely for his innocent sister.

Kit brought with him some interesting news of an unlooked for development in the opposite camp. In London on the 19th of December Parliament had introduced the Self-Denying Ordinance. "Briefly this means that no member of either the House of Commons or the House of Lords is allowed to hold any military command as from this time," he explained. "Conflict of interest."

"Then that includes Cromwell," said Sir James in astonishment.

"I was told that he resigned his commission immediately."

There was an incredulous silence as the news sank in.

"But Parliament cannot manage without Cromwell," William said. "He is the best commander they have. We faced his cavalry at Marston Moor so we know from personal experience how good he is."

"It can't be true," said Philip. "It must be a trick, some story put out by them in order to confuse us."

"Oh it seems to be true enough," said Kit. "Apparently Sir Henry Vane resigned from the Navy at the same time and the Earls of Essex and Manchester will also have to surrender their commissions."

The assembled company found it hard to comprehend the situation. Sir James said thoughtfully, "It sounds to me as if all this is a result of in-fighting amongst the Roundhead high command. It is well known that Essex and Manchester hate Cromwell and that this feeling is returned. It would appear to be a ploy to get rid of certain people in authority and perhaps the plan has been a little too zealous for their own good."

"What is to stop Cromwell going back on his word when he has got rid of his rivals?" said William scornfully.

"Yes it is easy enough to resign in the heat of the moment," confirmed Kit. "When he is needed they can always repeal the Ordinance."

"I think from what I have heard of the man he is sincere in his doings," said Sir James slowly. "If he cannot be both a member of Parliament and a soldier then I believe his inclinations lean more to the former."

"Cannot we perhaps see this as God's doing?" Lady Mary interposed quietly. "Perhaps by sowing discord amongst Parliament He will bring about their downfall and give us victory in the new year."

The Royalist men all knew that there was discord enough in their own camp to discount her theory. There was much discontent over the fact that Prince Rupert had been made Master of Horse in the Royal Household, a highly prestigious position and of long-standing English tradition not suited, it was thought by many, to a foreign prince. William could have told her how disappointed the Prince was however at being passed over for the post he really coveted - Colonel of the Life Guards - and could report from first hand on the feuds between Rupert and both George Goring and George Digby, resulting in non co-operation between rival Royalist commands. Sir James on the other hand could have told her of the indecision of the King, vacillating between one adviser and the next as they jostled for his ear. Also of the stream of criticism constantly flowing from Queen Henrietta-Maria in France about Royalist leaders she personally misliked or distrusted. But they all kept silent, hoping indeed that the year to come would herald a resurgence of Royalist strength. And with present developments the whole company did indeed feel more confident than they had done for some time so that they were able to eat and drink in good spirits as Yuletide passed.

The first day of January had brought Ambrose Hardwicke and his parents to join in the traditional New Year's Day festivities. Entering the Hall with her customary bustle, Mistress Hardwicke looked with dismay at the bare walls which used to hold some fine tapestries and pictures. "Oh my poor Lady Hesketh, how could you bear to lose such treasures!" she exclaimed. "They were so much a part of your beautiful house."

Lady Mary was not over-fond of Joanna Hardwick who, lacking beauty and charm, liked to flaunt her respectability and her affluence. The Hardwickes were nouveau riche having made their money through trade, for Ambrose's grandfather had been a merchant seaman with the East India Company. However in real terms they were much wealthier than the Heskeths as they had considerably enlarged their land holdings and their investments over the past generation. Lady Mary was well aware that they would presume she had been forced to sell some of their possessions to pay outstanding debts but she had no intention of enlightening them.

"I think your beautiful wood panelling shows to its full advantage, Lady Mary," said Augustine Hardwicke kindly, ignoring his wife's warning glance not to be over-effusive in his admiration of his hostess. "And I think you yourself look more beautiful than ever today," he ventured rashly, knowing he would have to face his wife's wrath later for her dominance was equal to the stoutness of her frame.

"Why thank you, Augustine," smiled Lady Mary in surprise. Without any jewelry apart from a simple emerald pendant (a treasured betrothal gift from her husband) nestling in the low neckline of her dark green taffeta gown, her slender elegance made Joanna's bedecked amplitude look vulgarly ostentatious. "I do hope we shall be able to replace the tapestries some day but in the meantime the girls and I have begun a new work for above the chimney piece, not of the same standard as our Flemish pieces but 'twill serve the same purpose," she laughed. She preferred the gentle Augustine to his strident wife, though at the same time deploring his lack of spirit. She could not help regretting that they had become church Papists, practising their faith in private but making their statutory appearances at the Parish Church to avoid penalties, unlike themselves who had paid their recusancy fines stalwartly over the years. It was true that Sir James occasionally visited the Parish Church, believing that as the local landowner it was not wise to cut himself off completely from his tenants, but she had staunchly refused ever to set foot in the place. She also could not help sharing her family's disdain that the Hardwicke men were not fighting with the Royalist army, though Ambrose had made a brief foray until suffering an injury in an early skirmish. Mistress Hardwicke insisted that this had brought about a recurring chest infection, and whilst understanding her anxiety for her only child Lady Mary nonetheless suspected they were wary of any active support so that whatever the outcome of the war they would not be obvious losers.

"Ambrose has bought Arabella a most beautiful gold necklace as a New Year gift," Joanna whispered confidentially as her hostess led them into the large parlour where the company was assembled. Ambrose however was most disconcerted to find Kit Verney amongst the guests and greeted him sullenly. Kit responded courteously but with a mocking smile for he had contrived to reinstate himself in Arabella's good graces. In fact it had been easier than he had anticipated and his neglect of her had made her more responsive to him once her displeasure had been manifested. He actually wished his conquest had been more protracted, for the game had been too quickly won for the stakes available. The most he could expect were stolen kisses, and though they were of a progressive intimacy the main interest came from seeing how far he could go with the flirtation while concealing it from everyone else. However he did not succeed in completely hoodwinking William and Ambrose, and when the latter saw how eager Arabella was to partner Kit in the games and the almost casual way Kit appropriated her he began to feel down-hearted. He felt dull and staid beside the charming Cavalier, while Arabella was looking particularly attractive in a pale blue gown trimmed with silver lace, her silvery blonde ringlets bobbing tantalizingly above her bare shoulders. Ambrose was not usually stirred by her appearance, having known her too long, but when she allowed him to fasten the gold necklace around her neck he realized again how much he wanted her and the realization prompted him into a sudden decision.

Abigail Hart was also realizing how lonely she felt without John Radcliffe, especially since there was so much companionship abroad in the house. She had kept to her chamber during her spare time over Yuletide, a celebration which her religion condemned. But she felt restless as she tried to read or sew. The laughter and music floated round the house and disturbed her, filling her with vague longings. She knew John would dismiss such revelry as inconsequential and this certainty forged a bond with him in his absence. But she longed for the days to pass quickly so that she could see him again. In bed at night she relived every detail of their passion and her awakened body ached for its repetition. She had done her best to discover what he wanted and hoped it would please him for she could not bear to lose him now. She walked restlessly up and down, unable to settle to anything, then on impulse crept down to the first floor landing and stood listening to the merriment flowing in waves of sound through the open doors below.

William too was feeling restless. Home was beginning to pall on him and he was ready for action. He would be glad to return to Oxford where the company was notoriously irreverent and where they would soon be planning the spring offensive. He had not been prepared for the lack of Philip's company, for his friend had temporarily forsaken masculine pursuits in an incomprehensible preference for Henrietta's society. If only Abigail had joined them her presence would have enlivened the occasion for William. Earlier that day he had given her a pair of gloves as a New Year gift.

"What on earth am I to do with these?" she had asked unhappily on unwrapping the soft kid leather in a delicate cream with ribbon bows.

"Wear them to keep your hands warm I should think," he said drily. "God's death, even you need gloves, Abigail. I have never met a girl who wants so little."

They were hardly gloves to keep her warm however, and such gloves were the traditional gift from a lover on St. Valentine's day. "You can always wear them when you get married," he added lightly, guessing her thoughts. "Why the sudden reluctance to accept a present? Ever since you came here I have always given you a gift at New Year."

She felt that this expensive gift was different to a box of sweetmeats but then he said tauntingly, stung by her unresponsiveness, "'Tis the custom to reward servants at such a time," and went his way.

Now as he came into the hall he caught sight of her on the landing and began to leap the stairs two at a time. Abigail felt ashamed that he should have found her eavesdropping but knowing that it would give an appearance of guilt to run away she stood her ground defiantly. She thought he would have mocked her about not being able to resist the revelry and she was preparing to confront him. But instead, before she realized his intention, he had gathered her into his arms and was kissing her long and hard. He snatched her coif from her head and as her glorious hair tumbled down he clutched and pulled at the long tresses with one hand while pressing her close with the other. At last she pulled away from him, trembling with anger. "William Hesketh, do not ever do such a thing again."

"Why what would you do?" he asked tauntingly.

"I would leave this house," she replied, quietly but emphatically.

"And go where?" His voice was mocking and his eyes insolently amused.

"Do you think I have nowhere to go?" she replied. "Do you think you own me? Do you think because you buy me a pair of gloves it gives you right to my body?"

"Oh no, you are worth far more than that, Abigail," he said challengingly.

"Leave me alone, William. I will never be your mistress," she cried vehemently.

He looked at her, more beautiful than ever in her anger with her cheeks flushed and her green eyes sparkling, her auburn hair all awry. "I always get what I want, Abigail," he said coolly. "I always have."

Abigail felt his eyes following her as she turned on her heel and left him but the encounter had disturbed her and she felt uneasy.

Arabella had been in her chamber splashing rosewater on her face which was revealingly flushed after one of Kit's more intimate kisses during a game of Hunt the slipper, and as she came out onto the landing she was just in time to hear William's final words and see Abigail run up the stairs to the upper floor. Catching her brother before he could descend she said, "You ought not to engage so much with Abigail. It isn't proper and you know Mother would be angry if she knew."

"Proper!" scoffed William. "You are a fine one to talk about what is proper. I have seen your flirtation with Captain Verney and he is a married man. I don't suppose you confessed that to Father Edmund."

Arabella felt her cheeks grow hot again and she bit her lip in vexation as William ran downstairs. Sir James was just entering the hall and surprised by his son's hasty descent looked up and saw Arabella on the landing. Wondering what the two had been in disagreement about he mounted the staircase and taking her arm said, "I want to talk to you for a while, Arabella. Let us go into the gallery where we can be alone."

The long gallery had originally been a storehouse for grain when the old house was first built but in the subsequent enlargement and refinement of the Hall now displayed the family portraits and was used for recreation when the weather was too bad to go outdoors. It was a long corridor, now oak panelled, leading from the first floor landing along the side of the old wing to terminate in an alcove with an oriel window overlooking the lake. It had always been a favourite place for the children who had romped along its length or played board games on the table in the alcove, and Sir James thought it would be a less formal setting in which to talk to his daughter than his own study. They sat down together on the cushioned window seat and looking out over the metallic surface of the lake he said almost inconsequentially, "We must not forget to fill up the ice pit when the lake freezes over again."

Arabella wondered why he had brought her here and beginning to be afraid that he had learnt something about her and Kit Verney her heart fluttered uncomfortably. But instead he said, "Today Ambrose has again asked for your hand in marriage, Arabella. He also intimated that if you continue to procrastinate he would feel free to look elsewhere for a wife."

This was certainly not what she had expected and for a moment she was surprised into silence. She looked out of the window to where the sun's pallid glimmer was beginning to fade, hoping to see in the wintry landscape some intimation of her fate but all was grey and colourless. She knew that she had delayed unreasonably in accepting a proposal postulated a long time ago, but although she liked Ambrose as a friend she had always looked upon marriage with him as an event from which some undefined happening would deliver her. Still she had never thought that he would consider relinquishing her, believing that her sway over him was sure and that their future lay within her deciding.

"He has many fine qualities of honesty and integrity, and he is a Catholic," Sir James continued encouragingly as she did not speak. "The Hardwickes' wealth is considerable and he is an only child with an uncle who is also childless so that he stands to inherit his estate also. I have no doubt he would keep you rich and comfortable, give you much of your own way, and you would be able to stay close to home."

Arabella knew all this. Ambrose was good-natured and generous without having any particular talents or skills, (William could always out-run him and out-game him), and he was genuinely fond of her and complaisant to her wishes. If a comfortable unadventurous existence was what she wanted then Ambrose Hardwicke could provide it. But unfortunately she had met Kit Verney and now knew that it was possible to have stronger feelings for a man, though she could not express herself like this to her father.

"It is not possible always to make a good match within the bounds of romantic love," Sir James went on gently, as if guessing her thoughts. "But often love grows after marriage. Your mother and I scarcely knew each other when our betrothal was arranged but through our life together and our children a great love has grown between us."

Arabella couldn't imagine anyone not loving her father with his gently handsome face, his elegant pointed beard like the King, still fair though his hair was beginning to fade and was lightly tinged with grey; her father who was so wise and cultured and sensitive. Ambrose was plain and dull and not particularly intelligent. Yet could she afford to lose him altogether? Her father would not give her in a marriage that was not advantageous to her and, as he said, she would be safe. If she refused again and Ambrose turned his attentions elsewhere, as he threatened, might she not be left without a suitor when the war ended. She was twenty one and young men of her age and class were becoming fewer. She was also afraid of the disappointment and shame it would cause her parents if Ambrose retreated from a contract they had hoped for and became public knowledge. And despite her dreams she knew there could be no future with Kit Verney. Yet notwithstanding these considerations something still held her back.

"Let me wait just a little longer, but please make my reasons clear to Ambrose," she appealed to her father, not realizing that she had given him no reasons and that the argument was all in her own mind. "We are both young and there is the war, how do we know what is going to happen?"

"I was thinking that it might be one way of protecting you my dear," her father said, though unwilling to express more clearly his worries about the Hesketh estate and their own fortunes.

Arabella took his hand. "Let me wait for just one more year. If nothing has happened in the meantime I give you my solemn promise that next Christmas I will marry Ambrose. Ask him to wait for just one more year and forgive me if I have disappointed you too."

Sir James studied her earnest face. For nothing would he persuade her into a decision unpleasing to her, and marriage was indeed a great and irrevocable step. She had always been his favourite child, his first-born who had followed him around devotedly, always seeking his approval. William had needed firm handling and Henrietta, happy-go-lucky and resilient, had plodded through life unconcernedly, but Arabella with her misleading fragile beauty had always charmed her way into his heart.

"Let us leave it this time then," he said rising. "I will give my reasons to Master Hardwicke as diplomatically as possible and try to stay his impatience for a while longer."

Arabella sat alone in the gallery for some time, watching the lake darkening in the early twilight and nerving herself to go back downstairs and face Ambrose. She felt badly about her treatment of him, especially since the extravagant New Year gift which seemed to be burning her throat. How convenient it would be to love him, for at least it would prevent her being further enmeshed by Kit Verney. Perhaps she had known him too long as a friend but whatever the reasons she knew she wanted some deeper passion, both to give and receive, within the bonds of marriage. Yet she was honest enough to admit she was probably being unrealistic. Her father's words held truth for with most people love and marriage were not mutually conclusive.

When she returned to the parlour the candles had been lit, the wine-red curtains drawn across the great mullioned window, and Philip and Henrietta were roasting chestnuts on the yule log burning merrily in the grate, so that Ambrose's sulky face was the more strikingly obvious as he sat listlessly watching Kit and William dicing. She went to sit beside him and the rising hum of chatter interspersed with peals of laughter half drowned her words as she said apologetically, "I'm sorry Ambrose, but I feel I am not ready for marriage just yet."

"You are twenty one, quite old really," he retorted bluntly.

"I hope that you will not lose patience for a little while longer," she said, ignoring his remark. "Let us wait until next Christmas when hopefully the war will be over and things will be different."

"I am afraid that you will find someone else in the meantime," he said miserably.

Arabella smiled to herself as she concluded his threat of rejecting her had been a ploy to force her hand and saying coaxingly, "I don't think that is very likely," she gave him a peck on the cheek. She knew she could always placate him. However this time he continued to look sulky and said, "I intend to go and fight again with the Royalist army. I think that is the only way to win your heart." She did not know how to reply.

They parted amicably but miserably and when at last they made their final farewells Mistress Hardwicke was undeniably cold in her leave-taking.

"You look troubled." Kit Verney drew up a chair beside her in the window embrasure when the Hardwickes had gone.

She wanted to confide in him and wondered what his reaction would be so she told him. "Ambrose Hardwicke wants to marry me soon." She did not know what she expected him to say but was waiting for some declaration of despair and demands to desist from such a course.

Instead his blue eyes quickened with excitement as he said, "Why that's wonderful, Arabella, this could be the answer to all our problems." She turned to him, hurt and puzzled, not understanding him. "As a married woman with your own household you would have so much more freedom. You would be your own mistress, answerable to no-one so that we could see as much of each other as we liked and stay within the bounds of propriety." Still she looked bewildered and he continued, "Provided we were discreet there would be all the opportunities which are at present denied to us." A dawning realization of his meaning swept over her as he put it more plainly, "If you marry Ambrose we could be together as lovers. The opportunities would be provided and the risks removed."

"Are you suggesting that I should marry Ambrose and then take you as my lover?" she asked at last, shocked and disappointed.

"Of course." His eyebrows arched in surprise at such a question. "It's the perfect solution to our dilemma. I am in love with you but cannot marry you. This way we can stay together and continue our relationship in the way we both wish."

"I thought you would not have wanted me to give myself to another man," she whispered.

"What does that matter if you don't love him," he replied. "And as for Ambrose Hardwicke, he has no cause for complaint if he marries you without assurance of that love, so long as he receives his due share of the bargain. Don't be prudish, sweetheart, everyone in our position does it."

Arabella knew that Kit's marriage had been arranged for him when he was very young but she wondered in dismay what he had been doing all these years when she had believed herself to be his one true love. If he was so casual in his ideas of fidelity how could she rely on his promises once his desire had been satisfied.

"Oh think about it," he urged. "It is a heaven-sent opportunity. What could we do otherwise?"

Arabella looked at him sadly. "It seems I am not used to the ways of your society. I think you have spent too long at the Court."

She was not so innocent as she appeared. Her taste for reading had acquainted her with a wider knowledge of life than she had actually experienced for herself, and William talked freely of life in Oxford. But the idea of taking a husband merely to accommodate a lover was a suggestion she found profoundly distasteful and Kit's blatant amorality had shocked her.

"You know I love you," he was saying. "Consider it my love, for my sake. It is our only chance."

The candles spluttered merrily and a peal of laughter rang from the settle where Henrietta was sitting with William and Philip. Sir James crossed to Kit with the wine decanter and Arabella slipped away into the hall to cool her flushed face and still her turbulent thoughts. She wanted Kit and she knew he was becoming increasingly frustrated by their unsatisfactory relationship. It now lay within her grasp to have both a comfortable marriage and an exciting lover. But when she finally gave herself to a man she wanted it to be to him only and for as long as she lived. She opened the front door and an icy blast took her by surprise. It was too cold to venture outside. The world had suddenly become a dark and chilling place.

Later that night when she was lying beside Henrietta in the big canopied bed they shared, cosy despite the empty hearth because Abigail had warmed the sheets with the warming pan, she told her sister, "Ambrose has been pestering me again to marry him."

"You ought to," said Henrietta sleepily.

"How can you say that when you have always been so critical of him, calling him dull and whey-faced?" Arabella cried in annoyance.

"Because you might not find anyone else," replied Henrietta, turning over and burying her face in the pillow from whence came a muffled, "Kit Verney is married already." She had thought of confiding to her sister that she was going to marry Philip Halsall but feared Arabella might scoff at their short acquaintance. The first time her brother had brought him to the house in the spring of the previous year she had immediately liked the young Cavalier whose thoughtful manners and quiet intelligence provided a foil to William's abundant high spirits. She had only been seventeen and he had taken little notice of her, but the determined Henrietta was not discouraged. She had carried his image in her heart all the summer and sworn that the next time she saw him she would make him aware of her. She was more than satisfied with her success for that evening he had made a veiled but unmistakable declaration of love. However it was unlikely that she would be allowed to marry before her elder sister so it now behoved her to change her opinion of Ambrose Hardwicke and encourage Arabella to consider his suit.

After Twelfth Night the company dispersed. William could not wait to be on the road for he had found the days between New Year and Twelfth Night tedious and monotonous. He was first in the saddle, his horse cantering and rearing, snorting in the frozen air and as eager as his master for some exercise. Lady Mary watched her son with regret, longing to have kept him at home and not knowing when she would see him again. Philip Halsall was leaving with a mixture of regret and satisfaction. He had no wish to leave the comfortable house and the acknowledged regard of Henrietta Hesketh but he knew that he would return as soon as he could. His visit had resulted in an unlooked for commitment to the young girl, not beautiful by conventional standards but intelligent, warm-hearted and high-spirited, whose round rosy face had become very appealing to him in the pleasant leisurely days of holiday. Kit Verney had left early after New Year having experienced a frustrating visit, and he wondered ultimately why he had bothered to come at all. He liked to play a waiting game but only if the waiting was not too long. He could only hope that he had been able to persuade Arabella to consent to marriage, and the possibility of making her his mistress still excited him but he could see no point in arranging any further clandestine meetings at the moment. This might precipitate her into action but with characteristic sanguinity he left all in the hands of fate and turned his attention to wondering what new delights Oxford held in store. Sir James Hesketh left home regretfully but well pleased with the success of their festivities. Also events at large seemed more hopeful as the Marquis of Montrose was making military progress on behalf of the Royalists in Scotland and was already preparing to march south and join with the King, while Parliamentary sources hinted at some disarray in their organisation. It appeared that the tide was turning again in their favour and the future might see a reversal of their fortunes once more.

John Radcliffe had promised to return to Hesketh Hall two days after the feast of the Epiphany (or the 6th of January as it was known to John and Abigail), when it was presumed that the Cavaliers would have returned to Oxford. Nevertheless Abigail had arranged to meet him behind the stables for safety's sake and when she arrived at the appointed time she found him already waiting. Three weeks of dreaming and longing had culminated in an anguish of expectancy as the day had crawled to its close and her heart leapt with joy at the sight of him. She greeted him rapturously saying, "All is well, there's no-one about, the men have all gone away so we can use the stable."

They slipped inside, accustoming their eyes to the darkness. The stable was empty apart from the pony who shuffled and snorted in his straw at the far corner, missing his recent companions, but the strong pungent smell of the newly-departed animals still hung in the air.

"I've brought you some food and drink, I thought you would have need of them," she said, producing bread and a hot pasty from beneath her cloak and going to find the jug of spiced ale she had hidden away earlier.

"This is welcome," he said, sitting down on a stall beam and immediately biting into the pasty. It had been a cold ride and he was hungry. Abigail perched close beside him, enjoying watching him eat with such relish, conscious of his nearness and anticipating the renewal of their intimacy. When he had completely finished he wiped his mouth with the back of his hand and asked eagerly, "Now what have you been able to find out?"

"Aren't you going to make love to me first?" she asked tremulously. His proximity had revived all the sensations of their last encounter and set her heart beating faster. "I've been longing to have you with me."

He nerved himself against the hunger in her eyes and said, "It's too cold, it's freezing in here," but he put his arm around her and drew her close.

"We could keep each other warm and I could get some fresh straw. Or we could go to my chamber, I told you they have all gone away."

He turned her face to him, touching her cold cheek gently to soften the refusal. "Don't tempt me, Abigail. What we did before was wrong. We are not wed and it is fornication. I'm sorry for it."

She gave a little gasp of dismay but swallowed her disappointment. "I am not sorry," she said defiantly.

He could tell even in the darkness that her face was without guile or coquetry and he liked her for it, but he was firm. "We dare not risk it again. I am not easy about the last time." It was worrying him that she could be with child though he had no doubts about doing the right thing if it should prove so.

"I am not with child, if that is what you mean. All is well."

He felt an involuntary sense of relief. "But next time you could be, and then what would happen to us?"

"It wouldn't matter if we were betrothed would it?"

John felt uncomfortable but he did not avert his eyes from her appealing face, pale in the darkness of the stall, and she saw her answer in that uncompromising gaze. A weight of lead began to settle on her heart.

"You should not trifle with me, John Radcliffe, and then draw back," she whispered, yet well aware that he had spoken no promises of love to her and merited no reproach.

But he knew she spoke truth and said softly, taking her hand in his, "I'm sorry Abigail. You are a very beautiful girl and I am most sorely tempted. But I have work to do, important work. I am not in a position to commit myself to anyone at this time and without that commitment it is not right for me to take advantage of you." His tone pleaded for her understanding, albeit undeserved.

She said simply, "I have missed you so much. I longed for you all over Yuletide when the others were all merry-making and I was alone."

He felt sorry for her, ashamed again of what he had done, and drew her closer. Her warmth was comforting for he had been lonely also, and as she nestled into his shoulder and he felt the silkiness of her hair against his face his pulses began to race. But time was precious and he could not afford to become entangled with Abigail so, although he kept his arm around her, he said firmly, "What have you been able to find out? Tell me everything you know."

Abigail realized with painful disappointment that it was no use trying to persuade him further but hoped that he might feel some gratitude towards her once she had proffered her information. She could not feel the intimacy of his body beneath the buff leather coat and thick cloak as she pressed closer to him to keep warm but their breath rose in spirals and mingled together in the chill air. She began to tell him everything that she could remember, some of it confused and half-digested, some of it trivial and some of it important, but John mentally sifted it and committed it to memory. And amongst all the chaff was an item worth all the rest, an item of stupendous importance that made his blood race as much as Abigail's sensuousness had done.

"Prince Rupert is going to try and retake Abingdon - a night attack on the first moonless night after the mid month."

Abingdon was the nearest Parliamentary garrison to Oxford, taken from the Royalists at the beginning of the war and of great strategic importance to both sides. The Cavaliers were beginning to be sure of their strength again, mused John.

"They are relying on the co-operation of the military commander there and it is believed he will betray the town because he is discontented with Parliament."

Is he indeed, thought John grimly. Aloud he said, "Abigail, you are wonderful! You don't know how much you have helped the cause."

She knew she had pleased him and went on to give him other scraps of news but his journey was already worthwhile. "You have done a wonderful job, Abigail," he said, kissing her now with genuine affection.

She clung to him, willing him to stay longer for she sensed his departure was imminent. "When shall I see you again?"

"That I do not know. I must make sure this news reaches its destination as quickly as possible. But always keep your ears open for news in this house."

She still looked downcast, as if something was troubling her more than his leaving her and eventually she said, "William Hesketh will probably be involved in the attack on Abingdon. I would not like him to come to any harm."

"He must take his chance as we all must. That is the hazard of war," he stated grimly but he looked at her carefully. "Have no regrets, Abigail."

"I shall see you again won't I?" she asked tremulously, feeling a chill beginning to settle on her heart, colder than the air in the icy stable, colder than the grass stiff with rime.

"I am off to Huntingdon shortly and after that.... well it depends on how matters fall. But I give you my word of honour that I shall return to Hesketh Hall, sooner or later."

She had to be satisfied with a promise she knew he would keep and did not try to hold him longer for she sensed that his attention was already from her. Urgency was paramount for him and he was strong and purposeful. He is as headstrong in his own way as William Hesketh, she thought, less volatile but as sure of getting what he wants.

He slipped away without further leave-taking or looking back, and after staring regretfully into the shadows for a while she returned slowly to the house. She had expected so much of this relationship and thought she could have bound him to her with a shared promise of intent. She had come as far as she could in stating her own love but there had been no reciprocal declaration and her only shreds of hope now lay in his promise to return sometime. Perhaps when he was less occupied with matters of war he would return to their previous intimacy.

John Radcliffe had spent a very uncomfortable Yuletide, mainly on the roads, always cold and often fatigued, but this evening had made up for it all. After his shoulder wound at Marston Moor, when a sword thrust between his back-and-breast armour had almost severed the tendons, he had volunteered himself as a courier, travelling between the various pockets of Parliament activity with important, usually secret, letters and messages and keeping his ears open for any snippets of information in alehouses and inns. His mother's cousin Keziah in Stratford had later provided him with a base and a convenient cover to scout southwards through the Cotswolds to Oxford, Royalist country, and the fortuitous encounter with Abigail Hart had presented him with a lucky opportunity to collect further information. But it had been lonely work and he was glad to be done with it. He was looking forward to returning to his command with the New Model Army, an entirely different military force of which Oliver Cromwell had been its inspiration though not its architect. Cromwell had realized that men hastily recruited for a short period when the need arose were not likely to have the mettle and commitment necessary to win this war, especially when called upon to leave their immediate neighbourhood and for payment which was, to say the least, unreliable. What was needed was a highly trained force of professional soldiers who would be paid a regular salary and would be willing to march under orders wherever and whenever they were called. So the New Model Army had been conceived and was now ready to take the field for its first blooding, with or without Cromwell himself though the soldiers were mainly men from his own regiments in the Eastern Association. However John was worried about the effect of the Self-Denying Ordinance because he did not think that Parliament could dispense with Cromwell's military leadership. Although he had always been subordinate to the Earls of Essex and Manchester there was little doubt that he was the genius behind Parliament's campaigns, and his own force of Ironsides a deciding factor in their victories. The Ordinance had been conceived in response to a speech Cromwell himself had made in the House of Commons. With his usual forthrightness he had stated that there was too great a concentration of power in the hands of men who were at the same time both civil and military leaders, a conflict of interest that resulted in some of them prolonging the war for their own ends and thereby antagonising the populace. He had made an appeal for the war to be "more vigourously prosecuted" by men who were soldiers only, and if this meant laying down his own command because he too was a member of Parliament then he had shown his good faith by being the first to do so. Everyone was aware of the quarrels between Cromwell and some of the other High Command whom he accused (rightly in John's opinion) of incompetence. It was no surprise therefore that his enemies were saying it was merely a ruse to be rid of his rivals and increase his own personal power. John reckoned he knew him well enough to believe that he would not renege on his word but he had no idea what would be the outcome of this defiant action. John Radcliffe also believed in a more vigourous prosecution of the war in order to bring it to a speedy conclusion because he did not think the country could survive another year of internecine strife and so had few reservations about the methods to be employed to that end. He was not by nature a soldier and the spectacle of Englishmen killing their own countrymen was as abhorrent to him as it was to most people, but the war had been entered upon and now had to be resolved. He had only enlisted after the Royalist victory at Edgehill when an armed struggle had become inevitable, a struggle which those who stood against the King seemed to have little chance of winning. He had enlisted because all he held most dear was at stake and he did not think it right to leave others to do the fighting for him. Now after two bitter years they had come too far to go back, and as capitulation was unthinkable without having achieved the aims for which they had fought so long and so implacably, the only possible conclusion was a victory for Parliament. And if a greater ferocity was necessary to obtain that victory then it must be so.

It was a dark, virtually moonless, night in mid-January when Prince Rupert's cavalry set out from Oxford for a surprise attack on the Parliament garrison at Abingdon and riding in the company were William Hesketh and Philip Halsall. They felt the familiar blood-tingling sensation of imminent danger, but also elation at the prospect of action at last and relief that the waiting was over. They had been expecting to ride for the last few nights but the nights had continued clear and sharp with frost and as long as the moon had illuminated the contours of the countryside with a dim radiance they had had to bide their time. Then the frost had temporarily relaxed its grip and the warmer temperatures had brought rain. Tonight was ideal, the sliver of moon veiled by clouds and a light drizzle hindering visibility as they covered the few miles southwards quietly and swiftly. In front was Rupert, his familiar scarlet cloak exchanged for a dark one. No-one could move a troop of horse as swiftly as the Prince and his ability to cover distances at seemingly incredible speed so that he appeared to be in more than one place at a time had earned him the title of "The Wizard" from his enemies. To those who had ears the sound of a large force moving in the darkness was faintly discernible by the clink of armour and the jingling of harness, but there was nobody about to listen to the muffled hooves as they avoided the roads, riding across the fields until they approached the town without being sighted.

There was no alarm given by any guards and they congratulated themselves on the success of the first part of their plan. Now they were relying on the renegade Roundhead commander to have left the gates unlocked with a sleepy and under-manned garrison behind the walls. The gates were open as expected but as they began their stampede into the town they were met by a volley of cannon fire and pistol shot from the large heavily-armed force awaiting them. Their horses recoiled in terror and the dismayed Cavaliers knew something was wrong. Prince Rupert pressed ahead, carving a passage through the unexpected opposition with his troopers following resolutely, but his brain was already working out the odds heavily stacked against them. As they passed through one wave of Roundheads another came to meet them with artillery at their backs and his men were either being pushed back or mown down. Rupert was trying to reach the artillery but could make no headway and in any case it was heavily guarded now by musketeers. The sheer speed and impact of the Prince's cavalry had devastated many Roundhead attacks of superior strength but here everything was against them. The confined space left them no room to manoeuvre, for the narrow streets were full of soldiers and they had put posts with iron chains between to prevent the horses' passage. The close fighting was as dangerous to his own men as to the enemy, because each trooper was in peril from his neighbour's sweeping sword as they slashed wildly in the darkness. They had relied on the element of surprise, the crucial factor in their daring plan. The key element in a surprise attack was surprise, but for some unaccountable reason this had been denied them. Somehow the Roundheads had got wind of their intention and set a trap for them. Prince Rupert was brave but not foolhardy. He knew he would have to call off the attack before his cavalry was decimated for no purpose and he began to give the order to pull back while all the time fighting furiously and supervising their retreat. He was the last to quit the town as they retreated but missed the grisly spectacle of the late commander's lifeless body swinging from the East gate, as harried and pursued some way by the jubilant Roundheads they left their own dead behind them.

Rupert led his troop at a furious pace back to Oxford, impelled by the rage which overwhelmed him. "We must have been betrayed, there is no other answer," he snarled, his lips clamped tight in a bitter line, his slight foreign accent more pronounced in times of stress or emotion. He was just twenty-five but already a veteran of Continental warfare before he became commander of the Royalist cavalry at the onset of the Civil War. The theory of betrayal was also voiced by William and Philip as they rode together, shocked by the events of the night.

"I wouldn't put it past one of our own side to have betrayed us for sheer vindictiveness and jealousy of Rupert," William muttered darkly.

Philip looked at him aghast. "You can't think that! None of Rupert's detractors, not even George Digby, would carry their jealousy so far."

But William refused to be convinced, for the other possibility was too painful to contemplate. He looked at Rupert, his tall figure rigid with anger, his saturnine face set in a scowl. Rupert's invincibility was legendary. Could it perhaps be just a legend? William, who admired Rupert with a loyalty bordering on idolatry, was horrified at the treacherous thought that had caught him unawares. Rupert's enemies who called him "The Wizard" and "The Necromancer" had attributed his early successes to black magic. The Prince's dog, Boy, they had nominated his "familiar", his evil spirit through whom he communicated with the Devil. But Boy had been killed at Marston Moor and it was being said that Rupert's luck would now change. William had seen the grief of the austere young man for the creature who had been his companion for many years and shared his three years' captivity in a German prison. He knew there was no magic about Rupert's success but tactical skills learnt through experience, plus great personal courage and the charisma that made young men feel honoured to follow him. However he had to admit that their past string of unanimous successes had now begun to be interlaced with failures and he reflected sadly that the new year had not opened on such an optimistic note as they had hoped.

At the end of January a peace plan was formulated by negotiators from both sides, and representatives from the King and the Parliament met to consider if some common ground could be prepared for the cessation of hostilities. Nothing could be agreed upon. The peace plan was rejected and both sides made a declaration to carry on the war with a greater ferocity.

CHAPTER 5

MARCH 1645

February was a wicked month with such extremes of bitter weather that it seemed as if Nature herself had turned her hostility upon a country already torn with faction. The inhabitants of Hesketh Hall shivered in the largely unheated house as the combined force of weather and circumstance imprisoned them, though they tried to keep busy and cheerful. They had heard about the aborted attack on Abingdon and Abigail was tormented by guilt and anxiety as she worried about William. Then he wrote to tell them that he had suffered no more than a powder burn on his chin and Philip Courtney a gash on the leg, and the inexpressible relief that engulfed her chased away for a time the unhappiness weighing upon her since John Radcliffe's departure. It was around St. Valentine's day when they received William's letter and it was accompanied by an epistle for Henrietta tied with blue ribbon and silver seals. She made no secret of what it contained and took to playing love songs on the spinet and lute. Arabella received no such communication from Kit Verney and had to be content with a pair of embroidered silk gloves from Ambrose, on each cuff of which was fastened a matching pair of brooches in the form of a phoenix and a turtle. She had to admit it was a sensitive gift. Abigail wished she could have received some memento from John as she feared she had lost him.

But the beginning of Lent brought the first tentative signs of spring with crocuses and wild daffodils appearing around the lake's edge. The days to Easter were eagerly scored on the almanac and as the earth quickened to new life each one of them was confident of the resurrection of their own personal hopes and dreams. Then on the first day of March, a day as calm as the previous month had been ferocious, a rider came with more letters bearing surprising and exciting news. The first was from Sir James informing his wife that Philip Halsall had asked to marry Henrietta. The second was from William to tell them he was bringing Prince Rupert to the Hall on the following day. Any news would have provided an occasion for excitement for a household starved of novelty but together it seemed too much to take in. Sir James spoke of his satisfaction with the young man's character and general worthiness but confessed his unease at what he thought might be precipitous haste and wished to know his wife's opinion on the matter.

William's letter was shorter, revealing his characteristic impatience with the task of sending missives. Rupert's cavalry were soon to leave Oxford for the Royalist garrison at Ludlow where they were to prepare for a new campaign in the north to retrieve the territory lost by their defeat at Marston Moor. With a brief pause for recreation the Prince had honoured William with a request to visit his home, an informal visit for one night only. Despite her son's laconic message Lady Mary understood his pride in this demonstration of the Prince's esteem for him. But she was also consumed by a sensation of panic, for her guest was not only her son's commander and comrade in arms but a Prince of the royal blood and nephew to King

Charles, and her thoughts were spinning as she realized how much had to be done in the intervening twenty-four hours in order to prepare him a worthy welcome. Yet though she was eager to go at once to the kitchens to get preparations under way she was also mindful of the other letter and first asked to see Henrietta alone.

Henrietta's excitement stemmed more from her father's letter than her brother's and even the prospect of a visit from Prince Rupert gave second place to a proposal of marriage from Philip Halsall. "I know that Philip intended to ask father but I did not expect him to act so quickly. Do you think they will give their consent," she asked Arabella, pacing up and down their chamber in an uncharacteristic state of agitation.

"I cannot see any objections," replied her sister. "He seems very suitable in both his character and his family connections. William thinks highly of him."

"That isn't necessarily a recommendation," Henrietta giggled. "But I know mother likes him and I think father was impressed too. I know he seems quiet and serious but he has great ambitions and I love him very much. I am afraid however that they will not give their consent to a marriage for me before you as the elder."

"Then I shall put forward my views in support of you," declared Arabella stoutly. "It is war time and conventions are relaxed of necessity. Besides I haven't met anyone I would really like to marry." (She thought briefly of Kit Verney.) "I suppose I shall have to settle for Ambrose eventually. You are very lucky to have made a love match and I am very happy for you." But she felt suddenly envious of her young sister with her round freckled face aglow with excitement.

Lady Mary was in her private parlour adjoining her bedchamber, a pleasant room with a view over the knot garden. Henrietta's exuberance had given way to apprehension and as she entered she composed her face into what she considered a dutiful expression. However her mother, seated at her writing table, recognized the set of her mouth and the tilt of her chin as indicative of determination. She studied her youngest child carefully as she stood before her. She had always been a little disappointed that her brown-haired daughter had not been blessed with her own good looks though she was forced to admit that Henrietta had a happy disposition and a resilience that more beautiful girls might lack. If Arabella would marry Ambrose Hardwicke and a land-owning Catholic heiress could be found for William then Philip Halsall was not a bad proposition for Henrietta. Though a third son he had some property of his own, his manners and demeanour were irreproachable and, most importantly, he kept the old faith as did most of the Lancashire gentry. "Tell me truly Henrietta, what are your feelings about Master Halsall's proposal?" she asked directly.

"I love him Mother," her daughter replied simply. She felt an urge to put her arms around her mother's neck saying, "Please, please let me marry him," as she used to wheedle treats as a child, but reflected that this would not give a convincing impression of maturity so she stood as composed and dignified as she could.

Perhaps it did not quite present the picture she intended because Lady Mary said, "You are very young."

"Eighteen is not so young, mother."

Nor is it, Lady Mary acknowledged silently. She herself had been married when she was not much older. She had not noticed how much Henrietta had grown. Many girls were married at fifteen or sixteen and though she herself considered it too young it was by no means unusual. "But you have known each other such a short time," she persisted. "An idea of romantic love is not a sufficient base on which to build a marriage partnership."

"You have often said how you and father hardly knew each other when you married. Well Philip and I are better acquainted than that. We know everything that is needful about each other and we are very sure."

Lady Mary knew from experience how determined her younger daughter could be. Henrietta had been named after the Queen who, twenty years earlier, had seemed the great hope for English Catholics, and she appeared to have inherited her namesake's obstinacy. She was afraid that if denied what she wanted then Henrietta might be tempted by unorthodox means and neither a runaway marriage nor a secret betrothal, which would grant them the rights of marriage without a religious ceremony, was acceptable. "I will give the matter careful thought before I write to your father," she said. "I will also make some enquiries with regard to Master Halsall's family."

As Henrietta was dismissed she thought uncharitably that her mother would want to discover how rich the family was and if they had any skeletons in their cupboards, but on the whole she was not dissatisfied with the outcome of the interview.

The remaining hours of the day until the light was completely spent were occupied in an unprecedented flurry of activity as they turned their attention to the other matter. Lady Hesketh harried her small band of servants into a frenzy of mopping and polishing, boiling and baking, while her daughters were designated the task of preparing the best guest chamber for the Prince's comfort. "There won't be enough time to see to our dresses," moaned Henrietta as they ironed the best sheets and put dried lavender between them. "The lace on my best yellow dress is frayed and I shall have to sew it myself because Abigail won't have time."

Her mother overheard her and said severely, "You need not spend too much time on your appearance, I would not wish you to convey a misleading impression to the Prince. No doubt he is tired of young girls trying to ensnare his affections." Henrietta's concern was not with impressing Prince Rupert but Philip Halsall who was accompanying William. However Lady Mary continued, "We must not forget he is a Stuart prince, for despite the misfortunes and hardships of his family I have heard that he does not allow anyone to overlook his high status." In truth she was apprehensive of his visit having heard so many conflicting tales of his conduct. It was reported that he was willful, arrogant, and ill-mannered and had antagonized many important people, Royalists as well as Parliamentarians, by his brusque and dismissive attitude. But William worshipped him and spoke of his kindness, his generosity, his staunch loyalty and his lack of ceremony, as well as the restrained, almost abstemious, nature of his personal life. She wished her husband could have been on hand. She also regretted momentarily the loss of their table silver and valuables. I hope he realizes our slender means are a result of our support for the Royalist cause she thought, then chided herself for her pride.

The following morning the whole household was agog with excitement. Arabella and Henrietta had been keeping watch in the bay of the parlour window and were the first to give warning of the arrival of the small party as they galloped up the driveway in time for dinner at mid-day. William had talked constantly of Rupert over the past two years and they all thought they knew him, but nothing had prepared them for this glorious giant. When he dismounted he stood a head over two yards in height with a breadth of shoulder and chest to match.

Beside him William looked only of average height and Philip small. His distinctive scarlet cloak swung open over a black doublet slashed with scarlet and there were ruffles of deep lace at his collar and cuffs. The whiteness of the lace against his throat emphasized his dark complexion which together with his uncommon, though faint, accent made him seem suspiciously foreign. His eyes were dark and hooded, his nose aquiline, the set of his mouth both proud and vulnerable, and thick brown curls fell to his shoulders beneath his wide-brimmed beaver hat. The three women curtseyed low to him and as they raised their heads they then had opportunity to study him closely. Arabella felt overpowered by his great size and reputation and for a moment was unaccountably afraid and wished he had not come. As she looked into his face she experienced a momentary sense of foreboding and shivered, as if someone had walked over her grave she later told Henrietta. Henrietta was more nearly concerned with Philip Halsall and after satisfying her curiosity that Prince Rupert was undeniably handsome and probably capable of all the feats attributed to him, she turned her attention to her lover. Lady Mary looked into his brooding eyes and an instant of awareness passed between them, the mutual regard of a beautiful woman and an extraordinarily handsome man. Yet beneath the imposing exterior she sensed also an inherent loneliness which aroused her maternal instincts and swept away all remaining traces of reserve or anxiety. He bent low over her hand then taking a small exquisitely-enamelled box from his belt pouch he presented it to her saying diffidently, "I have brought you some tea. I do not care for it myself but I believe it is a great favourite with the ladies."

She thanked him, laughing in genuine delight and he laughed also, revealing gleaming white teeth. As he looked into her eyes he had the strange impression that he had met her somewhere before but though he searched his memory all he could think of was a line written by one of his mother's favourite poets who had also been a friend of hers - "Nor spring nor summer beauty hath such grace as I have seen in one autumnal face." He drew his attention away from Lady Hesketh to her daughters, marvelling at how different the three Hesketh women were as they stood in the thin bright sunshine to welcome him to their home. Arabella Hesketh, pale and blonde, looked almost too fragile for a man to touch and her eyes held a slight hint of disquiet. With the influence of his resilient mother and his many rowdy brothers and boisterous sisters Rupert had a preference for women with strong personalities. Henrietta Hesketh, plump and rosy with a vivacious face, reminded him of his youngest sister Sophie who made them laugh with her malicious wit and her gift of mimicry. Their mother, serene and glowing in her amber satin gown, was more beautiful than her daughters, as was his own mother. He gave her his arm to escort her into the Hall.

Lent had decreed a fish dinner but there were boiled oysters, stewed carp, hot salmon, a dish of anchovies, followed by tarts, a custard and excellent cheese to compensate for the lack of fruit. Lady Mary was well pleased with their efforts in such a short time and Rupert made reference to the fact of their sacrifices for the Royalist cause. He was personally acquainted at his home in the Hague with the gradual disappearance of plate and silver from the tables and tapestries from the walls, not only to finance the wars to recover his dead father's lost kingdom of the Palatinate but to pay pressing debts. Seated at the head of the table with the Prince on her right Lady Mary wondered how she could ever have been worried about entertaining him, while William was beaming with pride and satisfaction at the way in which the prince so easily fitted into their family circle.

He told them the latest news of the war, both good and bad. Parliament had taken the Royalist garrison of Shrewsbury which was a great blow as it was an invaluable base on the Severn. But on the other hand France and Holland had promised to supply the King with troops. The news that Parliament's New Model Army was ready to take the field under the command of Sir Thomas Fairfax was of uncertain import.

"The New Noddle Army they are calling it in Oxford," William scoffed.

"They are fools to underestimate it," said Rupert sharply. "I have a great respect for Fairfax, and for Cromwell whose idea it was. Cromwell watches us and learns from us. He copied our cavalry tactics and improved on them. Perhaps we could learn from this idea of a standing army of professional soldiers, it is what I personally would like to see."

Rupert treated the women as equals in his talk of the war, feeling no more need to make polite conversation for their sakes than he would to his own family at home. This pleased him for he had neither liking nor aptitude for small talk and he began to feel happier and more relaxed than he had done for some time. Even Arabella lost her awe of him and wondered why a sense of foreboding had touched her in those first few minutes. William had confided to her that the Prince was suffering from a hopeless love affair. The lady in question was married and neither of them would behave dishonourably. Everyone was aware of it but it was a forbidden subject and Rupert had cashiered one of his officers for mentioning it in jest. The knowledge of their similar circumstances filled Arabella with a secret sympathy for him even if he was ignorant of it. Like her mother earlier, she began to be aware of the vulnerability beneath the stern exterior and surmised he could be easily hurt.

Henrietta was emboldened to recount their own brush with the Roundheads, embellishing Arabella's role much to her sister's embarrassment. Rupert studied her with new interest. She was obviously made of stronger mettle than had at first appeared. After praising her enthusiastically he went on to relate an experience of his own which involved a redoubtable lady. He had been trying to capture the desirable Caldecot Hall from a very obstinate body of defenders. "I had a fairly large force but we had been trying for a long time unsuccessfully to take the place," he explained. "We were being constantly repelled by persistent musket fire so I decided the only solution was to set fire to some outlying barns and gain entry under cover of the smoke. When we finally entered the Hall we discovered that our opponents were precisely one man, his mother-in-law and a handful of female servants. The redoubtable Mistress Purefoy, a grey haired lady of advanced years, could handle a musket with the best of them. I offered her a commission in my regiment but unfortunately she refused saying she could not desert the Parliament cause." They all laughed and other reminiscences followed including the story Philip had told Henrietta about the Countess of Derby's spirited defence of Lathom House until Rupert's cavalry had come to her assistance.

"I don't know what we would do without the womenfolk in this war," said the Prince.

Speaking of happier times Lady Mary told him how her father had taken her to London at the age of nine years to watch the fireworks in celebration of his mother's marriage to the Elector Palatine. "They lasted for three whole days and the one I remember best was St. George fighting the dragon, a piece which..."

"Went on for more than half an hour," Rupert interrupted laughingly. "Oh Lady Mary you do not know how often we have heard such tales of my mother's wedding and her early life in England. She filled us with stories of people and places until all we ever wanted was to come to England and see for ourselves." He thought suddenly of his mother exiled for thirty years from the country she loved, his beautiful, high-spirited, indomitable mother whose irrepressible laughter rang through the modest house at the Hague as she recounted to them English history and literature and made them believe that England was the most wonderful country in the world. When he finally came here to help his mother's brother fight for his crown it was to a country torn by hatred and he, his mother's son, looked upon as a foreigner and resented and mistrusted.

"I thought we could go hunt later, Sir," said William, who knew the Prince well and had seen the fleeting shadow cross his face. He knew Rupert would take the bait for both of them could only tolerate inactivity for short periods even though they had initially welcomed the respite from the demands and stress of action.

They were soon in the saddle again and galloping across the park then through the ravaged wood from where in the distance pistol shots could be heard. After a time Philip returned and walked around the lake with Henrietta, where they stood hand in hand and watched the primroses trembling in the light breeze.

Lady Hesketh had asked Abigail to help serve at table. She had trembled at the thought of meeting the Prince, commander of those Royalist forces which she hoped would be defeated in the struggle for the government of England. She wondered what he would do if he knew she had reported his plan for the capture of Abingdon. She had heard that he was called the Wizard and the Necromancer and she was afraid to lift her eyes to look at him in case he could read her mind. Yet as he talked she wished she might see John again and relate to him their confidences, trying to hold important information in her mind. At supper when she was carrying round the ewer of water and the napkins for them to wash their hands William pressed her toe with his foot as she stood beside him, trying to get her to look at him. She ignored him and concentrated on her task. Once she had known he had come to no harm through her agency he had ceased to have chief place in her thoughts and William had been too occupied since his return to pay her any attention. But when the meal was finished he slipped away to the kitchen where she was putting the dishes away in the closet.

"Would you like me to introduce you to the Prince?" he asked companionably.

"And how could you introduce me," she retorted scornfully, though the faint resonance of alarm in her tone was not lost on William.

"Why are you afraid of him?" he asked. "I'm sure he will not hold it against you that you choose to support Parliament." There was a challenging note in his voice as if he were daring her to openly proclaim her allegiance.

"I am not afraid to state what I believe in, William," she said defiantly. "I keep quiet because my opinions are of no purpose here, I am of too little account. Also I would not be ungrateful to those who employ me."

Realizing it was but a half-truth she turned away but he pulled her sleeve and held her back saying, "I'm coming up to your room later, I have a secret to tell you."

After supper Lady Hesketh retired into the parlour to leave the young people alone and to muse with satisfaction on the events of the day. It seemed incredible to believe that Prince Rupert, of whom they had heard so many tales over the past two years, should be happily settled in their home and at this moment playing a boisterous game of skittles in the hall with as much enjoyment as her son. She smiled as she heard his loud voice insisting that he had beaten William while her son just as strongly disagreed. Suddenly the tall elegant figure appeared on the threshold, stooping in order to pass through the doorway. She began to rise but he prevented her and crossing the room asked permission to sit beside her on the padded velvet settle. He did not speak further but sat gazing into the glowing heart of the fire and she looked questioningly at him, aware yet again of the incredibly handsome outline of his features - the strong hooked nose, the firm yet gentle mouth, the black brows contracted over the deepset brown eyes giving him a brooding look. She understood why people found him intimidating and yet for some unaccountable reason she felt perfectly at ease with him. His eyes met hers and held them, and once again they were both aware of something passing between them that was difficult to define in its complexity and the silence seemed to quiver with some inexpressible communication. When he spoke at last it was with the normality of courteous speech. "I would like to thank you for your hospitality. I have enjoyed this day so much. It has put me in mind of my own home in which I have spent so little time over the past few years."

She knew that he had been held in captivity in Germany for three years before he had come to fight in England and her heart constricted with an unfamiliar pain as she understood how this must have contributed to his sense of isolation. "It has been an honour and a great pleasure to have you as our guest, Sir," she said formally. "I hope you will come to us again for a longer stay perhaps, when the war is over and we can entertain you more fittingly. You will always be sure of a welcome here."

Rupert recognized the undercurrent of emotion which transcended the formality of her speech and was very conscious of her beauty as the glow from the firelight softened her face into youthfulness again. Her beauty and serenity and the warmth of the comfortably furnished room seemed to be working an enchantment on him, making him unwilling to leave. He remembered how his mother used to tell stories about knights-errant who accepted the hospitality of beautiful women only to discover too late that they had been ensnared in a web of enchantment that held them prisoner and robbed them of their strength. He loved soldiering, it was his life, the only life he had ever known, but at this moment it seemed strangely unattractive - the forced marches in consistently bad weather, the sleepless nights, the lack of co-operation and the constant arguments with other leaders, the indecision of the King who gave him the power of command and then curtailed his use of it, and worst of all the spectre of defeat. His longing to submerge himself into the sensuousness of the moment became stronger and he reached out to touch his hostess, placing his hand over hers so that she could feel the hard calloused ridges in the palm of his bridle hand. As she fixed her eyes questioningly on his face he suddenly realized why he thought he had seen her before. He had first thought that Lady Hesketh reminded him of his mother, his beautiful fascinating mother whose approval Rupert had fruitlessly sought in competition with his brothers. But now he realized that was only partly true. As he looked into her eyes and saw the golden flecks in the brown, he realized she also reminded him of Mary Richmond. In that moment all the forbidden memories came rushing back in a swirl of joy and pain as he thought of Mary Richmond, his best friend's wife. Mary, Mary, Mary, the name went round and round in his head, echoing in his memory, the name he had sworn never to say, Mary, Mary. He had said her name aloud without realizing it but did not know if he had whispered it or shouted it. He did not know where he was, time hung motionless. Lady Mary Hesketh was partly his mother, partly Mary Richmond, partly the enchantress of half-remembered legends, an ambivalent attraction hovering uncertainly on forbidden borders.

A log fell down into the red heart of the fire and hissed into sparks. The sudden explosion, magnified out of all proportion to his heightened sensibilities, seemed to shatter the stillness of the room and in that moment the spell was broken. Lady Mary withdrew her hand from his and he pulled himself up short. He rose from the chair and walked to the window, pulling aside the red velvet curtain and looking out into the unfathomable blackness. He heard his voice saying, sounding as if it were coming from a long way away, "I have to admit to you Lady Hesketh that I came here with the avowed intention of asking you to give your permission for Philip Halsall to marry your daughter Henrietta. I make no apologies for this stratagem, for in this matter I stand as deputy for my friend and kinsman Lord Derby. As you know, Philip's family are neighbours and tenants of Lord Derby and it was he who first introduced Philip into my service. I have the assurance that any such match would meet with the approval of all concerned." He was conscious of how stilted the words were but they began to sound more normal as he continued, "For myself I can speak personally of Philip's merit. Like

William he has been with me from the beginning and I know you need have no doubts of his character and good faith. Let them be married soon, before we begin our new offensive in the north. Who knows what the fortunes of war will bring. Let them take their happiness while they can." If he was unable to take his own happiness it was all the more reason why he should speak on behalf of a friend. He knew how tragically short some of the unions of the Cavaliers and their ladies had been.

"I had not thought of such an early marriage," Lady Mary murmured uncertainly though stirred by his sincerity. Besides, the recommendation of no less a person than the Stuart prince could not lightly be gainsaid.

"My mother arranged the Earl of Derby's marriage, speaking on his behalf to my cousin Charlotte, and they have been very happy. Let me speak now on behalf of one of the Earl's comrades. If you would consent to a wedding before we leave Oxford I would put my own quarters at your disposal for the ceremony."

Lady Mary was touched by his generosity and not unaware of the prestige in accepting such a concession. However she declined graciously. "I am most grateful for the honour offered to us, Your Highness, but if they are to be married then I would prefer it to be here in our own home, in our own chapel."

Rupert nodded his acceptance. "That would be most fitting I grant you. You have such a beautiful house and you obviously belong here together." There was regret in his tone that was not lost on her.

"I will speak to Henrietta and Master Halsall in the morning and if they are willing..." She stopped, realizing that almost without thinking she had given consent to his request. She remembered how people said that Prince Rupert always got his own way. Their tête-à-tête had shifted back to normality, a fact confirmed by the arrival of the others from their gaming.

Before retiring to bed William made his promised call on Abigail and slipped quickly up the back stairs to her chamber. She opened the door reluctantly to his knock, knowing he would take no refusal, but stood defensively on the threshold.

"What's the matter Abigail? You never used to mind my coming to see you," he said.

"It's different now isn't it? We are no longer children," she said, but she allowed him to come past her into the room and then shut the door. "Well what is your secret?" She knew it was only an excuse for him to see her.

"Henrietta is going to marry Phillip Halsall very soon, within the next month perhaps."

"That isn't a secret," she sighed, though the hastiness of the proposed match had surprised her. "You will have to do better than that."

"Well how about this then, I love you. Though I don't suppose that is much of a secret either." With a sudden nonchalant movement he flung himself on the bed and lay there with his hands under his head and his feet crossed negligently.

She regarded him in exasperation. "William please go," she implored. "Whatever would anyone think if they saw you here."

"They would think I had made love to you. Have you never thought of making love to a man? It can be a very pleasurable experience."

She flushed. "William please go, you are offending me. If I were a lady you would not talk to me like this."

"Of course I would. What difference would it make?" He was genuinely puzzled.

"Maybe it wouldn't make any difference to your fine ladies in Oxford. From what I hear they do not value modesty," she said, stung into uncharacteristic spite.

"They certainly aren't Puritans if that's what you mean," he retorted. "I wouldn't object to your beliefs Abigail if they didn't prevent you from having any pleasure."

She wanted to refute this but she realized that William knew it was not true. They had shared a lot of pleasure over the years with their companionship and their games. But he was thinking of only one thing now.

"Any kind of enjoyment is the work of the Devil, especially the sort of enjoyment I have in mind, that's what all the Puritan divines say isn't it?" he continued. "Well fortunately my religion is more tolerant of human weakness. All I need do is confess to Father Edmund afterwards."

Abigail was never sure when he was serious. His habitual gaiety and zest for mischief made his protestations of love confusing and she was disturbed by them.

"Very well then, I'll go if that is what you want," he said standing up, his golden head almost touching the rafters. "I don't know when you will see me again but I won't even kiss you. I will go and take my pleasures in Oxford where, as you say, modesty is not such a high priority and I leave you to dream about what you have missed. But beware you don't die a virgin!"

He went out leaving her biting her lip in frustration. She went to the bed and straightened the coverlet, removing his imprint, then she suddenly burst into tears as, sparked by his words, a rush of memories flared up from the still-smouldering embers of her love. "John, John," she sobbed, lying face down on the bed and burying her face in the pillow, and her tears could not quench the flame of her longing.

Early the following morning Lady Hesketh sent for Henrietta and Philip and talked to them for a long time in the privacy of her parlour. When she was satisfied with the sincerity of their replies she informed them of what the Prince had said to her the previous evening, concluding with "Father Edmund will be visiting us again at Easter. I suggest he performs the ceremony here in our own chapel on Easter day," an arrangement to which they both happily agreed.

After breakfast the men departed for Oxford with many words of thanks, of friendship, and of love, sealed with promises of letters to come. Abigail watched their leavetaking from her open casement. William put all his hopes on Prince Rupert, John upon Oliver Cromwell. She pondered on the differences between these two oddly matched adversaries - the one young but who had been a professional soldier for ten years, the other middle-aged who had only turned to soldiering late in life. Seeing Rupert in the flesh had demystified him and he was no longer either the supernatural hero of legend nor the devil incarnate of scurrilous pamphleteers. She wondered what Cromwell was like and who would be the one to lead his side to ultimate victory.

When they were alone again Arabella felt in low spirits after all the excitement but Henrietta was bubbling with elation. "I would love to have been married in Oxford with all those important people to see me," she said regretfully. "It would have been so fashionable and the Prince might have introduced me to some of the ladies at the court."

I could have seen Kit, thought Arabella, but aloud she said, "It matters very much to Mother that you should be married here by Father Edmund."

"Well it is of no account because Philip says I am to go to Oxford with him afterwards. He will stay there for a time helping to man the fortifications so we can find lodgings and live together. Then when he goes to join the Prince's army again I suppose I shall have to come back home. But when the war is over I am to go to Lancashire with him to his family and Philip says we shall build a new house on the estate. Oh Arabella I can't believe all this is happening to me. After this tedious winter I am beginning to live again, and live a life such as I dreamed about."

"I am very happy for you," said her sister. "And also envious," she added honestly. She felt she had no part to play in the drama that was enfolding.

Despite preparations for Henrietta's wedding Lady Hesketh was insistent that Lent should be kept with strict adherence to all observances. But the routine of prayer, penance, and fasting was lightened for the girls by the knowledge of the festivities to come. Lady Mary however was more stringent than usual and gave her household reason to believe that the utmost fidelity to each observance was necessary to procure a Royalist victory and consequent peace. In complete assurance of Father Edmund's visit the wedding was arranged for Easter day. It was to be a relatively small affair attended by their Catholic friends and neighbours, and also their Catholic servants and tenants who would have made their way to the Hall for an Easter mass notwithstanding. Others were welcome to share in the festivities afterwards and a general invitation was publicised by word of mouth around the little town, though veiled in some ambiguity so as not to endanger Father Edmund.

March drew to a close in a flurry of gales but April dawned warm and calm, the occasional soft showers forcing the springing earth into a wealth of blossom and wild flowers - daisies, primroses, cuckoo buds and ladysmocks spreading the park and the wood with a mosaic of yellow and white. In London the House of Lords passed the Self-Denying Ordinance and the former Parliamentary leaders, the Earls of Essex, Warwick and Manchester together with Oliver Cromwell, all surrendered their commissions. In Huntingdon Cromwell's own regiment came near to mutiny when they were told to march south without their General and John Radcliffe was one of those officers who calmed and reassured the soldiers. But the New Model Army was now on the move under the command of Sir Thomas Fairfax who had previously led the northern armies of Parliament. They did not celebrate Easter for they considered it a Catholic and pagan festival like Christmas.

On Holy Saturday Father Edmund kept his expected appointment at Hesketh Hall but his journey from the north had not been without danger. He told them how he had run into a Roundhead patrol and only escaped due to the presence of mind of a small boy who had helped him hide in a tree, "with great difficulty," he laughed. Lady Mary felt anxious about asking him to stay a day longer, especially since news of the wedding had now leaked abroad. However he refused to be dissuaded, though when he revealed his intention of seeking shelter elsewhere for the night Lady Mary insisted he stayed at the Hall so he took refuge in one of the garrets with Timothy set as lookout for unexpected visitors.

That same day William and Philip arrived from the garrison at Hereford where Rupert had been recruiting on the Welsh borders, though he was preparing to move on into Lancashire which had proved a fertile recruiting ground in the past. William would have preferred to accompany him but his parents considered a family wedding obligatory, and since Philip was his closest friend he rode home willingly enough, contenting himself with the thought that a few days' delay was immaterial. Sir James Hesketh made his departure from Oxford. On the same day Kit Verney also left the city but he was riding westwards, summoned by an urgent message from home informing him that his wife was dangerously ill.

Because of Father Edmund's protracted stay they celebrated the Easter vigil. But they were still up by daybreak and at an early hour family, guests, servants and tenants crowded into the tiny chapel, all dressed in their best clothes with knots of coloured ribbons attached to their sleeves. In her chamber Henrietta had experienced a moment of doubt as Arabella and Abigail put the finishing touches to her gown. They were fastening flowers amid her brown curls when she became overwhelming aware of the great step she was taking. "I shall miss you both so much," she cried. "It is the end of my life here and everything suddenly seems so strange, as if I am dreaming it all."

"It is a beginning not an end," Arabella comforted her, unused to seeing her sister anxious. But Henrietta had let her gaze wander slowly around the chamber, taking in all the familiar objects - the crucifix on the wall, the writing desk with parchment, quill and ink, a favourite book open on the chair by the window, the bed with its blue hangings and matching counterpane embroidered with roses. All her life she had shared this room with her sister. Tonight for the first time in her life she would not sleep here but would sleep with a stranger. She had clung to Arabella as if to the safety of the past and doubts had overwhelmed her.

Now however all doubts were dispelled as she knelt beside her bridegroom, her round face aglow with happiness and pride. As Lady Mary studied her daughter she realized that Henrietta was beautiful on her wedding day but yet so childish and innocent, like a spring flower herself in a gown of her favourite yellow, looped at the sides to display a petticoat of green silk embroidered with yellow roses. Philip looked ill at ease in his unaccustomed role of chief actor though resplendently dressed in brown satin and ruffles of foaming lace, with a broad brimmed hat adorned with curling ostrich feathers. Beside him William was hardly able to contain his laughter and tipped his friend an irreverent wink.

Ambrose Hardwicke was trying to catch Arabella's attention but she kept her face averted, suspecting he felt this an appropriate occasion to communicate something significant to her. Her dress of rose tissue gave some colour to her pale face but she felt it difficult to refrain from weeping, though the tears sprang from a vague unlocalised emotion that she could not share with anyone. Mistress Hardwicke, decked like a ship in full sail with all the best attire she could muster, pursed her lips in pique at the fine show the Heskeths had managed to provide and wondered with some malice why Henrietta, the second daughter, should be wed in such haste.

After the ceremony everyone trooped outside into the warm early sunshine, laughing now and congratulating the young couple. By the lakeside trestle tables had been set up laden with all kinds of meat and pasties, sweetmeats and cakes, wine and ale. Throughout the morning people continued to arrive, winding their way from the town and the surrounding hamlets, some of them with pipes and fiddles and many of them bearing small gifts in return for the hospitality. Henrietta accepted them all with genuine delight and loved being the centre of attention. When everyone had eaten their fill she began the country dances with her new husband, then sat in pride of place on a flower-decked dais to present prizes of wedding cakes to those who were winners in the games and contests that followed.

"Keep your eye on Wat Dacre and Adam Ashe, notorious tale-bearers and mischief makers," Sir James told William with all the wisdom of a Justice of the Peace.

"Is Father Edmund gone?"

"Immediately after the ceremony."

William commanded the assembly's attention to the announcement of a wrestling bout "between two volunteers, those two lusty young men, Wat Dacre and Adam Ashe. Place your bets now on one or the other while the contestants disrobe."

The two "volunteers" looked truculently at him and Adam Ashe clenched his fists threateningly but William outstared them. By this time the crowd were encouraging them noisily and already placing their wagers so the young men had no alternative but to comply. William laughed, well satisfied that the unlooked for activity would keep them out of mischief for some time since the crowd would allow nothing less than a full-bout serious contest as their money was involved. He then turned his attention to Abigail who had been kept busy serving the food and clearing the tables. Henrietta was standing beside her and he heard his sister say, "I want you to have my bridal favour, Abigail. I shall miss you so much because you have looked after me so well and I shall now have to find another maid." She took the favour from her sleeve and pinned it onto Abigail's plain bodice of grey wool saying, "I hope it will bring you happiness too."

Abigail looked at the knot of brightly coloured ribbons and yellow rosebuds and thought about John Radcliffe, where he was and what he was doing. Then she turned and saw William watching her with an uncharacteristically serious expression on his face.

Ambrose had also witnessed the action and seeking out Arabella asked, "May I have your bridal favour Arabella?"

"I thought I would keep it as a memento," she replied.

He was crestfallen and said sulkily, "You should have been the bride today, not Henrietta."

She felt sorry for him and added, "I promise I will give you my consent at Christmas. That isn't very long now, not much more than half a year." But like Abigail her own thoughts dwelt on a lover far away and she imagined herself as the bride today if circumstances had been different.

The afternoon wound to its close and people began to make their way home, jovial and not a little drunk, reminiscing about how it had been like the old days before the war when people were lighthearted and such festivities common at holidays. Wat Dacre and Adam Ashe had to admit no sign of any priests at Hesketh Hall and no servant had been able to give them any information. Everything had passed without incident and all that remained was for Sir James to go to the parish church the following day and for an exorbitant fee arrange for the marriage to be entered into the register.

Later as darkness fell Abigail performed her last service for Henrietta as she helped her to prepare for bed and brushed her hair as she had done every night since she was a child. Henrietta felt strangely reluctant to go into the guest chamber instead of her own room, but was relieved there would be no rowdy custom of accompanying them to bed with bawdy jests and drunken ribaldry as in her mother's day because only the family were now left in the house and such customs were distasteful to Lady Hesketh. She climbed into the strange bed and Philip came to her. They drew the curtains close so that they were shut away alone together in the small dark intimate space.

For Arabella it was the first time she had slept alone since she had been an infant and she felt lonely without the company of her sister. She couldn't stop thinking about Henrietta and wondered if she would ever find someone to love her. She was unable to stop the tears coursing down her cheeks and it took her a long time to fall asleep.

Many miles away towards Bristol Kit Verney could not sleep either. All night he stayed awake beside his wife's bedside, holding her hand and trying to imbue her with some of his own strength. Elizabeth Verney struggled to keep alive through the dark hours, gaining sustenance from his presence, but in the faint light of dawn her frail body found itself unequal to the fight. Kit shed tears of distress and regret as he held her lifeless body in his arms. They had been married since they were fourteen and although he had often been unfaithful and Elizabeth constantly sick he mourned her with genuine grief and a wish that things could have been different.

At Hesketh Hall next day Henrietta made preparations to accompany her husband, father and brother to Oxford. To Arabella's surprise her sister had looked no different when she came downstairs but Henrietta felt very conscious of her changed status. She was now Mistress Henrietta Halsall going to set up home with her husband, and though the night before had perplexed her somewhat she had no doubt that she would accustom herself to the conventions of married life in due course. She kissed her mother and sister but there was already a change in their relationship. She no longer belonged to them but to Philip and she rode away jauntily with her arms around his waist in the sureness of possession. She did not even look back as they left the Hall for her eyes were set upon Oxford, a place which seemed to her the fulfillment of all worldly happiness.

That same day Oliver Cromwell was at Windsor at the headquarters of Sir Thomas Fairfax where he had gone to lay down his commission in person to the Commander in Chief of the Army of Parliament. However the following day he received a letter from the Committee of Both Kingdoms, the administrative body of England and Scotland governing the war for the Parliament cause. They ordered him to take temporary command of a cavalry regiment and proceed immediately towards Oxford. He was to prevent the King from leaving with his army and joining up with Prince Rupert. Cromwell obeyed with alacrity. He had surrendered his commission in good faith, believing sincerely that if God still wanted him in active military service then He would surely send him a sign. Though he had been ordered back only on a temporary basis until a replacement could be found, he had no doubt in his own mind that such a sign had been given.

Chapter 6

APRIL 1645

Cromwell's men welcomed him back wholeheartedly. He had resigned his commission sincerely as a result of the Self-Denying Ordinance. He believed that the only way for Parliament to win the war was by the formation of a well-trained professional army, not a casual or pressed force, and by the leadership of men who were professional soldiers, not politicians or administrators. The fact that he himself had been forced to resign under the terms of the agreement had been an unfortunate but necessary consequence. However he had an unswerving belief that Divine Providence ordered all events and because he was convinced that God had called him to lead men in the struggle to establish the law of the land and the liberty of the Gospel he knew that sooner or later God would open up a way for him to return to active service. Consequently he had not been too surprised when the Committee of Both Kingdoms gave him a special dispensation to take command of his cavalry again for a campaign in which he was considered indispensable, and he had accepted joyfully.

John Radcliffe was one of the happiest to see him return. He had enjoyed being active again and training with the New Model Army since the new year had begun. But soldiering for him was only a means to an end and all he wanted was to bring the war to a conclusion as quickly as possible so that he could pick up the threads of his life again. The flat grain fields of Huntingdon were more to his taste than the battlefields of war, but he was prepared to do whatever had to be done and he knew that the next few months would be crucial if they were to end this struggle. Like most people in England he had not relished taking up arms against his fellow countrymen but his beliefs had been stronger than his misgivings, and over the past two years, as he mixed with like-minded men, his convictions had become stronger and he had hardened his heart to the personal miseries they were forced to inflict on an innocent populace.

Following the instructions of the Committee of Both Kingdoms Cromwell led his men into Oxfordshire. They skirted the periphery of Royalist territory but apart from small skirmishes with companies of Cavalier horsemen there was little threat to their progress. Cromwell's orders were to capture the Royalist strongholds around Oxford and within the salient of the Cotswolds so as to isolate the city and prevent the King's army from leaving to join up with Prince Rupert. They first made their way to Bletchington House, a strongly fortified Royalist outpost to the north of Oxford and prepared for a siege, but Cromwell also dispatched detachments of cavalry over the surrounding countryside to control other strategic bases and sustain a pincer grip on the area. Captain John Radcliffe was one of those given such orders. "Take your company and quarter them at the manor you know near Felton," the General commanded. "Ensure there are no pockets of activity in the region and clear it of draught horses so the King can't move his supplies or artillery. Also see what you can requisition for us, horses and supplies."

John had no qualms about going back to Hesketh Hall in this manner and the familiarity of the place and its inhabitants was a bonus in his favour. So a short time after Henrietta's wedding he made his promised return.

It was Arabella who saw them first. She had come from the herb garden but the spring sunshine was enticing and she had continued idly walking through the gardens to the front of the house where she stood surveying the tranquil surface of the lake and listening to the carefree songs of the birds. Then to her consternation she saw a large troop of mounted men come clattering up the driveway and as they swung along the curve of the path she knew from the orange sashes draped across their armour that they were Roundheads. Fear rose in her throat and her first impulse was to run but by the time she reached the main entrance she realized there was nowhere to run to. Lady Hesketh was sick and had been confined to her bed for a few days with an unidentifiable weakness, presumably caused by the strains and chills of the winter followed by all the upheavals of Henrietta's wedding. Abigail was busy in the kitchen garden to the rear of the house while Simon and Timothy were working somewhere on the estate. In that moment she realized that she was fully in charge of the Hall and its inhabitants and that she was quite alone in her responsibility.

The troop of cavalry had now reached the house. Arabella turned slowly and stood on the steps to face them, clutching the small bunch of rue in her hands to stop them shaking. She thought of the plant's old name, herb of grace, and whispered a prayer to the Virgin that grace might be given her for protection. All the stories she had heard about Roundhead soldiers came flooding into her mind and as she surveyed the menacing mass of armed men, the sun glancing off their steel helmets and breastplates, her legs felt as if they would crumple beneath her . The officer in charge, his orange sash fringed with gold to signify his rank, dismounted and approached her. The bulkiness of his buff leather coat and armour seemed to increase his size, his thigh-length riding boots and leather gauntlets, of which one was a metal bridle arm, and the steel helmet with its face guard all made him seem a threatening figure. Nothing of his face was visible and she could see only his eyes behind the bars of his helmet. Then he took off his helmet respectfully and to her amazement she saw that he was young, by no means thirty years old. His face was tanned, pleasantly featured, his short brown hair damp with sweat.

"My name is John Radcliffe, captain in the army of Parliament. I have to inform you Mistress that I am taking over your house for the quartering of my troops for as long as may be necessary."

From her advantage on the steps Arabella could face the captain at his own height and she found herself looking into brown eyes with a direct uncompromising gaze.

"And if I refuse your permission?" she replied staunchly, trying to keep her voice from trembling.

"It would make no difference," came the reply.

A hatred that was stronger than her fear consumed her as she faced his stony composure. "Then I want you to know that what you do is contrary to my wishes and those of my family and that you enter into our house only because I cannot stop you," she said. "I do not treat with my enemies and for myself I ask nothing, but for my mother's sake I ask that you will do her no hurt because she is not well, and as I am responsible for the servants I demand also that the young girls will suffer no harm."

John studied the girl who symbolized everything he despised. She was obviously one of the Hesketh daughters, only someone who did not work would wear a gown of such a pale blue to be almost colourless. Her fashionable hairstyle was à la mode Henrietta-Maria with tightly curled ringlets and a curled fringe, and her pale ivory skin bespoke the pampered existence of someone who need not spend much time out of doors. Her voice was haughty and she looked at him contemptuously even while she made her request.

"You appear to be under a misconception," he replied coldly. "The soldiers of the army of Parliament are godly men and we do not harm women. Neither will we do harm to your property. We shall require all your stores, your grain and your livestock, and I shall need to search the house for arms. I and my sergeants will sleep in the house though we shall have no need of beds, and my men will use the barns and outhouses. Now if I may examine the property." Without waiting for her permission he beckoned two soldiers and strode past her into the hall, his boots ringing purposefully on the stone floor.

The commotion had now brought servantgirls running and they looked in alarm at the soldiers.

"We shall do you no harm, nothing that we do concerns you, go back to your work," John said, not unkindly, but they looked to Arabella for reassurance and only when she nodded did they began to drift away, whispering uneasily and casting backward glances over their shoulders. At that moment Abigail came into the hall, having entered the house from the back but being alerted by strange sounds, and when she saw John her eyes widened in astonishment, especially as she saw him accoutered in the full panoply of a Roundhead soldier. She made to go to him but a warning in his eyes stopped her short. She understood he was commanding her silence so instead had to discover from Arabella the significance of this unexpected arrival. Arabella was glad of Abigail's support and after informing her of the turn of events sent her into the kitchens to explain the situation to the maids whilst she herself went upstairs to break the unwelcome news to her mother.

Lady Hesketh was sitting up in bed with a silk shawl around her shoulders and Arabella told her as gently and honestly as possible. "Try not to worry mother, they may not be here very long. I don't think they will harm us, we shall just be poorer when they have gone that is all."

Lady Mary's face paled even further but she began to rise saying, "I must get up and see to them myself, it is not suitable for you, Arabella." But a wave of nausea engulfed her as she tried to stand and she made little demur when Arabella prevented her.

"No mother, you must stay here, you are not well and there is nothing you can do," she insisted. "They have guaranteed our safety. I will go and speak with the captain again and come back to you shortly."

John was standing in the hall, still accompanied only by two sergeants, and he turned to her as she reached the foot of the staircase. "I think it best if we commandeer all the downstairs rooms. No-one will come above stairs save I myself, unless there is some emergency, so I suggest you keep to the upper floors. You have plenty of room and your meals can be served there so that you need not encounter my men and it will lessen difficulties. We shall try not to disturb you too much though I, and anyone else necessary to me, must be allowed access to every part of the house to keep it under surveillance." His warning was unmistakable. "Now if you will permit us we will make a thorough search of every room in the house."

Why do you use words like 'permit' when you know we have no choice in the matter, screamed Arabella inwardly but aloud she said, "You cannot enter my mother's chamber, she is sick, I won't allow it."

He was surprised by the determination in her voice and noticed the obstinate set of her small chin.

"Very well then," he acknowledged finally, "I trust your word but make sure you do not abuse my trust." Then ordering his sergeants to call in more men he divided them into groups and they began a systematic search of the house.

Arabella seethed with anger and helplessness as they began to familiarize themselves with every detail of her home, opening cupboards and chests and fingering their possessions with a heartless thoroughness. To her dismay she saw the pistols soon discovered and confiscated. John remembered the last time he had been in the house and recalled clearly every detail of the layout. Returning downstairs he gave orders for the rest of the men, who had been attending to the horses, to come inside. Suddenly a loud shout arose from the soldiers who had been searching below, followed by cries of glee and whistles. "Look what we've found! Come on lads, it's a chapel, a Papist chapel!"

There was a mad stampede as the soldiers now filing into the house followed their comrades' shouts and converged on where the noise was coming from. They were soon crowding down the narrow stairs into the underground chapel, struggling and pushing each other as they realized the impact of the discovery and eager to wreak destruction on what they considered an evil abomination. In an instant they were hurling down candlesticks and smashing them against the altar, breaking the crucifix into pieces, tearing up the altar cloth and missals, slashing the sacred pictures with their swords. With a fearful realization of what was happening Arabella ran down the staircase from the upper landing and stood in horror listening to the commotion. Almost against her will she made her way like a sleepwalker to the chapel but it was a seething mass of men intent on destroying every particle of what was contained there. The sacred pyx and the communion vessels were being fought over and tossed from one to the other and some-one had taken a tinder box and was beginning to set fire to the books. John was vaguely aware of the girl in the doorway as he pushed his way into the chapel. His voice rang out, "Stop this, all of you!" But the tumult was so great and the men so carried away in a frenzy of destruction that he had to repeat himself twice before he could make himself heard. "Stop this immediately or pay the penalty for disobeying orders," he shouted. "Put that fire out or we shall have the whole place burnt around us."

"And why not?" shouted someone. "Filthy Papist hell-hole!"

"Silence!" he cried, his voice controlled now and with an authority they could not dispute. But still there was muttering and some discontent amongst them.

"We are within our rights, Captain," growled Malachi Fen, one of the sergeants. "All images and idols are an abomination to the Lord and the altars of Babylon are to be cast down in His holy name."

There was concerted agreement amongst them and John said, "Well it is done now so let it be and return to your duties. Ensure that nothing is removed from this place. I will personally discipline anyone found with gold or silver on his person. You are paid a wage and there is no need for plunder. The Cavaliers plunder because they do not get paid."

"That does not apply to Catholic paraphernalia, Captain, as well you know," Malachi Fen persisted.

John was well aware that was true. "I want no discontent in this company because some have valuables and others not, so my orders stand," he retorted sternly. Yet deep in his heart he dimly recognized this was not the only reason for his prohibition.

Arabella returned sickened and shocked to the hall and found her mother clinging to the newel post at the foot of the stairs. Still in her daygown with her hair unbound on her shoulders and the silk shawl wrapped around her, Lady Mary had listened to every sound from the chapel, white faced and expressionless but with great shudders shaking her body as she visualized every thud and crash. Before Arabella could reach her someone had snatched the crucifix she was holding and hurled it to the ground, stamping his heels on it. John had been supervising the retreat of his men from the house but he witnessed the act and gave the offender such a blow with the flat of his sword that the man fell reeling to the ground, his head hitting the side of the livery cupboard. There was a stunned silence then Malachi Fen said quietly, "You exceed your authority John Radcliffe." But John exerted his authority even more strongly by calling his men into line and issuing them with a series of short, sharp commands as to their future behaviour in the house.

Arabella and her mother went upstairs to Lady Mary's chamber, visibly shaken and with the sense of participating in the nightmare they had always dreaded. "Perhaps father will come soon," said Arabella sinking into a chair and putting her head in her hands.

"We must pray that your father and William will not come," said Lady Mary firmly, putting her arm around her daughter. "Thank God that Henrietta is away at least. And that we already gave our valuables to the Royalist cause." Though she was sickened by all that had happened Lady Mary seemed to find new strength and the turn of events served to reassert her courage. She put on a beautiful gown of rich red satin and bound up her hair. "Outward forms only help us to know God, they are not a necessity," she said. "The images are in our heart and the prayers in our memory so that we can still worship without the chapel." Knowing how much the chapel had always mattered to her mother, Arabella was full of admiration at her reaction. "As for the sacreligious defilers they will receive judgment from God," she went on with supreme confidence.

Later hearing the captain mount the stairs Arabella approached him and making a great effort said courteously but coldly, "I thank you for trying to prevent some of the destruction."

He regarded her cool haughty face and replied in the same detached tone, "It was for no reason of personal conviction. The Bible tells us that images and idols are an insult to God and we offend him by presuming to worship in this way. I have no liking for the Papist religion."

Arabella flushed with anger and humiliation. She had humbled herself to go to him and offer her thanks and he had spurned her sacrifice. Her eyes flashed a burning hatred before she turned her back on him.

John knew he had been ungracious but the episode had unsettled him. He had taken part in the destruction of churches before, notably Peterborough cathedral. He hated Popery which not only sanctified pagan and idolatrous practices but was disposed towards treason and foreign domination. He did not understand why it had disturbed him to see the Heskeths' chapel desecrated because he believed they were mistaken and misguided individuals. The Hesketh girl had touched a raw nerve for he did not wish to be thanked for failing to do his duty and for a time he had come close to losing control of his men. It was not going to be an easy situation. He was also worried about Abigail after their brief encounter, for he thought her reaction could be unpredictable and he feared more problems on an emotional level.

Abigail had been amazed and dismayed to see John make his promised return to Hesketh Hall at the head of a troop of Parliament cavalry and was in a torment of confusion. She had thrilled to see his face again but wondered how she could now cope with her divided loyalties in such a close situation. She was also filled with guilt as to how far she was responsible for his being here with a force of Roundheads, for though he had often perplexed her she had never dreamt that he held that level of authority. She was longing for an opportunity to talk with him alone so seeing him go into the kitchen she waylaid him. "Are you going to come up to see me John?" she whispered.

He turned to her in exasperation. "Are you mad Abigail! Do you realize I should have a mutiny on my hands if my men found us together. And they would slash your face for a whore." She shuddered at the thought and reluctantly gave up all idea of love for the moment. "And why didn't you tell me about the chapel?" he demanded angrily. "It would have saved a lot of trouble if I'd known about it."

"I never thought to mention it," she admitted miserably. "I've been here for years and it's just a part of the house." She felt she did not know this stern hard John Radcliffe. But there was a matter pressing on her mind and she had to be honest with him. "I must tell Lady Hesketh that we are known to each other - only that I met you at Aunt Keziah's, nothing more," she added hastily as she saw the expression on his face. "It will out sometime and I do not want to deceive them."

He considered it briefly then nodded. "Very well then if it is troubling you. I warned you that you should leave this house. There is nothing for them, their lands will be sequestered. Why don't you go now? I could give you safe conduct up to Stratford."

She shook her head. "I told you before, I can't leave them. In a way I am part of the family."

He sighed. "Well so be it. But we mustn't meet so long as I am in this house. I'm sorry Abigail but I am on military duty and it is not the time to play the lover."

Looking at his set face Abigail thought how much he had changed from when they had played games together in the cottage at Stratford, when she had ridden with her head pillowed against him and when she had lain enfolded in his arms in her bed. Was this what war did to a man? She wondered if William was changed when he rode armed in Rupert's cavalry. What was the laughing, teasing, devil-may-care William Hesketh like when they besieged and killed and plundered and held whole towns to ransom? She spent a sleepless night worrying, for she did not relish what she had to confess to Lady Hesketh.

However next morning she plucked up courage and went to her mistress's chamber. "I did not tell you yesterday, my lady, partly because everything happened so quickly and unexpectedly, and partly because I was afraid, but I feel I ought to tell you now that Captain Radcliffe and I are not unknown to each other. His mother and my aunt are cousins of a sort and I made his acquaintance when I went to visit my aunt at Yuletide." She stood looking down at the floor and fearing how her mistress would receive the information.

Lady Hesketh was quiet for a time, studying Abigail who was obviously in some distress. "Did you know the Roundheads were to come to this house?" she asked at last.

"No I did not. I thought John Radcliffe had returned to his home in Huntingdon. I had no idea he was in this part of the country, in fact I did not know he was a soldier."

Lady Mary wondered briefly what information Abigail might unwittingly have communicated but she was sure of her loyalty to the family. "Why did you tell me this, Abigail?" she asked. "It was not necessary, no-one need ever have discovered it."

"Because I thought if ever it did come to light you might have judged me to be dishonest."

Lady Mary studied Abigail's downcast face and suspected there was more to the story. She sighed at the multitude of problems facing them. "I appreciate your telling me this, especially of your own volition. It is to be expected that you have relatives amongst the supporters of Parliament and I do not hold this against you. But I must command you to have no dealings with this man or with any of the Roundhead troops whilst they are in this house. However should you ever wish to leave our service you are free to go at any time."

"I do not wish to leave, I wish to stay," Abigail cried passionately, suddenly fearful that Lady Hesketh might dismiss her. Instead her mistress embraced her with an uncharacteristic show of affection, though Abigail was racked with guilt wondering what might have happened had the whole truth been known. John had been her friend and briefly her lover and she did not regret helping him but she had never suspected that he would bring the Roundheads here. She did want Parliament to win the war but she did not want the Heskeths to suffer and she was now becoming aware that the two facts were contradictory. Since the war started she had dealt with her divided loyalties by keeping them separate and burying her head in the sand to any implications. But it was now being made abundantly clear that she could no longer do this. She also knew that she wanted to stay at

Hesketh Hall because, although a simple life satisfied her, she had become accustomed to a comfortable existence and did not think she could go back to living in humble circumstances with Aunt Keziah. If only John would take her away with him as she had hoped then this would solve all the difficulties, but she knew that marriage was not in his mind. She longed for his company because when he talked everything seemed straightforward, but she had been forbidden to contact him and in any case he appeared at present to have no inclination for her company, either for talk or for love.

After their initial rampage the Roundheads were organized and disciplined, eating and sleeping in a well behaved manner and leaving the inhabitants of the Hall alone. During the daytime they were scouting and foraging in the surrounding area, clearing the ground of Royalist patrols, requisitioning any horses, especially drays, but always leaving a guard detail at the Hall to oversee stocks and ammunition and help with the cooking which would have been too much for the few servants. Lady Hesketh and Arabella kept to the rooms on the first floor, spending most of their time in Lady Hesketh's parlour, though Arabella sometimes walked in the gardens. But she hated to meet the Roundheads wandering about, feeling dishonoured by their glances and their contemptuous attitude yet angered by the casual familiarity with which they treated her home, the grounds of which were becoming to resemble more and more an army encampment. The worst times were early morning and late at night, on rising and before they retired to sleep, when the whole company sang psalms and prayed together. In the silvery dawn and in the darkening shadows their voices soared in a crescendo of powerful unison that proclaimed God on their side and sent shivers through Arabella and Lady Mary. They had been told by Sir James and William that this was what they faced when they met them in battle but now from their own experience they could understand their feelings of unease. Though they were in no doubt of the intruders' mistaken beliefs and found their own faith strengthened in the process, it was nonetheless a terrifying experience to have such a show of physical and mental solidarity so convincingly demonstrated. At night they lay sleepless in the same bed, alert to every sound, for Arabella was always fearful of being molested despite the captain's assurances and the subsequent good behaviour of the troops. She would fantasise that Kit Verney would suddenly appear on a white charger like a knight in shining armour and with great feats of daring deliver her like the heroes in the medieval romances she loved. But as time went on she realized more and more that the realities of war bore little resemblance to the stuff of romantic narratives.

The captain kept largely out of their way, busy about his own business, but he strode through the house as if he owned it, giving orders to soldiers and servants alike, and Arabella felt her hatred burning with ever increasing intensity whenever she caught sight of him. He would acknowledge her presence with a curt nod, scarcely deigning to look at her, but far from hurting her his disregard only served to fuel her defiance and she thought of ways to annoy him. She would hum dance tunes whenever she heard him approaching, made her devotions in a loud voice, and ignored his strictures on her whereabouts.

One day she felt an impulse to go down to the chapel despite his orders and stood inside the doorway grieving over the devastation within. She remembered Christmas Eve when her father unexpectedly joined them for the

Nativity Mass, and Henrietta's wedding such a short time ago when the chapel had been filled with happy worshippers. In front of her feet the beads of a rosary lay scattered like broken hopes.

"Can you not stay away from this den of iniquity, Papist witch," cried a soldier who had followed her. John had entered from the back of the house and was on his way down the passage but on hearing the words descended the stairs and brusquely sent the man about his business with a sharp reprimand. Then he said to Arabella, "Go back upstairs and do not put yourself to comment coming here."

She whirled on him furiously, two spots of colour burning in her pale cheeks. "Don't you dare order me about and don't ever tell me where to go in my own house," she cried passionately, her grey eyes glittering dangerously.

"If you behave foolishly I cannot protect you," he replied coldly.

"You promised that we should not be harmed. Are your promises like those to your King, made to be broken?"

His mouth hardened ominously but he ignored the taunt. "The men will not harm your body, they are honest and God-fearing. It is your religion they do not like and I am powerless to alter that."

"And insults do not harm me? Is it only my body that is important?" she countered. "*My* religion tells me that my soul is more important than my body." And with this triumphant assertion she turned on her heel and ran up the stairs before he could make any answer.

John was left in no doubt that her abrupt dismissal of any reply he might make was her way of showing contempt and his anger was fuelled by the awareness that she had won that round. Arabella, on the other hand, had made the discovery that mockery could rile him more than defiance.

The following morning he approached her saying, "I have received a communication which necessitates my staying longer than the few days I had first thought."

"Oh can you read?" she asked tauntingly. "I didn't think it was a necessary accomplishment for Roundhead soldiers."

"I can't read that," he pointed derisively to a French romance lying on the table. "I haven't had time for such luxuries."

"What a pity," retorted Arabella. "It might have improved your manners," and she had the satisfaction of seeing an angry spark in his eyes before he turned and left. But when he had gone a wave of depression engulfed her. There was to be no immediate end then to their captivity. Lady Mary refused to venture outside and was becoming increasingly edgy about being cooped up. The servants were feeling the strain of trying to live normally in abnormal circumstances, especially the girls surrounded as they were by so many men. Breakages and accidents to objects were common, an inevitable consequence of over-crowding and nervousness, and their provisions and stocks were dwindling rapidly.

"Why doesn't someone come to get news abroad," Arabella lamented. For the first time she longed for the appearance of Ambrose Hardwicke on one of his regular visits. It did not occur to her that the presence of a large troop of Roundhead cavalry was well known in the area and a serious deterrent.

It was then that Arabella made her decision. She had ensured that her mother's parlour had not been searched when the Roundheads first arrived and there was a pistol there. Inside the chimney was a secret place which Sir James had used as a store for valuables and it was there that they had hidden the pistol taken from the soldier they had killed in the autumn. When her mother was out of the room she retrieved it and charged it then waited. She had been prepared to fire a pistol once and she could do so again.

It was towards evening and the sky was sinking into a dark velvety blue, the shadows enfolding the tents and makeshift living accommodation in a cloak of anonymity with only sounds breaking the illusion that nothing had changed. She saw Captain Radcliffe go into the long gallery to look through the window at the rippling contours of the lake as the water slowly darkened, yet with quivering shafts of silver like shot silk. As she watched his still figure she noted that he was unarmed, with only a canvas jerkin over his shirt. It must be now, she thought. I cannot think of the consequences, I must do something. She had no doubt in her mind that William would do the same.

When John at last turned from the window he was surprised to find that Arabella Hesketh had followed him, and even more surprised when he found himself looking into the barrel of a gun.

"It is loaded," she said. "And do not think I cannot fire it because I have done so before."

John took a deep breath and looked at her implacable face as she stood like an avenging angel in her white dress. He remembered in a flash the one room he had omitted to search and blamed himself for his negligence while appreciating the resourcefulness of his adversary.

"Of what use is it to kill me?" he asked steadily. "There are fifty more men outside, one of whom would only take my place."

"Because you are the one responsible for taking over my home and I know my father or my brother would do the same. And because I hate you more than I have ever hated anyone in my life. I hate your narrow Puritan faith and I hate your domineering manner and your arrogance, especially as you are probably no more than a blacksmith."

"As a matter of fact I am a lawyer," he stated quietly and Arabella gave a start of surprise, though she remembered his slender unmarked hands.

"Nonetheless if I can kill one hated Roundhead I shall have done something for the cause I believe in," she said defiantly.

Despite her words John did not really think she would pull the firing bolt but he did not relish half the chance of having his head blown off. Her hand held the pistol remarkably steady and her eyes never wavered from his face. He resisted the impulse to knock it from her hand with a swift blow that would have broken her wrist. Despite her threatening stance she looked very fragile and, ironically, defenceless.

He kept very still, not moving a muscle and fixing her with his steady gaze, aware of the naked hostility in her grey eyes. Her fingers tightened on the trigger but he held her eyes with his. Silence hung between them, neither of them heard the constant activity outside. It seemed as if time stood still and the ensuing minutes stretched into an eternity as two strong wills battled for supremacy. Then he took the gun from her grasp and very gently put his arm around her. John was not overly tall but she reached only to his shoulder and he could feel her shaking. Then he led her to the window seat and sat her down.

"I know you hate me," he said quietly. "It is understandable and if I were in your place I would probably feel the same. I cannot even make the excuse that I am only doing my duty because you see I believe in what I am doing. I believe in the cause I am fighting for. I am sorry it is opposite to yours, but to me it is the right one and I must go on."

"You have made me look a fool," she whispered bitterly, tears of shame starting to her eyes. "You knew I could not fire it." I have wasted the pistol, she thought angrily, and for nothing but to look a fool. She tried desperately to hold back the tears for she must not cry in front of this man who hated her as much as she hated him.

"I knew no such thing," he said quietly. But she rose with as much dignity as she could summon and walked from the gallery.

In her chamber she sat in the chair by the window looking out across the lake, only discernible now by the flickering flames of the camp fires. She watched the soldiers crossing the park in groups, heard the ringing of harness and shouts of men, but neither sight nor sound penetrated her numbness. She felt empty inside now that her hatred had gone. For her hatred was no longer there and she did not know at what point it had left her, or why. Was it because of his unflinching courage, his ultimate gentleness, his honesty? Or even because of the awareness that he was no uneducated upstart from the working classes but a university trained lawyer. Her hatred has sustained her and given her courage and now that it had gone there was nothing to fill its place except a great confusion.

Arabella had longed for a visitor and soon her wishes were granted. William Hesketh had expected to be well on his way to joining Rupert by this time but in actual fact he had not left Oxford. His horse had stumbled and thrown him, resulting in a dislocated shoulder that was too painful for him to consider riding to a campaign until it improved. Then when he was well enough to proceed he learnt that the regiment had left Ludlow and were now on their way back south to join up with the King's army. As a result of this change of direction his father suggested he should make a short detour home to confirm that all was well at Hesketh Hall. William complied with his father's request, though he intended only the briefest of sojourns. So it was that he rode straight into the arms of the waiting Roundheads.

CHAPTER 7

APRIL - MAY 1645

As William rode up to the Hall he saw the Roundheads too late. On his approach into Felton he had caught sight of two Parliamentary officers but thinking nothing of it he had skirted the town and arrived at the Hall from the western side where it was sheltered by low hills. Now he cursed himself for his stupidity. It was only when he rounded the bend of the driveway that he saw to his astonishment the horses cropping the grass and the groups of buff-coated soldiers among the tents and paraphernalia of a military encampment. He immediately reined his horse and turned at speed but he had already been sighted. He was hotly pursued and his horse shot from under him so that he came crashing heavily to the ground. The pain from his injured shoulder was agonizing but he found himself dragged unceremoniously to his feet and divested of his sword and pistols. In a haze of pain and disbelief he tried to take everything in - Roundheads everywhere. He feared for his family while his favourite horse, Lightning, who had carried him into the fray since the war began and faced tumult, pike, and shot, now lay dead at his feet. His fury knew no bounds and it took three men to hold him. One of them twisted his arms behind his back and dislocated his shoulder again. The pain almost made him lose consciousness but he continued to struggle frantically, shouting the most fearsome oaths which further antagonized his captors as swearing was a punishable offence in the army of Parliament.

"Lock him up till the captain gets back," said the sergeant. So roughly manhandled, cursing and struggling, William Hesketh returned home.

Arabella had heard the commotion and was already on the staircase as William was dragged into the Hall, though she blanched at his language. "William, what are you doing here?" she cried in dismay.

"So it is Master Hesketh," Malachi Fen said with satisfaction. "Lock him in his chamber till the captain returns."

"Why don't you lock me up properly," said William sarcastically. "Why don't you put me in the turret room which has the only door you can lock. No barred windows but only eight foot square, enough like a cell for your satisfaction no doubt. Why give me the comfort of my own chamber? After all I am only the master here."

"Why not take the joker at his word," laughed one of the soldiers derisively, "Show him it doesn't do to jest with the army of Parliament."

"Yes do as he says," Malachi Fen confirmed vindictively and his companions roared with laughter for they had been appalled by William's blasphemous language. "We can always say he asked for this special treatment. You shouldn't make japes at your own expense," he added to William as they bundled him upstairs past the horrified Arabella.

"Bloody swine!" he shouted, continuing to kick and struggle as they hauled him up to the room in the turret above the porch and locked the door behind him.

The tiny room boasted only a table and hard chair, for one wall was taken up by the huge trefoil window of stained glass that was such an attractive feature of the front of the house. William dropped onto the floor, wiping the sweat from his face with the torn sleeve of his jacket. He clenched his teeth against the pain in his shoulder and tried to rest. He was unaware of how much time had passed when the door opened.

"I must apologise for the rough treatment you received but I believe you caused a lot of trouble," said John Radcliffe.

William struggled to his feet and said, "It might have escaped your notice but this is my house. My name is William Hesketh. Lieutenant William Hesketh of the Royalist army. Who might you be?"

"I am **Captain** John Radcliffe of the army of Parliament." He stressed the difference in rank then continued, "It might have escaped your notice but I have taken over this house."

"Like Hell you have," William cried, his eyes blazing and his fists involuntarily clenched.

"The facts are in my favour," said John calmly.

The two adversaries stood facing each other in the confined space. William saw the assured self-confidence of the officer, a few years older than he. He was shorter and broader with steady brown eyes in a tanned clean-shaven face and dark brown hair just touching his collar. A force to be reckoned with, he acknowledged. John for his part saw a tall slender Cavalier of about twenty, his long golden hair curling past his shoulders, a carefully shaped moustache outlining the scornful curve of his lips, grey eyes cold with anger. He dismissed him as a spoilt elegant boy.

"I shall have to keep you here for the moment," John informed him. "However you will be well treated. I will arrange for blankets and food to be brought to you, and you may have anything you require, within reason."

"Magnanimous of you, seeing I am in my own house", "William growled. "But you can send my servant Abigail Hart to me, I have twisted my shoulder and I need her to bind it up for me."

"I will ask her if she will come to you," John said pointedly, angry at the way William Hesketh had spoken of Abigail. Then as he was leaving he turned back and said, "As a cavalryman myself, I am sorry about your horse."

But his captive made no reply and gave him a stony stare.

When he had gone William sank onto the chair and rested his head on his arms at the table. A short time later Abigail arrived but only when she had closed the door to the accompanying soldier did she speak. "William what are you doing here?" she cried then, shocked by his dishevelled appearance and the grey pallor of his face.

"I can't explain everything at the moment. You must inform me what is going on here. How are mother and Arabella?"

She gave him a concise account of events but once he had got the gist of the situation he stopped her in mid-flow saying urgently, "I need you to do several things for me." He spoke low in a serious voice not at all like the bantering tone he often used with her. "Firstly I have dislocated my shoulder and I need you to bind it up for me so go and get some cold water and bandages. Also while you are in the kitchen get a sharp knife but don't let anyone see it, hide it in your clothes."

"What are you going to do?" she asked anxiously.

"I'll tell you afterwards. Just do that first. If anyone objects tell them they hurt my shoulder manhandling me and I need privacy while you dress it for me."

She looked troubled, as much by this unfamiliar intense William as by the predicament she found him in, but went to do his bidding.

When she returned William had managed to struggle out of his jacket and was sitting in the chair. "Help me off with my shirt," he commanded, and she took it off as gently as she could, feeling the surprisingly firm muscles underneath. "Now do exactly as I say. Get hold of my shoulder and pull it right back until it cracks."

She went pale. "I will hurt you."

"Yes you will hurt me like hell and I shall probably disgrace myself by fainting. But it has to be done. If I pass out splash cold water on my face."

"I cannot, William," she cried, visibly distressed.

"Don't be such a whey-faced ninny," he said impatiently. "I asked for you because I knew you wouldn't fail me. I have to get away from here and this must be done first. Now come on, speed is important. I will tell you exactly what to do but you must be very strong and don't worry about hurting me."

Looking at William's set face she knew there was no alternative so conquering her reluctance she nerved herself to do as he commanded. After it was done Abigail was the more distressed and she was overcome with a feeling of nausea. She wiped the sweat from William's face then splashed her own with the cold water so that her auburn hair that had crept from her coif fell in damp tendrils around her face, the drops mingling with her tears.

A soldier opening the door cried, "What's going on in here?" but all he saw was Abigail binding the bandage tightly around the Cavalier's shoulder.

"Can't you see I'm hurt, you dolt. Let me have some privacy while I'm being attended to," William roared. "God's blood, I can't run away can I." The door closed again and after a pause he continued in a low voice. "I'm going to get away from here but I need your help."

"How are you going to do it?"

"Why do you think I got them to put me here in this room. They are so stupid, not a brain between them - the new noddle army! This is where Father Edmund used to hide because from above the porch here you can see all the way to the wood. There's a concealed entrance behind the panelling, impossible to detect if you don't know where it is, and there's a narrow flight of stairs leading to a secret garret in the eaves. From the garret I'm going over the roof, the knife is to force the window open should it be stuck."

"You will kill yourself," she cried in alarm, thinking of the steep fall of the roof in this old part of the house.

"I've done it before. Don't you remember when I was about fourteen I terrified Arabella on All Hallows Eve cavorting on the roof with a white sheet on."

They both giggled at the recollection then Abigail said, "And you got whipped for it." She remembered Sir James's fury at the time and, sobered, she continued, "You will get more than a whipping if you are caught this time."

"Well I won't have to get caught," William stated grimly, aware of the penalty for escaping prisoners. They looked at each other seriously for a moment then he continued, "There is something else you must do. Can you get me a horse?"

"I don't know," she replied, aghast at the enormity of her task.

"Try and find a way to take one of them while they are eating perhaps, or they are asleep, there are so many of them they won't notice. If you could take it to where the land drops behind the bothy, where we used to play hide and seek, as soon as is possible after ten of the clock, I can hear the clock on the parish church strike."

"I don't know, I don't know if I can do it," she said hesitantly."Can't you wait for a short while until your shoulder is better, you are in no state for such a dangerous plan." She looked at him pleadingly and he saw the anxiety in her green eyes.

"I dare not wait, they could move me from this room. It has to be done tonight while I have the opportunity. If I fail, then I fail, but I must try. You know I can't stay cooped up here, I shall go mad. And I must try to get help to relieve this place."

Abigail remained silent, overwhelmed by the enormity of her task and the hazards for William.

"I know I'm asking a lot," he said, uncharacteristically humble. "If you are seen or encounter any difficulties then forget about the horse, I'll manage something. Just make some excuse and clear yourself, forget about me. I wouldn't for the world put you in danger." There was genuine concern in his eyes.

"I'll do my best for you," she said at last, realizing the depth of his trust in her and wondering what would happen if he discovered her relationship with John Radcliffe.

He smiled for the first time since their meeting. "I knew you wouldn't fail me. Don't worry about me, I can do it. Tell mother and Arabella that all is well in Oxford with father, Henrietta and Philip. I will come back with help as soon as I can. Now go, ...and Abigail," he reached for her hand, "I am most grateful to you." He was too tense for anything further but he kept her hand in his for a moment, looking at her beautiful troubled face.

"Please be careful," she implored.

"I'm never careful, it's not in my nature. Pray that the Roundheads are as stupid as usual that's all." His irrepressible temperament reasserted itself after the unaccustomed solemnity. "And Abigail, about the horse. If you could manage it the captain's horse would be ideal." He grinned wickedly.

John Radcliffe visited him again later. "How's the shoulder?" he asked, but William ignored him. John's face tightened. "I thought you might be able to give me some information about Prince Rupert but we can leave that till the morrow. You might like to know that your mother and sister are well and cared for."

"My mother's name is Lady Hesketh and I would ask you to refer to her by that title. What were you before the war, a cobbler or a tiler? No your hands are too fine, a tailor perhaps," sneered William.

John knew he should ignore the calculated insult by a second Hesketh but he couldn't resist the satisfaction of saying, "I am good at getting information out of people because I happen to be a lawyer. Though as a matter of fact my grandfather was a blacksmith."

So he was a university man and perhaps the Inns of Court, William reckoned with some bitterness, because both establishments were closed to him as a Catholic. This Roundhead was no mere bully boy.

"Times are changing Master Hesketh, - Lieutenant Hesketh. I think you would do well to be aware of the fact. The land will not always be in the hands of a few, passed on by birth and not merit."

"Yes, that is what this struggle is about isn't it?" William cried fiercely. "Land! It isn't about religion or politics but land. You Roundheads are supposedly fighting for the Parliament and for your Puritan religion but in actual fact you are fighting for our lands. And it isn't an even distribution of land you want but a redistribution - into your own possession."

John could feel his anger rising despite himself. What was it about these Hesketh sprigs that could force him onto the defensive? He knew that he should leave and not enter into an argument that was beneath him, but he knew that William, like Arabella, would consider it a victory for his contempt. "I cannot dispute that there are those on both sides, yours as well as ours, who are using this struggle for their own ends," he said curtly. "But I myself believe that it is God's work we are about, to establish a more just and equable society, and freedom from religious forms which degrade and enslave men."

"So you lock me up because you think my religion enslaves me," asked William mockingly, his lips curled in a derisive smile.

"I lock you up because you are troublesome and would cause my men more problems than they have time for. And also because I want some information from you," said John harshly, leaving the room exasperated beyond measure. William heard his raised voice reprimanding an unfortunate soldier who was chatting idly with a serving maid and smiled with satisfaction.

As darkness fell Abigail began to have further qualms about her mission. For one agonizing moment she was tempted to go and tell John and thus save William from further peril as well as herself from possible recriminations. She imagined John's gratitude and where it might lead. Then she thought of William whom she had betrayed before and suffered for it later. She felt torn between the two of them. She knew she was being disloyal to John but the Heskeths had given her a home and her friendship with William went back a long way. She had been aware that John's arrival in the house would bring problems but had not fully realized the severity of the implications. She felt as if she were being pulled apart by opposing forces but finally she decided to try and do as William had asked. However she baulked at taking John's horse. A cavalryman's horse was his companion, trained to every touch and command of his master, a relationship essential to his survival in battle. She would not harm John in order to satisfy William's malicious idea of revenge.

She was quaking with fear as she crept from the house by the back stairs, keeping close to the wall and melting into the shadows in her dark clothes, but her footfalls were drowned by the sounds of soldiers' merriment coming from the kitchens. She knew that if she was stopped she would have to invent some story and rely on John's relationship with her. Despite his present coolness he had lain with her and they had shared the closest of ties, surely he would not be too harsh. This thought gave her confidence and if she were caught with the horse she planned to say she had decided to leave the house and go to Stratford. Whether he believed her or not would be up to him. Perhaps her bravado influenced the path of fate, or perhaps the soldiers were too relaxed, for she accomplished her task without being apprehended and was climbing the back stairs again as the brass clock in Lady Hesketh's parlour was striking ten. Now all she had to do was wait. She did not undress but sat in her chamber, alert to every sound, every nerve tensed. She anticipated hearing William falling from the roof or his being taken, but there was no noise apart from the customary sounds of the soldiers preparing to camp down for the night and no unusual disturbances shattered the darkness. Every minute increased the hope of his success and when eventually so much time had elapsed that guaranteed all must be well she went exhausted to her bed.

Early next morning she was dressed and preparing to leave her chamber to attend to Lady Hesketh's needs when there came a sharp knock on the door. Opening it she found John Radcliffe on the threshold. He had not been in her room since the night they had made love but it was obvious from the expression on his face that he was untroubled by such remembrances.

"Do you know anything about the disappearance of William Hesketh?" he demanded abruptly.

"Why should I know anything?" she stammered, unprepared for the confrontation and biting her lip in confusion as she realized she had probably given herself away.

"I am asking you that question," he said, his suspicions now hardening into certainty in the knowledge that the news had not surprised her.

Her presence of mind deserted her in the face of his penetrating gaze and she was forced to drop her eyes, realizing how she had incriminated herself. John looked at her in consideration. He should not have treated her so harshly because he had misjudged her again. He thought her partiality for him would withstand his necessary neglect but she had put William Hesketh before him and the flash of insight was not pleasant. "It would seem you are fond of Master Hesketh," he commented laconically.

Perhaps more than I realized, Abigail perceived with surprise. But she kept silent, not looking at him, and he left the room without saying anything further. When he had left a sudden recollection sprang unbidden into her mind, the memory sparked by his words. It was of the day she had first come to Hesketh Hall. Lady Mary had taken her to meet the children and she had stood shy, nervous, and lonely, very conscious of her poor drab clothes though she was wearing the best she had. She looked at the three exquisitely dressed figures standing before her. The girls in their brightly coloured satin gowns with their hair curled and beribboned inspected her critically and she felt embarrassed before their cool surveillance. She had wanted to run away, back to the cosy familiarity of Uncle Jacob and Aunt Keziah, away from this overwhelming house with its rich and beautiful inhabitants. Then the boy, about twelve years old with golden curls and an angelic smile, had come to her with hand outstretched saying, "Would you like a sweetmeat? I'll show you the deer in the park tomorrow if you wish."

William's disappearance had first been detected by the discovery of the body of a Roundhead guard floating face down in the lake, and a missing horse. William Hesketh had left the house much quieter than he had arrived. John Radcliffe did not know how he had done it but surmised a priest hole somewhere and was angry with himself for not having thought of such a possibility in a Catholic house. He made a search of the turret room in order to satisfy his curiosity but was forced to draw a blank, though for the first time he noticed the cleverly disposed pieces of plain glass in the rose window, ideal peepholes for an unauthorised guest to view anyone approaching the house from a distance. William Hesketh had made a fool of him and had most probably already planned his escape when he was talking to him with such confidence, a thought not calculated to soothe his anger. He did not know why he had had a vague suspicion that Abigail might have been involved and he had gone to her room on impulse, but her reaction had confirmed his suspicions. He still found it hard to believe that she had put loyalty to William Hesketh, the Catholic Royalist who had openly proclaimed her his servant, before her feelings for him. His pride had been severely damaged even though he was aware that his coolness had upset her. But he had been right in surmising that her reactions could be unpredictable in this new situation of openly conflicting loyalties. He had not been so accurate in his assessment of Master Hesketh and John was honest enough to admit that he would have to revise his opinion. The young Cavalier's escape had shown courage, intelligence and extreme resourcefulness and John had to admire him for it. He was forced to concede that there was more to the Heskeths than had at first appeared.

Arabella had kept out of John's way since the incident in the gallery and when she had inadvertently crossed his path she had averted her eyes in order to prevent any contact with him. Now he sought her out to give her the information about William.

"I feel I ought to tell you that your brother has gone. It would appear that this happened during the hours of darkness and he is obviously well on his way by now. I do not think you need fear for his safety," he said, adding generously, "Your brother is quite a man."

A small smile of satisfaction and triumph touched Arabella's lips. "He has gone to get help for us," she said.

John did not tell her that the Royalists were far too hard-pressed around Oxford to spare help for anyone else, especially a country household. The New Model Army in full strength was now closing in on them. He decided to let Arabella live on hope and left her the pleasure of breaking the news to Lady Hesketh.

"It was kind of him to tell us," said Arabella, when she had done so.

"It was his duty," snapped Lady Mary uncharitably.

Nevertheless they were buoyed up by expectancy that relief could soon be at hand.

Later in the day Arabella was contacted by old Silas who was looking very agitated as he stood in the kitchen garden. "Wat Dacre and Adam Ashe are here reporting to the Roundheads that they have seen Father Edmund in the vicinity," he quavered.

"I will go and see what is happening," she said, thinking there was no end to alarms. "Do not repeat anything of this to my mother." She made her way hurriedly into the house where she found John Radcliffe seated at the table in the dining room with Wat Dacre and Adam Ashe standing before him, holding their caps in their hands but swaggering with importance.

"What do you know of these two?" he asked directly.

"I know they tend to make mischief," she replied hesitantly, not wishing to condemn them unjustly but mindful of what Silas had told her.

"Do they tell the truth?"

"I don't know," she said helplessly. "I know my father has had some trouble with them in the past."

"They say there is a stranger in the vicinity whom they believe to be a Catholic priest," he said studying her. He chose his words carefully. "I have no time to waste on a wild goose chase."

"It is the truth," cried Wat Dacre. "A Jesuit who has visited the Hall here on numerous occasions."

Adam Ashe corroborated the statement adding, "He must have found out the place was not safe for him. He is a notorious traitor and a danger to the State."

"If you are so concerned about the welfare of the State why are you not marching with the army of Parliament?" John snapped.

"Haven't we lived in a Royalist area? At least we didn't march with the Cavaliers," retorted Adam sullenly while his companion burst in, "We will march with you now if you will have us."

"You are too late," John rapped out. "My men are experienced and well-trained, we have no use for hangers-on now that the tide is turning in our favour. Get you gone, I will see to the matter."

"Don't we get a reward?" asked Wat Dacre resentfully, surprised at being dismissed so abruptly when they had expected grateful commendation, and his companion muttered in agreement.

"Your reward is the satisfaction that you have done your duty," said John, dismissing them with a curt nod of his head. Afterwards he honestly did not know if he would have let the matter alone had not Arabella started to plead with him.

"Please don't take any notice of them," she said, in her alarm forgetting herself sufficiently to appeal to him. "I told you they like to make trouble and if there is a priest what harm can he do?"

She was wearing a pale blue satin gown, the skirt open at the front to display a white silk petticoat embroidered with blue flowers, the bodice cut in a low curve revealing the lace edging of her shift and from where her small breasts peeped out in an effect both virginal and provocative at the same time. Her hair was arranged differently with a little knot of curls on top of her head. He despised her for appealing on behalf of a Catholic priest but other emotions were rising and he found himself struggling with a tension he could not resolve. He wanted to strike her and he wanted to kiss her and the violence of his feelings shocked him. "What harm?" he shouted furiously. "They are traitors plotting to overthrow the State. These travelling Jesuits journey from place to place with letters and information from Spain and France, intriguing with foreign powers under cover of their heathenish religion."

"Father Edmund is not like that, he is good and kind and only wants to lead us to God. He risks his life to minister to us, please, please leave him alone," she pleaded, so overwhelmed by her distress that she dropped on her knees before him, her hands clasped.

The action unsettled him further and he forced himself to retain his habitual clearsightedness as a wave of conflicting emotions washed over him. He was a Parliamentary officer on a military assignment and he must not be blinded to the fact that these Heskeths were confirmed and long-standing Papists who did not hesitate to equivocate and deceive.

"Father Edmund is it? Go down to Felton and see to the business," he commanded two soldiers. Then he turned to Arabella with a stony expression, "I must do the right thing."

She rose slowly and stood still for a moment, her grey eyes looking into his. Then she said, "You are the most insensitive and arrogant person I have ever met. You are always right - in your beliefs, your actions, your idea of God. It never crosses your mind that you could be wrong, or even only half right." His eyes flickered at her condemnation but his face remained impassive. She continued, "Our faith teaches us that we should have doubts, that it is right to have doubts, because without them we commit the sin of pride. We ought to be humble enough to have doubts. I pity you because you have none at all." When she reached the door she turned and said, "If you do find Father Edmund I have no **doubt** about this - that he will die for his faith with courage."

John turned back to his work for he had several important communications to attend to, but he could not concentrate and after a while he laid down his quill and went outside into the bright May sunshine which sparkled the earth with a clarity that defined every new blade of grass, every flower petal, every pendulous spray of fragrant blossom. He walked for a time as far as the ravaged wood and sat down on a truncated tree stump. Birdsong flowed over him and in the distance he could hear the muted sounds of the encampment but he was lost in his own thoughts. He had never considered himself arrogant. That was a quality he associated with the rich and powerful of this world. And he could not afford to have doubts. If he began to doubt God's purpose in what he had been doing for the past two years then life would be meaningless. Arabella Hesketh was wrong. His faith taught him not to have doubts but to believe wholeheartedly that the providence of God would guide those who put their trust in Him. That was the anchor of the Protestant faith. Why should it matter to him what a misguided Catholic, Royalist, rich, pampered girl thought. He made an effort to dismiss her from his mind and concentrate on his many duties and he strode purposefully back to the house, determined that the Heskeths should not unsettle him in this way.

However when the soldiers returned he felt a mixture of frustration and relief that they had found nothing. Father Edmund, if it were he, had disappeared as silently and completely as William Hesketh. Perhaps there was some truth in the accusations of witchcraft laid at the door of Catholics. He suddenly felt that he would be glad to be gone from this place so as not to be in danger of being bewitched himself.

His wish was answered the following day in a communication ordering them to leave Felton and proceed to Abingdon to join up again with Oliver Cromwell and he was filled with an overwhelming relief at the news. He ordered Malachi Fen to inform the men and begin preparations for their departure while he went to see Lady Hesketh.

"We shall be away within hours and I shall attempt to leave the place as I found it," he reported. He purposely made no mention of the chapel however. "I have to leave a sergeant here and a detail of a few men to await a further communication with regard to the deployment of some stores but they will be away by the morrow. Meanwhile they will confine themselves to the barns and stables and will give you no trouble. I will leave you enough stocks for your immediate needs."

Lady Hesketh acknowledged the information by a brief nod of her head but said nothing. She had made a point of never speaking to any of the Roundheads whilst they had been in the house and did not intend to change that now.

A few hours later they were away as they had come with John Radcliffe riding at the rear of the troop until they were clear of the house. Lady Mary felt weak with relief, even though their fields and their larders were stripped bare. Abigail also felt relief for it had been a great strain, yet she also experienced an overwhelming sadness for she suspected that a chapter of her life had ended, a chapter that had promised so fair. Arabella, who had been the first to see them arrive, was the last to see them go. She recollected how on their arrival she had stood trembling on the steps with a bunch of rue in her hand. She too had expected to feel only unspeakable relief at their departure. Instead she was jolted by a treacherous shaming feeling of loss as she realized she would never see the hated Roundhead captain again.

Afterwards John did not know what made him turn back. They had ridden for nearly two hours, some twenty miles, when he became aware of a vague disquiet which became stronger as the distance passed. He tried to ignore it as the inevitable feeling of some regret at the not entirely satisfactory completion of his task, but he became alarmed at its persistency which did not diminish as he rode. He had always listened to his inner voice, believing with the prophets of the Old Testament that God spoke to men in such a way, and after careful consideration he made a decision. He was aware that he could be acting irresponsibly and was mindful of the consequences should he be mistaken, yet he was confident of some prompting. He stopped their progress, then after a word with Malachi Fen placed the troop under his command and ordered them to continue on their way, saying that he had an unexpected duty to perform and would rejoin them shortly. They were surprised but did not question his orders, and after seeing them on their way again he spurred his horse and galloped back the way he had come.

As he approached Hesketh Hall he could see in the distance a thin column of smoke rising in a grey spiral against the hazy blue of the early evening sky and as he galloped at full speed up the driveway an acrid smell of burning assailed his nostrils. It appeared to be coming from the back of the house and turning his horse to the rear entrance he saw the men he had left behind wielding burning brands, while the household was clustered in shocked silence watching the house just beginning to be set alight. If they had started their firing at the front of the house then the curtains and wood panelling would have soon caught fire but their perverse notion of retribution had compelled them to begin where the chapel was.

He leapt from his horse and ignoring everyone else called to the men, "Stop immediately. Extinguish those brands and put this fire out!" He cared nothing for the effect his sudden appearance had caused amongst the onlookers.

"We are acting under orders, Captain," said the sergeant. "We were given clear orders to do this before we left, we are not acting independently."

"Then I countermand those orders," he said, realizing the enormity of his decision.

The men stopped to look at him in amazement. "The orders were from General Cromwell," said the sergeant, Peter Dawe, in an awed voice.

"At this moment I am in command and you take your orders from me. I will justify myself."

"You cannot justify yourself, Captain. Only God justifies," warned Sergeant Dawe, greatly troubled by his officer's presumption.

But John ignored him and began to give orders to everyone assembled. "Get this fire out before it spreads. Everyone get buckets, jugs, bowls, any containers you can find. Use the water in the house and from the lake. Quickly before it is too late. Luckily the wind is in the right direction."

The shocked household were spurred into action by the urgency of his commands and the group of paralysed spectators was transformed into a hive of activity with John as their leader. He methodically organized teams of workers to maximise their efficiency, working in relays filling and passing the containers from hand to hand, all the time following his orders as he assessed the situation. He had no time to register individual faces and was scarcely aware of the presence of Abigail, Arabella and Lady Mary. He was completely absorbed in the task in hand and urgent in its execution, never flagging as the shadows lengthened and dusk folded around the apocalyptic scene. No-one was sure of how much time had passed but finally as darkness fell the fire was out. The chapel was a burnt-out shell and the back of the house severely damaged but the fire had spread no further. Exhausted, dirty, emotionally drained, everyone now began to realize the enormity of what had happened.

John turned to his men who were now worried about the repercussions. "Have no fear, I take full responsibility upon myself, you will in no way be blamed," he attempted to reassure them, but they did fear and murmured amongst themselves. They admired and respected their captain who was just and courageous, but at this action they felt great unease.

Exhausted by his own personal efforts and half-blinded by dirt and sweat, John felt as if he were moving in a dream. The scene had taken on a hallucinatory aspect with dim figures flitting ghostlike through the gloom and the bitter pungent smell of smouldering wood choking the air. He was vaguely conscious of Arabella by his side. They had not spoken together amid all the haste and confusion. Now she attempted to thank him but he shook his head in despair, not finding the energy to voice his thoughts.

Noticing the vivid red weal down the side of his face where a piece of blazing woodwork had struck him she said, "There are ointments in the stillroom to dress that. Come into the house and I will tend it."

"It is nothing," he shrugged, careless of the smart.

"Why are you so stubborn? Do you never submit to the wishes of others?" Her voice had a weary exasperation and he looked at her properly for the first time. Her pale blue gown was now blackened and torn, her face even paler beneath the smudges of soot, her grey eyes sad.

He did as she asked and accompanied her into the house.

In the stillroom he sat on the bench by the table as she stood over him and by the light of a candle gently dressed the burn with a cooling salve. Her hands were tender and competent but he noticed they were red and bruised, the nails broken. When she had finished he took hold of them sorrowfully. There was so much to say but he could say nothing.

"Why did you come back?" she ventured at last, not removing her hands from his.

"Because I feared for you," he said simply. They sat in silence, their faces sad and weary in the flickering candle flame. "I had a premonition that all was not well and I knew I had to come back. You see I am not so insensitive as you thought." He smiled weakly.

"And I am more in need of your help than I had supposed," she whispered. Then she said, "I ought to go now," although she made no attempt to move and her hands were still clasped in his.

Her face was streaked with dirt and soot and there was a black smudge on her nose, her hair was awry and fell on her forehead and round her face in straggling wisps, and suddenly the incongruity of her appearance lightened his spirits. "You look like a chimney sweep." He smiled in genuine amusement.

She giggled and retorted, "And you look like a blacksmith."

Suddenly they were two young people caught in a war that was changing their lives. The spontaneity of their laughter echoed around the white-washed stone walls of the little room, warm in the candleglow. Then he stood up and pulled her into his arms, kissing her with a ferocity that bruised her face and lips and crushing her slender body so tightly that she was pinioned in his grasp and she moaned under his passionate assault. She resisted at first, rigid against him, then her mouth opened under the pressure of his lips and her body folded into his.

John was the first to draw back and there was both joy and fear in his eyes. "I am sorry," he said. "It will not do, I know. But I cannot get you out of my mind. I know so much divides us but my heart is drawn to you like a lodestone and I cannot deny it."

Arabella looked up into the direct candour of his brown eyes and wondered how she could ever have feared and hated him. In some inexpressible way, for some unfathomable reason, her life had become contracted into an all-encompassing need for this strong, honest, determined man.

Still neither of them could go further. For John, Arabella Hesketh was a girl out of his class whom he would never have encountered under normal circumstances. She was a Catholic whose beliefs were repugnant to him and a Royalist to whose family he was an enemy. And for Arabella the same strictures applied to John Radcliffe, a Puritan Roundhead of modest birth - an enemy to her faith, her principles and her social status. The gap between them yawned like a perilous chasm. But in this instance Arabella was the more courageous. She spoke for the first time, quietly and tremulously, "I love you."

John thought that in his need he had imagined the words as unreality washed over him. He took her in his arms again, gently now, kissing her tenderly and reverently and stroking her hair but as she responded to him he realized he was not dreaming. "You have made me ashamed of my fear," he murmured. "You are braver than I am." He had known a few women in the ten years since he had first lain with a girl in a Huntingdon meadow but he had never said he loved. Now he spoke the words for the first time. "I love you Arabella." He buried his face in the hollow of her throat and she stroked the back of his neck where his hair pressed damply, smelling the smoke and sweat on his body.

"What will happen to us?" she asked.

He did not want to say he did not know. "We will find a way."

She was comforted by his apparent confidence and did not want to think further of the complexities into which they had been drawn, shutting from her mind the faces of her parents and William. All she wanted was to be loved by this loyal, passionate, courageous man. She knew instinctively she could trust his word and with him she would know a faithfulness and protection that would never fail her. How could she ever have believed that she loved Kit Verney or that she could exist with Ambrose Hardwicke.

"Stay the night here," she pleaded. "It is late and grown dark and you are exhausted."

"No I cannot, much as I would wish it. I must be on my way, I have been gone from my men for too long." He began to be aware of the seriousness of his actions and a chill settled on his heart. He did not relish the long journey back, bone weary as he was, and the inevitable consequences that awaited him.

His anxiety was not lost on Arabella and she asked, "What will happen to you?"

This time he had to be honest and answer, "I don't know." He could expect a court martial and the loss of his command, for Oliver Cromwell was a strict disciplinarian. However he was relying on the urgency of the military situation to delay immediate punishment.

Arabella held onto him fearfully. When John Radcliffe had first ridden up to the door of Hesketh Hall she had been so afraid. Now she was more afraid to see him depart. They embraced a last time, reluctant to separate. Then it was time to go. He mounted his horse and taking her hand he kissed it tenderly. "I will come back to you, don't doubt that. And do not fear, because if you are ever in danger I will protect you with my body and my life."

He disappeared into the darkness and she could not see him round the bend of the drive, only hearing his horse's hooves grow fainter into the distance. She looked up at the stars and was comforted, knowing that John Radcliffe would keep the promises he made.

The road back to Abingdon was long and seemed longer than the thirty miles of cobbled roads, fields and pathways, silent in the lonely darkness. He had been occupied since first light, he had now ridden a total of sixty miles and he was wearied to exhaustion with many problems pressing upon him. He did not know when and how he was to see Arabella again and in what way they could stay together. He puzzled over how he had come to fall in love for the first time in his life with a girl he had thought he despised but who had overcome all his prejudices and captured his heart. Her fragility aroused all his protective instincts but her courage and determination, so at odds with her appearance, were in tune with his own temperament, and though he hated her Papist religion he could not deny that her faith was as sincere as his. But he did not know how their love could ever be fulfilled, though he was determined to seek a way. Equally worrying was the thought of his inevitable encounter with Oliver Cromwell. He feared the General's reaction to his defiance of him, which could only be construed as mutiny and merited the severest punishment. Yet despite all his problems he experienced a sense of elation that conquered his tiredness and gave him hope that he could resolve the confusion in which life had suddenly enmeshed him.

It was in the early hours when he rode into the garrison and he was past caring that his notoriety had preceded him and those on guard looked at him with awesome curiosity. For a brief time he slept a sleep of exhaustion and the only dream he could remember was of holding Arabella in his arms. However on awakening he was presented with the expected summons from his commander.

When he was ushered into Cromwell's presence in a room the General had requisitioned in the Town Hall, he found him seated writing at a table. John stood stiffly to attention and waited but Cromwell continued with his writing, not acknowledging him nor raising his head, seemingly oblivious to his presence. Time dragged on. John tried to hold his position, resisting the temptation to change the weight on his feet, but the waiting seemed interminable. The scratching of the General's pen seemed magnified above the confused sounds of military activity outside the room while a fly buzzed noisily above the bent head. He tried to stay calm and fixed his attention upon a knot in the wainscoting behind the desk, ignoring the beating of his heart which seemed to be counting every second as the minutes lengthened, drumming out his doom. Then without warning Oliver Cromwell laid down his quill and lifting up his head barked, "Well, what has been going on at the Felton manor?"

"I have done my duty to the best of my ability, sir," John said carefully, watching the reaction of the thick-set figure with the unruly brown hair and the large nose set in a mottled face. "I have discharged all the obligations laid upon me."

"I gave the order to burn that property. It is a den of Popery, a centre for all Papist and Royalist activity in the area. Why was it not done?" Then without waiting for a reply, he went on, "Encouraging others to disobey orders can be interpreted as mutiny and that is a hanging offence."

"The others are in no way to blame, sir. They obeyed me. I take all responsibility upon myself," John stated firmly.

"And who gives the orders around here, you or me?" his commander roared furiously.

"You sir."

"Then wouldn't you agree that it is a hanging offence?"

"According to military regulations yes, sir," John admitted. He had seen Cromwell hang men for less.

"So shall I hang you? Have you anything to say in your defence?"

John thought of Arabella. He could be of no use to her swinging on a rope and he did not want to die. He made a determined effort to marshal his thoughts, he was a lawyer after all. But he knew that all the arguments he could muster would carry no weight with Cromwell. He took a deep breath and said honestly, "I believe I am needed in the army of Parliament and there is still much valuable work for me to do. I believe I was called by God to serve in this way and I cannot believe the Lord intended to take my life before I have finished the course."

"So why did you not obey my orders?" persisted the General.

John swallowed hard then committed himself. "I believe, for what reason I know not, that I received a prompting from God to prevent it."

A muscle twitched in Cromwell's cheek. There was no answer to that and he knew it. He held a fervent belief in the validity of personal revelation, even though he was well aware it could be a convenient, and dangerous, justification for men's delusions. But he could not live in the conviction of Providence's direct intervention in his own life and deny the same prerogative to others of the faithful. He had known John for a long time and always found him dedicated and honest with a strong and sincere faith. There were many examples in the Bible of God prompting men to actions unfathomable except to the Divinity. He considered carefully and John knew that his fate hung in the balance. At last he said, not without a trace of sarcasm, "Well I have no authority to withstand the Almighty. We must wait and see what His Divine judgment has planned for the place."

John hoped that his sigh of relief was not too loud, but Oliver Cromwell had not yet finished. He had always been aware of the faintest hint of insubordination in John Radcliffe and considered him too much of a free-thinker, and for this reason had delayed promoting him for some time despite his undoubted courage and intelligence. "Don't make a habit of disobeying orders or you will find yourself in serious trouble," he warned sternly.

"No sir, thank you sir. I shall strive all the harder to keep the charge laid upon me."

Oliver Cromwell rose from his chair and walked over to where his captain was standing. He studied him carefully, not believing that he had heard everything about the affair at Hesketh Hall. His gaze was perceptive but everyone spoke of the gentleness of his eyes. "Don't lose your nerve, lad," he said kindly. "No man who puts his hand to the plough and looks back is fit for the kingdom of God."

John felt a rush of warmth for this blunt man who never failed to command the respect and affection of all who served under him.

Then his commander continued briskly, "There is much to do. We are on the move again. The Committee has decided we now have to march to the south-west where Taunton is under siege by the Royalists, and the main army with General Fairfax has already set out. For all I care the King can get out of Oxford, let's get them all out, into the open where we can force them to fight, one great battle to finish them once and for all. But I wish the Committee would make up its mind about where they want **us**."

John had the distinct impression that Oliver Cromwell would have sworn heartily if it had been his habit. Considering the General's frustration with the present situation he considered he had been very fortunate to get off so lightly and his heart soared. He was alive, and incredible though it seemed he still had his command in the New Model Army. As he left the Town Hall he could feel many men's eyes trained curiously upon him and as he passed through groups of soldiers he was aware of speculative whispers. He walked with a firm brisk tread, relishing the sun on his face, then he began to run to where his troop was waiting for him.

CHAPTER 8

MAY - JUNE 1645

Henrietta was enjoying life in Oxford. Their lodgings were simple and unpretentious being two rooms in an attic above a baker's just behind the High Street. The rooms were very small with a minimum of furnishings, one containing a bed, a large storage chest and a stand with a bowl and ewer, the other having a simple oak table, two chairs and a cupboard. The beamed ceiling sloped downwards and there were two low windows from where, if they bent their heads, they could see St. Mary's church - the back of the church not the front where the beautiful statue of the Virgin had been decapitated by a Roundhead bullet. It was cramped and hot as the heat from the baker's ovens pervaded the confined space, and even more so when the temperatures outside rose unseasonably high. But in comparison to much other accommodation in Oxford it was a palace, secured by Philip at great expense and effort when it was vacated by two high-ranking officers who had ridden north with Prince Rupert. The city was crammed to bursting with soldiers, the royal Court, Royalist Members of Parliament and government officials, refugees, and all the necessary extra servants, workers and tradespeople, as well as the normal inhabitants and students at the University. It was estimated that the population had increased tenfold and most of the strangers were lodged three and four to a room in the houses of the citizens, which did not make for a comfortable existence especially since most of the householders were not paid for billeting their "guests." But for Henrietta the stuffy rooms with the basic fare provided for them by the landlord constituted a paradise because she could be with the man she loved.

Philip's duties were not onerous so they spent much time together and Henrietta walked proudly on the arm of her young Cavalier as he showed her the sights of Oxford - the beautiful colleges and gardens taken over by the Court, or the stout fortifications of ramparts and ditches erected at the onset of the war and which his present duties involved helping to man and maintain. When Philip was occupied she wandered in the college grounds and paraded in the parks with all the liberty of a married woman, watched the musters of the garrison or the daily changing of the guard at Carfax, the central crossroads from where the news was also read daily. She particularly liked to walk in the cloisters of Christchurch or Merton where the ladies of the Court flaunted themselves in the latest fashions, for although Queen Henrietta Maria was now in France there were still enough representatives of the nobility to present a show of wealth and elegance. Sometimes she would catch a glimpse of the King, for he made a habit of riding out once or twice a week to make a tour of the city and inspect the fortifications and ordnance. As she watched his small erect figure riding with such grace and elegance she felt proud to be serving him with her husband.

But all was not elegance and civility. There were constant reminders that Oxford was not only the seat of the Court in exile but also the Royalist base for the conduct of the war, as demonstrated by the huge cannons parked in Magdalen Grove and the powder and arms magazines in the tower and cloisters of New College, whilst other colleges had been turned into factories and warehouses for the production and storage of military equipment. The crowded narrow streets were often noisy with undisciplined soldiers, and fights and riots were a common occurrence in the over-populated city, especially at night when soldiers and students were returning from gaming and drinking sessions. The gallows at Carfax was seldom without its grisly carrion, and the blackened ruins of a large part of the city to the west were witness to the autumn's great fire and presented a grim warning of the permanent fire hazard in the overcrowded dwellings made largely of timber and thatch. Disease was another constant danger. The city council had become so worried about the increase of filth in the streets that they had doubled the wages of the refuse collectors, but it was no wonder that there were outbreaks of plague and camp fever with so many unwashed bodies and such crowded living conditions and poor diet. As the weather grew unseasonably hot the dangers of such increased. Henrietta however was fascinated by the novelty of every aspect of the city, and in the company of her husband relished the new experiences every day offered. She had longed for such an exciting existence and this noisy, stimulating place was as far removed from the serenity and monotony of Hesketh Hall as anything she could have imagined.

She was quite unaware that of late Hesketh Hall had been neither serene nor monotonous. Lady Mary's recovered spirits had withstood the shock of seeing her house almost burnt to the ground, and despite the damage inflicted and the paucity of their stores it was such a relief to be alone again that other troubles dwindled in comparison. Her anxiety now centred on her family. During their ordeal she had wavered between dread lest Sir James should return and be captured, and hope that he would arrive with a large force and deliver them. After William's unexpected appearance and subsequent escape she was sure that relief would come promptly, but when nothing had happened she was convinced some mishap must have befallen him. "Your father would not have delayed once he knew," she fretted to Arabella.

"The Parliament army is all around Oxford. I don't think it is easy for them to get here," Arabella said gently, not wishing to alarm her mother more than necessary. She was consumed with worries of her own as she wondered if John Radcliffe was safe and where he was, feeling a traitor to her family as she did so.

In an irony of fate Ambrose Hardwicke rode over on one of his regular visits the day after the Roundheads had left and was surprised by the cool reception afforded him.

"We have had Roundhead soldiers billeted on us for two weeks. Where were you when we needed help," Lady Mary snapped.

"I am grievously sorry, Lady Hesketh, but I knew nothing of this," he stammered, quite put out by the news.

"It doesn't matter, Ambrose, there is nothing you could have done," said Arabella apathetically.

He was horrified by the sequence of events and made an early departure, sensing their disapproval. He was more than ever aware of his low-standing with Arabella and was depressed and frustrated at the way fate had excluded him from what could have been an opportunity for noble action. As he rode home he fantasized how he might have rescued Arabella and ridden away with her, to her undying gratitude. It was not his fault he had known nothing of their misfortune. Before he left he had given them news of how the King was trying to get out of Oxford to join Prince Rupert on his march north but the surrounding Roundhead detachments were preventing him. They had also cleared the whole area of draught horses so that the King could not move his artillery and without which he dare not march, a manoeuvre of which the Heskeths had had personal experience. However they realized now why no-one had been able to come to their aid. The news did nothing to lessen their anxiety, for they were well aware that if the King's army did succeed in leaving Oxford then their own vulnerability would be laid bare and further harassment was a possibility.

However after being cooped up in the house so long it was heaven to sit in the warm spring sunshine and breathe the air fragrant with the May blossom clothing the bushes with lace, and the apple and cherry trees pendulous with garlands of pink and white. They spent most of the daylight hours out of doors, reading or sewing in the walled garden where the roses were beginning to bloom or walking in the park with the daisies and buttercups beneath their feet. The blackened ruins of the back of the house and the chapel were a constant reminder of how close they had come to disaster, and for Arabella a constant reminder of John Radcliffe. She kept reliving in her imagination all the sequence of events since they had first met, trying to recall her changing emotions. She still could not understand how their mutual antagonism had blossomed into love as the bare winter trees now inexplicably burst into a fragrant flowering, but she knew without doubt the happiness she had felt in his arms. She no longer believed that life had passed her by, for love had sprung upon her in the most surprising way, unsought and unforeseen, flooding her existence with joy but bringing in its train heartache and fear, and her happiness was now laced with anxiety for his fate.

Abigail was alone in the kitchen garden trying to find enough ripened pea pods on the denuded shoots when she was alerted by the approach of a buff-coated soldier, armed and helmeted. For a moment she believed John Radcliffe had returned and her heart leapt with a mixture of hope and concern. Then she noted he was too tall and wore no sign to distinguish himself on either side, and she felt a stab of fear as she realized she was alone and hidden from view. She rose hurriedly from her knees, putting her basket down on the ground and wiping her hands on her apron.

"I can see the Roundheads have gone and that the bastards burnt the house." Only when he spoke and came closer did she see it was William. He tipped her straw hat to the back of her head so that he could see her face as he asked, "Are you well? We came to your rescue but I can see we are too late."

Abigail had wondered often how he had fared since his escape and a spark of elation caught her unawares as his eyes peered at her from beneath the bars of his helmet.

"I was sent ahead to reconnoiter," he explained, taking off his helmet now. He told her how he had already removed his identifying crimson sash as he approached the house from the rear, unseen and unheard, not knowing if the house was still occupied. "I'll go back and give them the news. Go and tell mother that father is here together with Philip, twenty of us altogether. And you can also tell Arabella secretly that Kit Verney is with us and has some news for her."

Lady Mary was overjoyed at the thought of seeing her husband and son, and also Philip who would be bringing news of Henrietta. But her first elation was soon allayed at the thought of having twenty more soldiers in the house to feed on their meagre resources.

Arabella was stunned by the news that Kit Verney was of the company. When the Roundheads were billeted in the house she had so often dreamt of Kit coming to rescue her, imagining every detail of his face and form as he swept her into his arms to deliver her from the hated captain. Now she had difficulty in bringing his face to mind and as she stood with her mother on the steps in front of the house to welcome them she relived the shock of that first encounter with John Radcliffe.

"I am sorry we have come too late to help you," said Sir James, dismounting and embracing his wife and daughter. "It was impossible to come sooner. The King has been trying to get his army out of Oxford for the last two weeks but now Prince Rupert has returned to his rescue and we marched out today, escorted by his cavalry. The commanders are in council at Stow where there is a muster of troops so we took this opportunity to ride here immediately. We have merely a day's respite so we shall be here for only one night."

"I wish you need not go away at all," said Lady Mary, realizing that she would gladly suffer the inconvenience of a house full of Royalist soldiers in order to keep her husband and son with her. But she held her emotion in check before the gathering of strangers and found an outlet in being able to greet Philip Halsall with a mixture of reserve and affection. Arabella noted Kit among the company and despite everything that had happened his quizzical smile could not help but revive memories as he came forward to greet her.

The men were led into the Hall for refreshment but Sir James's and William's first intention was to examine the damage to the back of the house. "Luckily they did not begin at the front," Sir James remarked when they returned, though he was sad at the thought of the distress caused to his wife by the destruction of the chapel.

"The house would all have been burnt had it not been for the captain," said Arabella, feeling compelled to relate John's part in the saving of the house.

Something in the tone of her voice made William regard her carefully. "And why should a Roundhead suddenly concern himself with the preservation of our property?" he enquired sceptically. He noticed his sister's pale face flush slightly as she turned from him and his eyes narrowed speculatively.

"He probably had an eye on the property for himself," Kit Verney ventured. "These Roundhead officers are accumulating substantial estates for themselves," an opinion to which the whole of the assembled company agreed.

Having the house full of soldiers again revived all the worst memories of the previous occupation, even though these were friends and not enemies. So when Kit asked Arabella to walk with him in the garden she agreed, albeit reluctantly. Although she did not relish a tête-à-tête with him she longed to be away from the house. They walked as far as the wood in the warm sunshine and he put his arm into hers, naturally continuing their past intimacy. They sat on the dry spongy turf amid a pool of wild flowers whose softly shading blue seemed to serve as a looking glass for the sky. The wood pigeons cooed and a blackbird trilled his song close by as if serenading them, so that the war and all its problems seemed far away and part of another existence. They sat in silence for a while, lost in the serenity of the moment and their own thoughts. Kit leant negligently against the growing stump of a tree with his long legs outstretched, fashionable lace-edged boot-hose draped over his boots and his beaver hat tipped rakishly to the back of his head. But when he spoke it was with an unaccustomed solemnity.

"I have something to tell you, Arabella. My wife died last month. I am now free to marry you."

Arabella couldn't believe she had heard aright and searched his face for confirmation of his words. "Oh don't worry, I didn't do an Earl of Leicester," he said sardonically, misreading her expression. "Elizabeth was always sickly and she died of a pulmonary infection which recurred from time to time. To my shame I admit that I had not always answered her appeals for my company when she was ill. This time I obeyed an urgent summons and although I was almost too late I was still with her when she died, painfully and too early, she was only twenty-seven." His habitual clipped tone wavered somewhat.

A confusion of emotions tore through Arabella. "Did you love her?" she asked at last.

"We married at fourteen. It was an arranged marriage. We were too young," he replied, looking into the distance and into the past. Then he made an attempt to answer her question. "We were fond of each other as two children who have known each other a long time. I never loved her as I love you," he said, putting his hand over hers.

She remained silent, feeling the lace of his cuff brush her hand gently, but wondering how far a man was capable of loving a second wife if he had not loved a first.

He took her silence for consideration and continued, "I would like to ask your father for your hand and then after a decent length of time we could be married. I have a fine house and a large estate near Bristol, you would want for nothing, and you could have complete freedom to practise your religion, I would not interfere."

Arabella knew it was a good offer. She broke a bluebell from its slender stalk and began to pluck the little bells one by one. She had loved Kit Verney and a marriage with him had been the stuff of her dreams, though seemingly impossible. His low cultured voice was working its old magic on her and the fingers that lay across her hand were long and elegant. He was a man of her own class and social circle, sophisticated, handsome and rich, someone who understood the conventions and obligations of their status. The match would no doubt please all concerned and deliver her from her parents' pressure to take Ambrose. Yet she could not rid herself of the uncertainty as to how faithful he would be once he had achieved his goal and she recalled his suggestion to her at Christmas.

She was hesitating much longer than Kit had expected and finally she said, "Please wait a little, it is all too sudden for me to take in. It is too soon for you too. So much has happened recently."

Kit was disappointed and surprised by her reaction. On past experience he had expected her to throw herself into his arms and could only surmise that the recent unpleasant episode had temporarily unsettled her. "I know you have been through a difficult time lately," he said, and there was no trace of the cynicism which often shadowed his face and was reflected in his eyes as he continued, "I am sorry we came too late."

She had absently plucked another of the blue flowers carpeting the grass and now saw that it was a tiny forget-me-not. Into her mind flashed a picture of the steady brown eyes and the resolute mouth, the regular features of a face neither cynical nor dissolute, and suddenly she cried fervently, "Yes you came too late. Oh why didn't you come a week ago? Why did you come too late?" She began to cry, great racking sobs that tore her slender body in a torrent of emotion as she realized what might have been if he had come earlier, early enough to prevent her falling in love with John Radcliffe.

Kit was embarrassed by the sudden outburst and did not know how to deal with this excess of emotion that seemed too extreme for the matter. After all, no-one had come to any harm. Arabella's delicate innocence fascinated him but he was more used to worldly women, and he felt out of his depth. He was also still surprised that she had not welcomed his proposal with alacrity, and rejection, even if only temporary, was an uncomfortable sensation for him. "Come, let me return you to the house. You are over-wrought and I should not have spoken to you so soon after all that has happened," he said, raising her up.

They walked back in an uncomfortable silence. She felt ashamed of the lack of control she had shown before such a sophisticated man of the world as Kit Verney. But the realization of the cruel trick played by fate had been too much. If only Kit had come earlier she would have accepted his offer of marriage joyfully, firmly believing that she loved him. But in those lost days she had met John Radcliffe. The final irony was that this second love was as impossible as her initial attachment to Kit Verney had been. It seemed impossible on every level, while marriage with Kit had now become miraculously possible and she had turned it down for what might be no more than a chimera of wishful thinking.

William saw his sister return to the house with her eyes puffed and swollen and began to speculate on the reason for her strange behaviour. He had known of Kit's intention and had expected them to return together in joyful union. As soon as he got the opportunity he sought out Abigail who had returned to her tasks after serving the soldiers with refreshments and was now spreading the linen out to dry on the bushes in the walled garden. "What is the matter with Arabella?" he asked, surprising her with his second appearance.

"How should I know? She doesn't confide in me." Her brusque tone covered an unusual feeling of disquiet and she continued spreading out the sheets, not wanting to revive the intimacy that had blossomed between them in the moment of shared danger.

"That isn't true. You used to be good friends together."

"Henrietta used to confide in me more. Arabella is quieter, more solitary. It is difficult to know what she is thinking."

"Did anything pass between her and the Roundhead officer?"

Abigail looked at him sharply because such a possibility seemed preposterous and she searched her memory before replying, "Not that I know of. Why?"

"It doesn't matter."

"You are the one behaving strangely, William. You seem different today."

He grinned suddenly. "Only because I was spoiling for a fight and I have been cheated out of it. I came here to get my own back on those God-damned Roundheads, especially the captain, and find that not only are we too late but I am actually indebted to him for not burning down my house. It makes me so mad."

"Oh William!" She shook her head resignedly then asked, "Did everything go to plan on the night you escaped?"

"Without a hitch. When did they find the guard in the lake? I really enjoyed killing him. He was the representative of the whole damned pack of them."

Abigail looked at him in horror and he laughed mirthlessly. "Don't look so shocked. This is war you know, not some sort of game. It isn't the first man I've killed and it was his life or mine."

She remembered how John had changed with the donning of his soldier's kit and she had wondered how William behaved in like circumstances. It seemed war changed people you thought you knew well. She was suddenly aware of how the war had begun to encroach upon their sheltered existence, from just before Yuletide when they had killed the intruder, then the meeting with John and his arrival at the Hall. Up until that time, apart from the death of Uncle Jacob and periodic alarms, the effects of the war had largely passed them by. Now they were being drawn more personally into the struggle that was dividing England.

Sensing her unease William moved closer to her and spoke gently, "I never thanked you for all the risks you took in helping me." Something in her eyes prompted him to kiss her and as he took her in his arms and fastened his lips on hers he found to his delight that she responded with unexpected warmth. A surge of excitement flowed through his veins and a faint smile of triumph flickered across his face. Abigail saw it and pulled away from him, ashamed that she had involuntarily responded to him as he caught her unawares. She felt a great urge to be loved since John Radcliffe had aroused her and she knew William desired her. But she was determined not to weaken in any way towards him and give him more power over her than he already possessed. William was untroubled by her sudden withdrawal. He had always suspected that beneath Abigail's cool demeanour simmered a latent passion, hinted at by her vibrant colouring and her enigmatic slanting green eyes, and now for a brief moment he had kindled that response. He could bide his time. He had waited long, he could wait a little longer, for he was sure it would be worth the waiting.

In the early hours of the morning Sir James Hesketh discussed with his wife the thoughts that had been uppermost in his mind since his return home. "I have been wondering if I should not go to Westminster and compound for our estates. So many others have done it," he said.

"No!" Her reply was vehement. "They must take it from us by force, we will never relinquish it willingly. We have held out for so long, we cannot give in now."

He was proud of her courage, and also surprised that his gentle protected wife should have revealed such strength in unforeseen adversity, as witnessed again by her behaviour during the occupation of the Hall. "I am afraid that if the worst happens then William will have no inheritance," he said. "Arabella must perforce marry Ambrose but if William is left with nothing….," his voice died away.

"Do you really have so little faith in victory that you talk like this?" his wife asked anxiously, trying to see his expression in the darkness. She thought of Rupert and the empathy she had felt with him that evening in her home. She wondered if he too had doubts of victory but was sure he had not.

"No, not at all, I think our chances are improving," Sir James reassured her. "Already we have confounded Parliament's plan to keep us penned in Oxford. Tomorrow we are on the march again with the objective of winning back the north while the Roundheads are occupied in the south, and if we can join up with Montrose's army marching down from Scotland then victory seems to be within our grasp. An astrologer has cast the King's horoscope and predicted great success for him," he added encouragingly, knowing this would cheer her. "However I do not think we should completely ignore other possibilities. In war, victory is a fickle mistress who grants her favours randomly. If we should be beaten there is little doubt the house will be taken and our lands sequestered and I think we ought to be prepared for any outcome."

"What shall I do if this happens while you are away?" she asked, fearful of such an eventuality but desirous of being prepared.

"No-one will evict you without fair warning or due notice to me. But if it did happen then we would have to ask refuge from some of our kinsfolk elsewhere, perhaps even those who have favoured the other side," he said gravely.

"Pray God that we do not come to such an extremity," she said fervently. "I do not know why victory eludes us when God is on our side. It is against the law of God that rebels should prosper. Do you think God is punishing England for abandoning the true faith?"

"We cannot read the mind of God. All we can do is to keep our own faith - to Church and King - and trust that will be enough."

Arabella could hear her parents talking in the chamber that led from hers, their low voices muffled from within the drawn curtains of the bed. She rose and putting a mantle over her shift sat in the chair by the window, watching the rosy streaks of dawn spread their reflections across the glassy smoothness of the lake. She recalled how she had sat there numbed on that evening when she had almost killed John Radcliffe. How could there ever be anything between them? Perhaps she might never see him again. He had said he would return but there seemed to be no way that he could do this, and he might even be killed and she would never know. Perhaps his attraction for her might have sprung from the lessening of her initial fear, her desire for his masculine strength born of her loneliness and confusion. Might it not be better to try and forget him, to marry Kit Verney and be safe with one of her own kind. The temptation to accept Kit's offer was considerable.

However next morning when the Royalists prepared to depart and Kit Verney took his leave of Arabella he spoke no more of an engagement at this time so that she had no necessity to think further of the matter.

Philip Halsall informed Lady Hesketh, "Henrietta should be back with you soon. I will return to tell her that all is back to normal here and make preparations for her safe conduct home before I rejoin William in the Prince's troop."

Seeing and speaking with her son-in-law had convinced Lady Mary that all was well with the newly married couple and she surmised that Henrietta would be in no haste to return home.

The little troop of Cavaliers were in high spirits even though they had been cheated of their expected action. They were eager to be blooding their swords again in a major engagement and certain they were on the brink of victory, so there was a great spirit of hope in the air as they rode back to the King's army.

The Royalist Council of War at Stow had ended inconclusively as usual with the commanders in disagreement. General George Goring was all for turning to the south-west in pursuit of Fairfax while he was separated from Cromwell. On the other hand Rupert wanted to march north to recapture the territories lost by Marston Moor and join up with Montrose and his Scottish army so that with greatly increased strength they would be in a better position to meet the Roundheads. The King was swayed by both arguments and eventually decided to try both plans, dividing his army into two even though the muster at Stow had revealed a disappointingly low count. Lord Goring's force marched south, and the King and Prince Rupert, with Sir James and William in their train, headed north.

In the meantime the Parliamentary Committee had altered their plans and recalled General Fairfax from the south west. He was ordered instead to go and besiege Oxford which now lay unprotected. If the King's army were to be cut off from its supply base then it could not long survive a northern campaign. They would be unable to join up with Montrose and at only half strength and without their reinforcements and supplies they would be forced to turn back and face the New Model Army. So in the second week of May the siege of Oxford began and Philip and Henrietta, who were making preparations for their departure, found themselves imprisoned there.

Earlier in the month Henrietta had watched the armies of the King and Prince Rupert march out of the North Gate with all pomp and ceremony. As the streets were crowded with spectators she had gone with other ladies onto a mound in St John's college gardens and from there she had seen her husband and brother riding with the Prince and had also caught a glimpse of her father in the throng. It had been a thrilling sight with all the colours flying aloft and the drums beating hypnotically. The plumes in the King's hat waved merrily as he led his armies, and Prince Rupert's tall figure in his scarlet cloak blazed his striking presence even amid the splendour of the long procession. Henrietta's blood was stirred by the pageantry, the brilliance of crimson sashes and the dazzle of light as the sun played on burnished armour and swords. For a time she had been able to forget the two preoccupations uppermost in her mind. The first was caused by the news brought by William that a detachment of Roundheads was billeted at Hesketh Hall, a state of affairs which her husband, father and brother intended to remedy so she had had few doubts that the small band of rescuers would soon rout the invaders. The second was her own imminent departure from Oxford and separation from Philip. She had been piqued that she had not been at the Hall when the exciting events were taking place and she had rather envied Arabella as she remembered the stirring tale of the Countess of Derby. But a visit home lost its briefly-held appeal when Philip returned with a report that all was returned to normal, and she was not relishing the thought of having to take up her old life of monotonous predictability without the presence of her husband. His return to Oxford gave them the opportunity to enjoy a day or two together before they had to separate, he going to join the Royalist army and she heading home. Then without warning came the Roundhead attack on the city.

It was a tremendous shock for the citizens to see the massed troops of the New Model Army beginning to surround them and moving their artillery into place around the walls. There was also much vocal resentment expressed at the civic and military authorities who were blamed for not being able to forsee such a manouevre and people took to the streets to demonstrate their anger. However the siege had little impact at first apart from making exit from the city impossible, and the sense of intimidation which was an inevitable consequence of being surrounded by such a large enemy force. There were fewer people to feed now that their army had left and with her husband fortunately at her side Henrietta suffered little alarm and enjoyed the frisson of excitement. But it was soon discovered that the city was very poorly stocked with food for the army had taken a great stock of provisions with them, and once the waggons bringing the regular supplies from the countryside were refused access, food very quickly became scarce. By the third week of May dispatches were being sent to the King informing him that they were seriously short of provisions and they could not hold out for long against the besiegers.

As the month of May wore on the siege began to bite. Henrietta began to realize there was nothing romantic about such a situation, especially as no-one seemed to be coming to their rescue. Walled within their fortifications, the hungry citizens looked out anxiously at the massed troops surrounding them. The Roundheads made little attempt to do anything but their very inactivity was alarming, as if they need do nothing but wait patiently. Sometimes they fired sporadic cannon shot onto the walls as a warning and though much of the artillery fell short, or did little damage, the thud of the guns was nevertheless alarming. Henrietta began to feel fearful as their landlord found it increasingly difficult to feed them. Suddenly the security of home no longer seemed such an unattractive proposition. Most of the shops were closed and if they were open they had little to offer. The pervading spirit of the city had changed from one of careless gaiety to a subdued anxiety as the citizens pondered on how long the siege would last and whether they really would be allowed to starve. Most people, including Henrietta, were also aware that if the city would not surrender then the enemy would be entitled to kill and plunder when they took control.

Philip Halsall felt guilty and frustrated - guilty for succumbing to matrimonial pleasures when he should have been riding with Prince Rupert, and frustrated because there was nothing he could do at this moment except man the defences and wait. He blamed himself for keeping Henrietta in Oxford in order to snatch a few more days together instead of leaving as they had planned.

"Do you think anyone will come to rescue us?" Henrietta asked anxiously as no answer to their appeals came from the King.

"I'm sure that with so many members of the Court still here, so many ladies, all effort will be made to break the siege," he answered encouragingly. "The King cannot afford to be cut off from his base for too long." But he knew that Rupert would consider other priorities more pressing - he was expecting them to hold out for at least another six to eight weeks so that he could complete his work in the north while the Roundheads were safely occupied here outside Oxford - in which case the sufferings of the citizens would take second place. Although to be honest it was doubtful if the Royalists had the strength to take on the New Model Army in their present circumstances. Philip's own hopes lay in the possibility that the Roundheads would be forced to withdraw to counter more pressing threats elsewhere, especially if Rupert should be successful with his northern campaign. However at the moment they seemed unconcerned about any further developments, in fact the Committee of Both Kingdoms sent reinforcements, ordering Oliver Cromwell to take his troops to the support of General Fairfax.

John Radcliffe arrived outside the walls of Oxford, no more pleased than his commander with this change of plan. They had marched towards the south-west to intercept Lord Goring, then before they could do so they had been peremptorily ordered to retrace their steps towards Oxford, and Oliver Cromwell was becoming increasingly frustrated and angry with the indecisive commands of the Committee. John hated sieges. He hated the long tedious breaking down of the defences through cannon, petard, and mine, and the slow wearing down of the inhabitants through hunger and weariness. He remembered that Arabella's sister was in Oxford and as he looked out across the barricade of stone walls and the encircling river he was conscious again of all the barriers dividing them. His spirits had been lightened however by two recent events. One was his troop's capture of three carts of canary wine and thirty accompanying horses and their riders as they tried to make their way into the city, a feat for which he was specially commended and which helped to reinstate him in the good opinions of his superiors. The other was the acquaintance of a little gipsy boy amongst the camp followers. It was difficult to know the boy's age (he did not know himself) as he was thin and undernourished, but he had a shrewd cunning that suggested twelve or thirteen years, though he looked younger with his skinny limbs and the thatch of untidy black hair obscuring the slanting black eyes deep-set in his olive-skinned face. His name was Luka and he had attached himself to John, begging to help with the grooming of his horse and the cleaning of his weapons in exchange for a piece of bread. John was happy to aid him, amused by his precocious audacity though he surmised the boy would be very unlikely to escape a hanging and extremely lucky to reach manhood.

Arabella was constantly in his thoughts. He still found it difficult to believe that she had said she loved him as he loved her, nor to comprehend just how or why he had fallen in love with some-one who symbolized everything he hated - Papistry, the privileged lifestyle of the landed classes, the concentration on adornment and superficial accomplishments. He could not recall a particular moment when the knowledge had struck him like a lightning flash. Rather she had inched her way into his heart with her directness, her determination, her courage - qualities that transcended the boundaries of class. And her delicate fragility, which at first had repelled him, paradoxically so contrary to her character, had unleashed all his natural instincts to defend and protect. The violence of his emotions confounded him and at the moment he could see no resolution of a situation into which he had been plunged so unexpectedly. But John, like his commander, believed that Providence ordered men's lives. He believed that God had directed his return to Hesketh Hall to prevent the burning of the house and this in turn had led to their mutual declaration of love. Though at the moment he could discern no future pattern for his life he had no doubt that understanding would be given to him.

In the meantime he thought and worried about Arabella who had known such anxiety and unhappiness of late. He considered that she must also be anxious about her sister imprisoned in the besieged city of Oxford. The woman was unknown to him personally but she was a link with Arabella and he wondered what danger might threaten her. Because he found himself with time on his hands Arabella was constantly in his mind and he began pondering if he could prove his devotion to her by getting her sister out of Oxford and back home with a message. What at first was an idle speculation began to employ his ingenuity in the tedious waiting demanded by a siege.

Henrietta made a point of walking down to Carfax each day to find out the latest news, though it was invariably depressing. On the way she would make a useless foray to the shops. She knew that Philip did not like her to walk abroad because cases of the plague had been reported again and he could bring any relevant news, but she hated to be cooped up alone in the small airless room when he had gone to his work on the walls. This difference in opinion had caused some friction between them of late and their frayed nerves had resulted in an increasing tendency to argue. But time hung heavily on Henrietta's hands as she found herself so much alone and though she enjoyed reading the hours were long and monotonous. In the beginning they had been so wrapped up in each other that she had made few friends apart from his comrades in arms who had now departed with Rupert. And lately Philip was absent so often that she might have suspected him of being unfaithful had circumstances been different, for she was well aware of the temptations Oxford offered to the young Cavaliers. But she knew he was busy with his military duties and when she had agreed to accompany him to the garrison as his wife she had made the decision to accept the limitations of army life, without really knowing anything about them. The strained and tense atmosphere was not helpful to all the adjustments that had to be made in the unfamiliar state of matrimony so she reverted to her usual headstrong impulses by walking abroad and braving his displeasure. But she was always depressed by the contrast of the listless deadening gloom to the bustle and gaiety of her first weeks here.

John Radcliffe found the game of stalemate played by both sides increasingly tedious, and found some relief in thinking about getting Arabella's sister out of the city as a pledge of his loyalty to her. Suddenly the idea of using the gipsy boy Luka came into his mind, and one day he asked him, "Luka, do you think you could get into the city?"

"I can go anywhere. But who wants to get into the city? Everybody wants to get out."

John thought carefully and later called the boy to him again. "Luka, I want you to do an errand for me. I want you to get into the city with a message for some-one. I cannot tell you where or how to find her, you would have to do that for yourself. Do you think you could do it, I will pay you well."

Luka's eyes sparkled at the talk of reward and he said nonchanantly, "Of course, that is easy. Shall I go now?"

John considered the implications and realized the operation would be better accomplished in one attempt rather than two. "No, I must think about it more carefully. Perhaps tomorrow."

He had no doubt that Luka could get into the city and, given time, use his ingenuity to find Arabella's sister. The problems would be twofold - to convince her to leave with the boy and then to get them both out together.

On the following day when he had finalized his plans he called Luka to him and made him commit to memory a message. "Her name is Mistress Halsall, Mistress Henrietta Halsall," he said, remembering what he had heard at Hesketh Hall. "Give her the message exactly as I have told you, neither more nor less. I will give you today and tomorrow to find her. Tomorrow night at eleven o' the clock bring her to the Folly Bridge where I shall be waiting for you. When you can repeat the message to me exactly I will give you sixpence. I will give you a further shilling when you bring the lady to me."

The gipsy boy's eyes widened at the thought of so much wealth and he could hardly contain his eagerness. When John was satisfied that he knew his instructions perfectly he let him go, confident in his abilities and his loyalty. Of his own principles he was less sure. Whether Henrietta Halsall left Oxford was a matter of little importance either to him or the besiegers. For his own part it was a gift to Arabella and a token of his faith and his care for her. To his commanders however it was a breach of security. General Fairfax believed in the strictest discipline for his soldiers and the previous day had hanged a trooper for stealing from a supply cart attempting to enter the gates. He was aware that once again his independent action was bringing him into insubordination and pondered once more on the way in which his passion for Arabella Hesketh was affecting his life. There was always a possibility however that Mistress Halsall would not be willing to leave the city and commit herself into the hands of strangers, and should that be so he would content himself with the knowledge that he had done his best and that this was not the path God intended him to take.

Henrietta was leaving the baker's shop for her daily walk to Carfax when she heard her name called. She turned in surprise and found a small dirty child with the look of a gipsy regarding her interrogatively. He repeated her name and when she assented he said, "I have come from a friend of your sister Arabella."

Thinking he was begging she said, "I am sorry but I cannot help you. We have no food ourselves. I could spare you a little black bread but nothing more."

"You much mistake me Mistress, I am sent to help you. I can take you out of the city if you wish."

"And how can you do that?" she asked in the tone of one humouring a child.

"I know the way. I can take you home to Hesketh Hall."

The shock at hearing the familiar name melted into an aching longing. But she asked in amazement, "How do you know about my home? Who has sent you to me?"

But the boy only shook his head saying, "I can take you there if you would like."

She began to feel disorientated talking to this strange child, wondering if he were mad or she. "You could not possibly do that, you are only a child and the city is surrounded by troops," she said, wanting to be free of his perplexing soliciting.

"I am not a child though I am small," he refuted in annoyance, "and Arabella's friend will help us. You ought to leave because you could be in grave danger here."

He spoke with intensity and as his thin reed-like voice began to work on her Henrietta considered him afresh, fearing that he was some elf changeling as gipsies were rumoured to be. "Who are you?" she demanded. "How do you know so much about me?"

But he merely shook his head saying, "Will you come?"

"How can I trust you," Henrietta said. "If you intend to rob me I have little to offer."

The boy's black eyes flashed angrily. "Cannot you understand that I am sent to help you. I do not rob those people known to my friends. Besides I have been well paid."

"You will have to tell me who this friend is before I can come with you," she persisted.

"I cannot tell you anything more except that I will take you out of the city and then you will be safe."

Henrietta began to feel faint and had to put her hand on the wall to steady herself. "I will have to speak with my husband. How can I reach you again?"

"It must be tonight. I have spent a long time finding you, much longer than I expected, it was not easy. I will come back here at ten of the clock. If you are to come with me then wear dark clothing and bring nothing with you. If you are not here when the clock chimes ten then I will go."

The boy disappeared so swiftly on his bare feet that he seemed to melt into thin air and Henrietta began to think she had imagined the whole incident, fearing that hunger and anxiety were causing her to hallucinate. She was confused and worried by the encounter as she continued slowly on her way to Carfax. There was no hopeful news and the crowds hung about dispiritedly while the only remaining bells in the city (all the others having been melted down for armaments) pealed their doleful knell for yet another funeral.

In the evening when Philip returned from his shift on the bridgehead she told him of the strange encounter. "I think it could be Kit Verney," she said. "I know of no other friend of Arabella's who could be here."

"You may be right," he said thoughtfully. "It is possible that Kit could be close on some mission, it has the mark of a well-thought plan and there seems enough proof that the person is someone who knows your family well. I think you should go. We do not know how long the siege will last and already there is much sickness, I heard today of more cases of the plague. It would be a great happiness for me to know you were safe at home."

She looked at him sadly. She had expected more regret for her departure, some declaration of how he could not bear to exist without her. Did he want her away? She thought about the letter, the letter written in French, that she had found carefully folded in the inside of his doublet. She realized with a spasm of pain how little she knew about him. "What about you, couldn't you possibly come with me?" she asked, feeling suddenly vulnerable.

"You know I cannot, the plan does not include me. I must stay here with the garrison and defend the city. We will never surrender it to Parliament."

"I do not want to leave you." She nestled close to him and for a time they recaptured the careless exhilaration of those first few weeks together.

He stroked her brown curls. "I do not want us to be apart either. But my concern for your safety is stronger than my desire to have you with me. If you love me then you should go. If the siege had not come about then we would already have been parted." She knew this to be true but then they would have parted in happier circumstances with perfect memories unalloyed by recent anxieties. "Besides you said you might be with child and you should not endanger your life nor his."

Henrietta had confided to him the possibility. She had felt sick a lot lately and had missed her signs, but was not sure if this was caused by the poor diet and the strain. However this was the final argument. The letter after all was unimportant and probably misleading.

"When the city is relieved I will return to you," he promised.

Neither of them mentioned the other possibility - that if the city were compelled to surrender he would be killed or taken prisoner. The rest of the evening they spent in making love and planning, in desperate hope, for their future together in Lancashire when the war was ended.

As darkness fell, dressed in a dark skirt and bodice and a black cloak, Henrietta was ready to entrust herself to a stranger. Luka was waiting as they came out of the baker's shop and though the curfew had long since sounded and there was no-one about, Philip accompanied them through the deserted silent streets as far as Christchurch. Luka was like a little animal as he led them scuttling and hiding in doorways and narrow alleys until they reached the Cathedral. There in the dark shadow of the building Henrietta and Philip made their farewells, clinging together, unwilling to separate now in the finality of departure. As Luka tugged at her skirt impatiently, Henrietta broke away and went with him. She had not intended to look back but couldn't help doing so and her last sight of Philip was of a dark unidentifiable outline in the stone archway, blurred through her tears so that he seemed but a faint shadow.

Now she was totally in the hands of the strange gipsy boy. They were to squeeze through a narrow breach that had occurred in the wall between Christchurch and Merton. Here the wall had not been defended so strongly because of the encircling river. Then they must cross the meadow to the river where they would be helped across. The problem was that the Royalists had flooded the meadow as part of their defences.

"Do not fear," Luka told Henrietta. "I know how to get across the meadow safely. I found all the shallow parts but you must be prepared for the water to come up to your knees. Hold my hand and trust me."

On the other side John Radcliffe waited. He had arrived at the Folly Bridge at the appointed time, hoping that the name was not prophetic of his own conduct. His eyes raked the darkness for any sign of two lone figures and because he was expecting them he managed to pick out the hardly discernible movement in the water. He had decided that audacity was the best strategy so when they were nearly at the bridge he strode across to the soldiers on guard saying briskly, "I am responsible for these children, they have been on an errand for me." Bored with their tedious task, heartily sick of the discomforts of the siege and noticing the officer's sash, the guards did not spare the small figures a second glance and John escorted them across the bridge until they were safe on the other side of the river.

To her surprise Henrietta saw no-one that she knew, but a stranger. It was a sturdy young man of medium height, bare-headed with short hair, though in the darkness she could not distinguish his features apart from scrutinizing brown eyes. John too was surprised because the bedraggled figure was much younger than he had expected. He had presumed Mistress Halsall to be Arabella's elder sister but in actual fact she was little more than a child with a round face that looked enquiringly up at him, an upturned mouth that indicated a propensity to laugh, and a nose slightly tiptilted and freckled. She bore no resemblance at all to Arabella.

"Who are you?" she asked wonderingly, but he didn't reply, being intent on the matter in hand.

"Get up behind me," he ordered Luka, "then when we are clear of the camp I will give you further instructions." He lifted Henrietta up in front of him and pressed her close to him as he took up the reins. Luka leapt excitedly behind him and the cavalry horse bore his increased burden effortlessly as they cantered away from the bridge, skirted the camp which was quiet apart from sleepy inattentive guards, and rode as far as an inn on a country road just outside the nearest village. There John dismounted and going into the stables brought out a small light horse. Luka had skipped down and John now gave him his promised shilling. "If you will take Mistress Halsall home now I will give you two shillings on your return," he said. "I can go no further, I must return to the camp."

Luka had already leapt onto the horse with glee, but John regarded him severely. "Bring him back or you could be hanged for theft," he warned him. If Luka did not return the horse it was no great matter for it was one captured by his troop.

"I'll come back for my two shillings," the gipsy boy promised, such a sum of money, a day's pay for a cavalryman, almost beyond his comprehension. "And besides, I want to serve you, master."

John then lifted Henrietta down from his horse and placed her up behind Luka, feeling the soft curves of her body beneath the wet clothes. Her hood had slipped from her head and her brown curls framed her childish face. She had nothing of Arabella's beauty but there was an appealing vivacity, clouded now by perplexity. John squeezed her hand reassuringly saying, "You will soon be safe at home now."

"Thank you. You are so kind," she said fervently. "And I don't even know who you are."

"It doesn't matter. Give Arabella a message. Tell her I will keep my promise." Then turning to Luka he commanded, "Follow the Stratford road. From Felton Mistress Halsall will direct the way to you. Now go."

The gipsy boy needed no further prompting, for to possess a horse was one of his wildest dreams. John watched them disappear into the darkness then turned back to the camp.

In the early hours of the morning the inhabitants of Hesketh Hall were awakened by a pounding on the front door. Fearfully calling for Silas to see who the unexpected caller was, Lady Hesketh was confronted by a weary and bedraggled Henrietta. There was no further sleep for a time as questions, answers and explanations poured back and forth, while as Henrietta talked she ate all the food she could find in the kitchen. Yet there were some things she knew she must keep to herself, for the journey from Oxford to Hesketh Hall had given her much time to ponder.

Later when she was lying washed and in a clean shift beside Arabella in the bed they used to share she told her sister some of the things she had kept from her mother. "Who was he?" she asked. "At first I thought it was going to be Kit Verney. But I think he was on the other side. Oh I know it's easy for a Royalist spy to change his sash but somehow I had the impression he was a Roundhead. How does he know you?"

Arabella did not answer and Henrietta was aware that there were developments of which she knew nothing. But she was too physically and emotionally exhausted to pursue the matter further at this time, tomorrow she would do so. Before she dropped off to sleep however she remembered something and murmured, "He sent you a message. He said to tell you that he would keep his promise, whatever that means."

Arabella felt ashamed, and tears rolled down her cheeks as she recalled how she had doubted him and almost accepted Kit Verney's proposal. John had most probably risked a lot to help her sister so that she might understand the depth of his commitment. How could she have believed for one moment that he would not keep his word. Everything she knew about him proclaimed his integrity. He was a Puritan Roundhead and she cared for nought except to feel his arms around her and his mouth on hers. She had almost failed him but she knew now without doubt that if there was a way for them to stay together then John Radcliffe would find it.

Captain Radcliffe only remained outside Oxford long enough to welcome Luka's return with the horse and the news that Henrietta was safely home. Cromwell had been ordered to leave the siege and proceed with his regiment into East Anglia where his home base was being threatened by a punitive Royalist force. They departed from Oxford with relief, eager to see some positive action. They scattered their enemies without too much difficulty, though the Cavaliers had inflicted substantial damage on Huntingdon and Oliver Cromwell was furious that such a state of affairs had been allowed to happen whilst he and his soldiers had been kept immobile outside Oxford. He mopped up the damage, fortified the approaches to the Isle of Ely, and by the last day of the month was in Cambridge.

On that same day Prince Rupert and his troops captured the important Parliament town of Leicester. The loss of this wealthy town came as a great shock and most shocking was the manner of its capture. The inhabitants had been given a mere quarter hour to surrender and upon their refusal had been subjected to cannon fire, wholesale destruction, willful slaughter, and a final orgy of pillage and looting by the Cavaliers. All the supporters of Parliament were consumed with fury at this outrage and their leaders decided that such a state of affairs could not be allowed to continue. All other considerations must now be forgotten and the Royalists stopped at all costs from retaking the north.

CHAPTER 9

JUNE 1645

The Committee of Both Kingdoms ordered General Fairfax to take the New Model Army and go immediately in pursuit of the King and Prince Rupert. Besieging the Royalist headquarters now seemed of less importance than confronting the Royalist army and halting their destructive passage to the north. On the 5th of June the siege of Oxford was raised suddenly and Philip Halsall watched the Roundheads begin to move away. He was ignorant of the reason but suspected it must be a Royalist strike of some importance, a possibility he had always relied upon for their deliverance.

Henrietta had been gone for almost two weeks and he believed she must be safe at home, resolutely banishing contrary thoughts from his mind. In the long waiting hours of daylight he imagined her at Hesketh Hall, drawing on every remembered detail of the house and visualising her activities. But in the long night hours he was tormented by visions of her lying dead by the side of some country road. It was after her departure that Michel Garolais moved in with him. Philip was glad of his presence. Michel was a professional soldier of higher rank than he, older and more experienced. He had withstood many sieges and in his company there was no need for guilt or worry, recriminations or anxiety, as there had been with Henrietta. It was like being with William Hesketh again and now that he was shorn of his marital responsibilities, which had proved more severe than he had expected, life became uncomplicated once more. The hazards and discomforts of war resumed their right proportions when there was no-one but himself to think of, or at least another man to share them. Philip had not realized how much in the past three years he had become dependent on male companionship.

Then suddenly the siege was lifted without warning. As the New Model Army marched away everyone began to stir themselves to renewed activity, for in the days that followed there was much to be done to get the city back to normal, especially once supply lines were re-opened. The necessary activity proved a release for the emotions of the citizens, relieved beyond measure that they would not have to suffer a prolongation of their misery into the increasing heat of summer. There was a spirit of elation abroad, though this was all too soon replaced by a sober appraisal of the problems facing them. However life gradually began to return to normal and with the resumption of communications Philip received a message from Henrietta informing him of her safe return. Now he could have no greater hope than their speedy reunion.

It was almost a week after the siege ended that William entered Oxford on a strange errand. Just before the siege was raised the King had, ironically, decided that they must relieve the city, and had put Rupert in charge of an attempt to get a herd of cattle to the near-starving inhabitants. His troopers had spent ten days trying to accomplish this task and by the time they succeeded the siege was already over. When they rode into Oxford with the cattle it was true that they were greeted enthusiastically, but there was an obvious underlying resentment that they had not come sooner, expressed more vocally by some of the citizens.

"It seems we are too late again," cried William in disgust when he had located Philip and they had been joyfully reunited. "When I joined the Royalist army I never expected to become a cattle drover."

"You don't know how fortunate you are," Philip returned wholeheartedly. "You should try being cooped up in a city under siege. You don't know how glad I am to be riding with you again." Even the regret at leaving Michel could not lessen his exhilaration at the prospect of being in action again with William at his side, especially when his friend regaled him with accounts of recent Royalist successes in the Midlands.

"'Twill be a mad ride," William warned him. "Rupert is in no fine temper."

The Prince was furious at the amount of time that had been wasted on the cattle-driving exercise, especially as he had been against relieving the city in the first place, considering other military objectives to be of greater importance. Now the fact that the siege had been raised before their arrival only served to justify his original opinion, and his temper had not been improved by the jeers and catcalls of some of the thankless citizens. He intended to waste no time on resuming his northern campaign and within a few hours they were out of Oxford, riding furiously as William had predicted.

William and Philip rode side by side exchanging news as much as they could in the headlong gallop, though Philip made no mention of Michel Garolais. William was buoyed up by the new developments and Philip exhilarated by the freedom of being on horseback again so the miles passed quickly. By the following day they had caught up with the King and the rest of the

Royalist army who were camped near a village called Naseby in the Leicestershire countryside. In view of the changed situation the King had ordered Lord Goring to bring his men back from the south to rejoin the main army, and they were expecting his imminent arrival, despite Goring's habitual tardiness in obeying orders. When Rupert's cavalry rode into the camp they found everyone in high spirits. The King had gone hunting and the Cavaliers were relaxing in the taverns or in the fields in the hot summer weather, their horses out at grass. Rupert, vigilant as ever, was not content to let his own troopers relax even after their long ride until he had sent out scouts to check the surrounding area, but when nothing untoward was reported they were allowed to take their ease. Rupert himself did not check the reliability of his scouts who had failed to discover that the New Model Army was on their trail and less than five miles away.

General Sir Thomas Fairfax on the other hand knew exactly where the Royalists were. He had been shadowing them for some days and was ready for a confrontation. He was aware that their reinforcements under Lord Goring had not yet arrived from the south, but his own reinforcements, Oliver Cromwell and his cavalry, had arrived early that morning. After receiving his orders they had had left Cambridge at a furious pace, John Radcliffe amongst the company, and after riding all night they had reached the Parliament encampment a few miles from Naseby at six o' clock the following morning. Tired after their punishing nocturnal ride but exultant that they had arrived in time, they were met by an extraordinary demonstration of regard as thousands of men rushed to greet them, leaving their tents and their duties to line Cromwell's path and cheer him with a fervour that resounded triumphantly in the fresh sweetly scented air of early morning. As they threaded their way through the lines of enthusiastic soldiers John could not help but feel proud to be part of Oliver Cromwell's Ironsides whose contribution to the imminent battle was considered essential.

Even at that early hour General Sir Thomas Fairfax was already holding a council of war. After the abortive march to the south-west and the ill-advised siege of Oxford he had become increasingly frustrated by the way the war was being conducted by a committee in London who did not understand, and sometimes did not even know, the real situation in the field. He had decided to take matters into his own hands and had presented them with an ultimatum. If he were to continue as commander of the New Model Army he demanded to be given total freedom to make his own military decisions, subject only to a council of war with his own officers. The Committee had been forced to agree and so now on his own judgment he had decided to bring the whole Royalist army into open battle, the battle that Cromwell had been urging for the past few months and which they both considered would be a final deciding engagement. Sir Thomas heard the tumult and guessing the reason he left the war council to go outside and greet his old friend personally. When they both returned to the meeting Oliver chose John as one of his aides to accompany him so he was able to hear the Lord General put Cromwell in overall charge of the whole cavalry of the New Model Army, second in command to Fairfax himself and a position which up till now had been left vacant. For the moment Oliver Cromwell's resignation under the Self-Denying Ordinance was still held in abeyance as serving a greater need. A smile of satisfaction passed between the two friends. They had now achieved what they both wanted and for which they had long striven - command of the New Model Army between them without interference. They had rid themselves of those commanders less competent and vigorous than themselves, of those men less honest and single-minded than themselves. Now they had acquired total freedom in military matters, the first time the army of Parliament had been commanded by soldiers in the field. The two skilled and capable soldiers, Black Tom and Old Noll, admired and trusted by those who followed them, both believed ardently in the personal guidance of God and the workings of Providence and there was no doubt that this new development was part of this manifestation for it was essential the war must be brought to a speedy and decisive end for the establishment of a more just and equable society.

"I have some interesting news for you Oliver," said Fairfax, and related to him how one of his patrols had intercepted a Royalist courier bringing a letter from George Goring telling the King not to fight until he could arrive with his reinforcements.

"We now have them where we want them, Tom," said Cromwell. "The King's army and Prince Rupert together."

"We bring them to battle tomorrow," said Fairfax with the utmost satisfaction. "We get the men prepared now."

After their punishing ride in the summer heat William and Philip had relaxed thankfully with their companions and towards evening went with many other Cavalier officers to have supper at a welcoming country inn in the village of Naseby. Everyone was in a carefree mood, intoxicated as much by the recent wave of successes and the hot summer weather as by the wine, and were sprawled negligently round the tables eating and drinking, laughing and joking. The jovial innkeeper, happy with the unexpected custom, was doing his best to provide them with the best fare, and the serving wenches were giggling at the bawdy talk and not averse to being kissed and fondled with the promise of more delights to come from the young Cavaliers, liberally dispensing their money. The din was raucous and an aroma of spilt wine and tobacco smoke filled the air. William and Philip were sitting a little apart from their rumbustious companions. Philip seemed in a reflective mood and William surmised that as a new-married man he would no longer be as eager to participate in the carousing so they had chosen to sit beside an open window because of the still oppressive heat. The casement was swinging on the latch and the scent of honeysuckle and rose drifted in from the climbing plants around the wall, a pleasant contrast to the stifling airlessness of the smoky low-raftered room. They were feeling pleasantly lethargic though were not as drunk as some of their comrades who had consumed a great deal of liquor and were now beginning to sing Royalist army songs, beating time with their tankards on the wooden table tops.

> "Charge it again boys, charge it again,
> Pardonnez-moi je vous en prie,
> As long as you've got any ink in your pen,
> With never a penny of money.
> And he who will not pledge me this,
> Pardonnez-moi je vous en prie,
> Shall pay for the shot whatever it is,
> With never a penny of money."

The French words put Philip in mind of Michel Garolais. Should he tell William? He might have done had he not been married to William's sister. He felt guilty but he still longed for Michel - suave, elegant Michel with his Gallic charm who had been unconcerned about the siege and sympathetic to Philip's concern for Henrietta. Henrietta had been so possessive of his time when he had been occupied with military duties and so demanding of his attention when he was preoccupied with problems. He had felt choked in the oppressive heat of the tiny rooms with their newly-sown relationship, a relationship that had not had time to bed roots, tainted by worry and uncertainty. It had been a relief to lose himself in Michel's undemanding society and the satisfaction of being man to man again. But he had grown dependent on Michel's affection. He should have seen the warning signs, he should have known. There was the Frenchman's easy way of making physical contact, the look in his deep blue eyes. **"Pardonnez-moi je vous en prie"**, the words were ringing loud in his ears. He had known! There was the letter Michel had written to him in the first early days of their acquaintance when he had been put under the French mercenary's command on guard duty, the letter he had carefully kept. He loved Henrietta and his whole desire was to take her home to Lancashire, to build a house and a business and live in peace with her and their children. But he kept remembering Michel's solidity and his strong capability, the way he took charge of everything. He never stammered when he was with Michel, he felt perfectly at ease in his company and he didn't have to force himself to be strong. Thinking about him now he longed for his comforting presence.

Suddenly there was a loud banging of doors and the thunder of booted feet through the narrow passageways of the inn as to their horror a Roundhead patrol burst in on them, armed, alert, and in deadly earnest. The Cavaliers leapt hurriedly to their feet as best they could though several had girls on their knees. Some of them put up a fight but most of them could not find their swords before they were taken, too encumbered by full bellies and the torpor of heat and drink. From their table at the far end of the room William and Philip had just enough time to take in the situation and weigh up the odds against them and fortunately they were not too drunk to act swiftly.

"Out!" cried William and they jumped onto the table, scattering the remains of their meal with mugs and trenchers clattering noisily to the floor. They dived more than leapt through the window for there was little space, and went crashing into the bushes below them. Their departure went unremarked in the general mêlée and the window being at the side of the inn there was no-one immediately in view as they scuttled to the rear to find their horses. Here they were met with such activity that it was not too difficult to reach their mounts before being sighted and they rode off with the speed of desperation, though only a half-hearted attempt was made to pursue them as the Roundheads were occupied enough with their more complaisant captives.

They went immediately to Prince Rupert who was horrified at the news and rushed to find his uncle. Everyone was dismayed to discover the Roundheads had entered the village of Naseby for nobody had the slightest suspicion they were so close. A council of war was called immediately. Whilst their commanders were in urgent council the Royalists began to bestir themselves and prepare for imminent battle which seemed inevitable now it was realized that the full weight of the New Model Army was close at hand.

"No reinforcements!" said Philip significantly. "We are unprepared again."

"Caught with our breeches down. Why didn't anyone know the Roundheads were so close," fumed William.

"It's Marston Moor all over again." They looked at each other, feeling their flesh creep unavoidably at the memory.

"Don't say that," ordered William furiously. "We mustn't think about that. This time will be different. This time we are going to avenge Marston. Goring is bound to be here soon, he's been sent for. If we can beat the Roundheads now we have been forced into battle again then the war is as good as won, and we've been riding on the crest of a wave recently so we should all feel confident."

But even as their blood began to rise at the thought of impending action they could not help but feel uneasy at this ill-omened beginning.

Rupert left the council of war abruptly. He stormed out of the tent shouting an oath at an unfortunate soldier who was almost knocked over by his headlong passage. Catching sight of his angry frowning face William knew that he had been thwarted in his opinion. Rupert was brave and headstrong but not reckless. It was his conviction that they should retreat swiftly and wait for their reinforcements rather than hazard odds which they knew were slightly worse than at Marston Moor. The King however considered it cowardly to run away. "We will stand and fight," he stated firmly and most of his advisers agreed. The commander of the cavalry, the most experienced soldier amongst them, must needs give way to the King.

Early the following morning, the 14th of June and a warm sunny day redolent with all the glories of an English summer, the army of the King and the army of Parliament faced each other. Ranged on opposing ridges just outside the village of Naseby, twenty-two thousand men were assembled on either side of a cornfield. They had been taking up their positions since dawn but by ten o'clock when the sun was high in the sky the battle lines had been drawn up.

William and Philip sat mounted with Rupert's cavalry on the high ground known as Dust Hill. They formed the prestigious right wing of the army. On the left wing the cavalry were under the command of Sir Marmeduke Langdale, while the veteran Sir Jacob Astley's regiment of foot held the centre supported by ten heavy cannon. Rupert's own regiment of foot together with the King's bodyguard were to be held in reserve. The Royalists had recovered their confidence after the first shock of finding themselves confronted by the Parliament army. Because George Goring's reinforcements had not arrived they were five thousand fewer in number than the Roundheads but they were all experienced troops and buoyed up by their recent successes. The New Model Army on the other hand was composed largely of new recruits as yet untried in battle. William and Philip had also regained their habitual optimism and were only hoping that there would be as short a delay as possible before battle was joined.

"Pray God we don't have a long wait," William said to his friend, for nerves were taut and they were already sweating in the heat in their buff leather coats surmounted by the heavy iron back and breast armour. William was also wearing a weighty barred helmet, known colloquially as an English pot, though Philip preferred the Montero, the hunting cap that Rupert also wore, though it carried a steel lining known as a "secret." What headgear the soldiers wore was a matter of personal choice. Some preferred the lighter broad-brimmed felt hats which gave better all-round visibility though left their faces unprotected, others liked the protection of the face guard on the barred helmets though they were heavier to wear and had limited vision on either side.

Suddenly Philip cried, "Here comes the King. It would seem we won't have to wait long."

King Charles rode his magnificent charger onto the field with supreme skill so that despite his small stature he made an impressive figure, stately and upright, his gilt armour flashing in the bright harsh sunlight. Prince Rupert rode to meet him and formally rendered up his position as Commander-in-Chief, an honour that was now the right of the Sovereign. Once his responsibility as overall commander had been shed, the Prince took up his position as head of his own cavalry and prepared to make the first move.

As the last minutes ticked by William wondered where his father was in the packed array of splendid troops and offered up a quick prayer for him. Philip thought for the last time of Henrietta, glad that she did not know where he was and what they had to do this day. Then they turned to each other. Wordlessly they clasped hands in a gesture that expressed all their feelings about their shared companionship over the past three years, and all their hopes for a fortunate outcome to the battle and a future that would be theirs to enjoy. They both knew how crucial this day would be. Then with nerves taut and every sense alert they fixed their eyes unwaveringly on Rupert and waited for the trumpets to sound the charge. Their bridle arm shielded by a metal gauntlet held the reins loosely but firmly, their right hand gripped their sword, the pistols in their belts were primed for later use, their knees were touching, so closely did they ride. They were ready.

On the opposite ridge of Red Hill farm John Radcliffe was in his place with the army of Parliament. Like

Rupert's cavalry, Oliver Cromwell's own regiment had been allotted the place of honour on the right wing with the cavalry of Henry Ireton, Oliver's forthcoming son-in-law, on the left. Cromwell's men were in formation on broken ground to the right of the foot regiments of Colonel Philip Skippon, a tried and trusted soldier with experience of Continental warfare and who had arranged his infantry in the new Swedish style of five separate blocks. John felt strangely calm, secure in the confidence that God would give them victory. He felt no fear, only a heightening of all his senses in anticipation of the great concentration needed. If he were to die in the battle then it would be with the assurance that he had done all that had been asked of him and the Lord had nothing else for him to do. He allowed himself only a brief thought of Arabella for nothing must disturb his single-mindedness, but he whispered a short prayer commending her to God's care. Thinking of her reminded him that her father and brother would be in place on the opposite side of the field and William Hesketh flashed momentarily into his mind with his insolent bravado but also his courage. One of them must be the loser this day.

Oliver Cromwell rode backwards and forwards amongst his men with a smile on his face, encouraging each one. "Smile out to God in the assurance of victory."

Then they prayed together and began the singing of the hundred and twenty-first psalm. Their voices rose in powerful and confident unison as "I will lift up my eyes unto the hills from whence cometh my help" was carried on a great wave of sound across the valley.

From the opposite ridge the Royalist army listened to the swelling chorus, "The Lord is thy shade upon thy right hand, the sun shall not smite thee by day." The rising crescendo sent a superstitious fear into the hearts of some of the Cavaliers, though many of them were lost in their own private prayers, but William commented mockingly, "They are even claiming God's protection against the weather." He could imagine the arrogant Puritan captain being amongst them. Then the singing died away and for a moment there was silence, a strange unearthly silence all the more telling after the resounding noise, a silence as if time stood suspended and history hung in the balance while God decided the relative merits of the two opposing sides. Then the sounds of horse and man, bridle and harness, foot and armour, recommenced in restless anticipation.

It was the Royalist trumpeter who blew the charge first and Rupert's cavalry began to move forward crying, "Queen Mary", the name by which Henrietta-Maria was known in England. The King had personally chosen the field word, an example of his habitual tactlessness because even amongst his supporters there was an avowed lack of enthusiasm for his queen. The charge gathered momentum as they rode down the hillside into the shallow valley and with every yard they increased their speed so that they were only vaguely conscious of the enfilading fire from the Roundhead dragoons in the hedges to their right.

With their battlecry of "God our strength," the left wing of the Parliament army under Colonel Ireton rode to meet them. Then all was confusion as the clash of horse and steel brought movement to a standstill. The fighting was furious as each side tried to break through the other's ranks. William could feel the surge of the Royalist army as Ireton's cavalry slowly began to give way against their impetus. He felt rather than saw Philip go down, slashed by a Roundhead sword. He twisted round and saw him lying motionless on the ground then in a moment he was being trampled under stamping hooves. William attempted to go back but it was impossible in the crush and in his heart he knew it was useless. But there was no time for sorrow or fear if he had to stay alive himself and he forced himself to keep his mind on the work in hand, knowing that he could be the next casualty if his concentration slackened. He followed the tall crimson-cloaked figure of Rupert who was fearlessly hacking with his sword in the centre of the mêlée and under whose leadership the troop was holding together. The Roundheads began to crumple under their ferocious assault. They began to scatter and flee as they were relentlessly beaten back by the Prince's cavalry and Ireton himself was wounded, blood streaming from his face from a sword cut above his eye. In the very moment of victory William came his closest to catastrophe. Just in time he saw the swinging blade of a Roundhead aiming for his head and as he swerved quickly the sword sliced through his horse's neck. As the horse collapsed under him William was thrown from the immediate danger but on leaping up swiftly in order to escape Philip's fate he realized he was in even greater peril. He looked around frantically for a riderless mount but the Royalist cavalry was now sweeping all before them and as Rupert's victorious troop chased their fleeing opponents from the field William could not join the pursuit. He looked around, trying to see some order in the seething mass of men, but the once clearly defined battle lines had merged into an indistinguishable heaving throng. In the centre of the field the two masses of infantry were locked in combat, but the Cavalier pikemen were pushing back the Roundheads and it seemed as if the Parliament foot was going to collapse. William pitched himself into the fray and continued fighting on foot, bringing his sword to the aid of the Royalist pikemen.

Fighting on the opposite wing John Radcliffe had followed Oliver Cromwell in his fierce charge against the Royalist cavalry of Marmeduke Langdale and experienced the exhilaration of seeing his enemies collapse under their onslaught. With no thought except to keep his own troop together under his example and wreak as much damage to the opposing Cavaliers, he had followed in Cromwell's ruthless path until they arrived on the opposite side of the enemy lines leaving a trail of death and destruction behind them. It took some time to halt their headlong passage and the cavalry being in disarray at that time it was difficult to see how the whole battle was going. Cromwell however had hastily found himself a vantage point on Dust Hill where he could survey the field, and at this moment the battle seemed equally drawn. Both he and Prince Rupert had been successful in their charges and both the left cavalry wings were in flight. The fate of the centre was still undecided, but the advantage appeared to lie with the Royalist infantry fighting under the command of old Sir Jacob Astley who were making headway against Skippon's Parliamentarians. Cromwell had seen Ireton's cavalry overcome, but also knew that Rupert and his triumphant horseman had left the field in reckless pursuit of their beaten opponents and in their headlong charge were now some miles away. However the Roundhead infantry were in danger of collapse and a defeat could be imminent should Rupert return to support the Royalist foot. Cromwell's judgment was shrewd and his decision swift. He had prevented his own cavalry from leaving the field but of necessity they were scattered and in disarray. He rode amongst his officers hastily, "Regroup. Make ready to charge again. We are going into the centre. Get ready lads, fast as you can. God bless you."

In company with the other captains John Radcliffe felt a momentary perturbation for a second charge had never before been attempted in a battle, riders and horses now out of formation and sometimes a mile or more away from the scene. But he had already been trying to call his men back into line, anticipating some further action. As well as commanding his own troop he had taken over the troop of an officer who had fallen and he worked swiftly on reforming them. He felt clear-headed as if breathing a rarefied air as he followed Cromwell's hastily shouted commands. The Parliamentary cavalry reformed, began to wheel, turn, and line again, and with his ordered and well-disciplined troops Cromwell accomplished the near impossible, a second charge with a mass of cavalry that had broken its formation. They hurled themselves into the support of their failing infantry and John followed his commander into the decisive action of the battle.

William was struggling amongst the contorting mass of infantry at push of pike when Cromwell's cavalry bore down on them. This is what Hell must be like he thought as he was surrounded by the screams of men and the terrifying neighing of horses, the clash of steel on steel, the grind of steel on bone, the squelch of pike into horseflesh, the repeated explosions of cannon and musket enveloping the infernal scene in a thick blanket of acrid smoke. It was impossible to move beyond one's own body space as, locked together, men hacked at each other indiscriminately, and impossible to see which were their own men. Their own men? Weren't they all Englishmen? Sweat was running down his face and into his eyes but he did not know if it was sweat or tears blinding him. "Oh merciful God help us," he cried, choking with the acrid smoke and his lungs bursting. For one brief moment William Hesketh and John

Radcliffe came within a hair's breadth of each other in the struggling mass of men until, oblivious to each other's nearness, they turned aside to counter other opponents.

Prince Rupert and his cavalry did not return to the field until too late as they were too occupied with rifling the Parliament baggage train encamped a couple of miles away. By that time King Charles, watching from the high point of the ridge, had seen his valiant pikemen being slaughtered by the New Model cavalry and realized that the battle, and perhaps much more, was lost.

When it was all over a dazed and exhausted William Hesketh, in company with other survivors, wandered the battlefield in search of his friend's body. It was not easy to locate him amongst the thousands of dead strewn across the cornfields, for friend and foe looked alike. But though half dead with sorrow and fatigue he persisted in his quest and at last he found him. He had a sword cut through his jugular vein and his bloody face was mangled almost beyond recognition where the horses' hooves had trampled him underfoot. He looked for some personal token on the body, knowing that he used to wear a locket with a curl of Henrietta's hair in it, but the body had already been plundered and his armour, his jacket, the rings from his fingers, even his boots and stockings were gone. William knelt down and wept helplessly - for the loss of his friend, for the loss of the battle, for his sister, for hopes that could never be realized, for the waste of life. He cradled his friend in his arms, his tears dropping onto the brown hair matted with blood, and kissed the face that bore no resemblance to the Philip he had laughed and joked and fought with over the past three years. He did not know what to do. He was in danger of being captured himself and he did not even have a horse. The Royalist army was broken up and scattered with many taken prisoner and the rest fleeing for their lives and he had no idea whether they would try to regroup later or whether all was irretrievably lost. In his loneliness and confusion he thought he might as well go home.

In the lengthening shadows of evening John Radcliffe also stood on Naseby field sick at heart. Though exhausted, blood-stained and aching, he had been exhilarated by their victory and full of heartfelt thanks to God who had granted it and made possible what must be a final defeat for the Royalists who were scattered in all directions with their army completely disintegrated. But then he had been informed of an act of such barbaric cruelty committed by his own side that had filled him with shame and horror. A large number of women had been found following the Royalist army, most of them from the Welsh borders where Rupert's main recruiting drive had been carried out. Because they were speaking an unfamiliar language they were suspected of being Irish and therefore Catholics. Some of them had been massacred instantly and the rest had had their faces slashed as whores, even though most of them had accompanied their menfolk, husbands and sons. John was full of grief and troubled in his heart. He could not believe that those who professed to let God rule their lives and had just witnessed the steadfastness of His promises could be capable of such wanton cruelty in His name, that men who trusted in God's all-encompassing mercy should deny that mercy to others. The deaths of those slain in battle could be justified. Most of them had taken up arms willingly and knew the odds as he had done. But these women were innocent victims, or at most guilty of nothing more than following their menfolk without whose support they could not live. He felt in some way implicated in the action because it had been committed by men beside whom he had fought this day, his comrades and fellow-believers. As he prayed for forgiveness, for those who had committed such an act and for his own involuntary participation in it, he felt sick at heart.

The following day he heard news which disturbed him the more. During the debacle of flight the King had lost his baggage which had been found by the Parliamentarians. On opening his personal correspondence they had discovered proof that he had been negotiating with the Irish Catholics. In return for their sending an army into England to support the King's cause he had promised to abolish all the penalties against English Catholics. To the Puritans this made horrifying reading. They were provoked to new fury by the deceit of the King who had always promised to withhold the Protestant faith, and by the vision of a foreign Catholic army fighting on their own soil. It was ordered that reprisals against Catholics were to be intensified. John had been neither able to give thought to Arabella during the extremities of the battle nor to wonder about the fate of her family in their defeat. Now however she was brought forcibly to mind. He felt a great fear envelop him and knew he had to get back to her as quickly as possible.

CHAPTER 10

JUNE 1645

The first the Heskeths knew of the battle was when Arabella and Abigail walked into Felton and read a news sheet which had just arrived. The townspeople were agog with consternation as the news was passed along and they gathered in groups on the green, in the market place, and under the arches of the moot hall to anxiously confer and consider the consequences. The girls hurried home immediately to impart the fearful information to the rest of the household.

"There has been a great battle in Leicestershire and Parliament was victorious," Arabella told her mother and Henrietta. "The Royalist army is scattered, the King has fled, and thousands of men have been either killed or taken prisoner."

They were stunned into silence. The news was too dreadful to take in and they were numbed by the impact. Whatever had happened to all their hopes and the auspicious fortunes on which they had built their dreams. Then as their senses begin to revive from the shock they were overwhelmed by fear. Who had been involved? Who was safe? There were so many of them to fear for - husbands, lovers, father, brother, son. The only comfort they could find was in each other's support, though Arabella alone could not be open in her fears. But it was fear that united them, though with a seal of helplessness. Never had they felt so much the woman's burden as the hours dragged excruciatingly onward and there was nothing they could do except worry and wait, pray and wait again in the debilitating sultry heat, letting their imaginations run riot in the sickening limbo of uncertainty. They could settle to nothing, no-one could eat, and they walked restlessly around the house and the grounds, sometimes alone with their own fears, sometimes clinging wordlessly to each other. They sent Timothy regularly into Felton but there was no further news, although each time they waited agonizingly for his return.

The first confirmation of their fears was the alarming sign of Sir James's valet and two of the house servants walking up the driveway without their master. Lady Hesketh ran to meet them with her heart hammering in her breast and all her fears writ plain on her face, though she could not put them into words as she waited for Alleyn to speak. He had served Sir James since he was a young man and he knew it was not the time to prevaricate.

"Sir James has been wounded, my lady," he said gently, "but you must not fear because he is now recovering and is on his way home."

Lady Mary held onto the wall for support as she asked faintly, "How? How badly?"

"He received a head wound but was able to get prompt aid from one of the surgeons and the worst has been prevented. He is mending well and should be home by the morrow for I left him not far behind." As Lady Mary breathed a sigh of relief, he continued gently, "However I would not have you unprepared. His speech is somewhat impaired and movement on his left side affected. But you must not worry for he is over the worst and there is much cause for thanks."

Lady Mary tried to cling to the hopeful parts of Alleyn's report knowing that he was an honest and faithful servant who would not mislead, but she knew she could not be at ease until she saw her husband. She continued her restless pacing, repeating endlessly to her daughters the message she had been given and begging for their reassurances. But at least Sir James was alive whereas of the others they knew nothing.

Late in the afternoon of the following day, a day of intense heat that hung airlessly beneath a lowering yellow sky casting a sickly hue over the parched grass and withered plants, a little party rode very slowly up to the Hall. Although Sir James had been transported on a litter for most of the way he had been determined to ride the last mile, but the heat and his paralysed arm and leg made the effort almost too much for him and he was sick and dazed. He was unable to focus clearly on the welcoming group awaiting him but they were running to him, helping him dismount and leading him into the house. He sank thankfully into a chair in the parlour and they were ministering to him with cushions and a footstool and a brimming glass of red wine. But they were all shocked by his appearance, his dull eyes and haggard face beneath his bandaged head which was shorn of hair in great uneven patches. His left arm and leg were partly paralysed and he spoke with a slurring speech as when he had drunk too much, though when he was rested and comfortable he informed them that the surgeon had said these disabilities would disappear with time. Lady Mary believed that now he was safely home she would be able to restore him to his former self with enough love and care, and her initial distress at being faced with this shadow was overcome by the joy they all felt at having him returned to them. Of William and Philip he could tell them nothing though he had seen and spoken with Kit Verney. Henrietta had cast a quick glance at Arabella at this welcome news but she felt no stronger emotion than a sincere gladness that he was safe.

After his initial despair William had met up with several of his former companions and learnt that though the King and Prince Rupert had fled to Leicester they were intending to re-assemble their scattered forces and march to the defence of the south-west. Although this was now the only part of England where the Royalists held control it was still a large area with the important cities of Exeter and Bristol, Bristol being the second most important city in the kingdom, and Rupert did not believe that all was yet lost. William decided to join them again. He had followed Rupert since the Prince had first raised his standard, dazzled by the courage and confidence of the brilliant young general. He would follow him to the end, even if the end should be bitter. William was young and despite his sense of utter hopelessness on the night of the battle his youthful optimism had gradually resurfaced and he found it difficult to believe that any failure, no matter how serious, was necessarily final. They had recovered from Marston Moor and perhaps they might yet recover from Naseby. Even his grief at Philip's death had settled into an acceptance of the inescapable tragedies of war. But he considered it his duty to break the news personally to Henrietta and not let his sister hear it from some other source, so he kept to his original plan of returning home before once again renewing his loyalty to the Royalist cause and marching south with the Prince's regiment.

As he rode up to the Hall a relieved Arabella came running to meet him followed by his mother who held him in a long embrace. Abigail watched from above stairs and experienced a great lightening of heart. They told him the news about Sir James but before he could go to see his father he knew that he had a much harder task to do and asked the whereabouts of Henrietta.

"She is lying on the bed resting from the heat. What is the matter?" asked Lady Mary fearful of his grave expression, while Arabella looked on in horror as he told them the truth.

"How much more, Oh God, how much more?" his mother whispered, but though shocked and grieved asked, "Shall I tell her?"

"No. He was my friend and she is my sister. I will tell her," William said unwaveringly.

Henrietta now knew without doubt that she was enceinte. She had suspected it for some time but wanted Philip to be the first to know and she had not dared to tell him until she was absolutely sure. But instead of the joy she had expected to experience she could only feel a deadening weight of foreboding as if the child within her was already full term and overburdening her. She supposed it was the breathless stifling heat oppressing her. She was tormented by worries of Philip and wondered why she had heard nothing from him. Did this mean that he was well and on his way or ? She did not dare to think of the other possibility. Because the heat outside was too much for her she spent much time lying on top of the rose- embroidered counterpane in her old chamber, too listless to read or to want conversation. She kept seeing in her mind the shadow of Philip standing in the stone arch of the cathedral at Oxford but was frightened because she couldn't recall his face clearly. Lying in her old bed in her bedchamber here at Hesketh Hall it seemed to her that she had never left home and that her marriage and her life in Oxford had been but a dream. The only proof of the reality was the presence of the child beneath her heart. She sat up with a start as William appeared in the doorway. Her face lit up with joy, then his expression told her everything she had dreaded in the long, weary, oppressive days since they had heard about the battle. She made no sound and her eyes were dry as her brother told her as gently as he could that her husband was dead, leaving out the grisly details of his killing and the callous treatment of his body.

"Did he mention me?" she whispered.

"There was no time. He died instantly. He kept your lock of hair close to his heart, I know that, but when I returned to his body someone had stolen it. I helped to bury him myself," he said, tears streaming down his face at the memory.

Still Henrietta did not cry and this control unnerved her brother. He had steeled himself for many reactions but this marble-cold stillness frightened him and he left her eventually, unable to comfort her because she had put herself beyond comfort. When her mother and sister came to her she preserved a stony silence and though Lady Mary understood she was suffering the effects of shock she knew there was nothing they could do at this time and they were forced to leave her alone, lying lifeless on the bed like one dead herself.

Then toward evening thunder began to rumble ominously in great swelling arcs around the house, interspersed with white forks of lightning. The storm that had threatened for days was upon them at last. Still it did not break but continued to encircle them with ever-increasing intensity. In the dead of night Henrietta was seized with cramping pains in her stomach and as the thunder rolled closer the pain rolled with it so she was soon crying in agony as the torment began to invade every part of her body. Lady Mary sent Timothy into Felton for the physician but she knew the cause and had indeed suspected that her daughter was with child. Arabella brought draughts of chamomile and pennyroyal from the stillroom and Abigail went to find old linen. All night they tended and comforted her as Henrietta tossed and writhed in agony, her face ashen and bathed in sweat. "Please God let me die," she cried helplessly when she could utter breath.

"You are not going to die, darling," her mother assured her. "But you must let go. You must let go your grief. Don't hold it in, let it wash away."

Amidst searing flames of pain accompanied by blue flashes of lightning that illuminated the chamber, Henrietta thought, what is my grief? Was it the fact that Philip was dead and she would never see him again, never lie in his arms again and have him kiss her lips and her hair, or the fact that it had all been so short and useless, the fact that she could not remember his face clearly, the fact that their last memories had been soured, the fact that she suspected him of something too terrible to name, the fact that she had finally left him alone and deserted him for her own safety, the fact that she had never given him the joy of knowing about the child who was now joining his father in oblivion. All was a maelstrom of confusion - sorrow, guilt, remorse, regret and agonizing pain for what was irretrievably lost. The unacceptable anguish in her mind had transmuted into a physical force that clawed and tore at her with relentless might while the lightning flashed around the room and the thunder seemed to shake the foundations of the house.

At last the first drops of rain began to fall and hung on the window pane like tears. Then the heavens opened and as the rain gushed down the window in torrents so

Henrietta's emotion swept through her in a releasing flood, bearing all before it. She began to weep, tears pouring down her face and great convulsive sobs shaking her harrowed body. It was all over. She lay weak and still, unable to believe that the pain had left her but with an empty space somewhere where her heart had been. The rain continued to fall and so did her tears.

After Abigail had washed Henrietta and found clean sheets and a clean shift she spent the last of the sleeping hours on a truckle bed beside her. The next morning she was gently brushing her hair when Arabella came in and sat on the edge of the bed. "Are you feeling better," she asked.

Abigail made to go but Henrietta took hold of her hand and restrained her.

"Yes, I'm feeling better," she said weakly. She could not explain to them half of what she felt. She was only eighteen but she felt old, so much older than they in their innocence with their dreams untarnished. "I find it so difficult to believe because I haven't seen his body. If I could have seen him dead then I would know he isn't ever going to come back to me," she said in part explanation. Neither of them knew what to say, each holding secrets and fears in her own heart. "I would like to have had the baby to remind me of him."

"It is better this way," said Abigail gently. "A child needs a father."

"But it all seems so pointless somehow. There doesn't seem to be any purpose in my getting married at all. I haven't got anything left."

"You have known love, if only for a short time. Isn't that worth it?" Arabella said, not able to keep her voice from trembling. She would probably never know the joy of consummated love with John, not even for a short time. "You have your memories."

Henrietta looked at her sister with worldly wisdom. Her memories of a few short months served no purpose than to intensify grief. "Memories are no comfort. They only serve to recall more poignantly what has been lost," she said. She thought again of the last time she had seen Philip outlined in the archway of the cathedral watching her as she left Oxford for safety. How she wished now that she had never left him.

Alone in her chamber Lady Hesketh looked with dismay at her face in the glass. The weariness of a sleepless night accounted for her pallor but lines of strain had been etched deeper around her eyes and mouth and she noticed threads of silver in her chestnut hair. She went to the window and leant out, breathing in the rain-washed air so refreshingly cool after the stifling heat of the past few weeks. She looked over the knot garden which was green and revived after the storm, and let her gaze go beyond the golden stone walls to where the fields of their domain stretched into the middle distance cut by the ribbon of the meandering stream. The year had fallen so short of all the hopes they had expressed at Christmas. What had gone wrong? They had kept their faith and sacrificed for the Royalist cause. Why was God forsaking them? Her husband had returned maimed in body and mind, and innocent carefree Henrietta was now a grieving widow. She should not have allowed Rupert to persuade her into consenting to the marriage. But the cool air revived her and the peaceful scene helped to still her turbulent thoughts. It was not up to them to question God's will. If He called them to suffer in order to bring them to a closer knowledge of His love then they must accept the burden with humility. After a few minutes of prayer to the Blessed Virgin, who never left forsaken all who had recourse to her protection, she went to see what she could do for her husband and her daughter.

John Radcliffe was wondering how he could possibly return to Arabella. He had no idea what had happened to her father and brother after the defeat at Naseby and he was greatly worried about the renewed hostility to Catholics, fearing some harm might come to her family. Whilst he was agonizing over what to do he was told that the New Model Army was preparing to march to the south-west to take the Royalists' last remaining strongholds, and presuming as William had done earlier that the route would pass not too far distant from Felton he decided to make a detour for himself. First however he had a matter to see to which he did not relish but which had to be done. He was on the point of asking for an interview with Oliver Cromwell when his commander forestalled his request by sending for him. He had no idea why the General wanted to see him but he knew that this was the opportunity he needed and went over everything carefully in his mind once more before answering the summons.

Cromwell stood up from his table when John entered the room in the inn that they had taken over as their command post and clasping him by the hand congratulated him on his promotion to major. "Well done, lad! You fought a good fight on Naseby field. I saw your quick thinking in taking over Major Anderson's troop after he had fallen. You can take over his command now."

John thanked him with sincere surprise and gratitude. He welcomed the opportunity to shoulder more responsibility and if the other matter had not been preying on his mind he would have been elated by his commander's recognition of him.

"But it isn't only for the one battle," Cromwell continued. "You have worked hard over a long period of time, even when you were wounded and away from active service. I wish I had more officers like you." He had not always thought like this. Although he had known John for several years and liked his honesty and commitment, there were occasions when he had been chary of his independent tendencies. But he had admired his foresight in the heat of battle and noted that he had already been regrouping his men before he had been given the order. Cromwell knew the value of a cool head at such a time. John Radcliffe was a good officer, trusted and respected by his men, and over the last few months he had grown in judgment and responsibility.

Feeling his commander's approval and knowing his standing was high at this time John realised he had been given an ideal opportunity. Without giving himself time to think he asked bluntly, "I was wondering if I might ask for some financial recompense." He was aware that he sounded brusque but he was unhappy with the request and could find no way of manipulating the words into a more agreeable form, for hypocrisy or sycophancy had never been his style. Oliver Cromwell was used to bluntness of speech for he used it himself and appreciated it in others, but he showed his surprise and looked at John questioningly so that he was forced to continue. "I know the Hesketh property will be sequestered. I was wondering if I might have an interest in it myself."

There was a long pause before Cromwell asked, "Do you fancy yourself a landowner, John?"

John found the sacrifice of his pride and principles the hardest thing he had ever done, even though he had prepared himself thoroughly, knowing what to expect. Oliver Cromwell was a percipient man and he must not let him suspect his ulterior motives, so he nerved himself to continue. "Why not when this war is over? Many have been given sequestered properties so why not I as much as the next man?" He was aware he could have phrased it in a more conciliatory way, damn him he was a lawyer, but the effort of even saying the words which were so hostile to his principles was forcing everything else from his mind.

Cromwell said, "Confiscated property goes to Parliament as you know." He paused then went on, "However it is not beyond the bounds of possibility for you to obtain the lease."

John breathed a little easier seeing that he had not been refused but he persisted grimly, "A permanent lease in perpetuity on the house and the lands, granted as a deed of gift."

Cromwell looked at him shrewdly. "I never thought of you as a worldly man, John," he said. He had known John was ambitious but he did not despise ambition. It was man's responsibility to God to develop his talents and capabilities to the full, but he had never thought of him as worldly.

In the sudden wave of revulsion that overwhelmed him John found himself struggling like a man drowning, but he knew that for Arabella's sake he must not give up. He forced himself to keep her small pale face in his mind as he continued, "It is a Papist house. It will be slighted. I developed a liking for the place when I was there."

"Is that why you refused to burn it down when I ordered it?"

The colour rose in John's tanned face and his voice shook slightly with the effort to control his anger, not quite concealed as he cried vehemently, "No! I gave you my reasons for that at the time and they were honest.

Whatever else I am, I am honest." But he burned with shame at the way he himself had cast doubt on his own sincerely-held convictions, and he knew that at this moment he was not being honest with his commander. He was a hypocrite, albeit for the best of reasons.

"Well perhaps this is why God stayed your hand then," said Cromwell equably but with a faint sardonic smile. "A nice irony. A Papist house converted into a bulwark of Puritanism, an example to believer and heretic alike. I will arrange for you to have a permanent lease granted to you as a deed of gift for exceptional services rendered to the Parliament cause. The property itself will belong in name to the Parliament, as a lawyer you know the procedure."

John nodded. He knew he could press no further and the concessions he had been granted were immense. "Yes sir, thank you sir."

"To all intents and purposes it will be yours provided you do not default," Cromwell added. He was vaguely suspicious that there was something more than he could divine to this matter. But Hesketh Hall was not a large estate and it would have been disposed of to someone, so why not to one of his own local men who had fought tirelessly for the cause for the past three years and for whom there was still much work to do. "Leave the matter to me and I will arrange it," he promised. "But don't settle down as a landowner yet. Get what rents you can from the property but we still have much to accomplish here and I have need of you."

When he had been dismissed John walked alone for a while, his emotions in turmoil. He felt shame for the way in which he had betrayed Oliver Cromwell's trust in his altruistic devotion to the cause and put himself on a level with those self-seekers in the Party who used the war for their own ends and whom he had always despised. Yet he could not help but feel elated that he had succeeded in saving Arabella and her family. He had not accomplished quite so much as he would have liked, and he had not thought through all the implications of his actions, the full severity of which was only now beginning to dawn on him. His over-riding impulse had been to protect her from harm and at least for the immediate future he had managed to do this for their house and lands could not be touched. But into what tortuous paths his love had led him. It had made him disobey orders, flout military regulations and finally behave dishonourably, contrary to all his principles. And for what? For one declaration of love from a girl out of his class, beyond his reach, of a faith that he hated, and who could by now have regretted her emotional response to him. Why had he not been able to love a girl of his own class who shared his beliefs? He had met several girls who could have served him well, beautiful girls like Abigail Hart. But he had reached the age of twenty-six without falling in love until he met Arabella Hesketh who was totally unsuited to him. It all seemed so illogical, and John Radcliffe's reading had not included those classical tales or those poems and plays written by native authors that would have told him his situation was not uncommon. Arabella's fragile refined beauty that had at first repelled him had inevitably aroused all his protective instincts and made him want to put his strength at her service. But he had also discovered that her fragility was misleading and she was as tenacious and resolute as he was, with as sincere devotion to her own misguided faith as he had to his. He was filled with a longing to hold her in his arms again and tell her what he had done for her. He was too intelligent and too much of a realist not to be aware of the problems facing him, yet too sure of himself to doubt his capability to succeed if only Arabella was still steadfast in her avowal of love. This was something he would discover within a few days.

Lady Hesketh was worried about Henrietta who was making a very slow recovery and not regaining her strength. Her face was no longer round and rosy and her brown eyes seemed huge in the pallor of her hollowed cheeks. She said she did not feel well enough to leave her bed and go outside though she would have benefitted from the long summer days of sunshine, and she lay lethargically on top of the counterpane gazing out of the window into the far distance. Arabella and Abigail came to read to her but she showed no interest and they were unable to persuade her into any activity. She did not seem to want to share her thoughts with them and appeared to be a different person to the vivacious and chattersome Henrietta they had known before. It was only William's company she sought because he could talk about Philip. Once she had accepted the tragedy she was filled with a desire to flesh out her remembrance of her husband with every small detail of his life, as if by continually adding to the picture she would keep it constant in her memory. Only William could do that but when she once asked him about Michel Garolais he said he had never heard the name.

Lady Mary was also worried about her husband. Some days he would seem quite well and they would walk together round the lake or sit in the walled garden, often in silence. He never spoke of Naseby, and though worrying tidings of current affairs filtered through to them neither of them felt capable of discussing long-term plans in the present circumstances. They lived from day to day, clinging to their faith and not knowing what the next day might bring. Sir James's speech was improving and he no longer slurred his words unless he was tired, and the use had begun to return to his left arm though he still limped badly. But just when there seemed to be a marked improvement in his condition he would relapse into a state worse than when he had first come home. He would either withdraw into a world of his own where he could remember very little and was confused about what was going on around him, or he would be apoplectic with anger over some triviality and obviously in pain. Lady Mary knew that such a severe head wound would take time to heal and they could not expect miracles, but she became increasingly anxious about how much permanent damage had been inflicted to his mind as well as his body.

Arabella was alone in having to keep her worries to herself. She dare not mention John's name and in any case no-one could have helped her with information about his whereabouts. For all she knew he could have died at Naseby and she would be served worse than her sister, for Henrietta had at least known the fulfillment of love if only for a brief space of time. Thoughts of his death tormented her, especially the fact that she would only know if he never kept his promise to return to her. The uncertainty created a silent misery and she forced herself through the days with an outward normality, carrying on conversations and continuing with routine tasks, that belied her inner turmoil.

When Major John Radcliffe rode up to Hesketh Hall it was already late afternoon. He stopped and reined in his horse to survey the vista as he rounded the curve of the driveway and the house came into view. It was certainly a beautiful house - the soft golden stone, the gracefully gabled elevation, the crenellated porch with its striking trefoil rose window, the large mullioned windows overlooking the lake. Flowers were in full bloom in the gardens and beyond the reviving wood the park rolled away to the cultivated fields of the estate. And it could be his. He felt tempted. His ambitions were stirring within him as he realized with a shock of excitement that the property was legitimately in his possession. What a great step for the grandson of a blacksmith, for a boy who had attended Cambridge University as a sizar, having to work for the masters and the richer scholars in return for his tuition. What a place to own and then to leave to his children. For the first time he realized the enticement of property, the lure of land, the greed that made men forgo their principles as many of his own persuasion had done during this war. Did he really care about the Heskeths who had lived a life of privilege for generations whilst others toiled and served them, who practised a faith forbidden by the laws of the country and who were potential traitors. Now because they had made the choice to support the wrong side they found themselves the losers like many other rich Royalists. The victors took the spoils, they always had. What was wrong with him owning the property when he believed that all men were equal.

The dream of possession did not last long. He knew that Hesketh Hall could never be his. He could never live here with Arabella because he knew she would never agree to the dispossession of her family, and he had no wish to live anywhere without her. But overriding all considerations was the certainty that his own sense of honour would never allow him to defraud the rightful owners of their title even though he dreamed of a land where all men had equal rights. His lease was a gift for Arabella, a safeguard for the family to which she belonged and, if the worst came to the worst, a bargaining counter for their marriage.

He rode up to the front entrance, nerves taut with expectation, and it was Abigail, returning from calling Timothy who had been catching fish in the lake, who saw him as he was tying his horse to the post and divesting himself of his sword which he laid trustingly across his saddle bag. Her heart leapt involuntarily and she was filled with joy at the realization that he was still alive and perhaps wanted to see her. "John, what are you doing here?" she cried, hope fluttering at the edges of her mind. "I'm so glad to see you safe after the battle."

He took her hand briefly but said, "I haven't time to explain at the moment Abigail, perhaps we can talk later," and her hopes began to subside. They were finally put to rest when he continued, "Can you ask Arabella to see me?" She suddenly remembered what William had said and a look of perplexity crossed her face, but she went away into the house to do his bidding.

It was William however who appeared on the steps and said in a harsh voice that managed to sound both belligerent and contemptuous, "Well what do you want here? How many of you are there this time?"

"I am alone," said John calmly, but William looked as if he did not believe him even though he was unarmed, clad in a black wool doublet without a sash and wearing a hat instead of a helmet. It was the first time they had met since William's capture and they stood assessing each other, wary and uncompromising, remembering their last encounter. William was flamboyantly attired in a scarlet doublet slashed with silver, grey silk breeches with lace foaming over his soft calf boots and blond lovelocks curling on his shoulders, but John now knew from experience that he was more than the dandy he appeared. "I wish to see Arabella," he said steadily.

"And why should you wish to see my sister? I cannot suppose she has any business with you." The tone was haughtily dismissive.

"My business with your sister is of a personal nature and, with respect, is no concern of yours."

William's anger rose as he recollected his previous suspicions. "Anything that concerns my sister concerns us all and we have no business with Roundheads or indeed with anyone of your ilk."

Arabella appeared behind him then, and coming into the glare of the sunshine from the dimness of the hall she looked as if she could not believe her eyes. Her first incredulity was transformed into a smile of welcome. Her eyes and every tiny muscle in her face spoke all that was in her heart and with a surging joy John knew that her love held strong. He smiled back at her, taking in every long-imagined detail while William looked from one to the other in disbelief. Had she been expecting him? Her rose satin gown and the pink ribbons in her low cleavage and round her knot of curls all demonstrated that she had prepared to meet her lover. A cold fury overwhelmed him. The Roundheads had killed his best friend, wounded his father, robbed his sister of her husband and child, wantonly destroyed his home. The personal tragedies, not national calamities, were lacerating him now. And Arabella was smiling at a Roundhead officer with the smile of a lover. He turned a look of hatred upon his sister but it was to John he spoke. "I suggest you leave immediately before I drive you out at the point of my sword."

John ignored him and kept his eyes fixed on Arabella. "Can we talk somewhere?"

"We can go into the rose garden," she replied. Then turning to her brother added calmly, "You have no right to behave so badly, William, before any guest of mine."

William could not believe his ears. "Your guest!" he roared. "You dare invite a Roundhead here after everything that has happened." He could not take in what was going on. What had happened at home during the occupation of the house?

John turned his attention back to him saying, "I am unarmed and I do not intend to abduct her. I will return her to the house when we have talked and I shall leave in my own good time."

Though burning with anger William realized he was powerless to do anything. If he tried to hold either of them back by physical means he would only look foolish and if it came to brute force he suspected the captain would be the stronger. He was forced to watch in impotent fury as they left the house together.

Once in the privacy of the walled garden they were in each other's arms and all the fears and longings of their separation were released in wild abandon. John was kissing her with a passion she had only read about, kissing her lips, her eyes, her neck, the top of her breasts where they peeped from her gown. His kisses on her mouth stopped her breath and he was tugging at her hair so that the little knot of curls she had so carefully tied tumbled down in disarray round her face. Her initial desire turned to fear at his unbridled ardour, then she found herself responding with a fervour equal to his.

"William might see us," she said at last, drawing away from him trembling. But he pulled her to him again and she felt her body dissolving and melting away like water. At last he forced himself to stop, knowing his desire was getting out of control. He led her to the stone bench in the alcove of honeysuckle and clematis and held her tightly in his arms while she lay passive with her eyes closed.

"I love you Arabella. I cannot exist without you. I want you to be part of my life but I have so little to offer you compared to all this," his gesture took in the expanse of the Hall and everything that belonged with it.

Arabella raised her head from where she leant against his shoulder and taking his tanned face between her small white hands she looked directly into his eyes as she said, "Whatever you have is sufficient for me." They had reached a stage beyond passion and they remained motionless, speaking only through their eyes, the windows of the soul.

At last John said, "I have an honourable profession and three fields of my own in Huntingdon where we could build a house. I must go on one more campaign because I have pledged my word but after that the war should be over. Will you then come home to Huntingdon with me as my wife? I cannot offer you as much as you will leave but I promise you I will love you more than any other man ever could."

Arabella's thoughts were far away from the huge divisions of class and religion between them and her family's certain resistance, as in that enchanted moment she nestled in the comfort of his body, the scent of the roses fragrant in the balmy air and the bees buzzing gently in the honeysuckle. "I will come with you anywhere you ask of me," she said, as if in a dream from which she did not want to awake.

John then told her about the house, about the new measures against Catholics and the reasons for acting as he had. "I give you my word of honour I will never take up my rights," he promised. "It was a way of protecting you. I promised to do so and it was the only way I could think of. Your family would have lost everything otherwise." Arabella understood what he told her because she remembered hearing her parents talking about such a possibility the night before her father left for Oxford. "When times are safe for you all again I will relinquish my title to the lease and everything will be as it was before," he promised earnestly, though he doubted within himself that times would ever be as they were before. But Arabella believed him because she loved and trusted him. She was moved beyond measure though she could never be fully aware of the sacrifices he had been forced to make, both in acquiring it and relinquishing it. "It is also to be used in the last resort as a deal whereby your family must consent to our marriage," John added unashamedly, a steely glint in his eyes.

"I think it best if we only tell William at the moment," Arabella said thoughtfully. "Our life is troubled enough just now." She related to him how her father had been badly wounded at Naseby and her sister's husband killed and John was shocked by the news of the latest tragedy to touch her life, thinking for a moment of the young girl he had taken from Oxford and who was now a widow. He privately considered William to be the least likely member of the Hesketh family to understand the situation and would have preferred to deal with Sir James.

"Today is not one of my father's good days," Arabella said, seeing his hesitancy. "William and I can explain to our parents later, at a time we think favourable."

"Very well," he acquiesced, "but they must be aware of the situation soon in case the Commissioners of Parliament come to take stock. I tried to do better for you and prevent confiscation but all I was able to manage was a permanent lease without charge, in my name of course for the time being."

"You have done a lot for us," she said warmly. "I'm sure my family must be grateful once they understand all the circumstances."

John himself was less sure than Arabella, for meeting William again had confirmed the depth of the animosity between them, and he well remembered Lady Hesketh's repudiation of him though he acknowledged that this was not without cause. Being back at Hesketh Hall had made him realize the dangers inherent in the transaction. However he was secure in his love and determined that no-one should deny them.

They returned to the Hall and Arabella called William into the small parlour at the back of the house where they would be unlikely to be disturbed. When William entered his face was full of bitter resentment and as Arabella explained that John had something of import to tell him he was immediately on the defensive. However what John said was totally unexpected as he outlined the situation in the same words he had used to Arabella.

William stood shocked and incredulous then he gave a mocking bitter laugh. "Do you expect me to believe that?" he cried, his face a mask of hatred and his eyes blazing with fury. "You have wanted this house ever since you first came here. You once admitted as much to me. 'Times are changing,' you said. All you ever wanted out of this war was our lands, you and all your kind."

"I have no designs on your property as I have explained to you," John said levelly. "I have three fields in Huntingdon, bought by my father as a free man. They are my own and quite sufficient for me. My profession is a lawyer and I have no wish to be a landowner."

"Yes a lawyer who knows all the tricks to swindle, an apt profession for you," William retorted sarcastically.

John ignored the insult and continued calmly, "All I have done is to protect your family from losing everything you possess. Can't you understand that your house would have been burnt or slighted, you would have been dispossessed and your lands leased to someone else. Better for me to hold the title than another for I hold it only on trust."

Something in John's face and voice sobered William slightly but only for a moment. "So I must be grateful to you for making me your tenant as I was supposed to be grateful to you for only burning down half of my house," he cried bitterly.

"I'm sorry about that," said John.

"No doubt you are, considering you intended the house for yourself," William sneered.

John felt his anger rising as it had when Cromwell had made the same accusation, though he acknowledged he had given both of them grounds for scepticism. "I do not have, nor ever have had, such pretensions," he said, trying to hold his anger in check. "I am a man of honour and when I give my word I do not break it. The fact that we are on opposite sides in this war should not prevent us from observing common decencies."

"Very **common** decencies. Like imprisoning me in my own home, desecrating our chapel and stealing all our stores," William shouted, for John's words had not made the slightest impression on him. "Do not forget that I have an example of your taking over my house before."

"What happened before was due to the exigencies of war. You are a soldier, you should understand that," said John. "This is a personal matter. I have acted only through love of your sister." This was the first time he had openly confessed his attachment and William eyes narrowed ominously but he continued, "I want to protect her more than anyone, but also her family because she loves you and she is part of you. I shall return the lease back to you immediately it is safe to do so. I shall not break my word."

Arabella stretched out her hand and he took it in his, clasping it tightly as he felt the depth of her trust in him. Seeing them together roused William to a greater pitch of fury and he whirled on his sister. "What kind of a person are you to be enamoured of a low thieving rebel? Must you have every man who looks at you? First Ambrose Hardwicke, then Kit Verney, now a Roundhead captain. You are no better than a whore."

John struck him hard across the face. He reeled back then shouted, "Get outside and we will finish this once and for all. Timothy, fetch two swords," he hollered going to the door.

"No don't," Arabella interposed. "There has been too much killing."

William ignored her, calling again for swords, but John's voice had the tone of a command, "You heard what your sister said."

"Are you a coward too?" mocked William.

"Perhaps. For some things."

A frightened Timothy had brought swords and William threw one of them to John.

Arabella ran between them. "No, don't! For God's sake do not fight over me. I love you both. Please, please do not fight, I do not want one of you to die for me."

John laid the sword on the table. "I will never fight you William Hesketh," he said. "But I tell you this - whether you like it or not I intend to marry Arabella."

"You will never marry my sister. While my father is sick I am master in this house and I will never give my consent."

"You do not own me William. I am of age and my own mistress," said Arabella steadily.

"You are mistaken," her brother replied coldly. "No woman is her own mistress. You are under father's jurisdiction and I stand in lieu of him. I will never allow you to marry a blacksmith's son, a Puritan, and a Roundhead. We Heskeths expect better for ourselves than to mingle our blood with base traitors." He turned then to John. "You will never have Hesketh Hall and you will never have my sister. I will kill you first."

John took a parchment from inside his doublet and threw it on the table. "There is a copy of my title. No-one will harass you again till I return. It is all legal and above board. As a lawyer," he stressed the word, "I have seen to that. Come Arabella, walk a little way with me, it is time I left."

William looked at them both furiously and stormed out of the room.

"You cannot go like this," Arabella murmured, visibly distressed. "Please stay a little longer, you must have something to eat."

"I think you have enough problems," he said ruefully. "And I must rejoin my regiment. The sooner my duties are done, the sooner I can return to you. But perhaps you could ask your parents if I might pay my respects to them before I leave."

Going first into the kitchen to command a parcel of food be prepared, Arabella then climbed the stairs to her mother's chamber. She informed her only that the captain had made a courtesy call to see if they were well but Lady Mary stubbornly refused to have any communication with the Roundhead officer.

Whilst John was waiting for a reply he noticed Abigail standing in the doorway where the back passageway adjoined the small parlour, almost hidden in her dark clothes. She had obviously heard much of what had transpired because William had made no effort to lower his voice, and she was pale and trembling for she had been shocked by much of what she had heard. Their eyes met. She saw the remorse in his and he saw the hurt in hers. He went across to her. "I'm sorry Abigail," he said, taking her hand. He had once said they were two of a kind. "It is a pity it could not have worked out differently."

"Yes it is a pity," she said, realizing that his gaze still had power to catch at her heart. "But I wish you well." The Heskeths had always had what they wanted. Abigail had always been used to having very little. She tried not to cry and on hearing Arabella approach she fled.

Arabella was distressed to inform John that her mother refused to meet him and putting the linen-wrapped portion of food into his hand she walked with him out of the house. Abigail could not help herself from following them at a distance, standing in the hall as John collected his horse and they walked along the driveway together. It was there that William found her. Still trembling with shock and hurt after the revelation about John and Arabella, some of her hurt had been caused by William. She faced him steadily and said, "I do not know if you are aware of this but John Radcliffe and I are distant kin. I heard what you said just now, that we are low and base and that the Heskeths do not mix with such. I had begun to believe you cared for me but I can see now how you denigrate me. Whatever feelings you have for me they are not of equality nor of respect. I am glad you have given me the opportunity to see your true opinion before it is too late." In her unhappiness and humiliation she was tempted to tell him that she and John had been lovers for she wanted to hurt him, but that would also mean hurting Arabella which she could not do. So she kept her peace and went to her chamber.

He let her go but continued staring after her in bitter resentment. She had looked so beautiful as she had faced him, tall and dignified, her low voice calm but her green eyes accusing. God damn him, he had destroyed all the recent advances he had made. He felt a surge of anger against himself and his unbridled tongue, against John Radcliffe who had been the cause of it all and, irrationally, against Abigail who had withdrawn herself from him again.

Upstairs in her chamber Abigail wept freely now, but for whom or what she was uncertain. Was it for John whom she had irrevocably lost. It had been a great shock to discover his relationship with Arabella. Was it for William whose professed regard she had begun to welcome and now knew herself to be nothing more than a menial servant. Or was it for herself who had been deceived by both of them.

As the sun began to dip towards the horizon Arabella accompanied John to the end of the driveway with her arm linked in his while he walked the horse.

"Are you sure everything will be well? I hate to leave you with the anger of your family," he said in deep concern, turning her towards him as the moment of parting arrived.

"Have no fear. William's heart is not so cruel as his tongue, he always speaks before he thinks. I will talk to mother and father as soon as I can and I am sure they will understand everything is for the best when it is explained to them fully."

John wished he could share her confidence and at that moment a shaft of fear pierced his heart. "You will come back to Huntingdon with me as my wife? You will not let anyone dissuade you when I am gone?"

"Nothing will dissuade me. I will come with you as soon as you return for me."

"You will leave all this for me?" he said, looking around at the park bathed in the lengthening rays of the summer sun and the house glowing with a soft radiance.

"More than anything else I have wanted to be loved. Not to be rich or important but to be loved. For many girls in my position it is not a viable option and I always dreaded a marriage with a man who might give me all worldly possessions but did not love me. I know you love me with a love I never dreamt I should find, and I love you with a love I never thought I would experience. Just being with you will make my life complete."

Her voice and her eyes dispelled any doubts and he felt humbled by her certainty. "We will start a new life together, a life that will fulfill our dreams. I will build you a new house on my three fields."

"With roses all around the house to remind us of the rose garden where we first promised to marry."

They clung together one last time, repeating their promises and their love. Then John turned his horse along the road to rejoin the New Model Army, and Arabella returned to the house to fight a battle of her own.

CHAPTER 11

JULY - AUGUST 1645

As June gave way to July William decided that he could stay at home no longer. After the trauma of Naseby, the distress of his father's condition, and the shock of Philip's death, Hesketh Hall had seemed the right place to be. But after a time he had largely recovered his spirits. He was not given to introspection and his natural optimism had soon revived, quickened by the fine summer weather and the unaccustomed comforts home provided. He was already beginning to chafe at the restrictions of being at the beck and call of his father and Henrietta when John Radcliffe had made his unexpected appearance. The devastating information, Arabella's betrayal, and Abigail's rejection of him all combined to make a longer stay intolerable. He would have to go and find Prince Rupert again. The situation became even more fraught when Arabella at last found the courage to tell her parents about the lease John had negotiated. She explained carefully that it was a stratagem to keep them safe for the moment and she had been able to argue the case fervently and eloquently though without fully revealing his reasons. Their father had seemed very confused and not able to take it in, repeating his bewilderment over and over again to a frustrated William. Their mother could see no further immediate danger and was therefore amazed and horrified, railing constantly at the Roundhead's perfidy but never suspecting that he might have any more personal motives than acquiring the property for himself. Henrietta was suspicious that something more lay behind the transaction, especially with Arabella's calm acceptance. She was sure that there was some serious involvement between her sister and the Roundhead, suspicions fuelled by Arabella's evasions when questioned. She remembered the strange circumstances of her escape from the siege of Oxford and surmised that her rescuer must have been this same Roundhead captain. She was hurt by her sister's refusal to confide in her and the lack of trust placed in her understanding, and shared much of William's bitterness, although even her usually candid brother was not being open with her.

For once William did not want to share his thoughts with anyone, at least anyone at home, for they were too confused, too angry and too bloody. He had not spoken a word to Arabella since his altercation with John and had refused all her overtures of friendship. He had also kept away from Abigail, fuelling his resentment against her in order to modify his feelings of regret and self-reproach, uncomfortable emotions for him because they were so unfamiliar. He could have unburdened himself easily to Philip but Philip was no more. But there was still Rupert. He rode down to Felton to buy a news sheet and found that the latest news was not all bad for the Royalists. The Marquis of Montrose was victoriously carving a path through Scotland and marching to their aid, there were many garrisons and fortresses preparing to re-muster their strength, and the King and Prince Rupert were recruiting in Wales with a view to crossing the Severn and marching to the defence of the south-west. He decided to make his way down there.

However his mother was horrified when he informed her of his intentions. "You cannot mean that you are going to fight again," she said aghast. "Haven't we done enough? You have been lucky so far but to carry on now is tempting fate. Look at your father. If anything should happen to you who will carry on the estate?"

"What estate?" he asked bitterly, and she turned her head away. It was difficult to remember that the property was no longer their own.

Everybody was filled with foreboding when he left to renew his allegiance to the Royalist cause but he noted with sorrow that Abigail was absent at his departure. He was not aware that she had asked Lady Hesketh for permission to leave their service. As William rode away he had no clear idea of where he was going. He had discovered that the King's armies had been re-grouping on the Welsh bank of the River Severn with the intention of crossing into the south-west peninsula where George Goring was holding out with his army. However he was in ignorance of whether they had actually done so. Rupert himself was supposed to be making for Bristol where he was governor, and because the city was of crucial strategic importance it was vital to keep it in Royalist hands. William decided he would go to Bristol in the hope of rejoining the Prince there. As he rode westwards he had leisure to think and for much of the time he thought about John Radcliffe. With the prospect of positive action again to rouse him, and with as much reflection as his generally uncontemplative nature could summon up, his white-hot anger had begun to evaporate. He began to unwillingly acknowledge that he might have misjudged the captain's motives, though that did not in any way lessen his determination to prevent any liaison between him and Arabella. He did not understand why he should feel so different about his sister's attraction to John Radcliffe and his own desire for Abigail, but reason was not one of William's strong points and his impulses and emotions generally determined his actions. Thinking of the tangle of relationships into which they had been drawn he suddenly recalled that Kit Verney's estate was near Bristol and a visit there might not go amiss. He hungered for Philip's company and realized afresh how much he missed his friend. They had shared so many experiences since the beginning of the war and William had never considered death might come to either of them, even though they had been in danger many times, because they were young and full of life and good fortune. He found it hard to believe that they would never again talk together, never ride together in the Royalist cavalry. The renewal of acquaintance with Kit Verney was a welcome thought and not bothering to reflect that something else might lie beneath the sudden impulse he swung his horse in a more westerly direction. Because the countryside was in a state of disruption with bands of marauders and deserters from both sides terrorizing villages that had already been plundered bare, he did not wear his identifying crimson sash and kept clear of towns as much as he could. But the country people were unwilling to trust any strangers, and doors were immediately shut on sight of such. At an inn he fell in with a small group of Royalist soldiers who said they were going to join the King but after riding with them for a time he suspected they were deserters and made an excuse to be rid of them, fearing for his safety if he had continued in their company. As he rode into the village of Compton Leyton he asked the whereabouts of Leyton Court and on learning that it was less than three miles distant he made his way to see Kit Verney.

He came upon the house unexpectedly as its tall chimneys suddenly appeared behind a high stone wall and he was faced by a crenellated gateway. As he passed through into a paved courtyard the house soared up in front of him, larger and taller than Hesketh Hall with four symmetrical gables of golden stone. It was a relatively new house as demonstrated by the preponderence of glass, the dominating feature of the façade being a huge mullioned window which soared aloft through two storeys, yet there was evidence of an original older building in the gatehouse and the outlying barns. On either side of the high walls of the courtyard were doors obviously leading to gardens, while behind the house rose a wooded hillside. As William gazed appreciatively at the fine building he considered it would be a suitable residence for Arabella, and now that Kit was a widower he decided to persuade him to renew his courtship of his sister for surely she would be tempted by such an elegant estate.

The house seemed deserted however and he was beginning to feel disappointed at his fruitless visit when a boy suddenly appeared from the direction of the stables to take his horse, followed by a solitary maidservant who admitted him into the house and retired to find her master. William was relieved to find Kit at home even if the house seemed unnaturally empty. While he was waiting he admired the finely proportioned hall with its elegant curving staircase, black and white tiled floor, and walls of pale blue plasterwork decorated with gilt ovals and lozenges into which doors where set symmetrically on all sides. From one of the doors Kit entered, surprised and pleased to see William. William was conscious of his travel-stained clothing as Kit clasped his hand warmly for his host was elegantly attired in a suit of kingfisher blue satin with collar and cuffs of impeccable white lace, white silk stockings and fashionable shoes with silver rosettes on the narrowly squared toes. Kit immediately called for refreshment though it was obvious he had already been drinking, then led his unexpected guest into the large drawing room dominated by the striking oriel window that William had seen from outside, reaching from floor to ceiling in a vast expanse of forty leaded panes. The floor was composed of marble tiles like the hallway and the walls were of pale rose-coloured plaster with a matching ceiling in an intricately worked pattern of flowers and fruit. Against one wall stood a magnificent white marble fireplace, supported by twisted columns of white and gold and surmounted by sculptured cherubs entwining golden pomegranates around a classical relief of two lovers in a sylvan scene. The furniture was largely of delicately carved walnut and rosewood, lighter and more elegant than the solid oak of Hesketh Hall, with caneback chairs upholstered in rose damask and green velvet. The effect was of wealth and elegance in comparison with which Hesketh Hall, with all its comfort, seemed old-fashioned, and William silently resolved to make changes there when time and money afforded, choosing to forget that his home was not at this moment in his hands. However the wine in a plain glass decanter was brought to him by the same maidservant who had admitted him into the house.

When they were drinking amiably together William explained that he was on his way to Bristol, though unsure as to whether Rupert had yet arrived there, and when Kit invited him to stay for a few days he accepted the invitation eagerly. But as they talked and exchanged news of Naseby and its aftermath, William began to deduce the situation.

"Things are very bad here in the West Country," said Kit. He told him how Goring had been trying to recapture Taunton but General Fairfax had come to its relief and he was forced to abandon the attempt. "I have already shipped out most of the possessions still belonging to me, few though they be after donating many of my family's valuables to the King's cause. They are in the custody of a friend in France, an advantage of living near a port." From his tone of voice William deduced it was a lady friend. "This is the only room still fully furnished," he said with a sardonic smile. "I will show you around my empty house later."

William was taken by surprise, even knowing Kit's cynicism. "Do you think all is lost then?" he asked.

"We can survive if we can hold Bridgewater and Bristol," Kit replied. "As long as these remain in our hands it will be possible to retake the south-west when the King has got an army together again and can move across the Severn."

They sat deep in thought while the light from the great window began to dim and the same girl brought a taper to light the lone candlestick on the long table in the embrasure. They had continued drinking and Kit had called several times for more wine. William then told him about John Radcliffe and related to him the full history. "Arabella is infatuated with the Roundhead. He seems to have some power over her that I cannot fathom." Then abandoning all attempts at tactful persuasion he said bluntly, "If you want my sister you will have to do something quickly."

Kit nonetheless recognized the appeal in the young man's voice, and with the stem of the wineglass turning in his elegant fingers he replied slowly, "I am afraid that I shall have nothing to offer your sister if the Roundheads get any closer. And I cannot go to visit her because I dare not leave the house at this time. That is the reason I am not fighting again. Though as you see I shall be ill equipped to defend it if things come to such a pass. Most of my servants have already gone, rats deserting a sinking ship. You must have noticed we are exceptionally short on labour." For a moment his thoughts drifted back to when Elizabeth was alive and the house, her domain for practically the whole of her sickly life, had been extravagantly and efficiently serviced. He also thought of how he had once dreamt of bringing Arabella Hesketh here, of displaying her in this beautiful setting and making his establishment a byword for fashion and elegant society. Now the truth was that he had more pressing problems on his mind than Arabella.

William continued to stay with Kit and when not drinking they attempted to clarify plans for a resuscitation of Royalist fortunes should the situation improve. Then a few days later they heard news of a battle at Langport where Lord Goring's army had suffered a crushing defeat at the hands of Fairfax and the New Model Army. The following day they learnt that the Roundheads had moved on to Bridgewater and put it under siege. The future was looking increasingly grim in the south-west. Kit and William waited for the outcome, riding out each day in the blistering heat which withered and parched what was left of the crops, as unrelenting in its ferocity as the winter snows and frosts had been. After a week of uncertainty when their expectations fluctuated between hope and despondency, the news proclaimed the worst - Bridgewater had fallen to Parliament.

"Can you fortify your house to withstand an attack?" asked William but his host shook his head.

"Neither the position nor the building is conducive to defence. Too much glass. It was built in a time of peace when the thought of war in England was inconceivable," he said sardonically. "Neither do I have the manpower. You and I could not undertake it alone." He paused, then looking into the younger man's grey eyes, which reminded him so much of Arabella, he said, "I am going to make for France. I have no family and some of my wealth is safe there as I told you. I do not really fancy an exile's life but I have no intention of becoming either a prisoner or a debtor to Parliament."

William understood that Kit Verney, together with many other active Royalists, was not choosing the easy alternative. He had decided to leave behind his country, his estate and his patrimony rather than submit to a regime with which he did not agree and against which he had fought long. William admired him for it, knowing he could never do the same. The life of an exile in another country where he would have to learn a foreign tongue, submit to foreign customs and live on the forebearance of others, was a prospect intolerable to him. When he had first seen Kit and noticed his flirtation with Arabella he had dismissed him as a totally improper suitor for his sister. Now he would have welcomed him with open arms. But it was not to be, and he witnessed the end of yet another hope.

As if guessing his thoughts Kit said, "I could never ask Arabella to share an exile's life with me. I had hoped to give her more than that." He thought wryly of his "friend" in Paris and saw in his imagination a succession of such women, eager when they believed he could offer them something then moving on when his purse began to empty, a decline of interest matched by his own dwindling passion as familiarity quenched the flames of his lust. He believed that he had really loved Arabella for a time and had lived briefly with the hope that her innocence and her artlessness would have made a new man of him. But cynicism was too ingrained in his nature not to suspect that it could have been otherwise, and there was no spare emotion to waste on regrets that were now superfluous. "What will you do?" he asked William.

Now that Bridgewater had fallen there was no doubt that hopes of holding the south-west had diminished. Apparently the King had a new scheme, for he was always susceptible to impractical solutions. He had decided to accept an offer from the gentlemen of Yorkshire who were promising to raise another army for him if he would bring his cavalry to their support. He had not relinquished hopes of rallying the north again and joining up with the Scots under the Marquis of Montrose so he turned in that direction once more. Rupert's cavalry were to be left to hold Bristol, because so long as the great port and second city of the kingdom remained in Royalist hands it would be possible to disembark the expected troops promised from Ireland and France. William decided he would keep to his original plan of rejoining Prince Rupert. He therefore bade an emotional farewell to Kit Verney, both of them realizing they would probably never meet again. Then he set his horse in the direction of Bristol. If the Prince had been told to hold the city at all costs then it would be a last-ditch stand and William had decided to stand with him, no matter what price he had to pay. He had an uncomfortable foreboding that the reckoning would be high.

Henrietta began to feel better as the month of July progressed and the weather continued hot and sunny and almost a month after Philip's death she left her bed unsteadily and came downstairs to greet the Hardwickes who had come to pay a call on the two invalids. They were shocked at how pale and thin the previously plump and rosy Henrietta looked and her mother's brown taffeta gown hung loosely on her. "I shall have to take in all your clothes," Abigail had said that morning, though Henrietta had no wish to wear all her brightly coloured gowns. But the Hardwickes were even more shocked by the change in Sir James. His hair had been tidied up to cover the unevenness but it was impossible to disguise the bald patches now his bandages had been removed, and his once handsome face was haggard and grey as he limped forwards to greet them. Lady Hesketh was her usual gracious self and behaved as if everything was quite normal, unobtrusively giving her arm to her husband or helping him to a chair, but Mistress Hardwicke found the sight too distressing for a long visit. However before they left she suggested that Henrietta might care to spend some time with them to aid her recovery.

"The change of scene will do you good," she said. "It is surprising how a new environment can help lift the spirits and we can feed you well and build you up again. I have an excellent physician who has taken good care of Ambrose and to whom I am indebted for my own mastery of my delicate constitution."

Lady Hesketh's brows arched eloquently. But Henrietta thought it might not be a bad idea to go away from Hesketh Hall for a time. There were too many memories here - her first meeting with Philip, his declaration of love, their marriage and their wedding night. Also she felt rejected by Arabella and hurt by her secrecy and mistrust. She was satisfied to take up the Hardwickes' offer of hospitality for a time whilst Joanna was happy in the knowledge that she had done her duty to the unfortunate Heskeths, considering that Lady Mary was occupied enough with caring for one invalid in their straitened circumstances. She imagined how she could display the tragic Henrietta to her friends and neighbours while at the same time demonstrating her own compassion and generosity.

Just before their departure Ambrose contrived to be alone with Arabella. She was very tempted to be perfectly honest with him for the first time and tell him about John Radcliffe as he once again declared his sympathy and his love for her. Yet a reluctance to hurt him held her back, as well as the fact that she had not yet confessed the situation to her parents and her sister. She could not see what was to be gained by revealing her secret at the moment. When John returned they would face everyone together. However with the departure of both William and Henrietta she was lonely and longed for John to come back so that she could put an end to the subterfuge. She wondered where he was and what he was doing and persuaded Abigail to walk into Felton to see if they could buy a newsletter, eager not only for news of the Royalists but for the Roundheads also because this might give some indications of John's whereabouts.

The matter was still also of some concern to Abigail. She could not entirely dismiss John from her affections even though she had now given up all hope of claiming his love and she sometimes relived the solitary hour of passion she had known with him. She felt ill at ease with Arabella as she pretended to be ignorant of her secret, envious of her happiness whilst concealing her own sadness. At least Arabella was ignorant of the secrets in Abigail's heart but this in itself proved a burden. Had circumstances been different she might have had a friend with whom to share her troubles. The strains imposed upon her lately by the behaviour of both John and William had made her feel that further residence at Hesketh Hall was impossible and just before William's departure she had made the momentous decision to ask her mistress for permission to quit their service.

Lady Hesketh, who was already worried and distressed by present developments, had been astonished by her maid's request. "You have been with us so long,

Abigail, do you really think our fortunes so irretrievably lost that you wish to leave us now," she said sorrowfully.

"Oh no my lady, it is for no reason so dishonourable," cried Abigail in agitation, aghast that her mistress should suspect her of such selfish motives. "I do not think your fortunes are lost, nor would I leave you for such a reason when you have always shown me kindness. There are personal reasons, my aunt is not so young as she was and might have need of me, and," she paused, twisting her fingers together nervously, "there is the matter of Captain Radcliffe who as I told you is of some distant kinship to me. Besides Arabella and Henrietta do not need me any more."

"You are mistaken Abigail, we all have so much need of you," said Lady Mary, surprised by a sudden realization of how much she would miss the gentle industrious girl who had been in their family so long. "Please do not leave us yet. I know I have always said that you may go when you wish, but stay a little longer while Sir James is sick and Henrietta is so fond of you."

Abigail was not able to resist the appeal in her mistress's troubled brown eyes, a strand of chestnut hair escaping uncharacteristically from her carefully arranged coiffure as she paced her parlour in disquiet. Yet resistance was not difficult for the simple reason that deep in her heart she did not want to go. She looked through the window to the knot garden and the fields beyond and thought how much she loved this place which, rightly or wrongly, she considered her home. "Very well my lady, I will stay a little longer while you have need of me," she said and to her astonishment was rewarded by a warm embrace from her mistress. She would have to forget all past associations with John Radcliffe and learn to ignore William Hesketh as she used to do.

However it was not proving easy, she reflected again, as she and Arabella leafed through the news sheets trying to ascertain real facts from the rumours and obviously partisan propaganda. On sale together with the news sheets was a publication of the King's private correspondence captured from his baggage at Naseby and which the Parliament had now printed for all Englishmen to read. They required all men to be aware of how the King stated that he did not consider Parliament a lawful institution, that he was negotiating for an army of Irish Catholics to invade the country, and that he was going to abolish all restrictions against Catholics in England. Arabella did not buy the pamphlet but the headlines were enough to convince her that much animosity against the King, and against Catholics, would be stirred up in the minds of ordinary people by these provocative revelations.

It was during the mid-day dinner on the following day that her forebodings were justified. She was seated with her parents at the long oak table in the dining room, which now seemed far too large for just the three of them, when she became aware of a strange humming sound, as if a swarm of bees had invaded the house. Lady Mary put down the spoonful of strawberries and looked at Arabella in perplexity, whilst Alleyn paused in the act of refilling Sir James's wine cup though he himself had noticed nothing and continued eating. The noise increased in volume so Arabella ran to the window from where she could see a crowd of people approaching the Hall, not orderly along the driveway but overspreading the grass in their haste. She looked in bewildered alarm at her mother who had quickly followed her and was instinctively fingering the gold crucifix around her neck. Alleyn helped Sir James to his feet and they all went outside, accompanied by Abigail who had been waiting on them. Other servants who had been roused by the commotion were peeping surreptitiously whilst not daring to leave their tasks. In the glare of the mid-day sun they could see that the crowd was composed mainly of men from the town, swollen by some strangers, all red faced and sweating in the heat. They were led at the front by a belligerent Adam Ashe and Wat Dacre and the most alarming aspect was that the men were carrying sticks and wooden staves and were obviously in an angry mood.

Sir James limped forward to meet them and asked severely, "What is the meaning of this intrusion?"

"We want no Catholic house in Felton," Adam Ashe said threateningly. "Traitors to the State and collaborators with Irish papists to overthrow the lawful government of this land."

The Heskeths could not believe they were hearing this accusation from local people who had often been recipients of their generosity and hospitality. But there was loud and concerted agreement from the mob and Sir James had to shout to make himself heard above the uproar.

"I am no traitor. My care has always been to preserve lawful rule in this land and protect it from rebels and malefactors. How dare you disturb our peace in this manner. Get you gone!" He shook his cane at them peremptorily, his face suffused with anger against the white lace of his collar.

The men made no attempt to move and Wat Dacre brandished a sheaf of papers as he cried, "The King's letters are printed clear for all men to read. We have proof that he was treating with foreign papists to make war on all true Englishmen."

Arabella wondered privately how many of them could read and who had stirred them up to this agitation but Sir James was too angry for rational thought. "There is no truer Englishman than I," he rapped out furiously but he was shouted down.

"All papists are traitors," cried Adam Ashe, and Wat Dacre echoed him. "We will not stand by while you plot to massacre us. We have come to put an end to this den of heresy and treason."

There was loud assent and Lady Hesketh thought sickeningly of the last time she had heard such words and sentiments and of the dreadful consequences that had ensued. She moved swiftly to her husband's side. In the old days before his injury Sir James would have reasoned with them, listened to their grievances and explained how he had always tried to help them and seek their welfare as a landowner and Justice of the Peace. But now all he could do was to answer anger with the like and he began to berate them with uncontrollable fury. This roused the crowd to a greater pitch of hysteria and they began to take out tinder boxes and light their staves. Sir James was shouting for someone to bring his pistols and Lady Mary heard herself screaming in a high-pitched voice she did not recognize as her own as she saw her beloved house on the point of being fired for the second time in a few weeks, and a troubled Abigail went to her side. Arabella was also trembling with an ever-growing fear but she realized she must find John's document with his deed of possession clearly authenticated and dashed into the house, scattering the wide-eyed servant girls standing agape in her path.

The crowd began to converge menacingly on the entrance, now excited beyond reason. They pushed aside Sir James and Lady Hesketh and moved forward in a mass of heaving bodies, burly bodies, thin bodies, reeking bodies with their sweat-soaked shirts and their faces red with anger and heat, their lighted brands making them hotter still.

Suddenly horses' hooves were heard pounding on the bone-dry ground and three riders came galloping up the driveway at high speed and throwing up clouds of dust. They cut through the assembled affray, scattering them with little regard, and rode straight to the front of the house where Sir James and Lady Hesketh, with Abigail beside her, had retreated onto the steps. The crowd fell back a little as they recognized Parliamentary commissioners in their sombre clothing with plain collars and wide brimmed hats.

"What is the meaning of this riotous disorder?" demanded the senior of the three, ignoring the Heskeths and addressing the mob from his horse.

"We are obeying the commands of Parliament," smirked Wat Dacre in the tone of one expecting praise for service rendered. "This is a Papist house."

"You are under a misapprehension," retorted the commissioner coldly, surveying him dispassionately. "This estate belongs to Parliament and the house is the property of a supporter of Parliament who has done good service for the likes of you. I suggest that before you take the law into your own hands you acquaint yourself with the facts. Extinguish those brands immediately and get you gone!"

The crowd looked thunderstruck and were slow to obey his commands whereupon the youngest man rapped, "Do you wish me to take your names for breakers of the peace and contravenors of the laws of this land?"

The threat was enough. The brands were extinguished and the rioters began to disperse. Lady Hesketh clung to her husband in weak relief though he looked completely bemused by this new development.

"Do not come near this property again!" was the final order of the commissioners, and the mob succumbed to authority and made their way home, chastened at their default of information yet not daring to doubt what they had been told. The silent one of the three followed them on his horse until they were clear of the property, ensuring that they took no time in the quitting of it. Lady Hesketh could never have believed that she would be glad to see officials of the Parliament. However she refused to speak with them and Arabella, returning with John's document, placed her in the care of Abigail who led her into the house, still trembling with shock.

Arabella knew that she must be beside her father while he talked to the commissioners and this he did angrily and unco-operatively, still confused by the assertions of the townsmen and unappreciative of their timely rescue. The Parliamentarians were well accustomed to such situations and expected no less. Once they had satisfied themselves that the Heskeths, in the person of Arabella, understood the procedure of confiscation and their position in law they made a lengthy examination of the estate and a valuation of the tenure.

"It is only a temporary measure to safeguard us," Arabella assured her father. "We will get everything back in time." She had kept close by his side until the commissioners had finished their business but he had understood little. His rage had now subsided into a lethargy of pain and weariness and he sank into his favourite leather-backed chair in his study as Alleyn came to minister to him.

"Light a fire in the grate Alleyn," he said.

"It is an exceedingly warm evening, sir," his manservant reminded him gently.

"I am cold," insisted Sir James.

Lady Mary came to sit beside him. For the first time she realized the full extent of the danger into which the worsening situation had plunged them and about which the Roundhead captain had warned them. She was forced to acknowledge that if his intentions were sincere and he did keep his word then he had helped them, though the acceptance did not alleviate her bitterness. "Why do all our mishaps take place when William is away," she sighed wearily, leaning her throbbing head against her husband's shoulder and feeling the cool silk of his doublet. Through the window the horrendous day began to fade away in a flamboyant crimson sunset.

As William rode towards Bristol he remembered the two times he had been there previously.

The first time was in the summer of 1643 when Prince Rupert had triumphantly taken the city from the Roundheads, one of the most spectacular feats of the war. The storming of Bristol, second city of England and major port, had been an exhilarating adventure for a young Cavalier on one of his first engagements, and had sealed William's devotion to Prince Rupert who had planned and executed it. William had also found the experience personally satisfying because the Parliamentary governor there had been Nathaniel Fiennes, the son of a landowner not too far distant from the Heskeths. With the intolerant enthusiasm of eighteen years William had heartily disliked him for choosing to support the wrong side and he had been overjoyed to witness Fiennes' humiliation when compelled to surrender the city, even more so when he learnt that the Parliament were threatening to execute him for his failure. William looked back regretfully to those early days when it had never occurred to them that they might be beaten by the untrained and disorganised Roundhead forces. It had all seemed a game then, a wonderful excuse for young Cavaliers to show off their horsemanship and swordplay skills which they had practised since boyhood. He recalled when he and his father first set off to follow the King's standard, well armed and resplendent on fine horses as they rode away to what they thought would be a few weeks' engagement, with his mother and sisters watching them with pride. Now three years later they had experienced loss of life, health, money, possessions, innocence, and hope.

The second time he had been in Bristol had been in the early autumn of last year in the aftermath of the defeat at Marston Moor. Philip had been with them then and the disappointed and frustrated Cavaliers had indulged in an orgy of debauchery that had called forth condemnation even from their own supporters. Rupert had been haunted by a sense of his own responsibilities for the failure of the battle and had sunk into one of his periodic fits of depression, and the dark memories of that time began to cast a long shadow as William rode into the city. He wondered how he would find the Prince now.

As he rode in at the South Gate he was aware of how the atmosphere had subtly changed. There was a noticeable air of resentful apathy in the city that had previously had the lively, noisy, bustling, cosmopolitan aura of a great port with cheerful citizens preoccupied with trade and industry. As he followed the cobbled thoroughfare along the waterfront the cranes and horse-sledges stood idle and people lounged listlessly in front of their silent shops and warehouses. Their stony stares bore into him and he felt their ill-concealed resentment. He had heard that there was plague in the city and the weather was intolerably hot but the general inactivity and the air of sullen animosity was more than that. As his horse slid and clattered up the narrow winding streets to the castle he was increasingly aware of the hostility of the people he encountered, and to his fury he was jeered and even spat upon. The truth was that the people of Bristol knew that their city was about to be fought over once again and, no matter who the victors should be, they themselves would be the losers. It mattered little to most of them whether the Royalists or the Parliament controlled their city for they had experience of both and knew it made no difference. But just now it was the Cavaliers causing their present distress as they were overtaxed to pay for the garrison defending them and now had to support and feed this further influx of soldiers, so it was upon them that they vented their anger.

On reaching the castle William was told that the Prince was up on the walls by the Priors Hill fort so he made his way up there. Rupert was working as hard as any of his lowliest soldiers to build up the defences in this highest and strongest position on the north side of the outer ramparts and William soon made out his tall figure. He was stripped to the waist, his naturally dark skin burnt almost black by the sun, and as he strained and heaved the powerful muscles rippled in his back and arms. "William Hesketh!" he cried joyfully, brushing the sweat from his face beneath the kerchief that tied back his long waving hair and offering him a grimy hand. "By all the saints, I'm glad to see you William. Get your jacket off and give us a hand. Do you know that nothing at all has been done to repair and strengthen the ramparts since we were last here. God's death, I was furious. I have been digging trenches with my own hands."

William could well imagine his anger but was relieved that one of Rupert's black moods was not upon him. Stripping off his own coat and shirt he fell in beside him, experiencing a surge of exhilaration to be back in the Prince's company. It was against Rupert's inclination to stop work for conversation but he invited William to sup with him later that evening.

William joined the Prince and a few of his trusted officers in his headquarters at the castle once it was too dark to continue working on the defences. There he informed him of the death of Philip Halsall and of the misfortunes that had overtaken the Heskeths. Rupert remembered his evening in the comfortable drawing room of the Hall, recollecting Lady Mary with her gold-flecked eyes and chestnut hair glowing in the firelight and reminding him of Mary Richmond, the vivacious irrepressible Henrietta who had reminded him of his youngest sister Sophie, and felt an overwhelming sadness. William saw his face darken and the melancholy hovering behind his brooding eyes. Others noticed it too and retired early, knowing that when the Prince was in a melancholy mood he was better left alone. They knew he was already worried by the poor state of Bristol's defences, by the overt animosity of the citizens who might very well throw in their hand with the Parliament, and by fears that in his absence his enemies in the coterie around the King were blackening his name concerning the defeat at Naseby. Most of all he was worried by the fact that the King seemed to have no awareness of how matters stood and appeared to be living in a dream world of his own, full of wild schemes that bore no relation to reality.

When he was left alone Rupert sat for a long time in silence, carefully going over everything in his mind. Then he went to the table which served as a desk in the small chamber on the second floor of the castle which had once been the constable's lodgings and which now provided his own sparse accommodation. Sitting on the hard wooden bench he lit a candle and then taking up quill and parchment he wrote a letter to his uncle. He asked him to consider making peace, saying that he honestly believed the King "had no way to preserve his posterity, kingdom and nobility but by treaty. I believe it a more prudent way to retain something than to lose all." He thought again, long and hard, before signing it Rupert P, affixing his seal, and sending off immediately by swift courier the letter that was to be his undoing.

Throughout August Rupert and his troops continued to work on strengthening the city's fortifications, building up wall and parapet, digging ditch and trench. It was hot work in the blazing heat but Rupert was indefatigable, working alongside his men at the hardest and most unpleasant jobs. He ordered provisions to be collected from the surrounding countryside and carefully stored, and supervised the making of ammunition, powder and lead shot, the manufacture of which he had an expert's knowledge. Every tower, church, and hill was deployed as a look-out and every weapon confiscated from the unreliable citizens. William renewed his acquaintance with his old companions and there was much jovial fellowship as the small band of a thousand or so Cavaliers drew on long-established ties, strengthened by Rupert's inspiring leadership. The worst hardship was the continuous pealing of bells from the city's many churches as more and more cases of plague proved fatal, until Rupert finally commanded them to be silent, an edict which further enhanced his unpopularity with the citizens who considered a funeral without the tolling of bells to be sacrilegious, though it gained him the gratitude of his own men. The Prince had by now received a reply to the letter he had sent to his uncle. The King wrote that he had no intention of making peace with rebels and traitors and that he would "neither abandon God's cause, injure my successors nor forsake my friends." He was full of new schemes to capture the north, buoyed up by increasingly hopeful news of Montrose's successful army marching from Scotland to aid him.

In the third week of August John Radcliffe found himself also at Bristol, though outside the city walls. Cromwell's cavalry was part of the force of 12,000 men of the New Model Army under General Fairfax who were now massing in preparation for an attack on the city. Bristol must no longer be allowed to remain in the hands of the King because, as well as its overall importance as second city of the kingdom, it linked the Cavalier recruiting grounds of Wales with the south-west and was also the port of entry for the foreign invading armies they were planning to deploy. Although it was always more difficult to take a city from without than to hold it from within, General Fairfax was not expecting too much trouble. It was only a matter of time because their forces were eight times greater than the defending garrison. First however there were formalities to be attended to and Sir Thomas Fairfax sent a polite letter to Prince Rupert asking him to surrender the city. Whilst he waited for a reply they set up camp and the preachers of the New Model Army regaled the soldiers with fiery apocalyptic sermons so that their spirits should not slacken in the lethargy of inactivity.

Inside the city the garrison of fifteen hundred men looked out at the massed forces surrounding them. However Rupert's spirits had risen at the prospect of action, despite the overwhelming odds against them. He was not unduly worried. He had contacted both the King and Lord Goring asking for their help so was daily expecting reinforcements from both the north and the south. He had ample supplies and ammunition and reckoned they were capable of holding out until relief came. So he answered General Fairfax's request for surrender by playing for time, prevaricating that he must first consult with the King. In the stifling heat of August the two sides sat and waited, playing a game of cat and mouse.

CHAPTER 12

SEPTEMBER 1645

August gave way to September but there was no such
surrender of the oppressive heat which lay upon the
thousands of waiting men like a suffocating blanket
under the ominous yellow sky. The New Model Army
remained immobile outside the walls like a beast of prey
waiting to pounce, whilst inside Prince Rupert waited
and watched for his expected reinforcements to no avail.
No-one could understand why they did not come for
Goring was not too far away. Like Philip previously,
William was not enjoying the experience of being
cooped up in a city under siege and often thought of his
friend who had spent his last few weeks inside the
besieged Oxford. Bristol seemed to have shrunk,
crowded in upon itself, with its narrow twisting streets
ever climbing to views of the menacingly immobile
Roundhead army or tumbling down to the silent,
shuttered, plague-ridden tenements by the waterfront.
The waiting seemed endless as the days dragged on,
with every look-out manned by eager-eyed scouts
raking the distance for signs of approaching forces. Still
no reinforcements came. Rupert never slackened in his
intensive preparations and kept his men constantly busy
on the walls and the ordnance. Every day he sent out
small sorties of cavalry to harass the enemy, plaguing

the supply waggons and picking off prime targets with pistol shots. William was constantly volunteering for such raids, his temperament being ill suited to waiting for action, and he found satisfaction in doing something while the element of danger provided a release for nerves strained to breaking point. Though they could inflict little damage and were always beaten back, Rupert knew that the activity kept his own men on their toes and reminded the enemy that they were not dealing with a cowed and frightened pack at bay.

On the other side of the walls John Radcliffe waited. The army of Parliament was not allowed to while away time in pursuits like cards or dice but instead were regaled with sermons or political speeches by the preachers and agitators who had increased in number and daring as the war progressed. Large captive audiences of men were ideal breeding grounds for radical opinions. Sometimes John attended such gatherings, indeed daily sermons were obligatory, for he liked to keep his pulse on the prevalent temper of thought. But he also spent much time reading for he was determined that he should not have forgotten his law studies after such a long period of enforced neglect. He also spent much time thinking and dreaming of Arabella. He was convinced now of the steadfastness of her love and her promise to marry him, despite all the obstacles that stood between them. He imagined her as his wife, caring for her, protecting her, making her lovely delicate body his own. He would dream of his own fields in Huntingdon where the harvest would now be gathered in, poor though it might be under the circumstances. Next year the war should be ended and he would be there himself, with Arabella and perhaps a child on the way, rebuilding a new life for themselves whilst the country returned to peace and prosperity, secure in the preservation of law and true government. But the war needed to be brought to a close before all this could happen and he longed for the action to begin.

As the days wore on General Fairfax's patience wore thin and he got tired of waiting for the Royalists to surrender of their own free will. He had sent several persuasive letters to Rupert, playing on the fact that he himself had fought for the fortunes of Rupert's family in the long wars in Germany and asking the Prince to reconsider his own obligations to the Parliament Protestant cause. But always Rupert refused to surrender the city.

Sir Thomas Fairfax decided at last that he would wait no longer and he would take Bristol by storm. Early in the morning of the tenth of September he summoned his officers to prepare for an assault on the city. John Radcliffe was one of them and knew an overwhelming sense of relief that the waiting was over and the time of reckoning at hand, a sentiment shared by all the men of the New Model Army as their shouts resounded in the stillness of the air to the accompaniment of the first cannon shots as the artillery began their breach of the walls.

Inside the garrison the sound of cannonfire signalled that the waiting was over for them too. As William armed himself with his companions they were all aware that they would have to defend Bristol themselves without any help from anyone, 1,500 of them against 12,000 Roundheads. Their thoughts were sombre but their hearts steadfast. There was no alternative so they must fight their best, even if it proved to be a fight to the last. William thought of home, of his parents, his sisters, Abigail, Philip, and wondered if this would be the last day on earth for him. He thought briefly of all his hopes and dreams and of everything he had wanted to do in his life. Then he buckled on his armour and reached for his sword.

Rupert had always known that he had not the numbers to man the five mile perimeter of the city defences so he placed his cavalry troops in the forts along the walls from which strategic points they would have to do as best they could. However this meant that there were many undefended places where the Roundheads could scale the walls unobstructed and before very long they had gained entrance into the city. They were also actively helped by the citizens whose only interest lay in shortening the conflict and minimizing damage to their own lives and property. William found himself in hand to hand fighting but the Royalists were overwhelmed by sheer weight of numbers. Rupert tried to pull his cavalry back into the safety of the castle, believing that he could hold out from this defensive position until his uncle sent the reinforcements which must surely come to their aid in this extremity. But Oliver Cromwell had realized that this must not be allowed to happen and his own cavalry were already in the streets leading up to the castle, cutting off the Cavaliers and preventing their passage there. For the second time John Radcliffe and William Hesketh came close to encountering each other at swordpoint, but both intent only on hacking down all who stood in their way they passed each other unseeing.

For hours the grim unequal struggle raged as the Royalists fought valiantly with their meagre resources. Then news was brought to Rupert that his garrison at the Priors Hill fort, the largest and most important fort along the defences, had been massacred to a man and he realized there was to be no quarter for any of them. Rupert was not afraid of death. He was a professional soldier and had faced death many times knowing it was an ever-present hazard. But he paused for a moment to survey his small band of men, most of them who had been with him since the beginning of the war, young, loyal and courageous. He could not, would not, sacrifice them heedlessly for the pride of not giving in when all was certainly lost. He would surrender. He sent a message to Sir Thomas Fairfax giving up the city of Bristol to the Parliament and asking for mercy for the survivors.

The following day William Hesketh rode with Prince Rupert's cavalry in circumstances entirely different from anything he had previously experienced. Because Fairfax was a just and merciful man he had granted the Prince's request that, as a condition of the surrender, they should be allowed an honourable retreat, although the Cavaliers had no bargaining power to exact such a concession and could have been made humiliated captives. Instead they left the city as if they were going into battle with trumpets sounding, drums beating, match lit and their colours flying. The townspeople jeered with much of their animosity directed at Rupert as they cried, "Give him no quarter," but he deigned them not a glance. The New Model Army lined their path in proud triumph, though many paid silent tribute to the bravery of their opponents. Rupert led the small procession, tall and erect on a magnificent Barbary horse with his silver armour dazzling in the sunlight and his scarlet cloak draped across his shoulders. His eyes looked straight ahead, shadowed with bitterness, and his mouth beneath the fine-drawn moustache was carved in a hard proud line. The carriage of his handsome dark head, the tilt of his chin, the hooked nose, all displayed the arrogance of the Stuarts and Palatines combined, an arrogance that called forth the mockery of the onlookers but which belied the hurt, the broken hopes, the guilt, the sense of failure and the inescapable all-consuming sense of betrayal piercing his heart like sword thrusts.

William had never experienced such humiliation in his life, a humiliation that for the moment surpassed the sense of relief that he was still alive. For three years he had ridden with Rupert's troop, often victorious, always confident, usually carefree, even in disaster for there was always another time. Rupert's cavalry were the pride of the Royalist army, supreme, unbeatable under their illustrious commander, the stuff of which legends are made. He rode with his eyes fixed straight ahead so as not to see either the triumphant looks nor the reluctant sympathy of the Roundhead troops, but the beating of the drums could not drown the cat-calls and vindictive comments of the common people who had now an interest in demonstrating to the Parliamentarians how much they hated the Royalists. William thought involuntarily of Nathaniel Fiennes and how he had exulted over the same humiliation meted out to him two years previously. A sadder and wiser William Hesketh now felt a belated sympathy for the man.

A detachment of Fairfax's cavalry under Colonel Butler and a detail of Cromwell's cavalry under Major Radcliffe were to escort them back to Oxford and as John reined his horse to one side, preparing to join the cavalcade at the rear, he had time to study the faces of the brave Cavaliers. It was then that he caught sight of William Hesketh. He had not known that William was in Bristol though he might have guessed he would be with Rupert. William did not notice John but if he had done so he would have seen a look of compassion in his eyes. At that moment John admired his Royalist opponents more than he had ever done. Rupert had always been a brilliant commander but this time they had fought to the end against overwhelming odds, valiant and unyielding and deserted by their own allies. He did not speak to William on the long road back and kept out of his way, considering his presence would only rub salt into open wounds. However when they reached their destination he rode up to him and said simply, "You were all very brave." Then he added, "If you go home perhaps you would be charitable enough to tell Arabella that I am on my way into Wiltshire but I shall be back soon." William made no reply and turned away.

William had had much time to reflect on the ride back to Oxford. He had no doubt that Rupert had done the right thing by ultimately surrendering. He had seen too much loss of life in the past year, culminating in Philip's death, for him to believe they should have carried on fighting to the last man when the city was already lost. But he felt an angry sense of betrayal that no-one had come to their aid and that neither the King nor Lord Goring had even answered Rupert's communications.

When they reached the gates of Oxford their escort left them and the little band rode into the garrison to weigh up the situation. Here however another shock awaited them, a profound shock for the Prince but one which reverberated through all his company. The King had at last written to his nephew who read with growing disbelief the missive delivered to him. Not only did the King condemn him in the strongest possible terms for surrendering Bristol, which he believed they should have continued to hold, but also accused him of making a deal with the Parliament for his own financial advantage and to save his own skin. The grounds for the accusation was the letter Rupert had written to him from Bristol asking him to consider making peace and which the Prince's enemies on the Council had leapt upon, suggesting to King Charles that he was already at that time negotiating with Parliament. The letter concluded with the peremptory statement that he was dismissed from his post as Commander-in-Chief of the Royalist armies and that he was to be issued with a warrant to leave the country immediately. Rupert sat stunned, unable to believe the words on the paper. Then after the first numbing impact he was roused to a terrible fury by the unjust accusations and the stain upon his honour. With a ferocious roar he stormed out of his apartments and strode around Oxford shouting for the blood of his enemies, not the Roundheads but those of his own party who had always been set on his downfall, who had never liked nor trusted him, who had been jealous of his successes and his influence, and who now in this moment of his greatest defeat had finally succeeded in turning the King against him.

William sat stupefied in the barracks as the talk centred on nothing but the devastating news which now superceded the impact of Bristol. Most of the Royalists realized the fatal consequences of dividing the central command at such a time, widening the rift in the factions competing for the King's favour, and could not credit the crass stupidity of dismissing their Commander-in-Chief who had a grasp of the military situation comparable to no-one else and who, despite his failures, had been responsible for their most spectacular successes. But William's reactions were more personal. He loved and worshipped Rupert and felt like weeping for him now when he remembered how he had struggled for weeks to make Bristol defensible and how he had fought to the end, encouraging them and inspiring them, and only when all was lost had he given in so that the lives of his men would not be needlessly sacrificed. He knew how much Rupert had suffered in the past from those who lost no opportunity to blacken his name. Now he had to suffer the shame of being publicly disgraced in front of all those lords who had never accepted him because he was a foreigner, because he was young, and because he thought he was always right. And the fact that it was his Sovereign whom he had served indefatigably, and his uncle whom he had loved with all the family feeling exhibited by the Stuarts, who had dealt this blow, was an unsupportable betrayal.

William felt the injustice and humiliation to his idol as to himself, and like his friend and commander burned with anger. For three years Rupert had fought for the King and the Royalist cause, driving himself beyond the bounds of duty, sacrificing sleep, comforts, leisure, love, and the pursuit of any life beyond soldiering. It was because of him that their battles had been won and because his advice had not been heeded that battles had been lost, and William and countless other young men like him had followed the Prince because they trusted and believed in him. The King had now scorned Rupert's sacrifice and loyalty, dismissed him from his service and from the country he had made his own, and in so doing had scorned and devalued all those who served under him. William felt bitter, angry, and disillusioned, too immersed in the hero-worship of the Prince to distance himself from the Royal quarrel. If Rupert was to go then William would go also. He would no more serve a king who was untrustworthy, ungrateful and deceitful. Others had realized this before and now William Hesketh experienced it for himself.

Arabella and Henrietta were seated with their mother in the large parlour at the front of the house when William made his unexpected and dramatic return home. Henrietta had recently returned to Hesketh Hall after staying a month with the Hardwickes and Joanna had pressed upon her several bolts of cloth and new trimmings since Henrietta would insist on wearing the suitably sober garments of a widow. So now they were putting the finishing touches to one of the new gowns though Henrietta was still displeased with the final result. "I think you have sewn too many pearl beads on the stomacher, Arabella," she grumbled.

"It needs something to liven it up," her sister argued. "If you insist on wearing these dark colours you should let me trim them with some contrast." Then she added encouragingly, "At least black is the fashionable colour at court this autumn."

"Probably because there are so many widows," Henrietta said tartly.

Suddenly the sound of a horse galloping at speed up to the front door made them hasten to the window where they saw William dismount and come running into the house. With cries of surprise they rushed to welcome him but he had already divested himself of his baggage and his sword, throwing them onto the hall floor, and had pushed past them into the room. By the look on his face they knew something was wrong.

The ride back home from Oxford had done nothing to calm his spirits but had rather intensified his feelings as in his imagination he relived over and over again the past three years. Without pausing to greet them he launched immediately into the whole tale of events from the siege of Bristol to the surrender, the humiliating return to Oxford and the final reaction of the King. "It was the only thing Rupert could have done save allowing every single one of us to be massacred but it appears that is what the King would have liked. He never sent us any help though he knew we were in dire straits and desperate for reinforcements. He accused Rupert of selling out to the Roundheads, of accepting a bribe - Rupert who has put all his money into the cause over the past three years and God knows he has little enough, he had less than ten pounds in his purse. He has dismissed him from his post as Commander-in-Chief and even ordered him to leave the country. He is blaming him also for the defeat at Naseby but it was Rupert who advised against fighting and he was over-ruled. After Edgehill it was Rupert who wanted to march on London immediately but the King would not. If the King had taken Rupert's advice over the past three years the war would have been over now, but he always disagreed with him and we have had to pay the price." William's words came tumbling out in passionate anger and he was almost beside himself as he cried, "I have finished. I will no longer serve such a king, such a man, I am changing sides."

There was a stunned silence and the three women looked at him in disbelief. It was Henrietta who spoke. "You are bound to be upset, William. It is only natural. Sit down and I will get you a glass of wine."

"Yes please get me some wine, but don't think it will make any difference to what I have said."

Lady Mary laid down her sewing and began to pace the room, biting her lip in anxiety. So many times she had seen her son in a passion over what he considered slights or injustices. She understood how hurt and disappointed he must be feeling and she wanted to put her arms around him and cradle his golden head against her breast as she had done when he was a small boy, but instinctively she knew she must leave him alone. Her heart also went out to the Prince, for in the brief time she had known him she had sensed his vulnerability and she grieved for the pain he must now be enduring. Turning to her son she said, "I understand what you must be feeling, I know how you loved Rupert," but he interrupted her brusquely.

"No-one knows how I loved Rupert, but that isn't the point. I fought *with* Rupert but I fought *for* the King and he has betrayed us."

"It is a terrible thing for the King to have done. You must stay here while you decide what to do. You will feel better after a good night's sleep, you must be exhausted."

She spoke soothingly but he burst out, "Did you not hear what I said, mother? I have already decided what to do. I am changing sides."

Henrietta had now returned with the wine which William drank thankfully while she exchanged troubled glances with Arabella. They knew their brother well enough to understand his impetuous temper and how difficult it was to dissuade him once an idea had taken hold of him.

"Think carefully before you do anything you will regret, William," said Arabella cautiously. "You know you always speak before you think."

"I have thought about it for two days. I am going to find the Roundhead captain."

William had not spoken to her since the quarrel with John, and Arabella now felt alarmed for this was a development that would not help her at all.

Lady Mary decided that it was now time for her to take a firm hand and she said sternly, "I have heard enough William. I understand your feelings but you are reacting too passionately. Now pull yourself together and go to find your father."

"I shall tell father exactly what I have told you," said William obdurately. "I intend to stay the night and tomorrow I shall go to find John Radcliffe and Oliver Cromwell." He remembered that the captain had told him they were riding into Wiltshire.

It began to dawn on the three women that William meant exactly what he had said. "You can't do this," cried Lady Mary in horror. "My God, we have lost everything we had in this struggle - our money, our health, our friends, even the house is no longer ours. If you really mean what you say then it has all been for nothing, all the misery and waste of the past three years has been for nothing. Do you think this is what Rupert would want of you? Are you going to answer betrayal with further betrayal?"

"You can't betray all those who have lost their lives for the Royalist cause," Henrietta broke in, feeling suddenly weak. "What about Philip? Doesn't his death mean anything to you? You would make a mockery of his death."

"I have thought about everything, and much of it distresses me," said William, quiet now. "But I am angry to think that for three years I have fought for a King who is not worth the fighting for. You know how he has broken his word to us Catholics, leading us on with vain promises when he needed our money and our support, only to renege when it suited his purpose. And so he does to all men, to Parliament whose rights he promised to respect in the first place and for whose denial this war was begun. Well he has broken his word for the last time to me."

Lady Mary began to cry. "Please, please William, don't do this. No matter how you feel, think about us, your family who have borne so much."

"Just don't do anything at the moment," pleaded Arabella, while Henrietta went to comfort her mother. "Don't go back and fight for the King, but stay where you are just now."

"Don't you see that to do nothing is to acquiesce," cried her brother. "It is a matter of principle now for me to make a complete break. Nothing you say will dissuade me."

Lady Hesketh began to sob hysterically as she realized the full impact of her son's resolution. "Holy Mother of God," she prayed, "Don't let this be happening to us." His birth had caused her so much pain, coming into the world backwards, but it was as nothing compared to the pain he was inflicting now. She continued to plead with him between her sobs, on her knees with her hands clasped as if in prayer, but though his face was ashen he turned away and looked out of the window into the fading rays of the mellow September sun. Henrietta and Arabella were horrified and went to lift their mother. Still sobbing she thought of the two sons lost to her, one stillborn, the other a few hours old. William was her only son but when she realized that nothing she could say or do was going to move him she said with a cold and dreadful finality, "If you do this William, I would rather you have died. Better you had died on Naseby field with Philip."

"Oh mother don't say that!"

"You can't mean that, mother."

Arabella and Henrietta were shocked and horrified and they began to cry also and in the midst of the sobs and consternation Sir James's voice sounded harsh and terrible, "What is the meaning of all this?" There was silence as they all looked at him standing in the doorway, his face suffused with anger as he cried, "How dare you make all this noise so that the servants can hear."

Lady Mary ran to him but he put her aside gently and turned to William. "No doubt all this coil rebounds from you. I refuse to discuss anything in the midst of all this hysteria. Come with me!"

William followed his father feeling as apprehensive as he had when a boy faced with a whipping for one of his more spectacular misdemeanours, but nonetheless determined to stick it out. His mother and sisters were left to comfort each other as best they could.

When he had dismissed his son Sir James sat with bowed head in his study, feeling the pain beginning to pound again and causing a sensation of nausea to engulf him. His interview with William was already beginning to be confused in his mind. He had done his best, using neither logic nor threats for he knew from past experience their limitations when dealing with his son, and instead had tried to understand him. At the final impasse he had been tempted to forbid him to enter the house again but William was his only son and heir and so even in the depths of his sorrow he had resisted taking a step that might have proved irrevocable. All he could do now was hope. He knew that William acted on impulse, often without considering the implications, and he hoped that when the heat of the situation had evaporated his son might recognize his folly and reconsider his decision. This was the only consolation he was able to give his wife and daughters in the midst of their latest catastrophe.

"Do you remember, Henrietta, how I felt a sense of foreboding when I first saw Rupert?" said Arabella with a sudden recollection. "As if I somehow sensed he was going to involve us in some disaster."

Lady Mary's thoughts were running along the same lines for there was a legend current in her younger days that those rash enough to become entangled with the Palatines were unavoidably touched by their misfortunes.

Supper was a disquieting affair with nobody speaking and Abigail, helping to serve, had looked from one to the other in surprise, although she had heard the shouting without understanding its import. She was struck by William's pale strained face that did not even acknowledge her, Sir James's stony expression, and the signs that Lady Hesketh had obviously been weeping. William made a toneless request to leave the table immediately the meal was over and went to his room. The situation was taking on the shape of a nightmare. He was already having fleeting doubts about the wisdom of his actions and a part of him longed to go back downstairs and be reconciled with his family. Then the memory of the King's betrayal and ingratitude flooded his consciousness and swept away all traces of hesitation.

Later in the evening he was lying on his bed when Arabella entered the chamber. She did not know what to say at first and sat on the bed in silence. Then at last she spoke. "I know you have been angry with me William and I have tried to heal the break between us. But I do not want you to think that because of my own circumstances I support the step you are taking because I don't. Nor do I want you to suppose you are helping me by persisting in this course. It will be far worse to have the family divided like this. I hoped that in time they might have accepted the fact that I want to marry John and we might have come to a tolerable agreement, but if you do as you say I cannot see any way of reconciliation. If you go to join him then they will hate him more than ever. I do not know what the outcome will be for any of us."

"What are you saying, Arabella? Are you trying to make me change my mind for my sake or yours?"

"For both of us," she said simply. He did not reply and she stood up to leave. "I love you William and you must do as you think best, it is your life." As she reached the door she turned and added, "If you do find John tell him that I love him too."

No-one else came to see him. He had half expected Henrietta but he was left alone.

Abigail almost went to William's room. She set off along the landing then thought better of it and went away again. Amongst the servants rumours were buzzing of his intended defection to the Parliament cause and his family's consequent disowning of him. She was in ignorance of his reasons but it seemed incomprehensible after three years of devoted service to the Royalists and his open and violent antagonism to the Roundheads. She wondered what had happened while he had been away. He usually came to see her to give her all the news but he had neither spoken to her nor even looked at her since his quarrel with John and she surmised he had taken her denunciation of him as final. She would have liked to go and talk with him because knowing him as well as she did she guessed at his suffering. Instead she went back to her chamber, lonely and worried, feeling part of the family's troubles yet unable to share them.

William couldn't sleep. His mind was a torment of raging emotions, most of them violent. He felt angry with everyone, with the King for his betrayal, with his mother for her rejection of him, with Arabella for her self-interest, even the servants who were eyeing him curiously and whispering behind his back. He was filled with a consuming desire to vent his anger on some-one. He got up and dressed and went outside, walking around the lake in an attempt to still his turbulent thoughts. Looking up at the black indeterminate shape of the house looming large in the darkness, he saw the faintest glimmer of light flicker in one of the casement windows under the eaves - Abigail's chamber.

He went up by the back stairs and when he opened the door he saw her lying in bed awake, her auburn hair spread over the pillow like ripples of liquid bronze in the flickering candle flame. She sat up, her green eyes wide with surprise when she saw him. Then something in his face made her pull the handworked counterpane up to her shoulders to cover the thin shift revealing the fullness of her breasts. William sprang with the lightness of a cat and was on her before she could speak, pulling away the bed coverings. He stopped her mouth with kisses, brutal bruising kisses that had nothing of love in them, and she gasped for breath, pushing at him frantically with her hands. He held her wrists in the iron grip of his bridle hand while he tore her shift away with the other, and her lovely body was revealed in all its glory, the colour of warm cream in the candleglow.

"Please, please William, you are shaming me," she managed to gasp.

His eyes glittered cold and merciless, like they did when he was killing in battle she thought. They followed every contour of her body like a wild animal before it devours its prey. He had let go of her hands and she put them over her eyes to shut out his expression and defend her modesty. His hands were digging into her breasts now and his knees pushing her legs apart so that she was pinioned beneath him, unable to move. "You have asked for this, Abigail Hart," he cried viciously. "You have always tempted me with your beauty, encouraging me then drawing back, playing the Puritan innocent. Well, no more!"

"Please William, this isn't you. Please let me go and we can talk. We have always been friends."

But he stopped her mouth again, biting her lips while he grabbed hold of her hair, tugging at it and twisting it round in his hands so that she moaned in pain. Then he was thrusting inside her with violent intensity. William Hesketh was slim but his body was like iron with every muscle and sinew taut and strong with fighting. He wanted to hurt Abigail and he wanted to humiliate her, and he succeeded in both as he emptied his anger, his frustration and his long-simmering resentment into her in unrestrained lust. In his feral possession of her he did not notice when her body ceased to resist him and instead of trying to push him away her hands moved to hold his golden head.

He left without speaking though he could hear her sobbing as he shut the door.

She tried to pull her torn shift around her as she sought ease for her throbbing aching body.

"I hate you William Hesketh," she cried. "I hate you, I hate you, I hate you." Her words and sobs became muffled as she turned her head into the pillow so that when she whispered, "I love you," it was an inaudible whisper. In the midst of her own pain she had recognized his, and while hating him for his violation of her she had understood his need and responded to it. His violent loveless possession of her had laid a claim to her body that John Radcliffe had not. The cruel irony was that William Hesketh had viciously taken what she would willingly have given. But in his wanton dishonouring of her he had demonstrated clearly that he had little respect for her, despite what he had often said. He was the master and she was merely the servant. This hurt more than the physical pain he had inflicted on her.

John Radcliffe was seated at a table working on the plan of how best to deploy his men at the imminent siege of Devizes when his deliberations were interrupted by a soldier entering the room and saying, "Major Radcliffe, there is some-one asking to see you. A William Hesketh."

John was startled as he put down the map he was drawing and ordered the admittance of his surprising visitor. "What has happened? Is something wrong at your home? Is it Arabella?" he cried anxiously, rising hastily as William entered for he could see no other reason for his appearance.

"No there is nothing wrong," William replied awkwardly. "All the family are well," considering it a fine irony even as he spoke the words.

He had found the New Model Army preparing to lay siege to Devizes castle and had no difficulty in locating Captain Radcliffe, Major Radcliffe he had been informed, who was quartered with other officers of Cromwell in a nearby farmhouse. Now he stood ill at ease in front of the man with whom his last encounter had been one of violent confrontation. He looked very much in command here on his own ground thought Wiliam, the table littered with papers and maps and minions within calling distance to do his bidding. John motioned him to sit and looked at him questioningly, perplexed as to what had brought William Hesketh into his company if not news of Arabella. He was fearful that it was bad news and that William was preparing to break it to him gently. "If it is something concerning your sister please tell me at once," he cried urgently.

"No it is nothing to do with Arabella." He paused then said reluctantly, "But she sent you her love." John looked at him in amazement and he continued, "I have come on my own business." John was even more puzzled as to what business William Hesketh might have with him though surmised it must be something concerning the house. However to his surprise William said with a great effort, "I behaved badly the last time we met. I would like to apologise for some of the things I said."

"Only some?" John asked with a laconic smile. Then he added generously, "No doubt my own behaviour was high-handed. Your sister once accused me of being arrogant but I am sorry if it seems so because it is not intended." Stretching out his booted legs he looked at William inquiringly, seeing in his face a fleeting resemblance to Arabella. They were interrupted with the delivery of a communication which John read swiftly and put aside before saying, "Does this mean that perhaps we can respect each other even though we are on opposite sides?"

"I want to change sides," said William abruptly. "I want you to help me because you are the only officer of Parliament that I know."

John was astounded. He searched the younger man's face for some clue to this incredible statement, trying to see behind William's stony expression with the direct regard that weighed up men and actions and never wavered before men's assessment of him. William was pale with signs of strain around his eyes and a hard set line to his mouth. He sat tall and too straight, as if held together by some inner tension, soberly dressed in a doublet of restrained russet beneath his buff coat. John was aware of how humiliated he had been at the siege of Bristol, salt in wounds still raw after the defeat at Naseby. The Royalists were losing now and it was natural for a young man to want to be on the winning side. Yet from everything he knew about William Hesketh, not only his avowed and bitter antagonism to him and the Parliament cause but the undoubted convictions that had made him dedicate three years of his life to the service of the King, he did not honestly think such considerations would affect him. He was aware of something else, some manifestation of deep unease that had been vaguely perceptible since his arrival. In a habitual gesture John pushed back the thick brown hair that had fallen over his forehead but did not speak, and as if guessing his thoughts William continued, "I thought you of all men would understand that I am not doing this for the wrong motives, knowing how much I have hated you and the things I have said." Then he went on to describe as clearly as he could the reasons for his change of heart, leaving out nothing but speaking in calmer, more measured tones than he had used with his family.

John listened carefully, impressed by his apparent sincerity but still not absolutely certain that an element of injured pride did not lie beneath it, even if unrecognised by William himself. "What about your family?" he asked at last.

William gave a bitter laugh. "My family have all but disowned me. My mother wished me dead, even Arabella is against it whilst….," he stopped and brushed his hand across his eyes.

"Are you well?" John asked in some concern.

"Yes, yes. But…," he paused again. "I've been guilty of one of the most heinous acts of my life and ….," he faltered and stopped.

John regarded him with sympathy for in this war they had all committed acts, often deliberately and cold-bloodedly, that under normal circumstances would have horrified their sensibilities.

"I do not think you should act in haste," he said thoughtfully. He was unwilling to encourage William Hesketh to take a step which, after the rashness of a hasty decision, his honour would not allow him to repudiate. Nor did he think it wise to widen the breach in the Hesketh family. Whilst he himself would welcome William as an ally he was of Arabella's opinion that a full-scale defection by her brother could only be detrimental to their hopes for a peaceful compromise with regard to their marriage. "Go home and lie low for a time," he advised. "You have been under a lot of strain, give yourself time to recover. No harm can come to you and your family at present so wait and see how events turn."

William sprang from his chair and looked at him in disbelief and anger. "You doubt my reasons don't you? You think I would renege again if circumstances changed? You think I am looking for an easy life after a year on the losing side," he shouted furiously. "Go home and lie low! Do you think that is what I would ever do in any circumstances whatsoever? I thought you of all men might have understood but I see I have wasted my time."

"I am trying to protect you from making a decision in the heat of the moment that you might afterwards regret, that is all," said John levelly. He did not yet know William Hesketh well enough to realize that reason and caution were ineffective arguments to use against him.

"Aren't I entitled to make my own decisions? And if I did regret it later, even renege on it, what is that to you?" William challenged him.

John weighed his words which had struck home. After a moment's consideration he nodded his head and said, "You are right. It is wrong of me to suppose you do not know your own mind or to assume that I have any claims on your conscience. What do you want me to do?"

"I want you to take me to Oliver Cromwell." He met John's steady regard defiantly and John realized there was no alternative but to take his one-time opponent to his commander.

"Very well, I will ask for an interview with him. But first of all there are some things I would like to make clear to you."

Oliver Cromwell had a busy schedule but curiosity impelled him to make time for William Hesketh, a prospective convert from Prince Rupert's cavalry was too good an opportunity to forego.

Before escorting William into his presence John gave him some advice. "He is a blunt man and no doubt will try to gall you, but do not lose your temper."

"I probably will," said William ruefully.

"He will also ask you to take the Covenant. It is supposed to be a condition of service but not everyone does and sometimes Cromwell ignores it so procrastinate if you can. Beyond that, just tell the truth. He is an honest man and likes to see honesty in others."

"I thought you would be pleased to have me renounce my faith, a soul saved from the damnation of Popery," William said with an edge of bitterness to his voice.

A year ago John Radcliffe would have thought so and rejoiced. But that was before he had been led into the labrynth of the Heskeths. He replied honestly, "As I told you before, I do not want you to do anything in haste that you would later regret. What you believe is a matter for your own soul and concerns only yourself and God."

"Shall I tell you something," said William, still with that same bitterness. "I don't think God cares. I don't think He cares whether I worship him with a crucifix or you look for Him in your heart, whether I pray in words I have learnt while you make them up for yourself, and I certainly don't think He cares about this bloody war. He is neither on one side nor the other and we have to sort out this mess for ourselves."

A year ago John would have been shocked at this heresy. Now looking at William Hesketh's young bitter face he was merely sad and troubled, not only for William but for himself. Although he refused to let any doubt take hold it seemed to him that his single-minded convictions had become disturbed since the massacre of the women at Naseby and his commitment to Arabella. Why had he ever allowed himself to become entangled with the Heskeths. He really should be glad that one of them at least was seeing the error of his ways. But he was still not wholeheartedly convinced that William's conversion was simply a matter of principle. How often were so-called principles governed by other factors of which we were not aware. John considered he had fought the war for principles, but in all honesty he acknowledged that his principles might have been different if he had had wealth and a large estate. As for religion, he had hated and feared Catholicism as a heathenish and traitorous practice, but now he found he could no longer hate with such vehemence the faith that gave quintessence to the girl he loved, or fear that her family were less English than himself.

William did nothing by halves and doubtless there was an element of self-mortification in his intention to see Oliver Cromwell, the devil of his family's imagination. But when he came into the General's presence he could see nothing immediately intimidating about the middle-aged squire turned soldier with his sturdy build, his red face marred by unsightly warts, his straight brown hair reaching past his plain collar, his gentle discerning eyes. However Cromwell grilled him unmercifully in his harsh voice with its country accent and he soon began to see why men went in awe of him.

"You worry me Master Hesketh. What reasons can you have for wanting to join us at this late stage save self-preservation. The war is nearly over." He drummed his fingers on the table and looked at William challengingly, a touch contemptuously.

But William replied to him defiantly. "How do you know?" he retorted. "The King is recruiting again in the north, Montrose is successful in Scotland, and there are countless garrisons and fortresses still in Royalist hands. Who knows when this war will end? Even if there is a truce how long will it be before the King ships over an Irish army or a French army to help him, he already has their promises."

Cromwell did not answer but said, "We don't need you. We have men enough now. Two years ago I would have been greatly in need of your service."

"Men are deserting all the time," countered William and saw Cromwell's eyes narrow. "Anyway I am no ordinary commonplace soldier. I am a trained cavalry officer who has fought for three years with Rupert's own troop." Nothing could keep the pride out of his voice.

Cromwell himself knew that this was the best training any man could have. His own cavalry, his own creation, was his pride and joy but he had learnt his skills and tactics from a careful study of Rupert then refined and improved his methods. "The King is a fool for dismissing Rupert," he said contemptuously. "He should have been fighting for us, Palatine Protestant that he is. And that brings me to another point. You are a Catholic, Master Hesketh. I do not have Catholics in my regiment." He paused to let the words sink in. "Will you take the Covenant?"

"Yes," said William without hesitation.

Once again he had amazed John Radcliffe who marvelled at the immediacy of his answer, without any trace of hesitation or reluctance.

Cromwell's eyebrows had also lifted in surprise, most converts made at least a pretence of consideration. But he said, "Attend church every Sunday and also listen to the regimental preachers," adding to John, "Make sure he does this." However he was secretly pleased with John Radcliffe for introducing him. The truth was that Oliver Cromwell liked having gentlemen as his officers, sons of the nobility or upper gentry, especially as they were sparse in his regiment. He particularly liked to show off the renegades to prove that the Parliament cause was winning not only the adherence of the common people but the people whose support and opinions mattered. He reckoned that John's influence must have been considerable and increased his good opinion of him. Letting him have the tenure of Hesketh Hall had been a successful gamble if a family of confirmed papists had been led to see the error of their ways. But he had not yet finished with William. "As you say, Master Hesketh, there is still a lot of work to be done. When you fight with us where shall I put you? At the front to make a public example of you or at the back where you will do less damage if you turn your coat again?"

John saw a muscle twitch in William's cheek but he kept his temper. "Wherever you will," he replied evenly. "But you would be a fool not to make use of my expertise."

To John's surprise Cromwell laughed. "Lieutenant Hesketh, you will serve under Major Radcliffe and for a time will be on trial, subject to reports directly to me. When I am satisfied I will raise you to the rank of captain."

William gave his assent, "Yes sir!"

John let out a sigh of relief that William had conducted himself in so controlled a manner. Then with the interview ended he heard to his horror William say, "I would like my estate back. There is no longer any reason for it to be confiscated if I am fighting for the Parliament and a Protestant."

There was a deadly silence and John thought Cromwell had heard his sharp intake of breath. His commander looked from one to the other with the piercing directness which made men quail in his presence, seeing the trace of impudence in the grey eyes and the apprehension in the brown eyes which nonetheless regarded him steadily. He was aware again of undercurrents that he could not fathom and as usual when he was out-manoeuvered his anger erupted.

"You think I have nothing else to do but pass confiscated estates from one to the other," he shouted, his voice filling the room and attracting the rueful attention of those outside. "Get out, the pair of you!"

John did not look at William and William looked uncertain as he followed him to the door.

Then when he was almost out of the door Cromwell called him back. "I suggest you get yourself a lawyer, a good one," he advised, with the faintest suspicion of amusement in his eyes.

"You nearly ruined it," groaned John when they were well clear of the building. "Why did you have to say that? Don't you realize it has made him suspicious of me and could well ruin everything. You accused me of doubting your good faith but you still do not believe me when I have promised to surrender my title as soon as there is no danger to you all."

"I want my estate back through my own efforts, not yours," said William stubbornly. "I'm sorry if I damaged your standing with Cromwell but I am not prepared to have my own property taken from me and handed back whenever you feel the time and situation is "convenient" like a schoolmaster confiscating a naughty boy's kickshaws. And besides there is the matter of the lease held by Parliament."

In a sudden moment of illumination John realized that this was something he had failed to take into account when pondering William's motives. He had seen no further than hurt pride without truly being aware of the depth of feeling he nurtured for Hesketh Hall, a depth of feeling that over-rode considerations of safety and expediency, even religion and perhaps life itself.

"And if you are thinking that is why I changed sides you are wrong," said William guessing his thoughts. "For the last time I will tell you that I made my decision on principle and I will now fight for Parliament with the same determination I fought for the King. But Henri Quatre once said Paris was worth a mass. Well to me Hesketh Hall is worth the Covenant."

They stood weighing each other up as they had done the first time they had met, both soldiers in buff coats and riding boots. One was tall and slim with mischievous grey eyes and long curling fair hair, the other some inches less and sturdier with serious deep brown eyes and brown hair cut short. William had been the better judge then for he had recognized his opponent's qualities while John had dismissed William as negligible. Now they were fighting on the same side and understood the similarities between themselves rather than the differences - courage and strong wills and a determination to achieve their ends though they employed different methods.

A smile began to hover around William's lips, breaking for the first time the bitter set of his lips. "By the way," he asked off-handedly, "are you a good lawyer?"

Traces of amusement began to crease around John's eyes also. "I told you I was the first time we met."

There was a faint stirring of feeling between them like seeds beginning to grow in the dark. Not so strong yet as to be termed friendship but a reaching towards comradeship, bridging the gap of birth and class and faith.

On the twenty-third of September the New Model Army rode to attack the Royalist stronghold of Devizes Castle, Lieutenant William Hesketh riding amongst the troopers of Major John Radcliffe's company.

CHAPTER 13

OCTOBER 1645

William had left very early in the morning, speaking to no-one and no-one had seen him go.

However the shock of his pronouncement still reverberated around Hesketh Hall, even the servants affected by the startling events of the previous day, though none in so intimate a manner as Abigail. Abigail's life had been shaken to the roots. Her modest self-esteem, nurtured by her Puritan faith and the approval of her employers, and the sense of security provided by Hesketh Hall, had both been destroyed in the space of a few minutes. She knew she could not possibly go on living there any longer and would have to make her escape at the earliest acceptable opportunity.

For the Heskeths it was like a nightmare though all of them had passed a sleepless night.

William's defection tore at the very heart of their existence, at their family unity which had withstood all other vagaries of fortune. Lady Hesketh had always maintained that so long as her family was together nothing else mattered. Now the family was no longer an entity but divided. William's action had also effectively negated all their life over the past three years. This was something that Lady Mary could not forgive. She remembered all the long weeks and months when the men were away and she and the girls waited and worried on events over which they had no control. Now William had gone off again, leaving them with an extra burden of anxiety which cancelled out everything they had previously suffered. She was haunted by the fact that he had left without asking her forgiveness, but was still bitter enough to have no change of heart about her rejection of him so long as he persisted in this course.

Sir James seemed a lot less well though his mind had cleared again and he now remembered every painful detail of the confrontation with his son, a recollection which did nothing to allay the increasing pressure in his head. Because he found concentration difficult he was not able to formulate any solutions and resorted to outbursts of fury against the Roundheads who had not only robbed him of his health and his inheritance but of his only son. In this mood of impassioned anger he was no comfort to his wife who previously had always relied upon his wisdom and his optimism.

Henrietta, who was just beginning to recover, slipped back into a deep despondency. The confusion of her emotions had been settling into a detached melancholy but they were violently disturbed again at what seemed her brother's callous betrayal in joining with her husband's murderers. Yet some part of her nature sympathized with him. She knew that Philip and William had both adored Rupert, though William with a more uncritical adulation than her husband. She wondered what difference it might have made at this crucial moment if he had Philip to talk and commiserate with, a speculation which only intensified her sense of loss.

Arabella could not rid herself of the strange sense of foreboding she had experienced when Rupert had come to the house and now, by some tragic irony, fate had made him the instrument to strike at their family unity. However she was honest enough to acknowledge that she had already done so with her secret betrothal to John Radcliffe, the secrecy in itself an affront to propriety, and in actual fact William had done no less. The violent reaction to his decision made her realize afresh the difficulties she and John would have to face. She thought of him often and wondered if William had caught up with him, or whether her brother had indeed thought better of his avowed intention. This was a hope uppermost in everyone's minds and for the first day they were half-expecting his shamefaced return. Then as the days wore on their hopes adjusted to the possibility that he still might have changed his mind but gone off to find the Royalist forces again.

In the days that followed William Hesketh did not find it easy to accommodate himself to the strict discipline of the New Model Army. After being forced to listen to a three hour exhortation from one of the more fanatical Puritan preachers in the regiment he vented his frustration on John Radcliffe. "Does Cromwell really think I am going to be converted to Protestantism by listening to such tedious doctrine? On the few occasions when my father attended the Parish church he would tell of one of the gamekeepers who would noisily clean his gun throughout the sermon. I think I shall be doing the same."

John merely shook his head in resignation, convinced that to try and make a Puritan out of William Hesketh was a fruitless endeavour. Though as far as military conduct was concerned William was scrupulous and exact and John's estimation of him increased, appreciating he would be a reliable ally in dangerous situations.

A short time later William was witness to a striking example of Parliamentarian morality. The weeks following the capture of Bristol had been spent in a series of mopping up operations, laying siege to, or storming, important Royalist garrisons on the main trade route between the West Country and London so that commerce between the capital and the port of Bristol could be recommenced. Cromwell's troops had successfully captured Winchester castle when five soldiers were caught looting. Oliver Cromwell ordered a military trial immediately and finding them guilty of the offence ordered them to be hanged. He commanded that they should be executed in full view of the castle where the offence had occurred and summoned the whole of the regiment to be present to take note of the grim warning. William sat his horse not far from John as Cromwell's troops waited in tense expectation, line upon line of wary faces. Cromwell himself sat with a stony expression as a noose was flung over a branch of a nearby tree. Then the five accused were led out to the beating of the drums, one of them attempting a look of defiance but the other four obviously terrified. The execution of the first man was about to proceed when the General suddenly rode forward and with an upraised hand stopped the trooper chosen as hangman. There was a momentary hush and everyone waited, breaths indrawn in anticipation. The convicted men turned looks of expectation upon their commander, not daring to show a flicker of hope at the interruption but hope nonetheless brushing the edges of their fear.

"I intend to hang one of you only," Cromwell announced, his booming voice carrying to the far reaches of the assembled troops. "You may draw lots as to who shall be the scapegoat."

Hope swept through the five men, but only for a moment. As the straws were brought the accused were overtaken by an even greater fear as each one saw his life hang no more on the judgment of a man but in the hands of fate. They chose their straws tremblingly. Four of them were faint with relief but the fifth man shook with horror as he saw his chance of life vanish for the second time in the space of a few minutes. For the man unfortunate to draw the short straw was the man who had previously had the noose around his neck, as if death had already claimed his prey and having once had him in his clutches was not willing to relinquish him so easily. As he was forced to suffer the repetition of his ordeal he turned to look at his ransomed companions, one evading his eyes, one guilt-stricken and two openly gleeful. However before the noose was tightened Cromwell spoke again. "Let this be a warning to you all. Soldiers in the Lord's army do not steal or plunder. You four should have an even greater guilt seeing another suffer for your sins. I have spared you the penalty of death but you will not go unpunished. You will be taken to Oxford to be sentenced by the Royalist governor there since your offence is against property under his jurisdiction."

This was a turn of events they had not bargained for but John knew his commander well. This was an opportunity for Oliver Cromwell to demonstrate to the Royalists the moral superiority of the Parliament army and his own punctiliousness with regard to military procedure. William could not but be impressed with Cromwell's fair discipline but felt a strong sympathy for the soldier who saw his hopes of life vanish for a second time on the whim of chance. John kept his eyes on the four men who had to watch their comrade die in their place and wondered what an effect such a redemption would have on their lives. Perhaps no effect at all he surmised, studying them and thinking that for him it would be an insupportable burden. Cromwell showed no feeling at all and when the man's body at last swung lifeless from the rope he delivered a homily to his assembled troops on the sin of covetousness and the necessity of loyalty to the faith they purported to uphold. "How can we be God's instruments for the retribution of His enemies if we bow to unrighteousness," he thundered.

For several reasons Cromwell decided that Major Radcliffe should escort the four prisoners to Oxford. For one thing he was a lawyer and therefore eminently suitable to convey to the Royalist governor the Parliamentarians' strict adherence to the code of military law. Secondly he was an ideal representative of the best sort of Parliament officer, courteous, intelligent and articulate, to demonstrate to the Royalists that the New Model Army was not merely composed of the meaner sort. In addition his integrity made him directly spoken and incapable of being either intimidated or flattered. There was little immediate business pending and John deserved a few days' respite. But there was also another element underlying his choice. "Take a detail of five men," he said, adding with a calculating smile, "and make sure William Hesketh is amongst them."

When John informed William he saw his face tighten. Cromwell knew that Prince Rupert was still in Oxford, trying to force the King to see him or at least grant him a court martial whereby he might defend himself from the charges levelled against him. He had as yet succeeded with neither. King Charles had resolutely refused him a personal interview, communicating with him through others or through correspondence, and was denying him the right of a court martial. Rupert however was adamant in his demands and refused to leave the country until he had been given the opportunity to justify himself personally to his uncle and his peers. It was unlikely that William could avoid seeing him but in any case it was certain that he would have to face many of his former companions. John felt decidedly uneasy about what effect this might have on him and considered it a cruel gambit on his commander's part to make his new recruit submit to such a severe test of his sincerity. "Shall I try to get you out of this?" he asked. "I could probably make a substitution without anyone being the wiser," though as he made the suggestion he realized he was considering disobeying his commander yet again for the sake of the Heskeths.

William however shook his head saying defiantly, "I am a soldier and subject to the orders of my superiors. They are my orders and I shall obey them. Cromwell thinks I shall renege again when I get to Oxford and I have a feeling you think so too, John Radcliffe. But I won't. I have given my word and I shall keep it. Any humiliation I may incur I have brought upon myself." But his face hardened and John privately considered that William Hesketh was getting more than his share of humiliation lately and it was an experience he was not accustomed to.

On the road John still felt troubled but William was in deceptively high spirits, laughing and joking when he found himself riding for a time in the rear with John. "This morality is killing me," he said. "Do you think there might be any pretty girls when we stop for the night?"

"Don't let anyone see you whoring," warned John, "it's a punishable offence." William swore colourfully and he continued, "And the penalty for blasphemy is boring the tongue with a hot iron."

"Does anyone carry out these punishments?" asked William in astonishment.

"Sometimes. In practice there is more leniency than in theory but Cromwell likes to make an example of individuals as a warning to the rest, as you have recently witnessed."

And as he is making an example of me, William thought, but he said jocularly, "More honoured in the breach than in the observance. That's a quotation, from a play by William Shakespeare."

"Yes I know. Hamlet Prince of Denmark." William looked surprised and John smiled. "I have never seen a play in my life but I have read Shakespeare's histories, there's a lot of wisdom in them."

William burst out laughing. "Plays are for entertainment, not wisdom. And playhouses are the best places for picking up whores, well they were until the Puritans closed them all down." Then unable to help himself he asked slyly, "Haven't you ever had a woman?"

"Not a whore. But occasionally yes, I'm no saint. But I don't make a habit of it. I believe you should only lie with a woman you love and I've never loved anyone until I met Arabella."

"What a strange man you are," said William in genuine perplexity. "I've never met anyone like you before. I'm sure if I were in love it still wouldn't prevent my taking pleasure where I could." Abigail's face flashed involuntarily before his eyes and he shut it out with an effort, saying with a vehemence he had not intended, "You'll never make a Puritan of me." Then after a time he said mischievously, "I cannot at all see why Arabella is attracted to you."

"Remember I am your superior officer," John said warningly.

As they rode closer to Oxford John became more convinced that it was not right for William to endure the mortification of meeting his former comrades and attracting their contempt. Despite William's apparent nonchalance he knew that he was still in an unsettled state, still haunted by the shock of the King's betrayal and his own defection, and John was sure it was not the right time for him to face another ordeal. It was too soon and he was afraid of the consequences. Also he had to admit that he was not absolutely certain that William would not defect back. Despite his assurances there was an element of unpredictability that John was uncertain about and if William should change his mind John was determined it should not happen while under his supervision. Yet for all his misgivings his genuine concern was most for William and not for his own credit. He had had a grudging respect for William Hesketh from the time he had escaped from his custody and now a tentative mutual companionship was beginning to grow between them as their differences shrank, coloured for John by the fact that he was Arabella's brother. William on the other hand missed his close friendship with Philip Halsall and without realizing it was beginning to fill the gap with a new experience of comradeship.

It was growing late and as they were still some miles from Oxford John decided they would stay the night at an inn in the village of Woodleigh. The innkeeper was none too pleased at having to supply free quartering, but John reminded him that he relied on the protection of the Parliament army to safeguard him from the raiding parties of the Royalist garrison so he grudgingly provided them with everything they needed. The men were glad to stretch their legs after being in the saddle all day and after they had seen to their horses they were able to wash and eat. However before they retired for the night John manacled his prisoners. This was not in accordance with their plans for they had been thinking that if they halted at an inn some connivance might be arranged for their escape. The boldest of the four decided to make a last-ditch appeal to the compassion of his fellow soldiers and addressed John directly.

"Major Radcliffe is this fair? We have given up everything to serve the cause of Parliament. Can't you let us get away? What harm have we done to warrant execution at the hands of our enemies?"

"Better to have received judgment from our own as this," said one of his accomplices.

Their faces expressed pitiable anxiety and John was aware that they had at least the half-hearted support of some of their guards. But he said coldly, "You received judgment from your own and the penalty was death, which penalty your comrade paid."

"And so we shall probably die, and in worse circumstances. Have you no mercy?"

He surveyed their faces and remembered their offence. "You have been given a merciful reprieve and the Cavaliers are not without mercy. No doubt you will receive a fair sentence," he said, unmoved by their pleas.

"But what harm did we do? What's a bit of plunder? Did we leave our homes and our work to fight for Parliament only to be rewarded like this?" There was concerted agreement from the other three.

"You are volunteers, not pressed men. You are paid a wage so there is no need for plunder which is but stealing and a criminal offence. You chose to enlist in the army of Parliament and it would have been better had you not done so, and all others like you," John retorted angrily.

Listening to his forceful denunciation William was cynically wary of such high idealism. But John was enraged by their dismissal of their crime as negligible and aware of the cost that had been paid by their unfortunate companion. He did not understand how anyone could live with such insupportable knowledge that someone had died in their stead, let alone dismiss it as of no account. And he also realized that his feelings were being influenced by the price William Hesketh was also having to pay for their actions. Looking at their officer's implacable face the culprits knew it was useless to appeal further or to consider, what had previously crossed their minds, a bribe. Cromwell knew what he was about when he placed them in Major Radcliffe's charge for he was incorruptible. "You have been granted a reprieve and I shall ensure that reprieve lasts until my duty is done," were his final words.

Early the following morning after a meagre breakfast of ale and stale bread with some greasy bacon they made ready for the final stage of their journey. John gave the innkeeper a bill for reclamation of his costs but he surveyed it sceptically, knowing that he would have to wait a long time for any reimbursement and only then if he was lucky. The men were mounting up when John called William back into the inn on a pretext about wanting to ask him some information about Oxford that he did not wish the others to hear. "Come up to the chamber, I've left a gauntlet there," he said, leading the way above stairs. John then hit him for the second time in their acquaintance, this time with clenched fist in a blow to the jaw that sent William crashing backwards to the floor and into unconsciousness. He felt a momentary qualm as William's skull hit the wooden boards but there was no time for regrets now. He manacled his hands, placed a letter inside his jacket then called a serving maid to lock the door and promise to release him only by mid-day no matter what threats were issued. (The generous coin he placed in her hand was of less persuasion than the stern words of the steel-helmeted Roundhead officer.) These were all steps that John had rehearsed carefully when he had made his plans the night before. Then he went to join his men and gave the order to proceed, taking the four prisoners on the last miles to their sentence and leaving his own personal prisoner behind. He was not without reservations about what he had done. He knew William would be angry but he honestly did not know whether his ultimate reaction would be fury or relief. He was aware that he had taken a calculated risk and that he might have destroyed any chance of their present truce becoming permanent, but he had weighed the risks and considered William's absence from this errand a necessity. He informed the rest of them that he had sent Lieutenant Hesketh ahead on reconnaissance and tried not to think too much of the lies he was being forced to tell. He did not think any word of this would come to Cromwell but he wondered how long he could continue crossing the General with impunity.

William awoke to a throbbing headache and as he tried to raise his head from the floor a wave of nausea overcame him so that he fell back, slipping into unconsciousness again. After a few moments the room began to swim hazily around him and he let himself go with the swaying motion until his senses began to clear. As his surroundings slipped into focus they were completely unfamiliar to him - the small room of wattle and daub with the high uncurtained window facing him - and he did not know where he was. He tried to think back and the last thing he could remember was being with John Radcliffe in the passageway but the effort of trying to think any further was too much and he surrendered to the sensation of drifting between sleep and wakening. The third time he awoke properly and when he began to move his limbs he discovered that his hands were manacled. Again it was too much effort to try and work out the implications of what had happened and he lay there for a long time. Then as the significance of events became apparent he began to fear that they had both been attacked and the prisoners escaped, a possibility that roused him with its awfulness so that he struggled to his feet, calling for John. There was no sound from anywhere so he began to hammer on the door with his clasped hands and eventually a small voice said, "I am not to let you out yet. I have orders to release you soon so please be patient till then."

"Where are the others?" shouted William. "Where is the major?"

"They are all gone."

"All of them?" queried William in surprise.

"Yes all of them."

It then began to dawn on him that he had been made a prisoner for the second time by John Radcliffe. He still felt sick and the pain in his head and jaw was severe so he crawled onto the hard bed and gave himself up to thoughts, confused though they were. He was furious with John Radcliffe and humiliated at being rendered unconscious by him, God he must have hit him hard! Yet there was also an overwhelming relief that he did not need to go to Oxford, a relief which would soon diminish as the full awareness of the implications overtook him, but which in his weak and confused state was momentarily welcome. He would not have to go to Oxford and see his former comrades. From the position of the sun shining through the high window he reckoned it must be near noon and by now his companions should be at Oxford, so acknowledging that there was nothing he could do he gave himself up to inertia. He lay on the bed, drifting between sleep and wakening, thinking about nothing but the throbbing in his head.

When he felt better however he began to reflect and his first reactions of relief gave way to anger. How dare the self-opinionated righteous Major Radcliffe take it upon himself to order his life and make his decisions for him. He obviously still believed he would renege when he reached Oxford and his old comrades, and that would have been a blow to John Radcliffe's prestige and to the representatives of the army of Parliament. He had been made to look cowardly and untrustworthy, not able to face the consequence of his actions or to be trusted to keep his word. He recollected furiously all John Radcliffe's arrogant behaviour in the past, from the occupation of Hesketh Hall to its conveyance in his name, his seduction of Arabella, his reluctance to accept his sincerity about changing sides, his vaunted moral superiority. As his anger boiled and seethed he couldn't wait to go and sort out John Radcliffe once and for all and hollered and shouted for the door to be opened.

However it must have been well after noon when the door was unlocked by a rather fearful maidservant bringing him something to eat and drink and he realized how parched his throat was. "I have come to let you out," she said in a broad country accent, putting a mug of ale and a platter of bread and cheese on the floor, and taking a small key from within the low neckline of her grey wool bodice.

William thrust out his hands belligerently and when she had unlocked the manacles he shook his wrists thankfully. Then he began to quaff down the ale and attack the food greedily while she stood watching him curiously, seeing for the first time the prisoner and finding him a very handsome young man. She was about sixteen years of age, small of stature but buxom and pretty with dark hair peeping from beneath her white cap and huge dark eyes that regarded him apprehensively under long fringed lashes. Aware of her enquiring eyes resting on him William asked, "What's your name?"

"Dorcas, sir," she answered, bobbing a curtsey and smiling at him provocatively when she realized he was not going to be angry with her. There was a small gap between her front teeth.

"Stay here a while, Dorcas," he said, pulling her down beside him, and she sat on the bed watching him eat and swinging a bare brown foot enticingly in its broken shoe. When he had finished the last crumb he drained the mug then asked, "Tell me Dorcas, does the door lock from the inside as well?"

She smiled at him knowingly and after locking the door returned to him on the bed, thrusting out her full breasts which strained in the low neckline of the tight-fitting bodice, and running her tongue along her full lips. William took her in his arms and bent his head to her tantalizing bosom but even as he did so he was brought up short by a sudden shock of revulsion. She looked Puritanical in her grey wool skirt with white apron and coif, but her face, for all its youth and prettiness, had a shrewd artfulness. Into his mind, clear in all its details like a portrait, flashed a beautiful face with anguished green eyes pleading with him. He dropped his hands and moved away while she studied him in surprise. He rose from the bed and murmured in embarrassment, "I'm sorry Dorcas. I have changed my mind." He found a coin in his purse, gave it to her then opened the door saying without looking at her, "Get you gone."

She surveyed him with contempt before leaving, though she pocketed the silver. William put his head in his hands. Outside in the passage Dorcas swore vociferously. Bloody Roundheads! They all wanted the same as other men but were afraid to take it for fear of their God-damned consciences. She had thought him handsome and ready for a little diversion but she had been mistaken. Now if only he had been a Cavalier!

When John Radcliffe arrived at Hesketh Hall he was met by Henrietta. After the satisfactory completion of his mission to Oxford he had informed his men that they were going to billet for the night at a property in which he had some interest so they had turned towards Felton before resuming their journey south. He could not let slip an unexpected opportunity to see Arabella again so soon. He had mounted the steps, taking off his helmet as he did so, but before he could reach the door it was opened by a young woman in a black taffeta gown devoid of all ornament except for pearl beads defining the stomacher which emphasized her small waist. She was not quite so tall as John but the brown hair fastened in a knot of curls on top of her head made her seem taller and older than she was. She was pale and thin, only the intelligent brown eyes and the sprinkling of freckles across her nose and cheeks giving him any clue that this was the same plump rosy girl he had taken from the siege of Oxford. He introduced himself carefully and she studied with interest the man she suspected to be her sister's lover, seen only briefly on that dark night. His inner tension gave his features a stern composure and she noted the uncompromising boldness of the brown eyes and the firm set of his mouth. If Arabella was in love with him she could see no reason for her sister's willful preference. He spoke formally and offered his condolences which she received with dignity though inwardly recoiling at the thought that this Roundhead officer might have killed her husband. She had been glad of his help and protection that night in Oxford but she had then been ignorant of his identity, and looking back now she wished that she had not been tempted to flee and leave her husband in the last few weeks of his life. Her manner was cool towards him as he explained that he had fulfilled a commission in Oxford and must billet himself and four men in the stables for the night.

"Then I will arrange food in the kitchen," she replied tonelessly, giving no indication of how she felt about the arrangement. "I will see to it and inform my sister and my parents." She did not invite him into the house but then unable to prevent herself she asked anxiously, "Have you seen anything of my brother?"

"Lieutenant Hesketh is close behind me," he said. "He has been unfortunately delayed but I think you may expect him before nightfall."

"Then I must prepare my parents for his arrival," she said soberly, and he recognized the tension behind the words as she re-entered the house, leaving him waiting outside. However she came out again almost immediately. "Please forgive my discourtesy," she said artlessly, "you must come in and wait in the hall until I find my sister."

But when she had left him again John stood uneasily in the hall gazing around at the familiar oak panelling, the flagged floor and huge stone fireplace, the heavy oak chairs and the great bulk of the livery cupboard, the oak chest beneath the robust oak staircase with its bulbous turned balusters and cupola-shaped newel posts. He remembered the turmoil of his last visit and was apprehensive for this. A young servant girl stared at him curiously then ran off to the kitchens agog with the news. Then suddenly Arabella appeared on the staircase, her footsteps dancing on the treads, and all his gloomy recollections were banished at the sight of her animated presence and the joy illuminating her delicate features.

"John, what a surprise. I never expected to see you so soon. What are you doing here?" she cried in delight.

"Where can we be alone?" he asked as they embraced furtively.

"I don't know. I can't take you to my chamber. There is the small back parlour."

"What about the garden? Is it too cold for you?" he asked, for already in the shortening days the nip of winter beckoned.

"No, wait a moment and I'll get my cloak."

He waited anxiously until she returned wrapped in a dark crimson cloak over her gown of ivory damask, then they made their way to the walled garden. The roses were dying now around them, their petals brown and shrivelled, and the fallen leaves crisped beneath their feet. They clasped each other tight and she could feel the hardness of his body against her while he sensed the beating of her heart as he put his hands beneath her cloak. "I have dreamt about you every night since we last met. I want you. I love you so much," he said, his voice hoarse with emotion. Arabella had never seen such naked passion in the eyes of any of the men who had said they loved her but she sensed that in John Radcliffe his desire was bound with a devotion that was infinite and she was no longer afraid of it.

"I have dreamt about you too. I lie in my bed and long to have you beside me."

He stroked her fair hair and gazed wonderingly into her uptilted face as he whispered, "I find it so hard to believe that you love me as much as I love you, that you still want to marry me."

"We are betrothed aren't we?" she said simply.

He clasped her tighter in his arms as a chilly blast shook the lime tree above their heads and a few leaves spattered down. "We have been told we must campaign through the winter. I had not counted on that," he said regretfully.

"Couldn't I come with you? We could be married and I could stay in inns close by where you are. I heard that Sir Thomas Fairfax's wife does."

John shook his head, kissing the blonde curls of her fringe. He understood the terrible hardships of army life more than Arabella with her romantic dreams. Even Anne Fairfax no longer accompanied her husband as she had done in the early days. "It is no life for a lady, especially in winter," he said.

"Perhaps we could meet in an inn somewhere from time to time," she suggested tentatively, recalling her secret trysts with Kit Verney. They were betrothed, they had vowed themselves to each other and it was their right to enjoy the fulfillment of their love provided their marriage day was set. She looked trustingly up at him. Times were too uncertain to postpone what was rightfully theirs, she had the example of Henrietta to warn her that life could be snatched away unexpectedly, especially a soldier's life.

"I want to marry you first, it is the proper way," John said. "I want to take you to Huntingdon and make you my wife."

In their talk of marriage neither of them had considered how they could accomplish this without the consent of her parents, unless it were by a secret elopement which would contravene all the conventions of society. Even if they risked this there was the problem of what form the ceremony would take, for John would never consider a marriage by a Catholic priest and to Arabella and her family the marriage would not be binding unless solemnized by the sacraments of their faith. In their complete absorption with each other these considerations played no part as they kissed and caressed. But John was still mindful of his duties and he knew he had to say, "I must first finish the assignment I have committed myself to, hard though it is for both of us to wait. I am no ordinary soldier, I am a high-ranking officer with responsibilities that I must fulfill because I have given my word. However when these are done I shall tender up my commission to Oliver Cromwell and although I believe the war will be ended by then, I shall serve no more even if it is not."

"Finish your campaign then and when spring comes we can be married," Arabella said. "We are both young and we have all our lives before us." The anticipation of their ultimate union would sustain her through the dark days of winter until then. She refused to consider the possibility that John might be killed. He had survived so far with skill and good fortune and it seemed to her that fortune was smiling upon them in the way they were continuing to be together. John began to kiss her again and it was much later before Arabella thought to ask of William.

William arrived at Hesketh Hall only a short time behind John, though unaware of the fact. He was still furious at the trick which had been served him in the latest manifestation of the Roundheads' vaunted moral superiority over the Cavaliers, the lack of trust, the assumption that he was too weak to face trials. Of course he had been instinctively relieved not to have to go to Oxford but that did not mean he would have shirked his responsibilities or would not have had the courage to face his old friends. He was ready for another confrontation with John Radcliffe who took too much upon himself in the ordering of events, as if he were God Almighty. John's letter had informed him that he intended making for Hesketh Hall and staying the night there before returning to Cromwell or William would not have returned home after the catastrophe of his last visit, still painfully vivid in his mind.

As he rode towards the house he noticed a figure walking by the lake, a grey wraith-like figure in the already deepening shadows of the late October afternoon. He hesitated, then feeling a desperation about the present course of events he dismounted and went towards her and she turned and saw him. They stood facing each other. A slow flush crept over Abigail's face at the remembrance of their last encounter but she faced him with dignity, her hands clasped close beneath her grey cloak. He took off his helmet and she saw that he had cut his hair and it curled around his face just touching his collar. In all the years she had known him his hair had fallen in waves past his shoulders, giving him an angelic appearance that belied his high spirits. Now he looked more boyish yet, paradoxically, older, and his face was grave.

"I am not going to say I am sorry," he said at last, "because such words would only insult you further. No words of mine could atone for the wrong I have done you, nor express my regret." He paused then said, "Instead I am asking you to marry me." Whatever Abigail had expected it was not this and she stood rooted to the spot, staring at him. "I know I am not good enough for you," he continued, "but I am a Protestant, a Parliamentarian and poor, surely that removes some of the obstacles you used to mention."

Abigail searched his face, looking in vain for some sign of further mischief, but his voice held no trace of the old teasing mockery and there was a hint of deep experience behind the grey eyes.

"You do not have to make reparation, William," she said at last. She closed her eyes as she struggled inwardly within herself, knowing she did not need to say the words but compelled to do so. "I was not a virgin. I thought men knew these things."

The revelation came as a great shock to him, yet instinctively he was aware of the effort it had taken to tell him and he was filled with a rush of pity. "So I was the second man to have abused you," he said with shame.

Her green eyes were unflinching though a faint flush stained her cheeks again as she admitted, "No. I gave myself willingly. Once only. But you see I am not as virtuous as you believed me to be."

William was astounded. He wondered who the man could be. He was not aware of Abigail having acquaintance with any young men although he had been away a lot of late. Was it someone from the town or perhaps someone she had met in Stratford when she went to visit her aunt there. He was compelled to revise his opinion of her though the revelation in no way lessened the condemnation of his own rape, or his feelings for her.

"My offer of marriage was not an attempt at reparation Abigail," he said gently. "It is because I love you. No matter what I have done or how ill I have shown it, I love you. I always have, from the day you came to this house in your plain clothes and I thought you had the most beautiful face I had ever seen, like the Madonna in my mother's sacred books. I offered to show you the deer in the park to make you feel happier but I don't suppose you remember."

"Yes I remember," she said, tears smarting in her eyelids. She recalled all the years she had known him, the way he had pursued her since he became a man, of how he had finally taken her brutally though she had entrapped herself by falling in love with him. For she did love him and perhaps had done so longer than she realised. She loved him wholeheartedly for what he was - generous and courageous, impulsive and high-spirited, strong-willed and selfish, and sometimes cruel. She loved him too much to let him ruin himself with a marriage that would be socially disastrous. He now supported Parliament and he said he was no longer a Catholic but the greatest obstacle still between them would be his ruin in the eyes of the world. "I am your servant," she said simply. Nothing could alter that. "You couldn't marry your servant. I would not let you put yourself in that position for me." I love you too much to let that happen, she thought silently. It was because she loved him that she could not bear him to suffer humiliation in the eyes of the world and she could make the sacrifice and refuse him.

But William was undeterred. "I am not the first and I don't suppose I shall be the last. Many men of higher rank than I have married beneath them. The Duke of Buckingham's father married his servant girl. Even kings have married their lesser-born loves if they could have them no other way."

"But you have had me another way, William," she reminded him. "I always said I would never be your mistress but circumstances are different now. You have already taken me. If you desire me so much then I will be your mistress."

"It would be against everything you believe in, I know that, my love," he said gently. "Besides I do not want you as my mistress. No, I must admit that is not strictly true because I would rather have you as my mistress than nothing at all and I know that is what I wanted of you in the past. But that is no longer sufficient for me, and it has nothing to do with my taking you by force. I want you as my wife, to be by my side continually and not as a pleasant diversion. I want to marry you Abigail. No-one else will do for me if I searched the whole world."

"I hope you did not think I withstood you in the hope of marriage," she said, suddenly aghast at the perception entering her mind. "I have never dreamt of such a thing, it was never my intention to tempt you in any way. I never ever thought such a thing possible."

William smiled in gentle amusement and taking her hands in his he said, "I know that of a certainty, such artfulness has never been in your nature. Oh my dear Abigail, you need never explain yourself to me, I know you too well." He took her into his arms very gently as if she were made of fragile glass.

She wanted to pour out all her love to him then. Ever since she had first come to Hesketh Hall he had offered her his friendship, lightened her life, teased and mocked her sobriety and introduced her to a gaiety her life had always lacked. Then he had hurt her and shamed her and now he was holding her with a tenderness she had never seen him show before. She wanted to be loved by him but still she could only think of the impediments to such a marriage.

"One day you will be Sir William Hesketh, owner of the Hall. I could not fill such a position as your wife, you must look for someone of your own class," she insisted.

"None of the women I know have your dignity and your beauty, no matter what their class. No-one could fulfill the position of being mistress of Hesketh Hall as you would do."

"What about your parents?" she whispered, moved by his trust in her but fearful of the reactions of others. "They have always been kind to me since they took me in. They would be shocked and angry if you were to marry me." She was well aware that Lady Mary sought a rich heiress for her only son.

William did not deny this fact but said ruefully, "I am so far beyond the pale with my parents that nothing I do can make matters worse." He touched her face gently with his fingers, a touch as light as thistledown. "I am not denying there will be obstacles, but you know I thrive on difficulties. I love you and that is all that matters. But you have never said you love me. I believe that you do and only circumstances prevented you giving me your love. I am not mistaken am I? You do love me, despite everything I have done?" There was an appeal in his voice and the slightest trace of apprehension.

"I love you William," she replied, and it was as if her heart suddenly had wings and soared into realms beyond her imagining.

As William looked into the enigmatic green eyes that had always tantalized him with their hidden depths he was compelled to say what he had never thought possible. "I promise you Abigail that if you marry me I will love no other woman, I will lie with no other woman, as long as we both shall live." He bent to kiss her and though at first she flinched as his lips pressed passionately on hers she put her arms around his neck and pulled him to her with an ardour he had always desired.

"I love you William," she said again, and it was a long time before she drew away.

"Who is in the house?" William said at last.

"Everyone," she replied. "Oh William I do hope you will be reconciled with them. I do not want to see you unhappy."

He held her close again. "I am so happy that nothing in the world can destroy that happiness," he assured her.

"John Radcliffe arrived with a few soldiers just before you did," she added. "Did you catch up with him? Is all well between you?"

At this news William's mind was racing on its previous course. "I'll tell you everything later," he promised. "I will come to you. But at the moment there is a matter I have to settle with John Radcliffe. Would you stable my horse for me?" He began to run across the grass towards the house, leaving her to watch his light bounding figure with a sense of high excitement coursing through her veins.

John and Arabella had returned into the house from the garden by the back entrance and were in the front parlour awaiting Sir James and Lady Hesketh, who had been tactfully informed by Henrietta of the arrival of both the Roundhead major and their son. Suddenly William burst in on them, having entered by the front door. To Arabella's amazement her brother approached John without preamble shouting, "You arrogant bastard! You thought I couldn't be relied upon to keep my word didn't you? You think you have the prerogative for that." His angry tone startled his sister and she looked from one to the other in surprise, believing them to have been reconciled, at least to some extent.

John was momentarily relieved to see that William had suffered no lasting harm, he had worried about the blow he had given him, but he replied firmly, "That isn't true. I knew you would keep your word and I wanted to protect you from what I considered undue and unnecessary pain."

He put out his hand to placate William but he ignored it and went on relentlessly, "Do you realize how often you talk about protecting people? The great protector, that's you. You think you are God controlling everyone's destiny, deciding what's right and good for people with no allowance for their own free will, whether it's the country at large or simple individuals. How can you presume to take such a responsibility upon yourself?

And does it never strike you that your judgments could be wrong?"

Arabella, puzzled and worried by this new quarrel, saw John's tanned face pale a little and a hint of disquiet shadow his brown eyes as he heard William's accusation but he said nothing, stunned by the impact of the words.

Still William continued passionately, "No, it never does occur to you that you might be wrong because you are in direct communication with God aren't you. There's no room for doubt in all your decisions because they are divinely sanctioned and this certainty in your convictions gives you an arrogance that is truly alarming."

The sound of William's upraised voice had brought Lady Mary into the room, closely followed by Henrietta. The first thing his mother noticed was his shorn hair, though his orange sash was in his saddle-bag, and she knew then that he had had no change of mind, a realization that caused a dull pain in her heart. But they were both perplexed by the sight of the two men, whom they had expected to be reconciled, still in seeming disagreement with each other. Lady Mary's hopes took another turn with the thought that William might have changed his mind after all for there could be no other explanation for this antagonism. Henrietta however was studying John Radcliffe's face and inferred some deeper conflict between the two men.

John had made no attempt to defend himself and still William continued, pointing his finger in emphasis of the words and oblivious to the entry of the two women behind him. "I think people need protecting from you, from your certainties and your pride, because I think you are a very dangerous man."

Still John said nothing, staring at William in dismay as the words sunk in.

"Now I am going to do something I have wanted to do for a long time," William said, "and return one of your gifts." He hit him hard on the jaw with his clenched fist and though John staggered backwards with the fierce impact he managed to stay on his feet, perhaps because he had instinctively been expecting the blow.

Sir James Hesketh entered the room just at that moment. He had heard his son shouting and now all that he was aware of was that they were fighting in his house, his son and the hated Roundhead who had caused all the trouble to his home and family- the destruction of the chapel, the possession of his estate, inciting his son to rebellion. A blind rage engulfed him. Arabella had gone to John's side as he recovered from the blow, putting her hand on his arm and looking at him with concern and love. Arabella his favourite child, his angel in her white dress. The Roundhead was taking her away from him too, as he had taken everything else.

"Stop! Stop!" he shouted wildly. Suddenly something seemed to snap in his head and a flash of white-hot pain seared his eyeballs. It seemed he was at Naseby again amid all the horror, the noise, the carnage, and the Roundheads were sweeping down on them and cutting them to pieces. The fragmented thoughts and emotions flashed through his mind in random and confused sequence and superimposed upon the scene was the image of John Radcliffe, in his boots and buff coat and yellow sash, magnified beyond all proportion and bearing all the sins of his fraternity. The descent into madness was for Sir James a long and agonizing fall, though in reality it was but an instant and everything happened so quickly that it was only seconds from his entering the room that the assembled company saw that he had his pistol in his hand. He levelled it straight at the Roundhead officer.

William sprang towards his father, but Arabella ran in front of her lover with arms outstretched just in the second that his finger touched the firing pin. She was going to say, "No father, I love him," but the last part of the sentence was left unfinished in the explosion of the gun.

John would not have believed that anyone as small and light as Arabella could feel so heavy as he sank to the floor with her in his arms. A dark red stain was beginning to spread across her ivory dress and her grey eyes were open wide in an expression of surprise. Terror consumed him as he fought the nightmarish horror that her life had been taken in that instant of madness. In the certainty of his abilities he had sworn to protect her with his body and his life, and instead she had protected him. The dreadful realization overwhelmed him and tore him apart as an animal roar of insupportable pain issued from the depth of his being and great sobs racked his body in a tearing agony of despair. He put his head down on her breast as he held her lifeless body cradled in his arms and his tears mingled with her blood.

CHAPTER 14

OCTOBER 1645

The sudden explosion renting the air, followed by the shocked cries, screams and sobs issuing from the parlour, brought servants running, the oldest and boldest into the room to see what could be done, the others clustered round the door in horrified contemplation of the scene within. William and Henrietta had rushed to their sister whom John, sobbing helplessly, was grasping in a frenzied hold. William was shaking with shock and emotion and tried to look into John's face but his eyes were fixed immovably upon Arabella. Abigail had joined Henrietta and they looked on helplessly, numb with disbelief. Only Lady Mary had thought of her husband. Sir James had sunk into the nearest chair and sat gazing straight ahead with sightless eyes, his mouth open in a grotesque expression of incredulity, his body hunched and limp like a rag doll which had been propped forgotten in a corner. His manservant Alleyn was next to reach him and saw at a glance that something was terribly wrong. Lady Mary, stunned by the shock and like someone sleepwalking, hovered indecisively between her husband and her daughter, totally overcome by a sense of unreality. Outside the last glimmers of the October day surrendered to the encroaching shadows and the room drifted into darkness as no-one bothered to light candles.

John refused to relinquish his hold upon Arabella but finally William managed to persuade him to carry her upstairs to her chamber. At the sight of her daughter's lifeless body in her blood-stained gown being borne from the room with her blonde head lolling against John's shoulder, Lady Mary crumpled into unconsciousness and Henrietta went to her aid. Abigail followed William and John to help lay Arabella upon her bed. John refused to leave her so after a whispered consultation they left him and went back downstairs where servants had lit candles and were hovering helplessly. Sir James was still sitting absolutely motionless like one dead himself.

"I fear there is something dreadfully wrong," said Alleyn who had taken charge of him, "but we shall have to wait and see whether it is merely temporary shock."

William tried speaking to his father but there was no flicker of response so he turned his attention to his mother who was sitting with bowed head in a chair by the empty fireplace with Henrietta's arm around her and Abigail looking on with tears trickling down her face. He remembered how only a short time ago he had told Abigail that nothing could destroy his present happiness. His mother did not lift her head and William did not know what to say to her. He had brought her so much grief and now his impulsiveness and hasty tongue had contributed much to this final tragedy. "I will go and find a priest, Mother," he said at last.

All night John sat beside Arabella, holding her hand until her fingers began to stiffen. They had closed her eyes so they could no longer reproach him and in the darkness she seemed to be asleep. He thought she might wake and smile at him, until his eyes were drawn once more to the crimson stain across her heart where her lifeblood had flowed away. From time to time during the night he was vaguely aware of others drifting through the chamber, but he neither recognized them nor acknowledged their presence. The overwhelming sense of despair pressed upon him like a physical weight, constricting his heart like a man being pressed to death under a great heap of stones, an ever-growing number being added relentlessly to the pile. Increasing the unbearable sense of loss was the knowledge that he himself had been largely responsible for the whole train of events which had culminated in her death, a knowledge made all the more painful because everything he had done had been with the intention of protecting her. And the final crucifying agony was that she had died for him, in his place. He could not accept such a burden of grief and guilt, it was beyond his capacity to bear. He thought of the lake outside the window and imagined its cold dark waters flowing over his head and drawing him down into oblivion. It would be a fitting conclusion to end his life here at Hesketh Hall where all his happiness and all his undoing originated. Only his unwillingness to leave Arabella before she was finally taken from him for ever stayed his feet from treading the path to the lake. He was unaware of the vigilance of his two guardians, for William and Abigail had both recognized the dangers of his distraught state and amid their other cares took turns in watching over him during the long night. At one time Henrietta had come to take a look at her sister and despite her condemnation she had felt a flood of compassion for the man her sister had loved so completely. She blamed him for his part in this tragedy but she also acknowledged the contributions of William and her poor deranged father, and in a moment of illumination she intuited the love that had lain beneath all his actions. She put a hand lightly on his shoulder in a gesture of shared sorrow, which he did not feel but perhaps subconsciously registered.

As dawn broke William came to him. "I am going to find a priest," he said. "I know all the channels. Mother will not allow Arabella to be put into the earth without the Catholic rites. You must go back and tell Cromwell what has passed. I will return as soon as I can."

John was lying beside Arabella on the bed like a grotesque travesty of a bridegroom but now he rose and got unsteadily to his feet. His face was drawn and haggard, his eyes dull. He shook his head saying, "I shall stay with her until she is buried."

"You cannot do that. You have men awaiting you in the stables. If they go back without you you will be accused of desertion," said William gently.

"Yes."

"Then what will you do?"

"I shall go back in due course and face my sentence."

"You could be shot."

"Yes," John said tonelessly, his face expressionless and his eyes stony.

William put his arm on his shoulder and drew him away from the bed with its burden of sorrow. "You cannot take all this upon yourself," he cried. "I am as much to blame as you and we must share the responsibility. If I had not been so hasty and unreasonable, if I had not picked a quarrel with you, then my father might not have acted as he did."

John could not begin to explain to William everything that was in his heart, the overwhelming realization of his own arrogance and self-assurance that had made him believe that he could order other people's lives to his own whim. He felt that William's words to him had been just and therefore his own share in the quarrel the greater. At this moment he lacked the strength and clear-sightedness to formulate all his responsibilities for what had happened. Instead he said simply, "She died for me. Not for you."

William, who had heard his words to the prisoners whose companion had been executed in their stead, knew that nothing he could say at this moment would alleviate John's guilt - no apportioning of blame nor his father's impaired mind. The irrefutable fact remained that Arabella had given her life to protect him. But now he had to be protected from throwing away his own life in recompense. "You must leave Arabella," he insisted. "She must be prepared for burial." He realized he had to be brutal to shake John from his stupor of grief. "It would be better for all concerned if you left. Can't you see what your continuing presence will do to our family. It is a further intrusion. You have no place here now."

As John lifted his eyes to him with the old unflinching regard, William almost had a change of heart. In their shared grief and accountability he felt John more of a brother than he would ever have done had he married his sister. He himself would have liked John to stay for some mutual support, but to the rest of the Heskeths he was the intruder who had been directly responsible for the tragedy in their lives. However this time John made no attempt to desist. With a sickening realization he knew that William was right for there was no longer any place for him at Hesketh Hall. His only tie had been Arabella and now she was no more. It was all over, her life and his.

"You are right. I will go," he said in the same toneless voice.

"You must return to Cromwell and complete your military orders," William insisted, still fearful that some further tragedy might result.

"I will do so," John promised. "But after that I do not know what I shall do."

He kissed Arabella for the last time. She already seemed like a marble effigy with her alabaster skin whiter than ever and her grey eyes shut. All her independence, her courage and her determination had fled and left never a sign on the cold purity of her form. His despair overwhelmed him again as he thought how he would never more see her smile at him, no more feel her body against his. They would never live in the house he had intended to build on his fields nor have their child. And he had brought her to this. His ill-starred intervention into the lives of the Heskeths had caused her death before her life had matured. But for him she would be now alive and carefree and probably in love with a man more suited to her. For her sake he wished with all his heart that he had never come to the Hall. He would leave it now for ever.

Lady Hesketh asked to see him before he left and he approached the parlour in dread at the meeting. He thought of all the times he had asked for an interview with her and been refused and now at this final concessionary encounter he feared her condemnation. She was seated in a chair in the bay of the big mullioned window, composed and elegant in a brown satin gown with a wide collar of cream lace, though her face was almost as white as Arabella's and there were dark shadows beneath her pain-filled eyes. She sat pressed rigidly against the tall carved back of the chair as if for support, with her hands gripping the arms so tightly that her knuckles shone white. He approached tentatively but before he could speak she said quietly, "I wish you to know that I do not consider you to be blamed any more than the rest of us. We are all to blame, each in our own way." Her thoughts had been ranging back over the past year, to the autumn twelve months ago when they had killed the Roundhead intruder and death had first invaded their home. Then the ill-omened visit of Prince Rupert resulting in the premature marriage of Henrietta, and whose disaster at Bristol and dismissal from the King's service had resulted in William's defection and so lit the touch paper of these subsequent events.

They were the first words she had ever spoken to John and he desisted vehemently, crying, "No, Lady Hesketh, not you."

But she interrupted him, speaking the words like one who had rehearsed a part. "I too. It was William I wished dead. God is not mocked. It is He who gives and He who takes away and we cannot usurp His authority and escape with impunity. I wished my child dead and God gratified me and punished me at the same time by taking Arabella instead of William, using as His instrument my husband who was not of sane mind by reason of the wound he sustained at Naseby."

"No, you must not think that, you cannot believe that," cried John aghast, kneeling beside her. "God does not punish us for one solitary mistake, for something spoken in haste that does not come from the soul. God only punishes us for continuous errors, for continually presuming to know His will and making that presumption the excuse for our own actions."

She really looked at him then for the first time, aware of the candour of his brown eyes and the strength inherent in his now weary face. "I have been guilty of too much prejudice, of too much hatred instead of trying to understand those things alien to me. I believe now that God sent me these trials to test my love for Him. Not my faith which has always been strong, but my love. And I have failed Him. If I had been more forgiving towards you then none of this might have happened. I know that you have always tried to help us."

"I should never have come here in the first instance," he admitted sadly. "I was out of my place. I shall never return. But I want you to know that I loved Arabella more than I thought possible. I have been responsible for bringing you much sorrow but I shall carry my punishment for ever."

She touched his head briefly with her hand as he knelt before her and for a moment they were united in their grief. She would never have given Arabella to him willingly but a misalliance now seemed of little import amidst the crushing blows life had inflicted.

"Go now and leave us alone," she said at last.

"Sir James?" he asked hesitantly as he stood up to go, loath to leave this woman until he could explain some of the things in his heart yet knowing they were now of no consequence.

"He is completely paralysed and seems to have lost his mind," she said in a matter-of-fact tone that did nothing to disguise the horror of the words.

John marshalled together his men who were bursting with suppressed curiosity about the events of the previous night, and quit Hesketh Hall. When he reached the end of the driveway he took a last look at the house which for a brief space of time had held all the happiness he had ever known and which fleetingly had been his. Then he turned his back on it all and rode south.

All the way back into Hampshire he rode unseeingly, almost letting his horse take him instinctively. He was overwhelmed, not only by his grief but by the magnitude of his offences. He had done everything wrong, from the day he had first come to the house and taken Abigail's virginity, then making use of the property to billet his company, falling in love with a girl who was beyond him, taking the lease of the Hall, disobeying orders, locking up William. But it was more than the cumulative effects of individual actions. It was the continuous sense of his own self-righteousness, the conviction that he alone knew what was best, not only for himself but for others, as if he were God Almighty William had said. William had always called him arrogant but Arabella had said it before her brother and he had not taken the warning. "You are the most arrogant man I have ever met. I pity you because you have no doubts," she had said early in their acquaintance. It was true, he had had no doubts. Three years ago he had left his profession and enlisted in the army of Parliament because his religious and political beliefs offered no alternative, and it had been impossible to continue fighting without retaining those beliefs. Now for the first time he was shaken by doubts as to whether he had been deluded in thinking his actions were directed, or at least sanctioned, by the will of God. The proof of that assumption lay in the successful ordering of events, the workings of Providence. But everything he had done had been wrong. Suppose, instead of Divine prompting, he, John Radcliffe, in his pride and self-importance, had been personally responsible for all the errors of judgment committed by him. If that were so then where was his God to whom he had prayed and asked for guidance. For the first time in his life he felt completely alone and adrift without rudder or anchor.

Arabella's body was committed to the earth on the fourteenth day of October, according to the rites of the Catholic faith administered by an unfamiliar though sympathetic and exceedingly courageous young priest. Towards dusk a requiem Mass was said in the blackened ruins of the chapel. A thin drizzle trickled down through the roofless sanctuary enveloping the mourners in a misty dampness - William and Henrietta supporting their mother, Ambrose Hardwicke and his parents, shocked beyond measure by the half-tale related to them, the servants clustered behind, and Abigail for the first time in her life joining the Heskeths in their tragic devotions. Sir James was a missing face, sitting motionless and unseeing in his study, watched over by the faithful Alleyn. Ambrose was devastated by the shocking occurrence, unable to believe that his former playmate and anticipated bride had been so cruelly snatched from him. As autumn had approached, heralding the advent of Christmas and Arabella's promise to him, he had become conscious of each passing day taking him nearer to his heart's desire. Now dressed in a mourning suit of grey velvet he shed the tears of a heartbroken lover and swore a lifetime of celibacy. As he wiped his plain flat-featured face with a lace handkerchief he was ignorant of the fact that her real lover was far away. William had neither time nor emotion to spare for Ambrose's grief but Henrietta pitied him and linked her arm in his as he wept.

The worst part of the day however was yet to come. In the dead of night the coffin was loaded onto a horse-drawn cart supported by William and Ambrose in dark cloaks and with spades and a lantern laid beside them. Silas drove the horse while Timothy walked alongside with the priest, his robes hidden beneath a long cape and a hat covering his face. They made their way quietly and quickly to the churchyard in Felton where Silas was left on look-out while the others swiftly dug a grave at the spot arranged by William with the rector. He had been co-operative enough for a sizeable fee, though too terrified of the authorities to agree to anything but a clandestine burial. So sanctified by Catholic ritual,

Arabella's body was interred swiftly and secretly in the graveyard of the Parish church.

The same night far away in Hampshire, unaware that Arabella had been laid ignominiously in her final resting place, John Radcliffe reached his lowest ebb. He had that day been present at the sacking of the Catholic Basing House. The seat of the Catholic Marquis of Winchester, one of the richest noblemen in England, lay two miles outside the town of Basingstoke. The great palace of turrets and towers, enormous in its extent and protected by a double line of fortifications, dominated the trade route between London and the south-west and served as a Royalist base for raiding parties for miles around. Throughout the war it had been a thorn in Parliament's side and had withstood several of their attacks. But it was now the last major Royalist garrison dividing London from the port of Bristol and could no longer be allowed to hold out. The aged marquis had resolutely defied Cromwell's call to surrender his fortress, as he had done many times before, declaring that if the King had no more ground in England than Basing House he would maintain it to the uttermost. Such insolent resistance by powerful Catholics was more than Cromwell could bear and still smarting from previous defeats that the marquis had inflicted upon the army of Parliament he gave the order, "No quarter!"

This time the house could not withstand the full weight of the New Model Army which was thrown against it. The walls were breached with cannon and shot and the Roundheads poured in thousands through every gap, every shattered gateway, every captured gun emplacement, crying "No quarter!" The house was attacked with a ferocity that eventually was to see it razed to the ground. The defenders, including women, were massacred without mercy. Then in accordance with the rules of siege warfare the soldiers were allowed to plunder the house of all its possessions. John watched sickened and helpless as men crazed with greed fought each other to secure valuable paintings, tapestries, silver and gold artefacts, furniture, rich clothes and jewelry, even snatched from the bodies of the dead and from fleeing survivors. For a small amount of plunder the four prisoners had been conveyed to Oxford, an undertaking which had led indirectly to Arabella's death. Now Cromwell's sanction of looting on such a scale of magnitude, because Basing House was a centre of Catholic resistance, seemed to John to make a mockery of his previous demonstration of justice. He had put his head down on his saddle and wept again. The desecration went on for hours in an orgy of violence and lawlessness, and John's only relief from the all-pervading horror was the fact that William Hesketh was absent and unable to witness the destruction of the great Catholic stronghold.

Finally he could stand no more and rode his horse as far as he could from the scene of barbaric brutality, smelling the stench of smoke and blood and death, still hearing the screams of the dying, the exultant laughter of the victors laden with spoils, the angry voices quarrelling over disputed gains, still seeing the leaping flames and the spread-eagled naked bodies. He sat his horse in the concealing shadows of a copse of beeches, watching the dews of evening moisten the fallen brown leaves and trying to bring his thoughts under control. On the night and day following Arabella's death he had lost faith in himself and in the belief of a God personally directing his life. Now he lost faith in the Parliamentary cause and the conviction that God was on their side. It was impossible that God was guiding men to do evil, no matter which side they were on or for what noble ends.

But where did this reasoning lead? God must be at best indifferent, at worst dead. The only possible conclusion was as William had said, that God was on neither side, that He did not care about this war and that men had to sort out the terrible mess for themselves. The other alternative was too terrible to contemplate - that God did not exist.

As darkness fell he rode into the village of Basingstoke and found the nearest tavern. Oblivious to anyone who might see and recognize him he ordered aqua vitae and sat in a corner until he was too drunk to feel anything. Then he picked up one of the whores frequenting the place and with her supporting him stumbled up the creaking twisted staircase to a chamber above. He collapsed onto the dirty bed but was totally unaware of the girl or what happened except her swearing at him and calling him vicious. He woke at dawn, cold and sick with a head full of banging hammers and a realization that nothing had brought him relief. He dressed with difficulty as nausea overcame him, noting that his purse was gone.

He returned to the camp, too wretched to care who might witness his condition, indeed hoping that Cromwell might discover his unacceptable behaviour and bring an end to his torment. He was indifferent to the fact that those who saw him retching and staggering to his pallet attributed it to illness, to camp fever, never suspecting that their abstemious officer was drunk. Only Nathaniel Farrington, one of the regimental preachers, noted the torment in his eyes and later, finding him sitting alone on a straw bale, went to sit beside him. For a time he didn't speak then he said simply, "Basing?"

John shook his head saying, "How can men of God do such things, Nat?"

"Because they are not men of God, John. We have lost our way from the simple faith and the ideals we had at the beginning of this war."

"I no longer think God exists," said John wearily.

Nathaniel Farrington was a man of forty, a carpenter before the war, with a wide experience of men's troubles after serving for three years in the army. John's words had shocked him for he knew Major Radcliffe as one of the most sincerely religious of the officers. "The fool has said in his heart there is no God, John," he replied admonishingly. Then something in the young man's face alerted him to the fact of a more personal trouble than disillusion with Basing House. "Would you like to talk?" he asked. "If you do, then I will listen. Otherwise I will go and leave you to the Lord's compassion."

John had listened many times to Nat Farrington's simple heart-felt sermons. Unlike some of the preachers who frightened the men with fiery exhortations of hell and damnation, Nat spoke encouragingly, stressing God's mercy and His care for all those who sought His aid, giving them comfort in the worst experiences of the war and strength for the trials to come. John felt suddenly weary of trying to carry his burden alone and began to try and explain the grief and guilt of his lover's death, while keeping secret some of the events that had led up to it. "As well as the unsupportable loss I cannot face the fact that she died for me, in my place."

Nathaniel was thoughtful for a time then said gently, "She died protecting you, that is irrefutable. But she did not die in your stead John. Only Jesus Christ died for you, in your stead, for your sins. Arabella died because her life was finished."

"No! No!" John cried vehemently. "Her life had barely started, she was twenty-one years old."

"Sometimes our lives are long, sometimes they are short, but we live the lives that are apportioned to us. We do not have to think of a life cut short but of a life completed, at whatever age it ends. Arabella Hesketh had finished what she had to do. We cannot question the reasoning behind God's will. His ways are not our ways and His thoughts not our thoughts."

"No, no, you are wrong Nat. I cannot believe that all the lives cut short by this war are in accordance with God's will. If that is so then God is a cruel merciless tyrant. It is better to believe He does not exist and all events are random accidents. I am finished Nat. My life is null and void. All I have done has been without reason and I have no longer any reason to live."

"You said your love died in your place. I do not believe that, but the fact remains that you are alive and I do believe that was meant to be. Don't let her death be in vain by throwing yours away now. You are alive because you still have much to do. God does have a purpose for your life and though you cannot see it now, He will show you in His own good time." Nathaniel paused then continued more tentatively, "Perhaps this terrible tragedy was a means to teach you something."

"That Arabella's death was solely to teach me that I am an arrogant self-righteous bastard?" John shook his head in despair and disbelief. "I don't know how you can even voice such a proposition."

"Perhaps I phrased that wrongly. I did not mean to infer that God brought about her death solely to teach you a lesson, but that He can use her sacrifice as a means of bringing you closer to Him and His purposes for your life."

"Then it has failed," John cried bitterly. "All Arabella's death has done is to make me lose my faith completely."

Nathaniel Farrington remained silent again for a time then said gently, "You admitted that you were out of your place there, at the Hall, with the family there. Don't you think this was God's warning and you should have reflected more, prayed more, perhaps acknowledged that your passion was unreasonable. You have said yourself that you did not think Arabella Hesketh could ever be yours." He stopped when he saw the tears running down John's face.

John brushed them away roughly with his hand as he said, "Well she cannot ever be now."

"Don't lose your faith, John," the older man made a last appeal. "It will return in due course."

"It will never return. It is gone for ever. I'm sorry Nat, I know you have only tried to help, but I cannot accept anything you have said. If it had been anyone else I would have called it lip-wisdom but I know you for a sincere honest man who speaks only what he believes. But as for me, I have lost my faith in God and in the Parliament cause."

"For the first I leave you to God's tender mercy. For the second I say we must stay loyal and hold to those ideals which for three years we have fought to uphold - a better fairer world for all Englishmen. We have positions of importance John, you as an officer, me as a preacher, and we must use those to influence men for the good and not let the cause be taken over by irreligious self-seekers. There is much for us to do."

John said nothing and seeing his implacable face Nathaniel Farrington laid his hand gently on his shoulder and walked away feeling sadder than he had done in a long while. But when he had gone John reflected on some of the things he had said. It was true that he had had many warnings that Arabella was not for him but he had forged ahead, trusting in his own pride to surmount undeniable obstacles. There were social conventions that had to be upheld and even though the war had slackened time-held bonds there were still recognizable boundaries. His misplaced passion and the way it had consumed him had brought about her death. The acceptance only served to magnify his responsibility and increase his guilt load.

When William Hesketh arrived at the camp a short time later he was shocked by John's haggard appearance, his blood-shot eyes and the unmistakeable smell of spirits. "Why don't you go home?" he said to him. "You are in no fit state to face a winter campaign." Despite the time of year the New Model Army had been ordered to march towards Exeter for a campaign in Devon and Cornwall. Because of practical difficulties the war had never been waged seriously during the winter months, but Fairfax and Cromwell were certain they had reached the last phase so it was necessary to strike while the iron was hot and crush the only Royalist resistance now remaining. "Plead sickness and resign your commission. For you are sick, John," William insisted. "You have done enough. Go home to Huntingdon and pick up the threads of your life there."

"I have no life there without Arabella," he replied. All his plans for returning there had been coloured by dreams of Arabella as his wife and the prospect of going home to Huntingdon without her was intolerable. "I will carry on fighting to the end." He had given more thought to what Nathaniel Farrington had said. He had lost his firmly-held belief that God's providence was working through the Parliament cause but he realized he still believed in the political objectives of their struggle. He had given three years of his life to that struggle and would not abandon it so near to its completion. Besides he welcomed a winter campaign. He welcomed the hardship as a penance. It might help to blot out all else from his memory and it would be an opportunity to court death in an honourable guise. With neither love nor faith to prompt him now there was only death.

"I still don't think you are fit enough to continue. In your present state you will be a liability," William persisted. "I will take on your share and fight for us both."

John realized that William was still trying to share the guilt-load with him. He felt ashamed to think how he had once doubted the young man's constancy, for not only was he willing to continue fighting for Parliament but to take his own place in a gesture of solidarity.

"We will continue fighting together William," he said, grasping his hand in a sudden rush of emotion. "But I shall need your help and support." He had been wrong again. Even without love and faith there was something more than death. There was friendship. It seemed as if he had not completely finished with the Heskeths.

CHAPTER 15

JUNE - OCTOBER 1646

On a fine warm day in June in the year 1646 Abigail Hart made ready to marry William Hesketh. Early in the morning Henrietta went to Abigail's chamber under the eaves. "You helped me get ready for my wedding, now I will do the same for you," she said.

"It seems very strange to be waited on," murmured Abigail with a little rueful smile. "I have always served others."

"You will have to get used to it," Henrietta replied, picking up the comb and wondering how best to arrange her glorious hair. "You will be mistress here one day."

Sitting in her shift with her hair loose and falling to her waist, Abigail looked about the room with her few possessions, the room where she had lived for the past eight years, where she had often leant out of the window to watch the comings and goings of the Hall in which she had no part. She felt a little afraid of the future and the responsibilities she would have to assume.

"I think I will put the pearls in your hair since you would not have it cut in a more fashionable style," said Henrietta consideringly. The pearls were Abigail's wedding gift from William.

The evening previously she had gone to him and given him a last chance to change his mind but he had only laughed. "I can't afford to recant now that I have spent all my money on the wedding," he teased her. He had been to London and bought himself a new set of clothes and bolts of cloth for the women, as well as enjoying a last batchelor fling. But he had no regrets at giving up his freedom. In the past four years he had experienced more of life than the past generation had known in a lifetime and he had drunk the cup to its dregs. He still could not believe that he had lived through that hard bitter campaign of the last winter, a campaign of brutal fighting, intolerable physical hardship and low morale. It had been a living hell which seemed to last for ever as the south-west was conquered, not in one great battle but inch by inch, every garrison, every town, every river, contested with great loss of life. The winter had been severe with torrential rain turning the roads into a sea of mud through which men and horses floundered to knees and fetlocks. Billeting could not be found in the sparsely populated areas and tents were few so most men had to sleep under hedgerows and awoke next morning to soaking clothes and paralysed limbs. Sickness was rife and men deserted in their hundreds. Then as the cold increased the rain turned to snow, clamped to the earth for weeks by the iron bands of a bitter frost. The mud caked into perilous ice whilst blizzards stung their faces and confused their direction in unfamiliar territory, adding miles to their journeys.

The Cavaliers had been fighting for survival and gone was the amateurish half-hearted skirmishing that had often characterized hostilities in the past. William still could not completely reconcile himself to the fact that he was helping to deal the death blow to his former comrades. He had carried his own guilt burden as much as John Radcliffe as they fought together. But he knew enough about King Charles to realize he would never yield willingly nor mediate with his opponents, regardless of how many men might die. The only chance of peace for the country seemed to be a victory for Parliament. William was not alone in thinking that it now ceased to matter which side was victorious so long as the war could be brought to an end and England could begin to heal her tragic wounds. Principles had been eroded by weariness and most people were desperate for peace, no matter how attained.

The winter had at last come to an end with the subjugation of the south-west and the defeat of the Royalist forces there. By the spring of 1646 only Oxford remained in Royalist control, though with the King and Court in residence there were still hopes that a revival of the King's cause might be possible. The capture of Oxford was to be the final act of the war. William Hesketh could not bear to deal the final blow to the city that had been his base for so long and considered the time had come for him to lay down his commission. He had fought for both the Royalists and the Parliamentarians and felt that whatever compromise could now be attained for the government of England he had earned his right to take advantage of it. He had started the war careless and confident, recklessly killing those on the side opposite to him because their beliefs were not his. He had finished it sadder and wiser, more tolerant of men's differences but more cynical of men's motives and, above all, sickened by the devastation of his country and the senseless killing of his countrymen. Now at twenty-two years old all he wanted to do was settle down on his estate with the girl he loved and retrieve his fortunes. Excitement and adventure no longer appealed to him.

He looked at Abigail for the last time in her plain clothes and white coif. "I know what I am doing," he reassured her. "I have never wanted anything so much as

I want you." Then he gave her the blue velvet box and when she opened it she saw a rope of perfect pearls.

"I have never had any jewelry before," she said, touching their milky whiteness in awe.

William watched her face with pleasure. The glowing purity of the pearls would complement her beauty more than any brilliant diamonds but he said, "You will have jewels a-plenty, my love. You should have had the family heirlooms but as you know we gave them for the Royalist cause. This is all I can afford at the moment but I will replace all our wealth in time. And don't say I should be marrying a rich heiress. I don't want to be bound to any woman by her gold. I shall reclaim the family fortunes by own efforts because that is how I prefer it. I am marrying you because I love you and I cannot wait for tomorrow. I once showed you my lust but tomorrow I will show you my love."

As Henrietta threaded the pearls in Abigail's unbound tresses she remembered how Abigail had festooned her own hair with spring flowers on her marriage day. Arabella had been there to help on that day and she could not believe her sister would not come running into the room now. Her presence still hung about the house and each festival and anniversary brought memories. William had invited John Radcliffe to his wedding but whether he would come was uncertain. She wondered what painful memories would be his on this day and doubted that he would return.

When Henrietta slipped the wedding gown over her head Abigail gave a tremour of delight as the soft whispering taffeta shimmered to the floor. There was also a sharp intake of breath from Henrietta as the new Abigail was revealed, no longer the demure Puritan maid but an astonishing beauty who would one day be Lady Hesketh. Her gown was deep green, neither light nor dark but which reflected the colour of her eyes and rippled with hidden depths like a tree-shaded pool speared by shafts of sunlight. Her tall slenderness was emphasized by the low-cut bodice with its ruched sleeves and full sweeping skirt, and her rich auburn hair, threaded with William's pearls, tumbled over her shoulders and fell to her waist. Abigail herself drew a sharp breath when she saw herself in the mirror which Henrietta had brought for her. All her life she had worn plain sombre clothes and now she had emerged like a butterfly from a chrysalis, not from any sense of vanity but through love of William Hesketh. She had brought him no dowry but her beauty and it was right that he should have that in all its splendour, no sin when meant for him alone.

Henrietta felt a stab of envy as she looked at her but said warmly, "You look so beautiful. You will have to take Arabella's place as my sister now. I cannot see it will make much difference because we have been friends for so long. But are you really happy, Abigail? When I gave you my bridal favour I hoped it would bring you good fortune. I know that William can be difficult but you know him as well as anyone and I am sure he will love you and be faithful to you."

"Yes I am happy," said Abigail, quietly but firmly. Her Puritan reticence still made it difficult for her to express her love and, unlike Henrietta, she had never read romances or poetry so was unacquainted with the language of love, a deficiency, together with much else, that William would make good. "Are you content, Henrietta, that I should be a real member of your family?" She still couldn't help feeling uneasy that she would usurp Henrietta's status.

"I would much rather have you as a sister than some spoilt shallow heiress that William might have been saddled with," Henrietta laughed mischievously as she kissed her cheek.

Lady Hesketh had asked to see Abigail before they left for the Parish church as she would never retract her stubborn refusal to enter there herself. She was still hurt that William had renounced the faith, though she knew his acceptance of Protestantism was a matter of expediency and that in his heart he still kept the old religion so she had no fears for his immortal soul.

"Which would you rather have, mother, landless Catholics or our inheritance preserved by a nominal acceptance of Protestantism?" he had asked bluntly. "It seems a small price to me."

Lady Mary herself would have preferred fidelity, even at the cost of Hesketh Hall, but she knew it was too much to expect the same sacrifice from her young ambitious son with all his life before him. Who knew what would happen in the future. She never ceased to hope and pray for England's return to the old faith.

When Abigail stood before her, glorious in her transformation, Lady Mary had the peculiar sensation of travelling back through time and seeing a reflection of her young self. How she wished she could turn back the years and look as Abigail did today, in her dress of her favourite green with her chestnut hair flowing over her shoulders. And William looked much as his father had done twenty years ago. Sir James had become like an infant, totally dependent on others for every detail of his existence, and Lady Mary had taken upon herself the burden of caring for him, rarely allowing the faithful Alleyn to relieve her. It was a penance for her sins and a labour of love for the man he had once been. As she fed, washed and dressed him, attending to his every need, she saw in the pitiable travesty of his person the man she had once known. As she combed his thin grey hair and wiped his sunken face with its sightless eyes, the figure she held in her memory was of a tall handsome charming man with fair curling hair and a small pointed beard. They had spent more than twenty years of happiness together in this beautiful house with three surviving children, and had been at the centre of life in the shire and the envy of all who knew them until the civil war had rent apart the country and their own lives. She sat for hours in his company, reminiscing aloud and recalling all the incidents of their life together, hoping that some particular memory might ignite a spark of life in him. Sometimes she imagined the light pressure of a finger or some flicker in his staring eyes and occasionally a strange moaning sound would issue from his lips. She persevered and clung to the hope that he could hear and understand her. But each day blurred into a sameness. She would awake each morning wondering how she would find the strength to face the day, then retire at night to bed, dreading the hours of lonely wakefulness.

In the midst of all her troubles it seemed of little importance that William had contracted a misalliance. She would have liked a rich Catholic heiress for him but since he had chosen to marry for love she considered he could have made a worse choice. She knew that Abigail was kindly and sensible, both gentle and strong, always used to waiting on others yet never with servility. No doubt she would supply all the needs of her selfish wayward son and would certainly grace his bed and his board. She knew also that Abigail loved Hesketh Hall and was familiar with the management of it. Indeed for the past six months she and Henrietta had run the household between them as all her own time had been devoted to the care of her husband. As Abigail stood before her now, all that remained for Lady Hesketh was to assure her one-time maid of a warm welcome into the family which in reality she had been a part of for so long. All else had been said between them when William had first informed his mother of their intention.

"I want you to have this as my wedding gift to you," she said, handing her an emerald pendant in a setting of pearls on a gold chain. "My husband once gave it to me and it is one of the few pieces still remaining to me. It will suit your colouring as it did mine and I am sure it would please Sir James for you to have it on the day you marry William." She fastened it around Abigail's neck where it fitted into the low neckline of her gown, glowing against her creamy skin.

Abigail was overcome with emotion and couldn't speak except to murmur, "You have always been so kind to me, Lady Hesketh, and I am most grateful for everything. I promise you I will always do my best for William."

"I have no fears for William, or you," Lady Mary said confidently.

When Abigail descended the staircase in her bridal finery all the servants were gathered in the hall to watch, marvel and envy. Clever girl to have so ensnared the master with her prudent modesty, was the common opinion. But as William watched her descent he felt his heart miss a beat. He had always been captivated by her in her plain simple clothes and used to fantasise about how she would look dressed as most ladies of his acquaintance. But the reality put his dreams to shame, taking his breath away and sobering him for a moment with the realization of his great good fortune. What he said to her however as he took her hand was, "Of course everyone thinks I have got you with child and am doing the honourable thing by you."

All the town had turned out to watch William Hesketh marry his servant and the church was crowded with curious onlookers and guests. Most of them were thinking as William said they would, though when they saw Abigail there was no-one present who did not understand why he was doing it. William had always intended to display his bride and had invited everyone of importance from far and near in order to demonstrate this was no hole in the corner affair but a liaison in which he took enormous pride. It was with immense satisfaction that he noticed the envy in men's eyes and the reluctant admiration in the women's.

Two unlikely guests had deep personal feelings of their own. Looking ill at ease amongst the landed gentry but nonetheless beaming with pride, Aunt Keziah sat behind her niece. She felt self-conscious in the new gown of grey satin with a real lace collar, her coif topped by a grey felt hat with a band of striped grey and white ribbon, for in all her life she had never had such a fine outfit as William had bought for her. She only wished that her dear Jacob could have been beside her to witness Abigail's unbelievable good fortune, for when they secured a position for her in the household of the noble Heskeths whoever could have believed it would have resulted in a marriage with the heir. The ways of the Lord were indeed past finding out. However she had no doubts at all that her niece was good enough for the handsome young spark in his doublet woven with silver thread, his grey eyes twinkling with suppressed excitement beneath his plumed hat.

At the back of the church a Roundhead officer sat alone. Up till the last moment John Radcliffe had been undecided about accepting William's fervent invitation, but he had been close by. He had been part of the Parliament army besieging Oxford, which had finally surrendered to Sir Thomas Fairfax though the King himself had managed to escape. Being outside the walls of Oxford again had brought back memories of a time when he had been happy, and he was suddenly overtaken by a desire to see Hesketh Hall once more before returning home to Huntingdon. Besides he and William had grown close during the shared miseries of that terrible winter campaign. The bond that had been growing between them for some time, at first unperceived, had strengthened in the common ground of shared tragedy, guilt, and hardship, to forge a tie of mutual respect. Beyond that they had discovered a genuine liking for each other's company, despite their differences. But their friendship had been dearly bought.

The winter campaign had been John's own personal Hell though Nathaniel Farrington had called it his Calvary. But in his distraught state he had welcomed every torment inflicted by the weather and the appalling fighting conditions. He wanted to be punished to the extremity of his endurance and the continuous physical agony drained the anguish from his mental wounds. He could see little purpose in living and though his first impulse for self-slaughter had passed he would have welcomed death in the guise of duty. He gave up his right to an officer's tent and slept with his men under hedgerows in driving rain or awoke freezing cold to a coverlet of snow, but his robust constitution held. He rode in the forefront of every action without any concession to his personal safety but the musket balls missed their mark and the pistol shots went wide. He volunteered for every dangerous assignment, climbing walls and breaching ramparts to reconnoiter, leading scouting parties into disputed territory, but by an irony of fate he always escaped unscathed. One night he was returning from a raid with a small troop when they were ambushed by a Royalist force. He received a sword wound to his neck but as he lay on the snow-covered ground the snow staunched the flow of blood and the severe frost held it in check, so that when they were discovered on the morrow by their own men his life had been miraculously saved. Once he would have attributed his preservation to the hand of God but now he considered it only as a perverse stroke of fate. But he concluded that he was not to die, that was too easy. His punishment was to go on living, and he accepted it as the most severe sentence he could have been given.

When on the first day of May General Fairfax brought the New Model Army up to Oxford William Hesketh had tendered up his commission and asked John his own intentions.

"I shall see out the siege then when Oxford has fallen I will go back to Huntingdon," he replied. "It shouldn't be a long siege and by then everything will effectively be over."

William was collecting together his belongings ready for his return to civilian life and had implored his presence at his wedding. "I know you will find it hard to return to the Hall but you cannot go on blaming yourself for ever. It is nearly a year now since Arabella died, you must learn to forget."

"I shall never forget," John retorted, angry that William should ever contemplate such a possibility, "and you are a fool if you think I ever could."

"You still have your life to live and you cannot live with such a burden for ever," William persisted. "Arabella would not wish it, not when she saved your life for you. I was as responsible as you and I too have suffered as you know. But I have now discharged my guilt and am looking to my own happiness. After all, even when reproach has been shared, you have to admit that the primary cause of all our tragedies was the war itself."

"What is war but soldiers? And what are soldiers but you and I?"

"Well we have done with soldiering now," William said.

And so he has, John thought, seeing him standing at the altar with his bride, his face vivid with pride and joy. He was now not sure that he should have come, the first time in almost a year that he had been inside a church. He was lonely and he envied William, for he too was dazzled by Abigail's beauty as he gazed on her perfect form in the flowing green gown, the flawless cream of her oval face, her long loose tresses glowing like burnished copper where a shaft of sunlight from a lancet window caught their radiance. She could have been his, beautiful and passionate, and he instinctively recalled the night he had made love to her. He immediately pushed away the unbidden image as unworthy, but in his low spirits he couldn't help wondering why he hadn't been content with a girl of his own class who had said she loved him. That was another link in the chain that bound him to William Hesketh but it must remain always a secret. Looking at Abigail's serenely glowing face he was sure she loved William so perhaps it was possible to love more than once and, incredible though it seemed to him, to love with a deeper intensity the second time. He also admired William's courage in flouting convention and couldn't help thinking that this uneven marriage could have foreshadowed his own.

William was aware of the envy of many men and relished it. When they were kneeling together at the altar he leaned over and whispered in his new wife's ear, "I once told you that I always get my own way," and when she lifted her head to look at him he was smiling triumphantly.

John had considered leaving after the ceremony but both William and Abigail had pleaded with him to return to the Hall for the wedding breakfast and he had reluctantly agreed. As he made his way through the churchyard he found Henrietta beside him and they continued walking together. She had relinquished her seat in the carriage to Aunt Keziah, which had further enhanced an event that was to provide unlimited matter for conversation for years to come back in Stratford. They saluted each other carefully, not having met since Arabella's death, then lost in their own thoughts walked silently through the fields of crimson poppies and corn ripening in the warm sun. Henrietta found herself speaking her thoughts aloud, almost without realizing it. "I wore yellow when I married and everyone said I looked beautiful."

"I am sure you did, Mistress Halsall," John replied absently, then the youthful ingenuousness of the remark struck him and he turned to look at her. She looked like a mature society lady in her brown satin gown with its wide spreading lace collar, until beneath her wide-brimmed hat of cream felt he saw her youthful face with its freckles and the tears glistening in her brown eyes.

"I wore a yellow dress when Colonel Griffin came to beg our possessions for the Royalist cause, and again when Prince Rupert came to the Hall. Then on my wedding day. I shall never wear yellow again." She turned her expressive eyes on him and said, "You should not have taken me from Oxford that time. I never saw my husband again and I always felt I deserted him in the last weeks of his life."

It was another thing he had done wrong for the sake of Arabella John considered sadly. He had never been aware of Henrietta before except as Arabella's sister. Now as he looked at her sad young face he felt a bond of sympathy with her, remembering that she had lost both a husband and a sister, and to all extent a father also. And she was no more than twenty years old. "We cannot think of what might have happened. We do our best at the time and no more can be asked of us," he said, comforting her with platitudes he did not take to heart himself.

Henrietta's quick sensibility heard the note of uncertainty in his voice. She had always treated him coldly as the unwelcome stranger whose imposition on their lives had brought tragedy and had never understood her sister's fatal partiality for him. Now she studied him carefully, noting the strong contours of his attractive face, his firm mouth and steady eyes of the same deep brown as her own. Her naturally compassionate nature sensed how difficult it would be for him to see Hesketh Hall again and she decided to stay by his side and try to divert him by neutral conversation, no great hardship for her as it helped to distance her from the glittering happiness of William and Abigail which reminded her all too vividly of her own wedding day here. They remained together, finding mutual support to endure their sad memories amongst the rampant joviality of the many guests, and John was agreeably surprised by Henrietta's intelligent conversation and her grasp of current affairs. He realized afterwards that the time spent in her company had helped him to face the scene of his tragedy unflinchingly. He did not wait however to see the couple bedded with all the bawdy jesting of the customary ritual and proffering his excuses and his good wishes set off again for Oxford.

Oxford was indeed John Radcliffe's last assignment as an officer in the New Model Army. There he tendered up his commission to Oliver Cromwell whom he had served faithfully for four years. "I would like to have kept you with me, John. There is still much work to be done. The King has escaped us and so long as he is free there will still be resistance. And we shall have to subdue Scotland and Ireland before we have finished. Go to Ireland with the army and I will make you a colonel. There will be great gains to be had in Ireland, land and estates bigger than Hesketh Hall," said Cromwell, eyeing him speculatively.

"I know you are not going to like this," said John carefully, "but I no longer believe you can solve problems by the sword."

"Oh! And how else?" was the brusque rejoinder.

"I don't know ...... discussion ..... greater understanding perhaps ..... compromise."

"And don't you think we have already tried all these," Cromwell barked. "You are entitled to your opinion because I have fought to make this a free country but I can tell you that you are wrong. To compromise with evil is the work of the Devil. Sometimes the sword is the only way. 'Think not that I am come to send peace on the earth; I am come not to send peace but a sword.' That is the word of God."

John knew it was useless to argue with his old commander and there was silence for a moment. Then when Cromwell saw that John was not going to be persuaded he went on, "However there's valuable work for lawyers too. Everyone is claiming compensation for loss and damage, or imagined loss and damage, now that we are the victors. I know we could refuse all civil liability - 'inter arma silent leges', that's the phrase isn't it? - but it is important for the Parliament to be seen as custodians of the law."

"I shall continue to work for the Parliament cause," John promised, "and should you ever have urgent need of me, send for me. I shall be in Huntingdon."

Cromwell grasped his hand in a gesture of friendship. "I have some land for you John, seeing you have lost the Felton manor. No, not sequestered land," he added as he saw the younger man's expression. "Near your own fields in Huntingdon. Old Jacob Fairlie died of late with no dependants and asked that his land be let to one of the faithful. It's yours for a nominal sum if you want it."

John accepted the offer gratefully and thanked his old commander. Oliver Cromwell did not forget those who served him loyally.

"My daughter Bridget is marrying Henry Ireton here in Oxford tomorrow," he said conversationally.

"Yes I have heard. My felicitations to them. Colonel Ireton is a good man."

"I have two more daughters growing up. Come and pay us a visit sometime."

"I will," John promised. "I will not sever my ties with what has been my life for so long. I have become so used to being a soldier that I do not know how I shall settle to being a lawyer again." He did not say how he had become accustomed to pain and discomfort, to brutality and killing, but instead he confessed, "One gets used to a sense of power."

"Oh yes, it is very easy to get accustomed to power," said Oliver Cromwell.

John Radcliffe found it more difficult than he had imagined to accustom himself again to his old life in Huntingdon. He had been too long away and changed too much from the quiet country lawyer with the unassailable Puritan beliefs. He found himself alienated from his family and his old acquaintances by his experiences of the past four years. After their initial joy at his return his widowed mother and his two older sisters and their families were bewildered by the change in him. They found it difficult to communicate with this morose and withdrawn stranger and were shocked by his neglect of the Puritan faith. For his part he was no longer content with their simple life nor could he share their religious certainties. He grew impatient at the naivety of their conceptions and chafed at the cramped conditions of his mother's cottage at the corner of the market place by the Grammar School. Everything seemed too small and constricting after the freedom of soldiering, even the busy little market town with its close-knit community. The neighbourliness was a threat to his closely-guarded reserve. When he never made an appearance at church he was summoned to the Parish council who were perplexed by his inability to give a satisfactory explanation for his absence and could only threaten him with the mandatory fine. There was no shortage of work however. He was overwhelmed by people clamouring for litigation on account of the war as well as the normal disputes over land and property, exacerbated now by confiscation and sequestration. There was a continual increase in the number of people who claimed the Parliament owed them money or compensation and it was a thankless task trying to sift the genuine claimants from the opportunists. But he welcomed the work and worked longer and longer hours so that his mind would be full and his intellect kept busy, leaving no time for introspection. His continuous working life also excused him from the necessity of spending time with his family or socializing. He was making money however and, despite having no wife to share it, decided to arrange for a house to be built on Jacob Fairlie's land just outside the town. This would be another way of finding some space for himself away from the intrusive demands of his former life.

Then his depression returned with renewed force as he recollected how he had planned such a project for Arabella, his melancholy nourished by the fact that he was overworked. He lived each day routinely from daybreak to sundown but during the night hours memories and images intruded into his restless sleep, tormenting him with conflicting illusions of horror and joy. The seasons changed but the days kept a uniformity, for to him the world was always grey and there was no discernible difference between the bright sunlit days of summer and the drab dreariness of autumn which brought the anniversary of Arabella's death. Then he was filled with an unsurpressible longing to return to Hesketh Hall.

He made the journey back in the closing days of a wet and cold October. As he rode along the familiar driveway he was suddenly overcome with trepidation, how would he be received, what further effect would tragic memories have upon him. Then the house appeared before him with all its associations. He reined in his horse as he had done many times before and sat with the rain dripping from his broad-brimmed hat and onto the shoulders of his cloak, loving every line of the beautiful building. He noticed that the wood was well on its way to new growth, and daisies and gentians still bloomed around the edges of the lake, its iron-grey surface dimpled by the rain. Light shone from the great mullioned window to disperse the grey murkiness of the gloomy afternoon and as he rode up to the entrance there was a sense of warmth emanating from within. Perhaps his visit could lay the ghosts of the past for him and he could begin to live again.

He was welcomed with a cordiality that surprised and cheered him. When his arrival was announced by a solemn manservant, William came running eagerly to greet him crying, "John, John Radcliffe, by all that's wonderful. How good it is to see you."

Abigail followed her husband with the same warm greeting and John noted her figure rounding with their first child. To his surprise a smile of pleasure also lit Henrietta's face as she joined the others in the front parlour where a fire was burning and candles were already alight. Henrietta no longer wore sombre mourning and was dressed in a cobalt blue gown with white lace collar and cuffs, but her adolescent plumpness was gone forever, her figure slender and her features well-defined. Even Lady Hesketh greeted him courteously though John was shocked to see her so gaunt with grey overtaking the chestnut of her hair. For the Heskeths it was the first time they had seen John not dressed as a soldier of Parliament. His breeches and plain doublet were of grey worsted but of good quality and well tailored and his collar and cuffs, though unadorned by lace, were of fine linen. He wore riding boots and when he took off his hat they could see that his thick hair was noticeably longer, reaching his collar, though his face was less tanned than when he had lived out of doors. But there was no sign of the Roundhead officer and the barriers that had once existed between them melted away. The unexpected reunion revealed to them all how close their lives had become entwined by ties forged by shared experiences, not all of them happy and not always noticeable at the time of their making, but nonetheless real.

John made a pilgrimage to Arabella's grave to lay down one of the last roses he had plucked from the walled garden, and laid his heart at rest also. There was nothing more he could do about the past. He had paid his debt as much as he could and now he must live in the present. He had begun to do so with the building of a house in his home town where he belonged, and he now realized there was still valuable work for him as he put his skills and experience at the service of those trying to rebuild England's future.

But then his intended brief visit lengthened into days. William enthusiastically sought his advice for a number of projects he had in mind. He was already planning improvements to the estate and the house, secure in the knowledge of Abigail's thrifty management of his household. His father was retreating further into the shadowy half-land between life and death but new life was already promised in the person of their child, and William was looking ahead to when the baronetcy would be his and he would have an heir. John was very conscious of the happiness existing between William and Abigail, the secret glances they exchanged, the message for him in her green eyes, the smile that hovered around his lips when he looked at her. But he was also perceptive enough to see a sense of longing in Henrietta's expressive eyes as they lingered on Abigail's contented face and swelling figure. Henrietta and John often found themselves seated next to each other when the family were together or sometimes encountered each other as they strolled in the grounds, lost in their own thoughts. They called each other by name and had discovered by accident how easy it was to converse together. John was surprised by Henrietta's readiness to talk about present political developments as well as the affairs of the Hall and estate, often spiced by an irrepressible wit, while she in turn was interested in his work and surprised by both his intellect and his sensitivity. With a sudden shock she realized she would miss his interesting company when he returned home while he had been pondering over an idea that had recently come into his mind.

On the day before his return he asked her to walk with him. They walked to the wood and around the lake, conversing generally as they had become accustomed to, until they found themselves at last in the walled garden. They sat on the seat in the arbour which offered some shelter from the chill wind, sitting in comfortable silence and watching a little sparrow on the grass in front of their feet pecking disconsolately at a fallen leaf, his feathers ruffled by the wind, until at last he flew away in annoyance.

Then John said carefully, "I do sincerely hope this will not offend you, Henrietta, but I have a proposition to put to you." He paused for a moment trying to put his feelings into words and thinking how like a lawyer he sounded. "I am twenty-eight and trying to build up my life again but I do not want to spend the rest of my life alone. I know that you also are lonely and I wondered if you would consider marrying me. I know that my birth and background is different to yours, as it was with your sister, but I am making money, I have a substantial new house that is almost finished, an honourable profession and one day I hope to be a circuit judge. I could offer you a life which, though not equal to the one you have known, would be one of comfort and respect and where you would lack for very little. I know we do not love each other in the way of lovers and that we could never be more than second best to each other, but we have a mutual liking and respect and we have shared the same sorrow. But please be honest and tell me if you find my presumption offensive."

Henrietta sat looking straight ahead, across the grass and the formal flower beds to the yellow stone wall where the climbing roses were dying, and beyond the wall to the flat expanse of the leaden sky. The proposal had surprised her but it touched a chord of yearning in her heart. She did not want to remain a widow and she wanted a child like Abigail. But she did not relish making herself available on the marriage market where the façade of courtship often screened the financial negotiations for someone in her position, and there was no-one amongst their circle of acquaintances with whom she wished to form a union. Her mother had tentatively suggested Ambrose Hardwicke but her feelings for him were as they always had been. She had married for love once and that was a privilege denied to many women, perhaps a marriage of convenience that promised practical advantages might be worth considering. It was what most women had to be satisfied with and John Radcliffe was as acceptable as many men would be.

"No woman could be offended by a proposal of marriage," she said gently but she hesitated to reply to his question.

"I would make few demands upon you. You would be free to follow your own religion. I think we could build a satisfactory life together and it would be a way of……," he sought for the right word, " … of transmuting some of the tragedy we have experienced."

Henrietta still did not reply but she was thinking of how great a release it would be to go far away from Hesketh Hall, away from the distressing sight of her father's deterioration and the feelings of helplessness it engendered, away from her mother's self-imposed sacrifice which she would allow no-one to share, away from the exclusive happiness of William and Abigail, whose role as new mistress inevitably reduced her own usefulness no matter how much consideration was shown to her. Yet it was such a big step to take. She hardly knew John Radcliffe, they were little more than strangers to each other. And once she had said she would never marry a man she did not love.

As she turned towards him, her face peeping from beneath the furred hood of her green cloak, he was suddenly struck by how young and vulnerable she looked. He had no right to make such an unexpected demand upon her without due consideration. If she had not already been a widow, responsible to no-one but herself, he would not have done so.

"I'm sorry to have startled you without due preparation. I will give you time to consider," he said humbly, realizing how much he was asking of her.

His lips were set in a tight line of anxiety and Henrietta remembered how she had once thought him stern. She admired his honesty and the way he had addressed her without any pretence of sentiments he did not feel. Instinctively she felt she could trust him, her sister had done so. Many arranged marriages where the parties knew little of each other (as in the case of her own parents) worked out as well as any other. He was young, honest, intelligent and trustworthy. She knew instinctively he would be faithful, a fair husband and a kindly father. What else could a woman wish for?

"I do not need any more time to consider. I will marry you," she said at last. "But I have nothing to bring you. I have little of my own and the Heskeths are no longer rich, as you know."

"That was never in my thoughts. That you bring me yourself and your trust is all I ask. And whatever I have is yours, little enough for your merit but I hope that in time it will be more."

Henrietta smiled tremulously, suddenly overwhelmed by the tremendous step she had taken.

"When the winter is over and spring comes, and William and Abigail have their child, I will marry you."

It was a contract entered into with rational deliberation, and yet it was a betrothal. They were both now surprised by what they had done. Henrietta remembered how she had at first disliked him and John wondered if he was only repeating the mistakes he had made with Arabella. However many of the previous obstacles were removed because as a widow Henrietta was her own mistress and he thought William would offer no objection. But he couldn't help wondering why he was getting involved with another of the Heskeths. What was it about this place that undeniably drew him back to it. He was forced to consider that behind his proposal might lie an unacknowledged need to continue the attachment.

They sat side by side in the walled garden, an unrecognizable pair of lovers, feeling a little uneasy with each other again as they considered the commitment they had made to the future. A chill wind cut across the grass and the last remaining leaves dropped from the trees and fell at their feet.

CHAPTER 16

SPRING 1647 - AUTUMN 1648

As Henrietta Mary Halsall stood beside John Radcliffe in the Parish church at Huntingdon she wondered, not for the first time, what she was doing there. All Saints' was an unfamiliar church and the medieval architecture showed obvious signs of damage inflicted during the war, for the Cavaliers had knocked down the thirteenth century tower because they thought it was being used as a Roundhead look-out post. Behind her she was aware of John's family in their severe clothes, their faces faintly disapproving of her Catholic name and her elegant appearance. Henrietta had considered herself to be most discreetly dressed in a gown of palest grey. What she did not realize was that the silvery silk shimmered like running water, rippling with incandescent gleams in the light from the clerestory windows, and the topknot of tiny curls perched atop the ringlets of her glossy brown hair was held in place by a pair of sparkling diamond pins, a wedding gift from William.

On the previous day when she had arrived in Huntingdon she had been surprised and disappointed by the suspicious reception afforded her by John's family - his elderly mother and his two older sisters, Patience and Edah, with their husbands Isaac and Samuel. It had never occurred to her that they might disapprove of John's choice of a wife, a baronet's daughter, a Royalist widow and a Catholic. She had always surmised that any opposition to the match would be from her own relatives, never suspecting that the Radcliffes would not appreciate the advantages of such a union. They had stood silently appraising her in her travelling habit of green velvet, her emerald ear-rings and her fashionably curled hair threaded with green ribbon, whilst the row of small solemn children in their white caps and aprons stared at her wide-eyed. Unnerved by their stern inspection she did not realize that the children were thinking she was the most beautiful creature they had ever seen, while their elders were astonished by her youth. Having only been informed that she was a widow they were expecting a woman of mature years and were confounded by the sight of an apparently frivolous young girl.

The sermon was very long. But above the pulpit was a medieval gargoyle with a mischievous smiling face and Henrietta was cheered by it, entering into its conspiracy of droll amusement at these solemn Puritans. Finally at the communion table, bare of all religious ornament and covered by a white cloth, she and John Radcliffe were joined together in holy matrimony, though without a ring as Puritans did not believe in such symbols, and found themselves man and wife. They looked at each other for the first time during the ceremony, brown eyes meeting brown eyes, and each saw in the other's a trace of apprehension at what they had done.

The wedding breakfast was in their own home, served by the two maids John had employed. He had taken Henrietta there on her arrival and she had liked her first sight of the new house. It was situated on the outskirts of the town, near the site of an old Augustinian priory and set in an orchard, though John was already planning gardens on some of the several acres of farmland that surrounded it. It was of moderate size with a kitchen and larder and a dining room on one side of the central hallway and a parlour and study on the other, with three bedchambers above, the matrimonial chamber, with a dressing room, stretching the full length of the back of the house with a view over the orchard. It was new fashioned in red brick with the newly popular sash windows giving more light so that the spacious rooms were bright and airy. The interior was sparsely furnished as yet but had new modern furniture and rugs on the floor.

"It is very pleasant John, and very tasteful," she had said and he had smiled with pleasure at her approval.

"We can always enlarge it later, and I have left most of the decoration for your own personal taste. You must choose what you wish and if you have need of more servants I will see what can be arranged."

She had thanked him politely but expressed her satisfaction with everything he had done.

Their wedding meal however was quiet and solemn, marked by an absence of laughter and a minimum of conversation. Although Henrietta had sworn she would not think of the past she could not help recalling the gaiety and excitement of her marriage to Philip with the games and dancing out of doors and the happiness of her family. If only William could have been here he would have enlivened the occasion with his irreverent merriment. He had been as surprised as anyone by the announcement of their intended marriage but had welcomed the strengthening of his ties with John who, during the time they had fought together, had begun to take the place of Philip as his friend and comrade and had now stepped more fully into his shoes as a brother. Henrietta felt a sudden longing for his supportive presence, having left him behind at Hesketh Hall, a proud father to his newborn son and even more enraptured of his wife. Remembering the baby cradled in Abigail's arms she reminded herself of why she had wanted to marry again, and discarding all past memories and regrets as a futile encumbrance she put her mind to presiding graciously over the table and making polite conversation with her new relations. John was solicitous in his attendance upon her but his conduct gave his family no clue as to why he had contracted such an unexpected alliance. Their original supposition that he must be infatuated with her was not borne out by his careful civility.

In the evening John and Henrietta were left alone. There was certainly no bawdy jesting, no accompanying them to bed with all the indecent revelry that had characterized William's nuptials. Henrietta felt very much alone. She stood in her shift in the bedchamber, looking out across the shadowy whiteness of the orchard drenched in apple blossom and conscious of the new bed behind her, as yet untouched, with pristine sheets and drapes of blue Dutch frieze that had never been drawn. She and John had never embraced or even kissed. Suddenly she was assailed by unbidden memories. She saw Philip on Naseby field, the valiant Cavaliers being crushed and slain by the Roundhead rebels and had a sudden vision of him being killed by John. She remembered a medieval romance she had read about a lady who married the knight who had killed her husband but couldn't recall what happened next except there was a violent thunderstorm. There was a thunderstorm at Naseby. No, that wasn't right, there was a thunderstorm at Marston Moor. But there was a thunderstorm when Philip died and she lost her baby. Everything was so confused.

When John entered the bedchamber he found Henrietta sitting on the bed shaking uncontrollably with her hands over her eyes and he drew back, unsure of himself. She felt his presence and taking her hands from her eyes looked up at him with tears wetting her cheeks.

"What is the matter?" he forced himself to say. "Are you afraid of me?"

She shook her head but was unable to tell him what she was feeling.

He sighed and ran his fingers through his hair in frustration. "I will sleep in the other chamber tonight," he said. "You are tired, and the long journey then having to meet so many strangers has been too much for you."

He made to go but she called him back. She knew instinctively that if she allowed him to go from her this night then their relationship was doomed. "No, don't go. Please don't leave me. All is well now, everything was strange that is all. You are my husband. Please stay."

She looked so young with her hair unbound and the tears drying on her freckled cheeks. He felt a rush of confused emotions - guilt, regret, desire. He was young and virile and it was his wedding night, and it was not as he had imagined it to be, as he had often imagined the first night with Arabella.

He climbed into the bed and lay still beside her, feeling her rigid against him. They lay together looking up at the plastered ceiling. Then his restraint cracked with his great need, for it was a long time since he had made love. She cried out with the fierceness of his possession and involuntarily resisted his urgent intrusion into her body, but he too had many demons to subdue and the confusion of his emotions overwhelmed him. His relentless vigour was like nothing she had known with Philip's gentle caresses and she moaned under his imprisoning strength, but when she finally submitted to his need she found herself drawn inexorably to an ecstasy she had never before experienced. Afterwards she lay trembling and amazed.

"Are you all right?" he asked when the physical and mental storm had passed and all he felt was exhaustion.

"Yes, I am all right," she answered.

When he slept she still lay awake. She could hear him breathing lightly beside her and she wanted to light the candle and look at him but she didn't dare. When her arms had been around him she had felt the scars on his neck and shoulder where he had been wounded and she felt a moment's compassion for the hardships he had experienced. She was filled with a desire to look at him closely when he could not see her. Now that she had given herself to him she felt bound to him though she still missed having a ring on her finger. But she felt strangely comforted and almost happy. She believed she could be happy in this house which, unlike Hesketh Hall, had no memories and no life other than what they would make for themselves. It was waiting for them to write its history, like a blank page, and she believed it was possible for them to create a satisfactory life for themselves. She lay still and contented for a time until she too fell asleep.

During the next few weeks John and Henrietta lived carefully as if walking on egg shells, trying desperately to please each other and give no offence. When Henrietta asked if she might have a spinet there was one delivered within the week, a beautiful instrument on a separate stand with elegantly turned legs. Now she could fill the house with music in her empty hours, for managing the small household with her two maidservants was not a time-consuming occupation after the responsibilities of Hesketh Hall and John was usually working. He made few demands on her after that first night and always asked her if he could make love to her. She was embarrassed and never knew how to reply except to say, "You are my husband," which response usually elicited a sigh from him. But he showed his gratitude for everything she did for him and she was warmed by his consideration of her.

The only cloud upon the horizon was the implied censure of his family who would never openly criticize her but would look askance at her way of dressing, and when they entered the house their eyes would linger disapprovingly on her books and pictures. The spinet was no objection for Puritans welcomed music in their homes, it was music in the church they considered a distraction from worship, but they frowned upon some of Henrietta's favourite pieces. She dreaded to think what would happen if they discovered the little shrine and prie-dieu in her dressing room. One evening when she and John had dined together she complained to him. "Your family consider me frivolous because I wear brightly-coloured clothes and don't cover my hair, and they think I waste my time reading romances and playing dance tunes. But I don't believe life should be dull and solemn and it doesn't prevent me from running the house efficiently. Well I think you should know, and tell them too, that I do not intend to change." She looked at him defiantly with her chin tilted challengingly and John faced another encounter with the Hesketh determination.

"I do not want you to change," he replied calmly. "I married you as you are and promised you the freedom to live as you wish. I will always support you. But if you are unhappy here we could always move away, perhaps go to London."

"No I do not wish to go away, I am not a quitter. I am happy here. I like the house and I like the town," she replied.

"I'm glad," he said warmly. At first he had felt unsettled in his home town and believed his wanderings had completely uprooted him. But now that he was married with a house of his own and a thriving profession he was beginning to find his ground again.

When Henrietta realized that she did not have to fight John she began to relax and establish her own pattern of living. She liked the busy market town where she was becoming a well-known, and pleasingly admired, figure as she shopped for their supplies or sometimes in the evening walked with her husband. The only place the Radcliffes were not seen was at the Parish church. But she was often lonely. She had nothing in common with John's family and they were uncomfortable with her. There was little opportunity to make friends as most of the townspeople also were in awe of the baronet's daughter with her elegant clothes and manners, and John mixed seldom with the gentry. He was always busy and had little spare time, or inclination, to cultivate eminent acquaintances. She also knew that he was worried about the political situation and when at rest was often preoccupied. When the King had escaped from the siege of Oxford he had made his way to Scotland expecting to find support in the land of his birth. But earlier this year the disloyal Scots had handed him back to the English Parliament in exchange for a considerable sum of money which they claimed was owed to them for expenses incurred in the war. Though he was now in Parliament custody the King was still refusing to compromise on the issues which had begun the war - religious and parliamentary freedom - and it was discovered he was secretly negotiating with France and Ireland to send him military aid. Meanwhile the division between Parliament and their army, always present but previously controlled, was now widening. The army had refused to disband at Parliament's request, ostensibly because their pay was in arrears, but they were fast emerging into a highly-organised autonomous group. John had personal experience of the extremists within the army and he was worried by the fact that they were now becoming a separate revolutionary body, at odds with the more reasonable aims of the Parliament. The situation was potentially dangerous and the deciding factor in the imminent power struggle could well be which party Cromwell and Fairfax chose to support. Henrietta too watched the developments closely, wondering what effect the succeeding events would have upon her husband who had believed the war to be over.

Henrietta soon realized she was was going to have a child but fearful of what had happened at her last pregnancy she did not tell John until she was sure it was safe. She hid the secret in her heart and every morning awoke to the hidden excitement. It would be a Christmas baby and she would have her own nativity. John was happy too when at last she told him, and it helped to cheer him when in the summer they learnt that the army had captured the King and taken him into their own custody. Sir Thomas Fairfax and Oliver Cromwell had decided to take their stand with the army.

It was whilst waiting for her baby that Henrietta found a new interest. She had always been able to talk to John about political matters and shared his concern about the new developments. Now because he was often shut away from her in pursuit of his work, even at home as well as the room he rented in the town, she began to give heed to what he did. She missed his company and found herself awaiting eagerly the time they spent together. So she began to question him, asking him to tell her about his assignments and got him to explain the complexities of the law. She had a quick intelligence and a retentive memory, which she had previously utilized for music and poetry, and she had always had boundless curiosity. Soon she was devouring John's law books with the same enthusiasm with which she had devoured Italian and French romances. Her avid curiosity found a fascination in the dullest tomes and the pursuit of knowledge began to quicken her with as much excitement as the feel of the child growing within her. John was amazed by her growing interest and her intelligence and found her companionship lightened the loneliness and tedium of much of his work. He found himself falling into the habit of asking her opinion and of using her as a sounding board for ideas and arguments that he had previously pondered in isolation. Sometimes she could intuitively see the answer to a problem and instead of sitting alone in the evenings he would sit with her beside him as they pored over books and papers, sifting evidence and refuting spurious claims. One day he said to her, "You would make a good lawyer if you were a man," and she flushed with pride at his praise. She would write letters and make copies, lightening his load so that on summer evenings they would be able to sit in their orchard with a cup of wine, listening to the soothing sounds of birds and grasshoppers, or they would walk by the river as a warm breeze shook the aspens. John was making a cradle for the baby from a tree he had chopped down. "You don't mind if I do most of the physical jobs myself instead of hiring a man?" he had asked her at first, for after his years with the army he needed bodily activity to counter the hours he spent at his desk. He enjoyed the times his work took him abroad and when in the open fields he would prick his horse to a gallop as he had done in a cavalry charge.

As winter approached Henrietta found it more difficult to go abroad and November was a bad month. John's mother died suddenly, being found already dead in her bed when Edah made her morning call. She was more than sixty years old but John was filled with sorrow that he had disappointed her during this last year and that he had not been able to reconcile her to the fact that the war had changed him. She had been hurt by his non-attendance at church and his neglect of religion, and had not been able to understand his marriage whereby he had overstepped the boundaries of his class. John was sad and guilt ridden. On the night of her funeral Henrietta was horrified to hear him call her 'Arabella' in his sleep as he turned to her and put his arms around her. She wondered how often he imagined her sister in her place when he made love to her. She was devastated and felt ill all the following day, not able to confide in him. She knew he was also worried about the increasing tensions between the Parliament and the army. At first he had tended to sympathise with the army, especially when Parliament had refused to pay them their arrears or give them indemnity for acts committed whilst under orders. He himself had requisitioned horses and horse-stealing was a hanging offence in civilian life. He knew that poor men would not be able to settle claims made against them and got himself involved defending many such, waiving his fee.

But on the other hand he was aware that there were agitators in the army who were using the present discontent to spread their radical views. His apprehension grew as the army increased its influence in the Parliamentary cause. In November the King escaped from his confinement but after a mere few days' freedom was recaptured and imprisoned in Carisbrooke Castle on the Isle of Wight. There were rumours that Oliver Cromwell had connived in his escape with the sole intent of providing an excuse to keep him in closer and less lenient custody.

Henrietta's own confinement was soon to be upon her though she had to wait until the new year before their child was born. Excitement and trepidation were equally mixed and one day she said to John, "If I am dying will you find me a priest?"

"I wouldn't know how. There aren't any Catholics in Huntingdon."

"Sir Henry Staunton's wife in Brampton is a Catholic. But you haven't answered my question."

John swallowed hard. "Yes, I would do my best if that is what you wanted."

Henrietta was satisfied and all over Christmas she waited in anticipation. But she had been disappointed and longed to be back at Hesketh Hall, the first year she had been away at this season which had always been celebrated with such enthusiasm. She imagined William and Abigail with their baby, and her mother and her poor father, and wished she could have been with them. But she was determined to keep the festival in defiance of her Puritan relatives. She made mince pies, festooned the house with bays, rosemary, holly and mistletoe, lit a Yule log on Christmas Eve, and played carols on the spinet, celebrating all the twelve days of the festival. For the first time in his life John Radcliffe celebrated Christmas and discovered that in indulging his wife's humour so near to her time he had enjoyed the experience.

Towards the middle of January their child signalled his approach. "I will go fetch Patience and Edah," said

John, discovering how alarmed he was at the imminent prospect, and for once Henrietta was truly glad to see her calm and capable sisters-in-law, so experienced in the business of child-bearing.

"Go out of the house John," said Edah briskly. "Go and find something to do."

He refused and went to his study, wanting to be on hand should he be needed. However Henrietta's cries soon un-nerved him and he came to the door of his chamber ashen-faced.

"Go and take a walk, there is nothing you can do," said Patience kindly. "Henrietta is all right."

"She says she is dying, I must see her," he said distraught, and remembering what he had promised.

"Henrietta is not dying," his sister reassured him. "She is young and strong and everything is going well. All women think they are dying at this time. Walk to the stile by the old oak tree. If you are needed I will come immediately."

"You promise?" he insisted, unable to bear listening any longer to Henrietta and realizing she was calling for her mother and not for him.

"I promise," Patience said, shepherding him out.

He walked over the fields to the stile, wrapped against the biting wind blowing across the flat landscape from the east and feeling more desolate than he had done for a long time. He leant with his head against the tree, the rough bark scratching his forehead. "Please God, don't let another of the Hesketh girls die for me," he pleaded in terror. "Exact any price from me, take anything you want of me, but not Henrietta Hesketh." It was the name he had thought of first, not Henrietta Radcliffe but Henrietta Hesketh, all the memories conjured up with the name. Would he never be able to break free from the tragedies of the past. Then he realized he had been praying, something he had not done since Arabella's death. Not a real prayer but asking a favour, making a bargain, but even the token gesture implied belief of a sort.

When he saw Patience's tall erect figure striding towards him with her grey cloak flapping in the wind he began to run towards her in alarm. But as she came closer he saw that she was smiling and before he could reach her she said, "You have a son."

"And Henrietta? Is everything well?"

"She is recovering and very happy. Your son is strong and healthy, small but with the most powerful pair of lungs I ever heard."

He began to run again, leaving his sister far behind, but on reaching the house he stood on the threshold of the bedchamber, suddenly awestruck. Henrietta was sitting up against the pillows and holding the little swaddled bundle tightly as if daring anyone to take it from her. Her curls were awry and her fringe plastered damply to her forehead but on her face was an amazing expression of complacency. Suddenly John wanted to laugh and in answer to her unspoken question he said, "You are wonderful. Nothing I have ever done in my life compares to this." He had taken life but she had created new life and he felt humble in her presence.

She laughed out loud and for the first time he saw her vivacious face completely alight with happiness. "Well aren't you going to come and look at him. He is just like you," she said, moving the blanket away from the little head. He bent over the tiny squashed face and could see no resemblance to himself, or to any other human being. Henrietta would not relinquish him. "I am so happy," she said. "Now I have some-one of my own to love."

She kissed the little forehead where the brown hair stuck damply and John felt a peculiar pain in the pit of his stomach as he had the sensation of being excluded from that mysterious bond forged between his wife and son whilst he was absent.

Later that evening when Henrietta was asleep he sat alone in his study attempting to read, but the flickering candle shadowed the words and distracted him. He had a son. It was hard to take in that the small red-faced bundle was his son, someone to live for and work for. Someone to protect. He brought himself up short. No, he would not protect him but encourage strength of character to face whatever life had in store for him. But for the first time in a long while he felt hope for the future, an assurance that life still constituted joy. And with the miracle of his son's birth he sensed the faint stirrings of faith. With this precious gift and the preservation of his wife it was difficult to carry on denying a benevolent existence somewhere beneath man's incomprehension.

The Radcliffes entered the parish church for the first time since their marriage for the baptism of their son who was named William, a request John could not deny his wife. Then the following Sunday John announced, "I think I will go to church."

Henrietta looked at him carefully then said, "I will come with you." John was surprised for she always made her devotions privately at the shrine and prie-dieu in her dressing room and he had never disturbed her, as he had promised. "I think now we have a child we should stand together," she said. "To attend church with you will not affect the way I pray in private and I know it matters to you that your son should be reared in the Protestant faith." It was after all what King Charles and Queen Henrietta Maria, her namesake, had done. John was moved by her decision, even though he reckoned he had little right to ask it of her seeing his own faith had lapsed.

There were some whispers and uplifted eyebrows when Master and Mistress Radcliffe entered All Saints, she going to sit on the left with Patience, Edah and the girl children whilst he joined Isaac, Samuel and the boys on the right of the aisle. Henrietta found her little gargoyle again during the long sermon, but the text, 'I have surely seen the trouble of my people in Egypt and have heard their cry for I have known their sorrows,' struck a chord in John's heart, while the singing of the metrical psalms reminded him of his time in the army of Parliament when he had been inspired and his faith strong. Later as they made their way home Henrietta said, "I do find the ways of your religion strange. I can lie beside you in bed but I cannot sit by you in the church. It seems very illogical to me."

"You are quite right but that is something I am powerless to alter, at least at the moment," he grinned. But he felt a peace in his heart and had been warmed by the welcome afforded him by the rector, and by the loyalty shown to him by his wife.

In the months that followed Henrietta lived contentedly, caring for her little son and supervising her small household. She still found time to share John's work, especially in the evenings when they would read and discuss together. She also found herself often being accosted in the High Street or the market place by people begging her to ask her husband for his help, so that she became well-known for her sympathy and her interest in their problems. Many people could not pay for the help they received and she supported John in his decision to waive or reduce fees for the poor and the genuinely deserving claimants.

"The more wealthy clients will compensate," he would say, "though I fear we shall never be rich. I thought when

I married you that I could eventually be a rich man and I'm sorry about that."

"You are a rich man, John," she said. "You are rich in intellect and largeness of spirit."

He looked at her in surprise at her commendation of him. "I am rich in having your help and support, and in the gift of a son," he replied.

Now that she had the child Henrietta felt more truly wedded to him. She was no longer nervous of his love-making and had grown to enjoy and look forward to his attentions though she could never bring herself to tell him and he was sparing in his demands. She knew he was worried about the gathering clouds on the horizon. It was discovered that the King had made a secret treaty with the Scots who were promising to restore him if he would establish the Presbyterian religion in England.

"There is going to be another civil war," John said, as they sat one warm spring evening in the garden they were making together in the part of the orchard nearest to the house.

Henrietta held the baby close against her breast as she asked anxiously, "You won't go and fight again will you?"

"Not unless the situation gets desperate," he assured her. "But I am saddened when I think of all the time and effort and loss of life, and we still cannot reach an agreement between our two sides."

"You think the King is largely to blame don't you?" she asked, bending to tie the baby's bonnet strings.

"Yes I do. He will neither compromise nor negotiate openly. Instead he relies on deceit and intrigue, feeding on divisions and encouraging insurrection."

"Many people are dissatisfied with the way Parliament is running the country," she countered strongly, riled by his old dogmatic tone.

"It isn't easy to re-establish law and government after such an upheaval as we have had. It will take time and if only the King would consent to a reconciliation instead of refusing to accept defeat, then both sides might be able to work together," he continued heatedly.

"You cannot blame the Royalists who have nothing left to lose for refusing to accept defeat," cried Henrietta. "They are very brave."

They could feel an argument building up between them and sat with stony faces, both set in their beliefs. Then John acknowledged, "Yes they are very brave and the King is brave, I do not dispute that. I have always admired courage." Henrietta's chin was tilted defiantly and he remembered all the Royalists known to her who had paid a hard price, including her husband Philip Halsall. But he felt compelled to say, "Perhaps it is foolhardiness however and not bravery to plunge the country into bloodshed again."

They sat alienated, Roundhead and Royalist once more, as old memories surfaced in a wave of anxiety, loss, regret and remorse, and the baby began to cry.

Anxiety put them both on edge during the next few weeks and their differences intensified for a time. Their worst fears were realized as civil war broke out again. In South Wales the governor of Pembroke declared for the King, and in May rebellions followed in Kent and Essex. Then as summer progressed an army of Scots invaded England in an attempt to reinstate the King. Fairfax and Cromwell were kept busy with a conjunction of forces more threatening than at any time since Marston Moor.

"I think I might have to go and fight again," John said, looking ruefully at his child in the cradle, his new house that had become a home, the evidence of his work piled on the desk.

The shadows upon Henrietta's new-found contentment grew longer. The letters that passed between Huntingdon and Hesketh Hall, with opinions on the worsening situation by John and William and on the care of babes by Henrietta and Abigail, one day brought news of Sir James's death. It had been a sudden end with no warning so that Henrietta could not have been appraised in advance and he had already been buried by the time the news arrived. She was desolate that she could not have seen her father again before he died and she cried for days. John comforted her by assuring her that he would have been unaware of her presence and it were better for her to remember all the happy memories she had of him. But in her dejection at this new sorrow John was made aware of how much he had come to rely on her gaiety - the tinkling of the spinet, her singing to the baby, her laughter bubbling up at so many of the things that caused her amusement. He had never before realized just how merry a place his home was until Henrietta was sad.

Fortunately he did not have to consider going to fight again. The alarms and anxieties of the summer were short-lived. Fairfax subdued the south again, while Cromwell conquered Wales then in August went on to disperse the Scots at the decisive battle of Preston. The second civil war came to an end after a mercifully brief duration of six months. But it had come at a price. There was a growing bitterness against the King for his intransigence and a hardening of attitudes towards him. There was also a deepening division between the Parliament and the army who had put down this new insurrection swiftly, but in some peoples' opinion too ruthlessly. For John and Henrietta however there was only relief, a relief manifested in the calming of their spirits and a new appreciation of the joys of life. The wet and wasted summer transformed itself into a golden autumn, an Indian summer that was to stay in their memories for ever.

John always remembered the September day in the year 1648, a year and a half after their marriage, as if it had been burned into his memory like a brand. The revelation had come upon him as suddenly as St. Paul's blinding light on the road to Damascus, though he supposed the seed had been growing in the darkness of his heart without him realizing it. He was riding into Cambridge where a fellow lawyer had invited him to share some of the load of his thriving practice, an opportunity to increase his income and reputation which he had leapt at. It was a warm, golden day, as warm as high summer yet with a mellow radiance that bathed in a lambent glow the yellowing trees and the fields ripe to harvest. As he rode past the cornfields he was aware for the first time in three years of a startling brightness in the world around him and a leaping joy in his heart. He reined in his horse looking at the promise of the waving corn, the blue sky with the wispy white clouds above him, a lark piercing the purity of the air with its song, and felt the radiance flowing over him and through him like the Old Testament prophets described their encounters with God. He was overcome with a certainty that such beauty, such happiness, such assurance that there was good in the world, could not possibly exist without some vital principle behind it all. It was as if a sudden heavy weight had left his heart and sent it soaring free. And at the same time he was illumined by a joyful revelation so sudden in its impact that he knew he must return home immediately, and turning his horse around he galloped back to Huntingdon.

He ran into the house calling, "Henrietta", but she was nowhere to be found so he went through the back of the house to the orchard. She had taken off her shoes and was dancing. She was wearing a sleeveless bodice like the maids wore and had kilted up her green skirt and her shift almost to her knees, the long grass tickling her brown legs as she danced and sang a Royalist song, a satire on the Roundheads.

"They raise their valiant prentices
To guard their cause with clubs,
They turn their bishops out of doors
And preach themselves in tubs,
The cobbler and the tinker too,
They will in time advance,
God take them all in His Mon Dieu,
Tis à la mode de France."

The baby was seated on the grass beside her, clapping his hands and laughing in delight. John stood silently looking at them, unobserved in their joyful absorption, the little brown-haired child with his round rosy face and Henrietta skipping and twirling in light-hearted abandon. Then she became aware of his presence and stopped, reaching for her shoes in the grass. "Oh dear," she said, but she was laughing and there was no sign of repentance in her mischievous face as she continued, "You see how silly I am when you are not here." Then noting his serious expression she asked in alarm, "Why have you come back?"

"I came to tell you that I love you," he said.

She regarded him in amazement and felt suddenly embarrassed, giving a little nervous laugh as she said, "Only for that?"

"Yes only for that! And yet it isn't 'only', it suddenly seemed very important to me." Her heart lurched and she began to slip her feet into her shoes, not knowing what to say. He came close to her and pulled her into his arms. "I once told you, very stupidly and cruelly, that you would only ever be second best to me. I want you to know that isn't true. You are first, first in my life and first in my heart."

Her brown eyes which a short while ago had been dancing with merriment were now filling with tears as she fixed them on his face. Her heart was beating fast and she did not know how to reply, but she whispered, "I did not think I should ever hear you say that."

A shadow crossed his face momentarily as he acknowledged how he had once thought the same. "I'm sorry," he said, "sorry that it has taken me so long to say it, to realize how much I love you, how much you mean to me, but love you I do, Henrietta, with every particle of my being." Looking back he could now see how his love had grown gradually from the way he had begun to depend on her and value her companionship, to the birth of his son when he had been filled with terror lest he should lose her, and the jealousy he had felt as she lavished all her devotion on the child. But although it had grown gradually it was no lukewarm affection. Holding her in his arms and looking at her lovely young face, for she was barely twenty-two, he was conscious of such an overwhelming passion, a deep burning need for her, that he had felt for no-one else, not even Arabella. She satisfied every part of him. She satisfied his body with her loveliness, his mind with her intelligence, and his spirit with her warm-hearted vivacity. She lightened his life with her gaiety yet understood his deepest fears. He tightened his hold on her warm body, the vivacious face with the upward curving mouth that laughed at him so often, her skin pale gold with the sun and the deeper gold of her freckles spread lightly across her nose, and in his longing for the vibrant girl who was his wife, the pale angel of her sister sank for ever into the deep recesses of his memory. But one matter of crucial importance was still outstanding and there was fear at the reaches of his heart as he asked apprehensively, "And you, Henrietta? Can you love me? Can you love an egotistical blind fool?"

She nestled into his arms and smiled up at him. "I love you, John. I love you so very much. I think I loved you before you loved me." When she had promised to marry him she had trusted him and he had more than repaid her trust with his care of her, which would have been enough for their initial bargain. But as her growing regard for him turned into a deeper emotion, nourished for her by his lovemaking and the birth of their child, she had longed that he might love her as she had begun to love him, but not thinking it possible she had instead poured out all her feelings on the little being who was so like him.

Her brown hair was hot from the sun as he pressed her close against his shoulder. He now knew with certainty why he had been led to Hesketh Hall, because he believed once again that, without denying the mistakes he had made, he had been meant to go there.

"My dear, dear love, do you believe in destiny, or Providence, call it what you will? I believed that I had been drawn to your house, to Hesketh Hall, for some purpose. After the tragedy I couldn't see any sense in anything and thought that I had been deceived in why I should have been led to the Hall and entangled in your affairs. But I have come to realize that there *is* a pattern to life and God *does* have a plan for us if we will listen to Him and not drown out His voice with our own conclusions. I now believe that I was sent to Hesketh Hall to find you, my love, not Arabella but you, and for you to change my life. What a long time it has taken me to find my way, I am thirty years old." Then with sudden clarity of vision, realizing that his assurance about God's purpose had not been replaced by doubt but by another conviction that there was no purpose at all, he added, "You know it is harder to find one's self through a path of certainties than through a path of doubts."

As Henrietta looked into the brown eyes that had always faced reality fearlessly, she believed she understood the symbolic significance of him taking her away from Oxford from her first husband. She had been a child and it had been a childish romance that would always remain with her other early memories, but it was only a prelude to the mature passionate binding love she had now found. There was an inevitability about the whole pattern of events. She replied, "Yes I believe in destiny, or Providence as Puritans call it, and I too believe we were destined for each other, we are kindred spirits. If it hadn't been intended, there is no way we could have crossed each other's paths. I always dreamed of love but I never thought it possible to love anyone as I love you."

They had been married for a year and a half and they were as new lovers, totally absorbed in the wonder of each other, trembling with the excitement of their mutual avowals. They were kissing as they had never done before, until disturbed by their child whimpering at being forgotten and trying to pull himself up by his father's riding boots. John lifted him up and held his wife and son close to his heart, happiness overwhelming him. It was possible to love more than once and to find the second time a love stronger and more profound, forged in the fire of experience and beaten into unbreakable links by the hammer of adversity.

It was late when John returned from Cambridge but Henrietta was waiting for him with the candles lit and the house silent. She helped him out of his riding clothes but he was impatient.

"This is our wedding night, our real wedding night, my love," he said. Even knowing him well, Henrietta never dreamt that such passion dwelt beneath his controlled exterior and realized how much restraint he had previously shown. "We have no need of these," he cried, tossing away his shirt and pulling off her shift as she leapt into his arms. He was familiar with every curve and hollow of her body and she knew every scar and toughened sinew of his, yet it was as if they had never touched each other before. All contact was a joyous exploration of wonder and each fulfillment an increasing revelation.

"Where did a strict Puritan learn these things?" she teased him.

"Instinct," he laughed. "Not practice I can assure you, my love. I had to wait for you but I never knew it. Neither of us was ready."

The rosy fingers of dawn were already streaking the sky when at last they fell asleep, enclasped in each other's arms as if they would never be separated.

The following weeks of autumn were a source of great wonder. For both of them it was as if they had come alive from a long sleep. They could not bear to be out of each other's sight or touch for long. Every night they lay entwined and every morning awoke to the joyful realization that the day was theirs to spend together.

One day John came home with a present for Henrietta and invited her to open the large mysterious box which he had placed on the table. She looked at him questioningly but he refused to speak so, eyes sparkling in anticipation, she removed the lid. Inside was a yellow gown. She lifted it up, catching her breath as its splendour unfolded - yellow taffeta with flounces of gold lace on the ruched sleeves and a wide pointed collar of gold lace.

"Oh John it's so beautiful," she breathed. "It must have cost a fortune."

"I don't know if it's the right fit, I've never bought a gown before," he said in some embarrassment. "But you once told me you would never wear yellow again even though it was your favourite colour, because of all the sad memories associated with it. I want you to wear this for me."

It was a test. Could she bury all vestiges of past tragedies as he had done, and walk with him unencumbered.

Henrietta realized the significance. "I shall be honoured and proud to wear it. It is the most beautiful dress I have ever had," she said seriously so that he understood. She stood looking at it, fingering the glowing material. Then her natural impulsiveness overtook her and she cried excitely, "I'll put it on now, you can be my maid."

When she was dressed he said softly, "You are so beautiful. I have a pain in my heart just looking at you."

"I was never beautiful," she said. "I was plain and fat." Then she said deliberately, "It was Arabella everyone admired." He didn't flinch and the expression in his eyes never wavered as he shook his head in disagreement. He went to fetch the looking glass and seeing her reflection Henrietta knew it was no longer true. "If I am beautiful your love has made me so," she said. She turned up her face for his kiss, and he knew that and amid all the confusions and vicissitudes he had found the girl who was meant for him. "We are twin souls, destined one for the other and drawn together, despite ourselves, when the time was right."

The emotion that flowed between them hung heavy in the air like a rich perfume that would always remain there, discernible to all who entered the house.

Then Henrietta's face broke into a teasing smile. "Of course you will now have to discard your Puritan objections and learn to dance so that you can partner me in this glorious gown. William is sure to have a ball when we go to Hesketh Hall at Christmas and I expect we shall be invited to the Hardwickes and other places. I know you believe that dancing is the Devil's work but if you don't dance with me you will leave me at the mercy of all the young gallants." Her sparkling brown eyes held a mischievous challenge and the freckles on her nose wiggled as she tried to refrain from laughing.

When John's brother-in-law Samuel arrived at the house a short time later he couldn't believe his eyes. His knock had gone unanswered for the maids were busy outside, and he had followed the sound issuing from the dining room. John and Henrietta were dancing and she was singing the tune with a loud emphatic rhythm. They had removed the chairs and pushed the table in front of the window where the sun streamed through on to the large bowl of dried flowers and rose petals.

"Oh John you have two left feet," Henrietta cried and they collapsed into gales of laughter, helpless in each other's arms. Then John was kissing her as no man ought to be kissing his wife.

Samuel was rigid with shock but worse was to come. John pulled Henrietta down onto the floor and inbetween their laughter she was shrieking, "My new dress, you'll spoil it, let me take it off first."

Samuel retired hastily to inform Edah of the wickedness taking place in her brother's new house.

John Radcliffe was most certainly going to the Devil.

Chapter 17

CHRISTMAS 1648

"I don't think you should have called him William, dear," said Lady Hesketh, as she took away from Henrietta's year old son the stick with bells on it with which he was attempting to hit his elder cousin.

Henrietta laughed and retrieved her little boy who was just learning to walk, sitting him on her lap and stroking his thick brown hair. "You must play happily with your cousin Jamie, Will, now that we have brought you such a long way in this cold weather to visit him," she explained.

James Hesketh was almost two years old, altogether quieter than his little Huntingdon cousin with his father's blond curls and an angelic smile which so far appeared to complement his nature, not belie it as his father's had done. He offered Will Radcliffe his wool lamb as an invitation to play again, first taking an anxious peep at his baby sister sleeping on his grandmother's lap. Three months old Maria Hesketh had her mother's auburn hair clustered in little damp curls where her head rested snugly against Lady Mary's breast. Will struggled down from his mother's restraining arms and Henrietta let him go, knowing that Lady Mary's careful attention was upon her grandchildren. How she loves having them near her she thought, watching her mother as she gathered them close around her skirts. She had been shocked at first to see how Lady Mary had aged visibly over the past eighteen months of absence, with deep lines etched on her fine-boned face and her hair almost completely grey, but today there was a satisfied contentment in her eyes.

They were all gathered around the Yule log burning in the big stone fireplace in the parlour of Hesketh Hall. It was not yet time to light candles and the curtains were undrawn, revealing a light sprinkling of snow across the park and dappling the lake. It was the first time they had all been together since Henrietta had surprised them all by marrying John Radcliffe and Lady Mary's attention drifted from the little boys playing happily together now, Jamie following the younger Will's lead, to study their parents.

William was smoking a pipe and talking earnestly to John. Sir James would be so proud of his son now, she thought. He had settled down into a responsible and dedicated landowner and was doing well for himself. He had begun to enlarge his land holdings, having taken in some fields from a neighbouring estate which was in financial difficulties, and had plans drawn to extend the Hall with a new wing. He had already rebuilt the damaged portion at the back of the house, though as new service quarters instead of a chapel. Abigail's careful housekeeping and unconcern about personal luxuries, together with William's skillful management of the estate, were paying dividends and allowing surplus funds to be put to good use in the improvement of the property. Lady Mary's confidence in Abigail had been justified and she discharged her duties as if she had been born to them. Having helped with the running of the house for so many years there was no area of government with which she was unfamiliar, while her association with Arabella and Henrietta had given her an awareness of social niceties which she instinctively reproduced. She was neither educated nor cultured in a fashionable sense but she entertained the important people William cultivated with a gracious and generous hospitality and won them over with her unselfconscious beauty so that any gossip which had at first circulated on their marriage had been completely stilled. William made no secret of the fact that he liked to display her, though she resisted all forms of ostentation both in her dress and her household. She wore the jewels William bought her in order to please him, but it was the rich simplicity of her attire that served as a foil for her ever-increasing loveliness and made men gaze in envy and women feel overdressed.

Abigail and Henrietta were in animated conversation about the problems and delights of child-rearing. Not having seen Henrietta since her marriage Lady Mary found her daughter's blazoning happiness a revelation. She looked as if she were lit from within by a radiance illuminating every part of her - her sparkling eyes, glowing skin and the shining warmth of her brown hair all offset by her gown of deep ruby red velvet. She had always been disappointed that Henrietta had not inherited her own beauty but now it seemed that as her own beauty faded its glory had been rekindled in her daughter. She had been amazed by the undeniable evidence of a deep mutual love between Henrietta and her unlikely husband, not understanding from whence it had originated. But equally obvious was the companionship that pervaded every part of their relationship together with a visible manifestation of equal respect. There was nothing proprietorial in John Radcliffe's manner as there was with William, and as Sir James had always shown towards her, and Lady Mary knew how well this would suit her strong-willed daughter. She had not been happy at the announcement of their marriage and was still in ignorance of how the unlikely romance had blossomed, but there was no doubt of its fruit.

"Have a game of cards, John. Your free advice on how to get Guy Carleton off the west leas pasture against the new foal for my little namesake," William suggested.

"No gambling, William. I'll play cards with you but I won't wager," John replied.

"Still a Puritan!" William sighed. "Even Henrietta hasn't been able to change you completely I can see." He was surprised to see how much John had changed. He was wearing a doublet of dark wine-coloured velvet and his hair almost reached his shoulders, the stern set of his features had relaxed and he laughed a lot. Even more surprising was the fact that on the previous evening he had danced creditably at the Heskeths' Christmas ball.

"Being a Puritan is merely a matter of how I worship God and has nothing to do with wearing sober clothes or disliking music and dancing," said John severely. "Those who think in this way are mistaken, as I was for a long time. There is nothing in God's word that says we should not be light-hearted, in fact joy is one of God's greatest gifts. But the whole idea of wagering is against my personal convictions."

"Sermon ended," said William drily. "We will play for the pleasure of it then, but it takes away all the excitement. Still, as you're a novice I suppose it's only fair."

"I've been teaching him, William, so you had best beware," warned Henrietta. "He is a novice but he's cunning, he wouldn't be a lawyer else." She thought how her husband's family would be shocked to see him dancing and playing cards, blaming her for corrupting him. "What shall we say if the Parliament commissioners come and ask if we are celebrating Christmas," she said, glancing at her husband with a mischievous smile.

"I shall inform them that I am Sir William Hesketh, Parliamentarian and Justice of this shire. My brother-in-law is a strict Puritan so how can we be celebrating a forbidden festival. But if we are, what business is it of their's," William said and they all laughed.

When the game was finished with William the expected victor, he went to fling himself on the floor at Abigail's feet, leaning his head against her while she ruffled his curls affectionately.

The afternoon shadows began to lengthen into early evening and servants came to draw the curtains and take away the little ones. Abigail bent to take the baby from Lady Mary's lap and for a brief instant Henrietta thought she was looking at her mother as she used to look when they were young, even to the same deep brown of the taffeta gown she loved to wear because it brought out the copper glints of her hair. William was also studying her slender figure and her burnished hair. She resisted a fashionable hairstyle and bound her hair in coils so that at night she could let it down in all its glory and he could bury his face in its richness. As she straightened she caught his eye and a smile passed between them, a smile full of promise that made his blood thrill with expectancy. For both of them the happiest part of each day was when their duties were done and they could shut the door of their chamber and be alone together.

Lady Mary also retired with the children and William said, "Henrietta, go and talk babies with Abigail, I have something of importance to discuss with John."

"Don't order me about, my husband doesn't. And whatever concerns John concerns me," retorted his sister, going to sit beside her husband on the settle and nestling against him.

William turned his eyes up. "I don't envy you," he said to John. "She was always a pest."

John smiled and thought how he no longer envied William. Once, briefly, on his wedding day, he had done so. But he didn't envy him his fine estate, his increasing wealth and his growing importance in the shire. Or even the beautiful house which he had grown to love and which he had believed he could never again enter. Hesketh Hall was the home of his kin now, friends where there would always be a welcome and he could visit with pleasure. He could look around at the familiar surroundings without seeing the shadows of time long past. The ghosts had all gone and the place was no longer haunted by past tragedies for the guilt had been paid for and expiated. William was resolutely changing and updating the old furniture and furnishings and the house was beginning to take on a new aspect with its young inhabitants and their growing nursery. Hesketh Hall was the home of his brother and friend, where John could enjoy the company of his one-time opponent whom he had come to like and respect, and where his family could come whenever they wished. But their own home was far away, a place of great contentment and love. He thought Henrietta might have felt a sense of regret on her first return to her old home but that morning, lying in bed together, she had said, "I have loved coming back here and meeting everyone. But when the time comes I shall be glad to go home."

"Where were you? You were far away. I have spoken to you twice." Henrietta had slipped her arm about his neck.

"Oh I was thinking that I would plant some more cherry trees in the spring. And perhaps make the house bigger."

"Why do we need a bigger house?"

"For all the children we are going to have," he said, putting his hand on her belly where their new little child lay, the child conceived on that night of passionate love-making, their real wedding night when they had first expressed their love for each other.

"Not too many children. I don't want to share you with too many others," she whispered.

Shadows still lay across their content however, and the Yuletide season was clouded by an awareness of serious considerations facing them when the celebrations were over. The longest shadow was the knowledge that the King was to go on trial at Whitehall in January and now the implications had to be faced.

"This is what I wanted to discuss with you," William said. "What is going to happen?"

"There is to be a trial - but no means have been provided for an acquittal," John replied solemnly.

There was silence as the gravity of John's statement sank home, though he had already talked of the matter to Henrietta and they were aware that people were talking openly of the King's death.

"You mean that the King will be pronounced guilty?" asked William in horror.

"It means there can be no other verdict," said John. Then with a sudden rush of passionate anger he cried, "If this proceeds it will be a travesty of the law, a betrayal by Parliament that I cannot condone nor forgive."

"It may not proceed so far," William attempted reassurance. "From what I hear there has been great difficulty in finding lawyers to participate in a trial."

John nodded. "The law as a profession has emphatically refused to be involved. Even Cromwell's friend and kinsman, Oliver St.John, one of the most notable lawyers, won't comply." He thought of his old comradeship with Oliver Cromwell who had now taken a path he could not follow, and was glad that his old commander had not contacted him and forced him into an open breach. Cromwell was desperately trying to summon up support from lawyers but John surmised he would be well aware of his own undoubted opposition to a course that was legally dubious.

"What should we do?" William asked.

"I have already decided what I must do," John replied. "I shall go to London and register a formal protest. I did not fight so long for the establishment of rightful government and the upholding of the law to see my cause end like this. I can in no way be party to such an action and to stand aside and do nothing is to agree by default. If necessary I shall attend the trial and make my opposition known there."

"You must not do this John," said William warningly, seeing his set face. "You have your family to think of. Don't let him go Henrietta!"

She looked into her husband's eyes and saw there all the honesty and integrity that was in his soul and for which she loved him, and though her heart leapt painfully she put her hand in his saying, "I cannot ask him to be less than he is."

"Then I will come with you," cried William impulsively.

"No!" John's eyes flashed him a warning and held with the old unwavering regard. Abigail had come back into the room. "We must never be involved in anything together William. Not any more. Each of us must have the assurance that, if need be, our families are in the care of the other."

There was silence for a time and the Yule log crackled merrily, spitting off sparks. Then William said at last,

"I think I may have to change sides again if things fall out as you fear. I cannot support the murder of the King."

John did not reply immediately then eventually he said, "Nor I. I have blamed the King for much and my opinion is not changed about him. But I will not accede to judicial murder. I shall have to give the matter careful thought."

The room was warm and comfortable with the new curtains of deep blue wool drawn on the mullioned window, shutting out the snow which had begun to fall again softly. The wood panelling reflected the glow of the leaping flames, and the candlelight sparkled on the pewter bowl of russet apples and the crystal wine glasses which were set on the new walnut table inlaid with mother-of-pearl. Over the fireplace an oil portrait of Abigail had replaced the old tapestry donated to the Royalist cause. The parlour no longer looked as it had done when John had first come to the Hall and the inhabitants had changed also. Their hard won reconciliation had removed barriers of prejudice in religion, politics and class, and they had all learnt to think with open minds, to see with unblinkered vision and reassess those attitudes their upbringing had bestowed. It was difficult to believe that the civil war still rumbled ominously around the borders of their lives.

"We must always stand together, no matter what happens," Henrietta said fervently. "Never again must we be divided."

"Let's drink a toast to that," William proposed. "Together we will survive. Let us drink to peace for our country and happiness for ourselves."

John thought of the children in their cradles above stairs and the baby beneath his wife's heart and said,

"I think we shall have to wait for a new generation to reap the blessings for which we have suffered. At least we have our children to inherit the better land for which we fought."

The promise was implicit and they all drank hopefully, pledging themselves, their children, and their country in the golden liquid.

When Lady Mary opened the door she saw them grouped together with their hands clasped tight. They had all been divided at some time by misunderstandings, mischance, pain and tragedy, but now they stood united in a knot of love and friendship. She thought of the missing faces - of Sir James and Arabella lying beneath the turf in the churchyard, of Philip Halsall buried with so many other young men below the battlefield of Naseby, of Kit Verney and Prince Rupert, wandering exiles. She pledged them all in her memory. Then she went to join those who had survived, for the future was theirs and they had much to live for.

FINIS